Mermaid Rising

(Book 1)

C. L. Savage
Mermaid Adventures

A SeaRisen LLC Publication
2014

Mermaid Rising

Author: C. L. Savage

Publisher: SeaRisen LLC, Boulder, Colorado
– SeaRisen.com

Cover Photographs by Sassafras Photography
– Superior, CO 80027
– www.sassafraspics.com

Paperback: ISBN 978-0-9909258-1-1
eBook: ISBN 978-0-9909258-0-4

Printed in the United States of America

First SeaRisen LLC Printing December 2014

10 9 8 7 6 5 4 3 2 1

To friends, old and new …

Dedication

I could not have accomplished this book without the wonderful guidance and help of the Glorious Father, the Illustrious Holy Spirit and my Savior Jesus Christ. Together they have inspired, kicked me out of bed in the morning and kept the book upright and good. I honestly do not know where the ideas come from, if not from their dedication to the topic through me. It couldn't be me, or why would I be moved to tears while reading my own book?

Then I would like to thank my friend Charlie Darrah that has reviewed most of the writing as it came from my fingertips. His steadfastness is much appreciated. Then there is my long-time friend William "Bill" Crane, who is now in Heaven, who dedicated one of his iPad's to me as a gift on his passing on which most of the book was written. His wife Judy inspired me in the development of the girls, one of which was to be getting her friend, the lead Jill, into trouble – which I haven't developed well enough; there is always the next book Judy!

Next I'd like to thank my dad Kent Savage who also has moved on to greener pastures. His love of nature and the environment has definitely influenced my life and is reflected in the writing of this book. Then there are my many lady friends, I do hope I was able to capture some of what it means to be a woman in the hearts and characters of the women portrayed within, because of them.

Table of Contents

1 It's Just a Dream

– JILL

11:32 p.m. The quiet after the storm. I sat up in bed. What had awakened me? I tried to sit still to listen, but my heart was pounding. Throwing off the covers, I turned to look out at the rising moon shining brilliantly through the departing storm clouds. Silver light fell into my room in my family's apartment on the roof of Goldie's Gym, the gym named for my mom.

My whole life I had spent in and around the gym. Right at that moment, I felt the moonlight as if it were the sun. Goosebumps rose on my arms, and I tried to rub them down. At moments like this, I experienced visions of a sunny beach. Tonight it was of the pool below, like I was standing on the diving board. Broad windows wrapped the pool on three sides and the rising moon cast its light across the floor. As the moon rose, its light trailed into the water of the pool and bubbles began to rise from the bottom in slow motion. Each bubble rippled as it filled with air, its inner surface reflecting the blue moon.

There the vision ended and I was left sitting on the bed staring out into the moonlight. In a trance, I watched myself from above, as if I were a marionette on strings. I climbed out of bed and tip-toed out of our apartment, down the stairs and into the gym proper. Through every window I passed on the way to the gym's pool, I could feel the silver moonlight. It reached even here, making the air glow and my night shirt luminous. Even the bits of dust floating in the air held still for that which was about to happen. The door to the pool flung itself open. The pool was aroused by the moonlight and its water called to me.

1.1 Sunken Treasure

Through the open door, I ran to the pool, doffing my night shirt. The wind of my passage caused the shirt to float away and dance in the moonlight. It continued prancing on the deck of the pool, caught up in the moonlight's song as I dove. The bubbles still lazily floating up from the bottom filled with moonlight bright as day. The surface of the pool was still like glass, seeing as that the many moonlit bubbles had not reached the surface. The surface reflected an image of myself, the moon, and then the reflection shattered. Blissful waters greeted me, calling to me as one of their own. It was a thrilling experience as I became one with myself, and instead of the expected pool bottom, a sparkling undersea vista welcomed me. Figuring this to be a dream, I accepted the transition from pool to ocean without question.

I dove down twirling through a school of multicolored tropical fish in wonder. They created a pillar some thirty feet up to the surface, but a group of them separated out and began swimming with me. Their enjoyment matched my own, dancing with me as I flashed this way and that, exulting in the freedom of infinite energy, water, space and sea. As we swam together, they entwined so closely that they looked like an opaque gown of moonlight, replacing my garment which still danced above.

Swimming through the sea, a clear blue sky color, I finished my long joyful undersea arc and broke through to the surface, the salt-scented air intermingled with the fragrant smell of flowers from a distant tropical island greeted me. I gazed in wonder around me. The island had sands of pearl, rocky outcroppings that caught the waves and a verdant jungle echoing with exotic sounds. Then as I cast my eyes around, they were arrested by an image as striking as a fly in milk – a beaten-up yacht lay at anchor, drifting mysteriously nearby.

Like a cold splash to the face, the vision lost its dreamlike luminescence but none of its improbable strangeness. I, a girl barely thirteen years old, was treading water out at sea. If this was real, I was no longer in Boulder, Colorado. This had to be a dream, but it was like no dream I'd ever had before.

None of the joy was gone, but when the dreamlike state that I'd been indulging in vanished I took stock. A light wind kicked up the sea, and the cries of birds caused me to look for them. Eventually, I saw them lazily circling overhead. Shading my eyes from the sun, I squinted. There was no moon.

I felt like I was in a movie, the empty-sounding ship riding at anchor in this picture perfect setting, with its metal chain clanking against its sides in the lazy sea. The sound of it carried easily to me over the water, but the yacht itself sounded empty, forlorn, which made me think nobody was aboard. A chill ran up my spine at the possibility of the people being dead, but I pushed that out of my mind.

As a dream, it would be too creepy. Let's go with it being nothing like that. So if they were alive then they were too far from the island for it to have been their destination. That is, if they had wanted to go ashore. It seemed to me, that since they weren't above, then they were below in the water someplace.

When I had walked through the gym, I'd felt the moonlight all through myself. Now, too, I can feel the sea itself and through it the ship pulling at its anchor. There was something to this, and it was in the sea below. Time to go see. Raising my hands over my head, I descend into the deep, trailing bubbles for a little while as I gaze in wonder into the world beneath the surface. How different it is from the surface above.

Again, I'm thrilled to be swimming in this vast undersea world in all its variety. Over there is the tornado of fish twisting on itself, lost in its own dance, that I'd swam through earlier picking up the fish that swam with me now. An infinite variety of colored and striped fish swam all about, though most were swimming near the coral below, there were yellow, silver, red, blue and orange fishes. Through them swam three giant turtles who disappeared into the distance only to be replaced by a giant manta ray as it swam like the old man of the sea, saying "Come swim with me child, and I'll show you life abundant – the things the fast-paced world forgets with its cell phones and designer clothes."

Following the manta ray, my gaze was drawn to the great dark shadow cast by the yacht. There, I observed the sea anchor and another line going straight down towards it. I paused in wonder, staring at an unbelievable image. Like a reflection of the ship above, there on the bottom of the sea lay an old yacht from a bygone era of elegance and romance.

This sleek old wooden galleon had once roamed the sea, perhaps a hundred years ago or more, fast enough to prey upon slower vessels like an ancient raptor, but now it was rotting and home to sea life. Here and there, coral had built up around it, mostly keeping it upright where it had settled. Strangely, it rested there remarkably intact.

On the seafloor beside the sunken galleon lay the yacht's bent and tarnished anchor, carefully placed, so as not to wreck the coral. The diver who placed it was careful not to disturb the surrounding sea life. I had drifted down by then to hover over the landscape. I lost track of the second line coming down from the yacht above. Where was it?

Eventually, I saw it dangling loose some meters above, which again made me wonder. The lack of bubbles over the shipwreck had me turning in circles, looking for a diver, but there was nobody to see, only many sea animals going about their lives unconcerned. So, I aimed for the wreck and set off in an easy glide towards it. I delighted in the easy way I was breathing. There was water on my lips, and as I breathed air came in and out. I had no bubbles like a diver with scuba tanks would have. How delightful! I required neither a diving suit nor air tanks.

I came down upon the wreck searching for some clue. But what was I looking for exactly? Upon seeing the remains of the galleon's wheel on the aft deck whereby the ship had been guided, I glided towards it imagining myself at the helm. Captain Jill, I'd call myself, doffing my hat to the waving crowd as we set to sea. I could just see myself in silks, knee-high boots, and a scowl yelling at the crew to put on more sail. Grinning at the thought, I swam up onto the railing and cast about.

"Ahoy Captain! Mind moving that barge? Real traffic coming through!" I looked about until I spotted a line of puffer fish getting all indignant at my taking up their sea lane. Apparently they'd been waiting a while, as this ship hadn't moved in a long time. "Go around," I suggested. "You've sprung a leak you know," they replied spinning around to swim back the way they came.

Before I could become engrossed in the thought, I heard a sound from below deck, causing me to remember the divers. I wanted more than anything to meet these divers who, like myself, breathed water and talked with the sea life. Since none had appeared, it was time to go find them myself. Perhaps they could help me find my way home. That would be the perfect dream. I did so hope to remember all this upon awakening.

1.2   In Too Deep

The way into the ship from the deck was blocked, so I searched for another way in. Swimming effortlessly through the sea, I felt like a strange sea-bird as I flew over the edge of the ship. I hovered over the edge, scanning below. It took me a moment to see through the schools of fish going here and there, that some were coming and going through several ports along the sides of the ship. Surely, one of those portals would be large enough for me.

Going from one portal to another, I kept sticking my head in, but only saw sand and coral. Eventually though, I came upon one that opened down into the ship. I kept thinking I should be seeing bubbles, dream though it was, but seeing none, I knew the divers were in trouble. Taking one last look up towards the roof of the sunlit sea, I entered and pushed off from the ceiling downwards when a way down presented itself. The hull was cavernous and dark at my end, but light came through the darkness. As I wove my way through the floating barrels that had been stuck there for who knew how long and nets overgrown with seaweed, I came to the source of the light – a dive torch floating.

As I came around to see better, the light shone in my direction blinding me. I swam around to the side in those cramped quarters, sea life scooting away into the darkness, in an attempt like myself to get out of the light. These items that had been floating in the hold undisturbed for ages made it hard to navigate. Over and under I crawled until, pushing aside one floating barrel, I was able to see the lone diver, limp and unmoving.

Apparently, in an attempt to pull a chest from where it was lodged underneath other ancient belongings, he had caused the debris to tumble down, pinning him there. The dream was remarkably detailed, and I wondered at the metaphor as I gazed upon the drowning man – it didn't make sense that I could breathe and he could not. Now it also made sense that I'd seen no bubbles, as he wore no scuba gear or dive suit. He was wearing beach shorts, and he had curly brown hair and dark skin from time in the sun. His eyes moved under his eyelids, and he twitched slightly. Good he still lived, I'd been afraid it was a creepy dream after all.

I could see that the man was drowning. He was attempting to breathe the water and he looked cold. Cold? This was such a strange dream. He was cold, but I thought the water delightful, silky smooth, and... warm. Until then I had not considered its temperature. In no dream could I recall temperature being a concern, even though I'd had dreams with snow, rain and sunlight. The water was perfectly warm like silk sheets – completely comfortable.

A free diver dived without tanks and gear and went hundreds of feet down on a single breath. The depth of this wreck was hardly a feat by those standards, yet trapped as he was, he would expire unless I helped. I would have to give him air, in an intimate embrace. I felt this intuitively. What kind of dream was this anyway? It wasn't fair that I should live and he should not if I failed to act.

Reaching out to his outstretched hand, I tugged myself closer to him. Greatly underestimating my dream strength, the pull caused him to float free and I spun upside-down, careening toward the opposite end of the ship, pushing aside everything I'd passed through and crashing into the debris there. A great cloud of silt rose up obscuring the light, and it would have obscured my vision as well, but as I reached out towards him, my hand mysteriously pushed the silt aside like a drop of soap in oily water. Then I was able to swim back to him and take ahold of him again.

Thinking to use the mouth-to-mouth training I'd learned from my step-dad Lucas, I drew him close. Pulling him up where I would have to breathe life into him, I felt air instead spring from my heart to his, and his lungs cleared of water. He was breathing like I was. I felt him reviving as he drew life from my heart until he'd fully revived and his eyes flew open. He searched my eyes and I searched his in a last ditch effort to hold to the dream figuring this was the end – he would live.

1.3   Not Possible

After a bit I realized the dream wasn't going to end as his eyes traveled every which way, probably feeling like he was awakening from a bad dream. Without thinking, he asked "What, where...?" and then realizing he was hearing himself speak underwater he begged the question from me, "What, how?" I had no answers, I didn't know speaking underwater was possible, dream or no dream.

Speaking kicked something loose in his throat and he coughed and began to turn purple. The thing I'd done to get the water out of him apparently hadn't taken the silt out with it. Trying to feel for the silt in his lungs, I focused on it through the connection we shared and watched the silt lift from his lungs to be expelled with his next cough. His breathing became normal and he leaned back exhausted from the experience.

Feeling strange about still holding his hand, I tried to pull free, but when I did he gripped my hand desperately. To him, the touch was how he knew that he was drawing on me, like an umbilical cord and if I let go he might perish, but I knew it was different than that.

I could see how important it might be to him to maintain a connection to another living person in this dark place. Letting him hold my hand felt completely strange, especially with the heart-to-heart attachment we continued to share. At least through it I felt him needing me as I'd thought.

As the moment lingered, the attachment I felt for him kept growing with each breath he took. Because he continued to draw on me for air, I was becoming more acquainted with him and his internals. For instance, knowing the strength of his liver, heart, and internal organs. Though it was not something I'd ever wanted to know – even though I knew how to revive someone that was drowning, I'd never had a desire to go beyond that to become a nurse or doctor.

Even so, I was being taught, sensing little oddities as his heart taught me more about him. Once I began interpreting his nervous system, I understood that the red impulses racing up his spine were pain. Following them down, it seemed a mere second had gone by, by the time I knew his leg was broken. I had to break the sensory exploration as I was repulsed by the intimate knowledge I was getting of the fracture.

Reviving from his stupor, with the back of his other hand, he wiped something dark from his lips. It floated away before I had a chance to identify it, though it didn't look like blood and he seemed to be getting better with some color returning to his cheeks. Still, I had to get him to the surface because I couldn't stay here with him indefinitely.

When I next met his eyes, he saw that I knew his condition. Something in his expression said he was relieved that I knew, even though he was doing his best to ignore the pain as he again searched my eyes for understanding. I had none to give him. When I offered no explanation for any of his inquiries, he asked, "Are you an angel?"

"I'm not," I answered, but at that moment I wasn't sure for something truly extraordinary was taking place. Then, to put it into words to what I'd seen, I explained, "But you are hurt. So we need to get you to your ship," and I waved upwards.

"Ships are big," he corrected me with a half-grin half-grimace. "The Lazy Cloud would be best described as a yacht, but 'boat' will do. Though when thinking of a boat, one would normally think of something smaller. Because usually you think of boats as two-man boats, four-man boats, et cetera." He coughed again lightly, wiping his mouth again with the back of his hand. He had piercing eyes, and I found myself avoiding them as if he were challenging me to contradict him. Picturing his yacht floating at anchor and awaiting its captain, I just wanted to see him up there, but he could continue this discussion forever.

Seeing that he couldn't bait me, he stopped trying to hide the pain he was feeling. Then because it was so intense he blacked out and let go of my hand. I felt him drifting away emotionally and physically. At that moment, I had to reach out to him through my heart and not let go. In that way, I was able to steady the two of us and take stock of the situation. I almost laughed at the thought. I was being swindled into thinking that this was real. Surely, I could just leave and he would live, or never have really existed, but my conscience wouldn't let me.

Not knowing how long I had, I realized I'd have to do this myself. To get him out, I was going to have to bind his leg, or risk injuring it further. Using his lamp and looking around, I searched for something to bind his leg with. It didn't take long to find the rope he'd planned to use to hoist the chest he'd found and then some boards that were floating in the corner.

Since I had plenty of supplies, I decided to bind his legs together for added support, to keep his limbs from flailing. At first, while I searched for supplies, I worried that he might continue drowning when I drew away. But I discovered that if I put conscious effort into our connection then I could continue to share with him the life he needed. Also, though, as I swam into the recesses of the wreck, the connection drew thin. I realized it would be easy to let go. Why would I want to do that? Yet, the longer I kept the connection, especially the further away I got, the more it drew on me and the more I was tiring. I definitely wouldn't have time to wait until he awoke again.

Fleetingly, I wondered what was so important to him that he'd risk his life for it. Treasure hunter or enthusiast, it really didn't matter to me. I knew enough of the second type being similar in my love of swimming. I hoped he was more the latter, but seeing the chest that he had probably been pulling out, I decided he was probably the former. Also I wanted none of what the chest might contain and continued getting him ready to leave.

Once I had him bound in a makeshift harness, I tested it and found it sufficient. In my exploration for materials, I'd found the hole through which he'd entered, far closer and fortunately bigger. It was toward that one that I began guiding him through the debris that had drifted back into place after my tumble. I had to be extra careful not to trip and send us sprawling. At the exit, I turned off his lamp and strapped it to him for the journey up.

With a last look around, I scooted him through the hole. He probably wasn't going to be happy that I would be leaving his find down here. But he could come back once he'd recovered. Once we were out in the sea, and seeing that I would no longer need the rope, I freed him and coiled it up. I wouldn't leave it here though. Putting the rope over my head and under my right arm, I took a hold of him and began swimming up towards the dark underside of his boat.

In the hold, I'd felt unnatural strength and now I felt like I'd gained diving flippers on my feet to propel us upwards. Even my hands felt like they were webbed, guiding me with gentle turns of the wrist. I felt born for this environment and knowing I would soon be hoisting him aboard, I was reluctant to leave it. I took no time for this consideration, for I had to get him to safety and his craft seemed the best place instead of the tropical island I'd seen when I first arrived.

Near the surface, I could see that the waves had been kicked up by stronger winds. Moving around to the back of The Lazy Cloud, I saw a ladder hanging from the stern but couldn't just carry him aboard no matter how strong I felt. No additional ability manifested itself, even though I expected wings to materialize on my back. I guess I wasn't an angel, though, as nothing of the kind was available – instead I had fins. "Think, Jill," I chided myself, still half-hoping he'd wake up and tell me what to do. But no, I would have to use my noggin this time to figure it out and get him aboard.

Then I saw what should have been obvious from the start – a glint of light reflecting from the back of the boat. I'd mistaken it somehow for another anchor, but it was attached to what looked like a winch. Of course, that was how he hoists heavy things from the sea such as the treasure chest. Maybe I could do the same with him. I glanced at him, then back at the boat. I would have to recreate the harness, but one that would hold up out of water.

Finally, I decided on one that would hold him under the arms and around his chest, since his leg was injured. Once I had the sling wrapped around him, I had to move quickly and went for the ladder to search for the controls. Taking ahold of the ladder, my invisible fins mysteriously disappearing, as mysteriously as they'd appeared. I climbed rapidly to the top. Then seeing the deck clear, I jumped aboard.

It wasn't a pretty yacht. That much I already knew. Yet now I knew why. He wasn't a treasure hunter but probably a marine biologist who couldn't turn down a treasure chest when he'd found one. There were a few more objects around that he'd recently hauled up, but I ignored them. Instead, I went quickly to the winch. It was electric and had simple controls. It didn't take me long to get the hang of it and wind it up until I had the hook, then unwind enough slack.

I jumped over the side of the yacht with the hook end of the winch wire, landing with a splash and then swam back to the diver. There I knotted the rope to the hook and then climbing back aboard, I went to the winch's controls and hoisted him aboard. The motor whined at his weight, but didn't balk at drawing him out of the water.

Once he was high enough, I swung the arm around and lowered him down gently, doing my best not to aggravate his leg. He'd be safe enough here for now.

Somewhere in getting him from the sea to his ship, he'd awakened, but it wasn't until he'd touched down onto the deck that the pain brought him back to the here and now. Hearing him moan, I quickly unwrapped him. "Hey, you... what?" he gasped as he saw me untie him, taking a glance at his surroundings.

I'd accomplished what I'd set out to do – he was aboard his ship. Now, I had to leave. His hand reached out for me, but I pulled back. I couldn't let him detain me. I had been uncomfortable enough holding his hand underwater, but aboard his ship I felt my strength had lessened and didn't know if I could resist him.

Turning, I ran to the side of the craft. The instinct to run overwhelmed any desire to stay, and I simply reacted by diving overboard. When I was in the air, I heard him call out, "Wait!" That was the last I heard of him before I entered the sea. Had his cry been a desperate call for help or an attempt of a marine biologist to understand me? The former may have swayed me, but the latter disgusted me. Either way, I couldn't go back.

Yet, for some reason, I stayed underwater, watching him as he eventually came to the side of the boat, searching for some sign of me. At last, our eyes met, as there was but a handbreadth of water between me and the surface. We held our gaze again, me half-expecting the attachment I felt before to return, but instead I felt nothing more than I might feel with anyone else, even though he was pale-faced with pain. So, instead of returning to him, I flipped about and dove downwards. It hurt to leave him, but it seemed the thing to do.

Perhaps one day we'd meet again. There was a mystery to all of this, but I knew I'd done what I had come for and on reaching the seafloor I turned and swam away.

2 There Be Mermaids, Captain

2.1 June 6th, 2009 (Flight and Arrival PNG)

My name is Arlo McKenzie, and this is my personal journal. A personal outlet for the following events. Which I hope are fruitful. After months of preparation, I'm here at last. I sometimes wondered if something was wrong with me as I found it so easy to leave my brother Jeb and my niece. It was nice of them to let me stay while I was away from The Lazy Cloud.

Research was my mistress, my love, and I had surrendered to the wanderlust years ago. When I was stateside, it was usually to the university at Boulder that I went. Jeb put me up. It was good to have family, the only ones I really felt close to. Yet, I knew there was no way I could ever return the favor. Being a drifter and going wherever the university sent me.

The flight from the US was long, boring, and tiring. During the journey, I had a chance to re-read Dr. Killian's writings on marine biology. A lengthy and somewhat tiresome read, as tedious at times as wading through thick seaweed.

Dr. Ryan Killian – DK – is the head of marine research at the university and nominal leader of the expedition and he is a dedicated researcher. Even though his book is lengthy, it goes through all the processes he takes to reach his conclusions. DK reminds me of Edison (wish I'd met the man), 1600 some attempts to discover the filament in lightbulbs. The two of them were like a dog with a bone, chewing away at it until it reveals its meaty center. That's the main reason we got along so well.

So here I am in Papua New Guinea – PNG – to follow up on leads from the last expedition. PNG is a pleasant enough place, but I spend little time among the locals as I'm anxious to head out to sea. Down at the port, my research vessel, The Lazy Cloud is waiting. I spent a day putting away the supplies I've been purchasing for two months at sea. I'd be making stops among the many islands in the region to talk with the natives and buy fuel, fresh fruits and veggies.

A bit about me, I'm the son of Henry and Carlotta McKenzie, born 1970. I'm 39. This is my second expedition in the areas surrounding PNG. I'm on a contract with the university in Boulder, Colorado working for Dr. Killian, the head researcher for all sea life in these parts of the world. His pet project is to be on the lookout for unusual aquatic sea creatures of abnormal size or appearance. DK has convinced me with a large amount of evidence, and the human in me agrees, but the scientist in me rebels at the idea, of there being huge unknown creatures. Like leviathans from ancient folklore, hiding in the deep below.

The argument goes, because the world is covered with more than seventy percent water and much of it too deep for continual human observation, that these creatures exist and are rarely seen. Thus giving rise to myth. It would only be by sheer chance, and likely a fatal one at that, that I'd encounter ever any such creatures. Still, my vessel is equipped with numerous cameras, motion sensors and recording devices to help pinpoint any such activity. (On the up and up, they were for recording everyday sea life because getting funding for researching mythological beasts wasn't available.) For that is how DK had sold the project to the university and got the funding for this trip. Realistically though, I am looking forward to two months of diving in the beautiful waters surrounding PNG and the many isles in the region. I rarely come back without discovering something nobody has seen before, so perhaps there is a discovery waiting for me here.

2.2   June 8th, 2009 (Port of PNG)

The locals at the port give me a hard time, though my papers are in order. I spoke with DK before boarding, and after syncing the computers and navigation, I pushed off. With the coordinates for my first dive at hand, I set the auto-pilot and went about stowing and organizing.

Finally, I have the wind of the sea in my face and not the stench of the port. Most places where you find washed humans, you also find a spoiled land and sea.

DK and I both believed if we were to find anything unusual, it would be where the locals had left the world pretty much unchanged and lived closer to the mythological, and didn't wash religiously. Though, theoretically, in a truly civilized magical culture, they'd live closer to the land and would know the importance of keeping their lands and themselves clean. Where magical creatures would feel comfortable.

When in college, I'd traveled the world and had found the South Pacific to be the closest thing to Paradise possible. It was still my opinion if there was something to find it would be in these parts. Still, there were places close to the poles where few humans were around to abuse nature, and if we found nothing here I'd likely find myself going there.

2.3 June 11th, 2009 (Diving in Wrecks)

Two days of diving revealed six wrecks of WW2 planes and one wrecked transport ship – nothing of real interest. Did DK really expect to find a lost civilization in these parts? Me and the other three researchers out on different rigs, had, on our last trip, only found a few pottery shards. Not that it really matters, but marine life is abundant. I have tons of samples already on the way back to the university, and this is just the beginning. So far, nothing on the damaged crafts hint at the kind of structural damage I was looking for.

2.4 June 16th, 2009 (Murky Waters)

Stormy seas means murky waters – this is normally a time of relaxation for the island natives, but for me it meant that the undersea world would be alive with activity. I donned my scuba gear for the first time, as vision would be impossible without it, and dove. Most finds DK had emphasized in our last meeting were to be found when the sea was rough. I hesitated to use the word "monster," but it was then that "they," according to DK, typically came out. They were supposedly active then, using the turbulent seas to hide from human monitoring.

If "they" were that sophisticated, these creatures, what made DK think our cameras would catch them in the act... the act of what? Feeding or playing pinochle?

During this dive, the cameras caught what may have been a giant sea serpent, or rolling clouds of silt stirred up by the storm above. I personally saw nothing and spent hours cleaning out my mask, camera filters and lenses. A waste of time. But, I'll keep that from the official journal. Fortunately, everything was digital and was easily copied and radioed home for the team there to study.

Most finds were a combination of two things – perseverance and luck. The first meant being there, and the second meant that whatever happened would be caught on camera.

2.5   June 26th, 2009 (There Be Trash)

I've investigated a dozen locations. I've hauled aboard enough garbage to fill a museum if anyone was interested. Not the truly disgusting kind found in dumps, but real garbage like twenty-year-old tin cans, miraculously preserved and therefore worth studying. Gathering the substance, whatever it was, was difficult, tedious and boring!

If DK didn't have me diving in one of the most beautiful seas of the world, and paying me to do it, I'd have fled his research team long ago. Still, it has its benefits, the research. It also keeps me hoping I'll be the one to discover some new kind of sea life.

2.6   July 1st, 2009 (Syreni)

I've taken on fresh supplies from the Island of Syreni. It wasn't hard to determine where they got the name – the port's taverns and gift shops were lined with carvings from coconut trees of shapely women with the tails of fish. Several locals gave locations where someone vaguely related to them (like an aunt second-removed married to their third nephew) had seen a real mermaid.

But the people were too clean for my tastes. They bathed too much, and who could blame them? Perhaps in that river that flowed into their deep harbor? I wasn't likely to find anything interesting among them. Also, they must not have much to offer the world to have so little traffic. But they were friendly enough.

Nobody gave me any hard data. I hadn't expected any. It was like their local version of a tabloid. Since there were enough people talking about it, maybe there was something to it, though I doubted I'd find a mermaid myself. All legends derived from some kind of truth, and that truth was what I was looking for. But would I know a mermaid if I saw one?

Their tails were legendary. But there was enough myth to suggest they could walk on land the same as anyone. If so, would I know one by appearance alone?

2.7   July 6th, 2009 (Mythical Mermaids)

I've exhausted the rumored locales of mythical sea-women. It is no wonder, and I tend to agree with what others over the centuries have concluded. That the observed "mermaids" / bathing beauties were no more than locals taking a dip. They not wanting to be seen hide behind rocks making them all the more alluring.

There were certainly enough of the local variety. But when they emerged on land, they had legs like any other woman. Most, if not all, movies portrayed that mermaids when wet had tails and not legs. These women while wet had legs, and it wasn't like I could ask them for a DNA sample.

2.8   July 8th, 2009 (Uncharted Island)

A particularly nasty storm drove me for some time, my instruments playing games with me. It seemed as if I were going south but at one point the sun broke through on my right when I thought it should be to my left. Through the break in the clouds, the sun highlighted an island that wasn't on the charts.

There was no hope of returning to course if I couldn't get the instruments working, so I decided to make for the island. On my way in, the clouds parted for good and I saw there were no visible ports and when I tried using the radio there was no response. Once anchored on the lee side of the isle, I decided to make the best of the remaining day and do some diving.

2.9 July 9th, 2009 (Uncharted Island – Day 2)

I'm still around the island. I had a strong need to feel firm ground beneath me, so I spent the morning ashore. There is a particularly beautiful waterfall not far inland. It was nice to shower in it while visions of rainbows danced before me in the spray.

My navigation equipment is still not responding and I'm slightly worried. Honestly, I'm a city boy at heart and the fact that my equipment is unresponsive is difficult to swallow. Fortunately, the cameras all seem good and the pictures from this morning at the falls seem excellent.

2.9.1 Late Afternoon

I've located what appears to be a sunken galleon. It's hard to determine its proper age, but I guess it to be a Spanish galleon anyway. Of course pirates would have prized a sleek vessel such as this. Thoughts of pirates have me wondering what I'll find within. I've placed cameras around the wreck and surrounding coral to film the sea life. Since it was too dark to explore the vessel by the time I finished the camera placement, I reluctantly left that for the morning.

2.9.2 Late Night - Two a.m.

I cannot sleep. I've tried all the relaxing techniques I know, but it is no use. I'm wide awake. I expect it's a combination of the mysterious island, the failure of my equipment and the unexpected find. I pace the confines of the interior before going out to witness the marvel of the rising moon. I've never seen it so glorious in all my life. I had the feeling that I'd never see it again, and used the permanently mounted ship cameras to focus in on its odd appearance. Even the stars were spectacular, like there wasn't an ounce of pollution in the sky. That got me excited all over again. I will have to spend more time around here.

I finally yawned and decided to call it a night, having already forgotten about the cameras, leaving them to capture the moon's beauty. I descended to find my hammock. It seems I'll sleep after all.

2.10 July 11th, 2009 (Mermaid or Angel)

A mermaid has rescued me. I'm in shock. I'm in awe. I'm alive! My leg is broken – I'm speechless and I'm coming down with a fever. I think it was the silt I breathed in while unconscious, though it might be something from the island when I visited it. An honest to god mermaid!

The fact that I'm a scientist means I'm not about to lend credence to the notion of mermaids, but the mysterious appearance of the girl beneath the sea – it bends my understanding completely. If not a mermaid, then perhaps an angel?

For she displayed powers that are unknown at best, but certainly not divine like a god – that would just plain freak me out.

Nor did she display miraculous strength, for she used the winch to haul me aboard. (She'd been in the process of releasing me from the rope I'd been using, using it via the winch cable.) If I hadn't spooked her, perhaps she would have stayed. I wonder how intelligent mermaids are, or are they animals? No, that can't be, she used the rope with decent knots and the winch. How on earth did she learn to use electronics, being from the sea? Am I assuming she's a mermaid then?

I had more questions than answers. Oh, and then she disappeared over the side as soon as I recovered consciousness. If only I could repeat the encounter. It boggles my mind that I was face to face with a mermaid and she escaped me. But the cameras! Surely, they filmed the girl underwater. If not, then she's a guardian angel. I've heard of them and as far as I know this is my first encounter with one.

I've only just woken. Having a broken leg has taken it out of me. I'm bone-weary.

My mind is in shambles and I'm feverish, but I need to get an orderly account down before I pass out again and forget anything important. I may be losing details already. I have to write it down before it slips away entirely. I lift my pen and begin from when I awoke yesterday.

2.10.1 July 10th, 2009 (Yesterday)
Still no longitude or latitude, I'm afraid I'll never find this place again; thus my reluctance to leave it. The fact that instruments don't work and I've encountered a mermaid... anyway, the facts.

I awoke at approximately 9 am and went about preparing for the dive. The sea was clear as glass, not a ripple of wind to disturb the view of the undersea world. What a great location! I checked everything and made sure the anchor was hooked, and kept at a safe distance so as not to disturb the find. Everything was ready. I took to the sea. I love free diving, a trick I picked up years ago. It has saved me loads of time.

After about ten minutes of scouting the exterior of the galleon to be sure nothing had changed from the day before, I began looking in one porthole after another. The ship was remarkably intact after what must have been centuries of abuse from Mother Nature. Barnacles and other sea life have made their home within and without, making me unable to determine the name of the ship from its nameplate, but I was certain that with some effort I could determine its origin. In time perhaps. I found evidence of antiquity buried in its cargo hold. Another puzzle – how did artifacts that appear to be Roman end up on this ship that was at most three hundred years old and obviously of Spanish design? I put aside all other concerns as I worked at recovering the artifacts.

Perhaps this was a lesson for me to learn about free diving. I'd recovered a few items before finding a small chest with strange markings, still discernible after so much time. In my haste, I was unaware that the material in the hold had shifted and before I knew it, I was pinned under a load. I can hold my breath phenomenally well after years of diving without gear, but no man can hold his breath forever. To top it off, a load of silt wrapped around me, so when I eventually blacked out, my body responded by trying to breathe and I inhaled some silt. I expected to drown. I imagined all my research lost, and this discovery left for another along with my bones.

I'm not sure how long I was out – seconds, minutes? I don't think there was a real miracle of bringing me back from the dead, but I'm still forever changed by the encounter. I'm in shock and have no way of explaining that girl, probably fourteen years of age. She'd been wearing ... a school of fish – and why should she, a mermaid or angel have such things? Where would a mermaid get clothes and wouldn't an angel of divine nature be beyond such concerns? Whatever the case, the fish swam gracefully about her organically, a tiny colony of intricate sophistication. Giving her the appearance of having exquisitely perfect clothing, a dress that moved of its own. Always changing, yet always swaying like cloth, like a dress might underwater, but of its own accord and extremely beautiful. That alone would have taken my breath away.

I really must have been out of it, for she was exquisite in her perfection. I knew that she had magic of a kind that extended to her clothing, for fish never acted so. Her hair and complexion were otherworldly as well, but it was her eyes that were the most beautiful and pierced my being. I'd been cut to the heart by her gaze. She saw everything, down to the broken leg, without me revealing anything.

The cameras showed her to have a darker complexion than what I remembered, which makes sense if she spends any time on beaches, and there are plenty of those around these parts. Any mythical story would confirm such activities.

Anyway, I digress. Somehow I was breathing, and talking – she said little in return, but enough to tell all, direct and to the point. All the water that had filled my lungs was gone, and air was in its place, but the silt residue was there to choke me. I'll never take air for granted again!

I passed out again, this time from the pain. I would have liked to live that moment forever. I'd tried keeping my mind from the pain, but it was too strong.

The events that played out on camera showed her getting me out of the wreck and up to the ship above. I'd fortunately had some cameras aimed upwards or I'd have none of her winching me aboard. Then there's a small gap when we were both aboard before she dived back down. She turns to see me from beneath the water, before diving deeper into the sea below.

I'd have loved more than anything to see her swimming away, or better yet swimming towards the island like any normal woman – but no, she heads towards the open sea and literally disappears, no more than ten feet out from camera number six! I've studied the video several times, and it appears like she just vanishes. I'm intrigued by her already and I try to come up with possible explanations for the disappearing act, but I'm at a loss.

I've erased the memory card of the camera in the hold where I was trapped and made personal copies from all the cameras and stored them online just in case. I can't bring myself to delete those, as they are my only hope of finding her, this mysterious girl, mermaid or angel.

Also, this may sound strange to say, but I have this nagging feeling I've seen her before.

3 Mermaid Awakening

I awoke tired and in the depths of the pool, the strangest of circumstances. Clear-headed, I looked about, pretty sure I should be in my bed, but instead I found myself floating underwater. I remembered then how it had started – the dream with the storm and the moonlight's call practically floating me from my bed, to the pool, to the ocean. Yet as I looked about, where was the ocean? The boat? The island?

I wanted them back, especially the tranquil magical sea with its fish, talking manta ray, and the tropical fish that made a gown for me. I mean, it wasn't a bad way to enjoy the pool, lying in the middle of it on my back as if it were a bed. Still if it were between sleeping in a bed and in the pool, I would choose the pool every time. Curling on my side, the water formed a kind of pillow that propped up my head comfortably. This was too amazing, I felt sad at that, pretty sure that this was a dream too. Looking at the rays of moonlight like laser beams in the pool before me sizzling the water into bubbles – it surely was magical. I must be the envy of every underwater sleeper.

Of course, this was a dream within a dream, the bubbles that didn't reach the surface allowing me to breathe underwater and feel totally at peace. I watched how the bubbles formed spontaneously from where the moonlight fell within the pool and nowhere else.

Reaching out, I tried to pop them like so many soap bubbles, but they merely rippled around my hand and continued upwards. I felt mystical as the bubbles warped around me, blessed to be experiencing it. Never had the pool been so beautiful and one with all the waters of the world.

The pool was a frame to give my mind boundaries, but really I was floating on the surface of the great sea where all water connected, and it didn't stop at the surface but continued into the depths. It seemed I was on the edge of a great discovery. There was a truth floating right under this dream that I couldn't put my finger on.

The sense was great that the pool extended to the world, and somewhere there was a door to these other places, but I couldn't find it. Seeing only the normal walls of the deep end and the rest of the pool, it was a feeling, a strong feeling, but only that – a feeling that if I reached out, I could go to Italy, Paris, the lakes in the Rockies or the steppes of Russia.

I wasn't going crazy! It had been no dream – the ocean and that man. It had been as real to me as this very moment. Yet, this had to be a dream too! I swung my hands about in frustration. Causing a current to slam around me with the motion, I felt the whole of the pool slosh cresting over the rim as I jostled. I heard chairs scraping across the cement patio at the sudden wave.

"What have I done?" I cried, and with a kick tried to surface and have a look. Instead, I shot up out of the water. Like a breached whale, I couldn't sustain my upright pose upon the water and fell back down bewildered, creating a splash that ran out from me to the far shallow end. From there, it crested over the edge and ran like a tsunami shoving everything along, up against the walls.

Around me, a whirlpool had formed as water began to swirl. Every motion was creating an unintended wave – a flick of the wrist, a turn to look, a kick – and the water slammed out from me getting even more violent.

"What is happening?" I cried, astonished.

Forcing myself to hold still, I sank, looking at my hands and feet. I've seen tantrums, but this was a vortex and I was its cause. In all my life, I'd never jumped out of the water without pushing off from the bottom, and I lifted myself clear out of the water with the simplest little kick. But now wild water was rushing to and fro across the room, all of it my fault.

Stunned by what had happened, I felt the water like an extension of myself splashing against the walls like waves on rocks, creating a riptide as it retreated to pass again up against another wall. The doors to the lobby were battered aside. Without me moving, the force abated and at last the waters retreated back to the pool. The shifting water around me slowly settled, dirty with debris. Uncle Arden was going to have my hide.

Keeping myself from moving, I eventually drifted to the bottom, so that now I lay upon the bottom of the pool. From there, I saw the distorted moon winking at me – what was it trying to tell me? Was there more to come?

Then a powerful wave of exhaustion passed through me as I laid still, afraid to move. Already tired and further taxed by what I'd just done, I slept. Dreams took me and I experienced open seas, a continuous looking glass of infinite waters and endless hot sands to bask upon and walk along. Even the ancient waters of the great Polar

Regions invited my soul to wander. Somewhere within the greatest trove of sunken vessels, a sea snake named Penelope gave me a tour.

3.1   It Was Not But Whales

The sound of conversation, my Uncle Arden and Lucas my stepfather talking, pulled at my unconscious mind. It took me a while of listening before I realized they were discussing things from my dream but were bewildered by how it had happened. Together they were setting the room right, discussing possible explanations for how it had occurred, talking as if some kids had broken in and moved the chairs around crazily while everyone slept.

Somewhere in their discussion, I realized a few things. One, I was awake, really awake. Two, I was still floating on my back underwater and at the bottom of the pool. And three, I hadn't dreamt up the crazy pool experience. Instinctively, I reached out to the water as I had in the dream and strangely I could feel the water, what it occupied and what lay within – mainly me. It filled the entirety of the pool, but not beyond. The whole room and even some beyond had been swamped, but the sense didn't leave the pool so I realized that the patio must be dry.

It didn't make sense to me though, because the whole room should have been wet. I didn't have time to figure it out. My uncle and stepfather were making their way around the room and if I stayed here much longer they would discover me at the bottom of the pool and how could I explain?

Like a shadow, I passed along the edge of the pool hugging where the wall met the bottom, keeping myself from view. Then, when I thought their backs were towards me, I slipped out of the water and made for the ladies' lockers. As my wet feet left a trail of water, I knew for sure they'd find me out and with regret I entered the locker room figuring I was going to have to explain myself.

3.2 Foreseen Consequences

– LUCAS

First, there was a moment of silence as the two men continued to clean up. Then Lucas turned to Uncle Arden, asking, "Is she gone?"

"She is," Arden said, but it was already obvious from his expression. They'd known each other for many years and got along surprisingly well considering their differences.

Arden had surprised him the night before, warning him that it was going to happen – something to do with the moon and the storm. It made no sense to Lucas. Lucas was much too logical for the mumbo jumbo that came from marrying Goldie, but his love for her surpassed the occasional oddities. Give him something quantifiable and he could make sense of it, make order of it, and even sell it. However this, all of this, was beyond his reckoning and he was glad that Arden was here to make sense of it for him.

They'd watched her sleeping on the bottom of the pool, and formulated a plan to give her an escape. If Lucas hadn't known any better, he would have run and dove in to see that his baby girl was alright. They had long ago agreed that Jill would have to figure this out for herself. Though it was really his wife Goldie that was adamant, that Jill choose and not to interfere. Jill would have to decide if this was the life she wanted.

Long ago the two of them – his wife Goldie and Arden – had foretold that one day 'this' would happen. Nonetheless, it was still a mighty shock for it to finally have happened. *Affirmation* is what they'd discussed over coffee one morning after learning that their baby mermaid was going to be different.

They had found her that distant morning swimming on the bottom of the pool like a fish, much to the surprise of everyone. They, Goldie and Arden, had assured him that she would continue to seek these watery experiences and that they were to support, guide and help her fit in. That was then.

Lucas had always been accepting that Jill would grow up different, but it was important to him that she should have a 'normal' life. That she should have 'normal' childhood experiences.

"Get her teaching others, and on a swim team. Get the schools to have their teams practice here," had been Arden's recommendation, and it had worked. She'd made friends who taught her by example, how to be normal. Unfortunately, though, this was at the expense of losing touch with her maiden self. This is what Arden had predicted would be the result.

In addition, having the team here meant more revenue – steady revenue – and that was something Lucas understood very well. It had meant expanding the pool, taking on loans, but ultimately it had been a sound investment.

Thankfully, Jill had taken a liking to teaching others and being part of a team. Having friends close by helped her as she was an only child (likely the only child Goldie would have). Heaven knows why he had failed as a parent. Lucas knew he was distant, knowing numbers and not understanding emotions, but he did what he could to support her. Still, it pleased him how he felt right now. On seeing Jill on the bottom of the pool, business no longer seemed important.

The two men, long accustomed to each other's signals, sank together wearily into the chairs, facing one another. Lucas had questions and hoped for some answers. Arden sometimes knew things. Where he got his information he never revealed, but his idea with the pool had been the right thing to do. More than anything now, Lucas needed assurance that the girl he loved most would turn out alright.

"How did you know it would happen tonight?" Lucas asked, still bewildered at the devastation that Jill had caused in the first day of her awakening. "She seemed fine all yesterday. Shall we tell Goldie? She won't take it well. This wasn't supposed to happen, for what, at least another five years? And this," he said, unable to find words to describe what he saw, waving his arms about. Everything was in disarray, the chairs, benches and kick boards had all been scattered about. Some had even ended up in the pool. The lane stringers were lying about like an octopus. In a hushed voice he whispered, "And not one thing wet!"

"Oh, it was," Arden said, "Look here," and he lifted a pamphlet that had been washed off the bulletin board and was lying at his feet. The paper showed water stains and was seriously wrinkled.

With another sigh, Lucas looked about and then down at his hands. After a moment, he glanced up at Arden for an answer he wasn't likely to get. Lucas tried explaining how he felt to his friend, "This is tearing me up, you know. I'm more emotional now than ever. It was all I could do not to dive in after her, even knowing she would be breathing on her own down there."

"Funny that," Arden laughed lightly. How Arden could find humor in this was explained by his words, "To think you're the one having trouble. I find it laughable that she's attached to me at all, the least deserving. She's even taught me how to laugh," Arden said. Lucas couldn't help but agree to that. Arden had been dourly stoic when they met, never showing any emotion. Arden had hardly been human then.

Lucas felt he had a sour disposition too, too logical and unable to bond with his daughter as he figured he should have, even though Goldie said he was humorous. "I wouldn't have married you if you didn't make me laugh," Goldie had explained once.

It was obvious that Jill was changing them both. Lucas smiled at that and of course it made him want to hold her and not let go. That was another surprising emotional response for him. Emotionally detached all his life, it had only been upon meeting Goldie that he'd ever felt like holding anyone. Then looking about them at the devastation his 'baby girl' had committed left him at a loss, and so he retreated mentally to what he knew.

Lucas decided to get on with putting the room in order, and let the supernatural be handled by Jill's confidant. "You go after her. Oh, and take her shirt to her, too," he said pointing out the shirt that had washed up near where they sat. She'd left the pool wearing a young version of the tropical fish swimsuit, the final straw of proof that his daughter was like her mother if he'd had any doubts. Standing, Lucas said with determination, "There's little I can do here, but I'll do what I can."

3.3   Triton

– ARDEN

"You do well," Arden said with respect for Jill's stepfather. Actually, Lucas was more like a real father for the care he showed her. "And remember, she loves you. Hold to that." With that, Arden got up, leaving the man with his doubts. Stepping up to the locker room where he knew the showers were going, and could hear the distinct sound of the girl he had watched all her life. Why his King had set him to his task he didn't know, but it wasn't his to question.

As a triton, his duty had ever been the same. Since the beginning, he'd stood at the springs of the Atlantic Ocean, had been the wielder of the Horn of Grenosh. With it, he'd controlled the tides and all the motions of the sea, seldom leaving his post and only at his King's request.

Even without the horn, Arden's power was vast. Having studied all the varieties of the sea in its many courses. He knew its beginnings and its end. Yet now he was powerless as he'd given his heart to his ward. Now, he felt each tear she shed, so attuned he was to her. Those precious salty tears ran down her face to mingle with the shower water. He knew them as they found the drain. Each one made its way to the sea. Since dawn immortal, he'd kept a special cache of things he'd found interesting or never wanted to part with. Every one of her tears, ten thousand leagues they might travel, but each made it into his collection as if they were drawn to it with a will of their own.

When the first of her tears had arrived, he'd dropped to his knees knowing that his master was giving him a gift too precious for words. That had been years ago, but he ached as each one arrived since, and now too. Knowing with certainty where each one traveled. Every one was a dagger in the shield that had encased his heart until he could withstand it no longer and opened his heart to her.

In his long life, Arden had experienced many things. He'd beheld wonders that few could comprehend. But not until the day his heart opened to her had he experienced love. That day had been the best day of his life. She had taught him so much since then. Now he cherished every moment. Even the conversation he'd just had with Lucas, was precious to him. She had helped him see that life was to be enjoyed.

At first, he'd seen his assignment as punishment for some infraction he'd been unable to comprehend. For several years, until that first tear settled into the treasure cove that was his heart, life was duty and service in the honor of his Lord. Black and white, no variance in color or life. Over the millennia since he'd been given his initial duty, he'd lost his ability to empathize, to feel for another and to love. He'd been unable to recover it since, because he didn't even know that he'd lost it. She'd restored it to him and had asked for nothing in return, how could he not give her the world.

He listened with his back to the wall. She wasn't crying anymore, and that was good. Whatever had gone on last night was a mystery even to him. Rarely was he surprised anymore, but it was with a pleased look that he surveyed the room. It had been his joy to teach this young one and her friends. He'd grown close to the lot of them, and he'd not thought that possible. All of that was her gift to him.

The devastation didn't bother him, it was insight into her untapped talents. He was amused at the mess she'd caused. It must have been a shock for her as well, if her reaction in the lockers was any indication. They had planned a camping trip for a few weeks later. He lost himself in planning the details. He'd have to come up with a way for her to display some of what had happened here tonight and begin to help her master her abilities. There would be no more mental breakdowns on his watch.

3.4   No Hiding
– JILL

Uncle Arden was hovering nearby, I could feel him. Whenever I acted out or needed someone badly, he was there. From my earliest memories, he has always been there to pick me up whenever I fell and scraped a knee. Then he'd set me back on my bike and help me start again.

Uncle Arden, faithful protector, faithful friend. Dear, dear, dear friend. I wanted more than anything to go to him and tell him everything, but I held back. "What was he to think, what was anyone to think?" *I'm a freak!*

"A superhero freak," I had to smile at that, "rescuing men..." He'd been kind of cute, old for sure, probably forty something. "But, sweet almighty... Ugh," hormones! I was tight all over. "Relax, Jill," let it go into the shower. "Was it just my racing hormones, a genetic spasm?" I felt different, changed. Feeling the water as it raced over me, and through the drain. I could see, a vision, from the microscopic view of an individual water atom, to the room as a whole as if each water molecule had eyes everywhere. My mind was fracturing to take it all in – in addition men, boats, storms, moonlight and waves crashing over it all. I felt like I had to become a woman right then. There seemed such a rush to grow up. I was strangely giddy. Tears of joy and sadness ran down my cheeks all at once. Ugh, why am I crying?! I wiped my forearm across my face, but the tears would not stop!

What were my friends to think about me? Would I lose them? For sure, I couldn't keep it from them. Or from Arden for that matter – my uncle, friend, and coach.

If I closed my eyes, he'd gather me in. I wanted to be a child again, for him to wipe away my tears, but that wouldn't be what he's been teaching me all along. "Stand up, walk forward, and hold back the darkness," he always said (strange advice). I couldn't run to him. So, I wanted to be back on the bottom of the pool looking up at the world, my cares held at bay and not to have to think about them for a while.

I stood there for as long as I could holdout. But, knowing that he was waiting, kindly hanging out of sight, I turned off the shower and headed out. I was unable to deny my need for his heart, his arms and his warmth any longer. Along the way, my hand landed on a pile of towels, pulling one off the top and holding it as I walked towards the pool area, only stopping on the other side of the dividing wall because he was on the other side, placing a hand on it and then my forehead. My heart wanted to be near, but I couldn't go closer. My desire for him to comfort me was warring with my reluctance for him to see me like this and I was frozen in place. He was a lighthouse in the midst of my storm, I was drawn to his rocklike presence and I felt the emotional turmoil being soothed by his steady acceptance.

I'd come to realize as I showered that running from him and Lucas was a mistake. Along with Mom, they were the loves of my life, my everything. I could tell Mom anything that had to do with girl problems. Lucas could explain anything having to do with school and the world over, but it was to Uncle Arden I turned to when I was troubled. And I was troubled.

If it were not for Uncle Arden, I would live bouncing between the carefree life of Mom and the strict business of Lucas, but uncle was different. Never would he let me run from a problem. I knew he was standing on the other side of this wall that I had my head pressed against. Just around the corner I could hear him, just where I knew he would be.

As if I'd passed a test I sensed him place a foot against the wall that divided us and push off to stand upright from where he'd been leaning. He called in to me, "Your father could use your help straightening up." From the corner of my eye, I saw his shadow drift out from beyond the end of the wall along with my shirt, which was wafting out as if still alive in its dance.

Never with a reprimand, always with the right word for me, he always caught me off-guard. I'd fully expected a scolding. Surely I deserved it, no kids had been destructive in here. That story of there being kids had been for my sake, to help me save face, but it had clearly only been a story.

I almost stepped out but stopped for a second still wondering if I was still wearing the fish. It wasn't the fish, or so I thought at first. No – something like my team swimsuit but a lot more comfortable.

He'd have to wait a minute, for I still dripping wet stood there grasping the towel before me as if it were a baby blanket. Lost in the moment, with the closeness of him, there on the other side of the wall, I lost all sense. Vulnerable, I stood waiting for what I thought was to come, but instead of a storm he brought me out of one.

In the time I stood there, the waves that had been crashing against my consciousness stilled, the storm finally breaking up, my tears abating without my being aware of it.

In the midst of his expectation, I shifted moods and bent down to dry off. I would go out and face the day and even be cheerful about it. I hurried as fast as I could, but putting on the shirt was not easy while I was still damp. Before I could round the corner, he was gone.

Instead, Lucas was out there stacking kick-boards, and I ran over to join him. There was a tear in his eye as he greeted me. I pretended not to see it as I stooped to gather boards and hand them to him. Together we worked until the room was set right.

There were no requests for explanations, and at breakfast I was given a hint that night swims were not off limits. Somehow, I'd graduated to something akin to adulthood by turning thirteen, and I liked it.

3.5   Stretching My Tail

The buoyancy of young adulthood succumbed to the routine of life. We – mom, Lucas (dad) and I – had eaten breakfast. Lucas and I went to the gym where I'd spend the majority of the day filling in where needed and teaching lessons. Then, there was swim team later in the day. I spent the morning helping with those who were registering their kids for the various classes that were starting next week, and then giving them a tour of the facility. I saved the pool for last as it was my favorite. I had been on so many adventures, mostly in my mind, that I normally had no problems conveying my love for the place as I talked and talked through one presentation after another.

Today was different, though, I couldn't get the dream out of my mind and the thought of the guy I'd rescued only to abandon weighed heavily on me. He had a broken leg after all. But a guy like that, out diving – free diving, mind you, on his own – was a capable guy. Surely, he could take care of himself. Around and around in my head went these feelings and arguments. I was anxious. I didn't feel my normal cheerful self later as I explained to one couple and their six-year-old girl the joys of the place. Thankfully, they didn't need much convincing or I'd have lost them.

I tried explaining my dream to my friends: Melanie and Lucy were working the front desk, but they were too busy with everyone coming and going to give me much attention. It was a typical busy morning. Cleo, who worked the sport shop, listened to every word wide-eyed, and told me, "Too bad it was a dream. It sounds exciting! But since it was a dream, I wouldn't give it much mind." Then she apologized as she moved to help some people who were looking at protein powders. I listened to her for a bit as she expounded on the various products. My mind wasn't there but rather on the feeling of the sea. I felt as if I was still in it, but in a strange bubble that at any minute would pop.

In that ocean was a boat, and in that boat was a man. Was he well? I couldn't get him out of my mind, and these thoughts floated with me throughout the day.

In a last-ditch effort to get my friends to join me before I came apart at the seams, I asked, "I'm going to hit the pool for a little while before the meet, anyone want to join me?"

"I want to," said Lucy, "but your dad has been getting upset when we abandon the desk." Melanie nodded agreement.

"Okay, laters," and I went through the glass doors to the poolroom. On the other side of the doors, it was like a cloud had descended on the room. I heard the distant sound of the kids playing within and pushed through it. When I had walked through the fog into the room, it was devoid of anyone and I looked around. It was oddly quiet. There should be screaming kids having fun in here at the least. Standing there, and seeing that I had the room to myself, I thought it an opportune time to see if I'd been dreaming.

I would have to duplicate what I remembered, and perhaps I could recreate the experience. What I wanted to do was to dive in, go into the sea with The Lazy Cloud – the guy's yacht, and see if it was still there. To see if it had been a dream. At least, because of the fog, the air had a dreamlike quality. This might work!

Going to an empty chair I put down my things and then sat on the edge of the pool. I had a great sense of expectation, but when I entered the water, it felt sluggish, like I was wading through a river flowing past me and dragging at my swimsuit. Maybe if I removed it, like I had removed the shirt in the dream that would change. I'm pretty sure it wasn't a coincidence that I'd done that.

I double checked that I was alone, yes it was strange, I was all alone in the pool. I still had to gather the courage to shuck my suit, because technically at any moment a horde of people could descend on the pool. As I ducked under to remove it, something tickled my legs. Color swirled around my feet, and I jumped back a step.

I recognized the color – it reminded me of the moon gown from my dream. But I didn't trust the swirl – it was nowhere else in the pool. Of course had it been everywhere, I wouldn't have gone in at all. Backing up I pulled myself up and out, watching the swirl follow alongside me. It was not a shadow, for I recognized stray bits, swimming in arcs. Were they fish? And how could fish have gotten into the pool? They swam out a little ways, as if inviting me to swim with them, continuing to swirl, waiting to see if I would join them.

Deciding to chance it, I went to the steps, sat down on the edge, and put my feet in again. They swam over cautiously. Then seeing that I wasn't going to flinch away again, several fish, varying in size from goldfish to guppies and smaller, swam up and touched my leg. Then they one by one attempted to swim up my leg, as if it were a stream, but then they fell back into the water when I was repulsed at the idea of having fish for a swimsuit. I wanted a normal everyday suit, but then here I was planning on ditching my normal suit to try and re-experience the dream. Where they wanting to help me with that? Because, in the dream they, the fish, had been the gown I'd worn. I'd been dressed with them when I found the diver.

I still wasn't comfortable with the idea, of having fish for clothing, but I was talking myself around to the idea and in the end I needed them. I kept wanting to swat them away, but now I restrained myself and watched them make the journey one by one up my leg, and then disappear under my normal suit. Before I knew it the pool was empty of fish and I felt no different. How did they all fit under there?

Opening my suit at the neck and glancing in, I was surprised to see another suit inside. Which was the real suit and which one was made of fish? They were similar.

Having the room to myself, I got up, I went to an empty chair and removed the outer suit and compared it with the one I was still wearing. Which I assumed was the one made of fish. On close examination, I could tell the difference. The one I still wore had no stitched seams and felt naturally comfortable, unlike the one I'd put off and held in my hands. At the moment I couldn't say why it felt more comfortable, so I shrugged and put the normal suit with my other things. Now I was in the perfect attire for dream activities.

As I dived into a lane, suddenly the cloud that had given me privacy lifted and the lanes were full of swimmers and the pool room echoing with the shouts of kids when I surfaced. I thought to see if the fish had abandoned me too, but on seeing them swimming alongside me, I laughed. Some were swimming with me making the suit ripple with color.

Thinking to descend into the dream and the sea, I found myself in my favorite place instead, the gym's pool. My love for the place had me easily fitting myself in among the other swimmers in the lane I shared. A few of the kids on seeing me, tried to jump on me as I flashed and flipped at either end. I dodged their attempts, but I couldn't help but laugh at their antics.

In between dodging kids, sensing through the water where they were about to land, and the adults I swam with, I tried to make sense of the fish's behavior. I wondered where the fish I'd had this morning had gone between then and now. I had a feeling it was probably my fault that they'd left. But then we hadn't been properly introduced. I was determined to permit them to stay now that I knew what their purpose was. They weren't icky but beautiful and friendly.

I swam with the fish, getting used to the magic moment until I felt ready for the swim meet. I was going to need my team suit on for it. When I left the water, they made of themselves an elegant, light and perfectly comfortable one-piece suit. I couldn't even tell where they overlapped – they looked like they'd become a second skin to me, but I couldn't have one of the fish falling off at random.

Since I was no longer alone, I ducked into the ladies' lockers and found a quiet corner. The fish hid themselves under the suit as I put the old normal suit back on, though I felt like they were upset with the treatment – almost like they were saying they could be my team suit, but I wasn't going to chance it.

3.6   Swim Meet

The whistle blew. I was off the starting block and pierced the still water. As I arched under, I saw that I had a firm lead. My swimsuit felt like it had in practice, sluggish. I should have gone with just the fish, but now it was too late.

So, thinking next time I'd wear the fish, I put all I had into the race. I wouldn't be held back by a normal swim suit; I hit the turn, I flipped and streamed back towards the start. I only came up for air because it would have been remarked upon if I didn't. By then, I was powering forward with easy strokes. I was in my element and my kicks like twin propellers. Four laps done, and it was the easiest I've ever swum. I didn't even feel winded as I was cleaning up on the last lap. I was crushing everyone.

While I swam that final lap, ideas crept in disturbing my elation. "Finish the race with the others," I heard and, "When you finish, stay in the water." Finish with the others? I looked up, seeing that I was catching the tail racers. They were flipping to go back. "No," I was swimming too fast. Looking over my shoulder at the clear pool, I realized that I was a full lap ahead! Impossible. Instead of taking first, I'd be disqualified, I thought as I hit the end, flipped and went back again, this time trying not to outrace everyone.

When I finished, it wasn't last but nobody was looking at me. Almost forgetting the warning, I was about to pull myself up when I stepped on something squishy. Looking down, I saw that it moved. It looked like a squid, and I dropped beneath the surface to scope it out. It looked like a swimsuit as it darted along the deep side of the pool. I tried to grab it, but it darted out of reach. "No you don't," I thought, recalling my true speed, and grabbed a hold of it.

The turquoise pool bottom disappeared, and suddenly I was looking down at the very distant seafloor. Seafloor? I was in the deep ocean somewhere, the pool was gone along with the meet. I almost screamed at the sudden change, but then the thing tried to get away, tugging to get out of my hand. Kicking, I surfaced, pulling at the thing. It fought like a wild fish, but I finally wrangled it to the surface where I was able to look around. A stiff wind blew across the surface making the sea roll in huge roller coaster waves and mist whirled cold from the tops of the waves. I'd never seen anything so beautiful.

Where am I? Dark clouds covered the sky. When I rolled to the top of a wave, the sea was all about me, and there was nothing but the great ocean in every direction. The sea was dark, but I was unafraid. The thing I held squirmed again, and I looked at it puzzled. It looked like our team's swimsuit. Then, I realized I was holding my swimsuit. No wonder I'd swum so fast, I'd been wearing the fish suit all along. Why was my suit fighting me?

Then something bumped into me, and suddenly realized I was looking at Ri'Anne's perplexed face in the middle of her lane. Even I was confused – what was reality? I felt her and saw her, but it was somehow distant. Then the swimsuit in my hands tugged hard and the pool was gone again, along with Ri'Anne. It pulled me under the surface as I wrestled with it. "I will put you on," I told it in anger, feeling the pool waver nearby as I struggled, figuring if I put it back on I would regain my life and it would stop fighting me. I had to keep the swimsuit or lose my grasp on reality. Were those my only options?

As I fought with the normal swimsuit, I had a sudden vision of the yacht tossing in a similar sea, but this time the storm was within – the man's health grew worse because I struggled so. I had a chance to save him, and I knew if I let go of the suit, I could go to him. I would have to let go of the suit and disappear from the swim meet. But if I didn't return, I'd lose my way home.

Trying to put the swimsuit on, it fought and had me swimming in circles. Then I was going head over heels, and it almost slipped away. I was reaching for it, had it, and then lost it as it slipped downward but I pinned it between my ankles.

Paddling downwards and tossing my hands upwards, I spun down feet-first into the sea chasing the swimsuit and a reality I wasn't entirely sure was my own anymore. It flashed away like a fish, trying to unhook from my ankles. With renewed effort, I swept my hands so that I descended faster and faster. Down I plunged into the sea. All around it grew dark, yet I wasn't blind. My view of the sky dwindled as the great deep surrounded me more and more.

Then the suit tried to dodge sideways, but that was a mistake and my legs finally jammed into the holes. I had

49

a brief second as I suddenly saw why the suit had tried to dodge – there was suddenly a dark metallic and giant submarine at my feet, and the dark blur of its tower passing before my face. Bending my knees just in time, I took the shock of impact with my legs from my rapid descent. If I were made of metal, there would have been a resounding clang, but instead I felt it through my bones, as my teeth rattled. I wondered what the crew of the sub felt or heard as I saw the submarine slide past.

Suddenly, I had another problem – a great whirling propeller moving quickly towards me. Grabbing the straps of the suit, I held on tight and kicked as hard as I could flipping over behind the submarine as it passed. I would have both life at sea and at home in Colorado.

As the straps of the normal suit snapped onto my shoulders, I suddenly saw the pool back on the surface. Having dodged the submarine, I looked about. I was some thousand feet down, impossibly deep. There was that word again, "impossible." I should have been crushed at this depth, yet I felt normal, even natural. Looking down, I could see some thousand or more meters to the sea floor, a rocky underwater canyon. There was life down there, but my life was up.

Before I could leave, I had to thank the crew of the submarine. With a smart salute and a wave, I called out to them, "Thanks, Sailors." It was the least I could do. If not for them, I would have still been plunging downward.

As I glanced back up toward the surface, the pool was the only light I could see. I kicked towards it, and my feet were twin propellers again. With determination, I held to the straps at my shoulders so it wouldn't escape, unwilling to stay here. The man would have to wait, I had a swim meet to return too.

Arriving at the surface, the pool around me was dreamlike, and the ocean was real. The sky had gotten darker, I'd spent too much time here. It had to be nearing evening where I was at, which meant I was somewhere in the Atlantic Ocean. I guessed at my location. That I was east of the United States or Canada and below Greenland somewhere, a long way from home.

It took me a while staring at the pool to realize that there must be a connection between this place and that one. It wasn't just a projection, but really was just a step of a certain kind away. Swimming about it, did nothing, I was still in the sea. "Please," I found myself saying, "I need to get home."

The normal suit made another wiggle and I knew I'd struck a nerve. Attempting now to go through, I took a small step and kick, and the pool was suddenly equally real. Again I stepped, this time onto the pool floor, seeing the ocean disappearing, and by the third step it was gone. The normal suit collapsed limply, just as light as a feather, and stopped fighting me. Just in time, too, for I saw the team gathering around Coach Arden. The meet was over. I'd missed my last two events.

Ducking under the lines, I swam to the pool edge before emerging. As I stood at the pool edge, I felt waterlogged in more ways than one, but it all slipped away and I became dry as I climbed out of the water. The water didn't want to let go of me, but having no choice it slipped away taking with it the captivating sea. I felt the loss but forced myself to turn my attention to Coach Arden.

3.7   Let's Breathe Water

Then it was back to the gym. I tried saying something to those I sat with in the van about the submarine and the war with my suit, but I couldn't bring myself to open my mouth on the subject. Instead, I listened as they boasted about how well they'd done. Nobody seemed to have noticed I'd only swum one event too wrapped up in their own victories, and I decided it wasn't worth explaining.

Stewing on it until free swim later that day, when my friends Melanie, Lucy, Cleo and I were hanging out near the tall glass windows that were great for sunbathing in the winter months but they were impossibly hot now. As a result, we had the area to ourselves. I decided it was time that I told them about the dream, but this time I emphasized that I no longer thought it was a dream. I needed their advice.

They listened quietly, only shifting to adjust the towels we used to hide ourselves from the sun, and then the story continued. I'm not sure what I expected, but it wasn't Cleo's comment, "I want to breathe water." Or Melanie's, "Let's go!" The three of them got up from the chairs, walked over to the pool, and dived in. I couldn't believe their reaction, like it wasn't as farfetched as I had thought. Maybe they weren't understanding the impossibility of it all.

When I saw their faith in me, I wondered if I was somehow leading them on. I wasn't sure myself if I wanted it to work – what would that mean? I got up and felt like I was suddenly wearing a sack of potatoes and sat back down. My emotions piled on top of me. I was embarrassed to admit it, how was I going to demonstrate it. I didn't even know if I could.

To top it off, my suit was feeling sluggish. "Not again," I complained, thinking of how the suit had abandoned me during the swim meet. It had stopped its odd behavior until now. Did it think, my getting back into the water was going to cause me to return to the ocean?

As it turns out, it wasn't that far off. As I sat there thinking of the sea, an undercurrent flowed beneath me. I knew if I closed my eyes I'd be sitting on a rock in the sea.

Instead, I stood up expecting my emotions to restrain me again. Walking quickly, I sat down at the pool's edge, dipping my feet into the water to be safe. During my confession, I hadn't told them how my shirt had been replaced by fish the night of the dream, or yesterday before the swim meet. With the renewed effort of the normal suit to resist my swim, I was reminded of the need for the special fish suit. Why wasn't my normal, everyday suit sufficient? I didn't want to be protected by fish, elegant as they were.

But then I thought if I saw that guy again, did I want him to be able to identify me by my team's suit? I thought the whole point of me slipping away the first time was so that he shouldn't know me...

"Are you coming in?" Cleo called, interrupting my thoughts. My best friends were waiting in a semi-circle, expecting a miracle. Honestly, I wished I was the angel the guy had thought I was, with a direct connection to the divine and able to manifest these things on demand.

"Yep," I said slipping in and swimming over hoping I could do this. The short swim reminded me how tired I was, which was strange in and of itself. The events of this morning and the strange outbursts of power made no sense. At least I hadn't flipped out of the water with a single kick while swimming in my swim meet event. To top it off, my swimsuit felt like I was swimming in my winter coat, completely soaked and weighing me down. It couldn't be the swimsuit, for it weighed almost nothing.

"You're a deep thinker today. What's going on?" asked Lucy with concern all over her face, sliding over and putting a hand on my shoulder. The other two joined us.

"I'm fine really," I said, trying to be upbeat, but I could see that they weren't buying it. Yet they ignored it, because they wanted to try the experiment. I could see the excitement and hope on their faces. "Ready?" Melanie asked with a thumbs down indicating we should dive, I shrugged as we went under.

I could breathe, but it felt difficult and I could feel the fish indicating it was the outer suit. I'd noticed it in practice, and thought nothing of it at the time and had continued to breathe normally pushing through it to breathe as I had all my life while swimming. But the underwater breathing wasn't working for them. I could see their struggle, the normal team suit was blocking my ability from going out to them so they could get air from the water as I was. After a few seconds, they pointed upwards and we surfaced.

"What's the problem?" Cleo asked full of faith in me and determined to experience it. Melanie sat back floating in the water, ready for anything, and Lucy simply watched with just her head exposed. When Cleo finished her question, they looked at me pointedly. It was time to confess.

With a sigh, I looked down at the water and then to them. "Honestly I don't know how it works, but what I know is this," and I explained to them the whole story. How I'd left my room and appeared miraculously in the ocean wearing a ballerina suit of fish, though it meant little to me at the time, and I explained how it made me uncomfortable having to wear only the fish as a swimsuit.

They were nodding, and Melanie turned as she floated on her back and looked at me upside down. I wanted to be doing the same, but I was too uptight and knew I couldn't. From that vantage she said, "Do you have them with you now?" To which I reluctantly nodded. "Oh cool, I want to see them. Will we get them too?" And I shrugged at that.

I would have to remove the normal team swimsuit under which was the fish one. It continued to bother me that it was a condition of these abilities. It made about as much sense as any story ever told of true mermaids, and they were confusing at best. As often as not the mermaid wasn't wearing much. I could be thankful, I guess, that I had been given the fish for a swimsuit.

They all thought about it, and then Lucy said, "That guy you rescued, he probably thinks you're a mermaid."

Cleo countered, "But mermaids all have fish tails, and we can clearly see that you do not," and after a pause asked in a whisper after looking around to be sure nobody was listening, "You didn't, did you?"

I shook my head, "No, not a mermaid tail. I did feel when I was carrying the man up to his boat that I had fins on my feet like a scuba diver, but I couldn't see them."

"That makes sense," Melanie added, and when the three of us turned to stare at her, and she asked, "What? No mermaid is born with a fish tail, she has to earn it, and everyone knows that!" With a huff, she turned a somersault and came back up facing us.

"So, you're a mermaid," Lucy and Cleo said at once.

I answered with, "Am not!" and turned away from them. Emotions were piling up again – I needed their support, but they were basically calling me a freak. In a heartbeat, the three of them were around me, holding me close. Yet, how could I deny the evidence? It was all happening so fast. I'd been a thousand feet down in the Atlantic, impossibly deep. As much as I wanted to deny it, I couldn't shake it, but their arms helped my nerves to settle down.

"You don't have to be one," Cleo said, looking beyond me to the other two with a determined look. Her argument sounded good. Right, I don't have to be a freak if I don't want too. It's good to have friends you love, no matter the circumstances.

"Right, you don't have to be," said Lucy agreeing reluctantly, but Melanie added, "Remove your team suit, and let's be sure," shooting it all sky high. I wanted to turn on her and push her underwater, and I would have had it been Lucy or Cleo. Instead I did what my friend told me to do, I'd lost control of the situation. Actually I lost it when I'd told them about it in the first place. Knowing it could come to this.

When I began to get out of the team suit, Melanie continued, "Besides, even if you're not a mermaid, breathing water is a cool thing and so is that suit, wow. It's so beautiful!" The fish had reorganized themselves, no longer appearing as my team suit, but a multicolored variation that suited my feelings. Her voice trailed off putting out a hand to touch it where it was revealed, "And soft. There's no seam on your shoulder, like its paint, but not." She meant it stretched in the right places.

"You're right. It can be fun," I said thinking a thousand feet under and the pool forever away could be fun. I finished stepping out of the suit that I had fought to keep on earlier. I stood there afraid I'd be many miles away in a second, but instead there were a half-dozen tiny fish swimming in the palm of my hand. "What is it, guys?" I asked them feeling silly, under my breath so even my friends couldn't hear me.

They replied by spelling out the message, "Could we be bikinis for you and your friends?" Where they the fish that had been with me all day? I'm pretty sure they were.

I knew I shouldn't go around without clothes, but I asked, "Will my friends be able to breathe underwater when you are on me?" They rotated in place, which I hoped meant yes. "Okay then, but be cute and protect us," giving them permission. "We will." They swam up my arms and to my friends. So quick I don't think my friends noticed. The swimsuit I wore changed to a bikini. It seemed they could become any kind of swimsuit.

Meanwhile, Cleo grabbed up the suit I'd taken off saying, "Here," meaning to toss it far away, like that would help. "No, let me," said Melanie. They fought for the privilege.

"I got it," I said strongly, and Cleo let it unwind into my hands. The act of throwing it away was symbolic, that I was throwing away my dependency on normal girl ways.

I balled it up, feeling the sheer nylon spandex. It felt so artificial now – I'd never noticed that before. When I threw it, it left my hand like I'd cracked a baseball with a bat, and it smacked against the window fifty feet away with a loud thud. As it flew through the air, I decided right then that throwing it wasn't such a great idea, but I'd crossed a bridge of no return with the throw. As it hit, drawing everyone's attention, the four of us dove underwater so that no one would know who had done it. But it was fairly obvious, if they cared to identify the culprit, as we were the only ones hightailing it underwater to the deep end.

"It's working," Melanie said and smiled joyfully as the four of us stopped underwater at the deepest part of the deep end.

"My ears aren't popping, and, and... we're talking!" Cleo clapped excitedly looking around. Then looked at me, asking in a hushed whisper, "Nobody can hear us, can they?"

"We should be fine," Lucy said.

Then Cleo asked, "But how come we..." and she gestured to her swimsuit.

Lucy answered flippantly, "It's Jill's mermaid powers that are enabling us," momentarily forgetting my sensitivity to the issue.

I wasn't paying attention to them, for when we'd zipped for the deep end, the bottom of the pool was becoming transparent. Then, when we stopped, a whirlpool swirled around the base of the pool. It had no sucking feel, but as it slowly swirled, it acted like a big eraser and it started erasing the bottom of the pool in wider and wider arcs. Through the hole, the same seafloor was revealing itself as in my dream.

"Go ahead," and I felt like I was giving them a gift greater than simply breathing water, "and remove your team suits too. You have fish suits now." I laughed at their surprised looks trying to ignore the effects going on around us.

"Come on," Melanie said to the others and pushed off the straps of her swimsuit oblivious to the whirlpool and the results of her actions. She was half out of her suit by the time the other two joined in removing theirs. "Wait," I pleaded as the whirlpool leapt up the walls of the pool in reaction to their actions. As suit after suit came off, the seawater rose to encompass us.

I may not be able to have the full gown anymore, but we were all decent. By the time the last suit came off, my friends saw they we were all "suited" with fish, but by then we'd been cast out into the sea. The ocean was all around us except for what looked like an oil slick overhead where we could see the pool though it wasn't to last, oozing away like the oil it appeared to be, dissipating in seconds. They hadn't listened and now I knew we would be stuck here until we could figure out a way back home.

"What are these?" Melanie asked holding up a bunch of fish, and gesturing to the fish that swam about her and each of us.

"They're the fish suit, silly," I added kidding with her. "What did you think I meant?"

Cleo said in amazement, "They certainly are pretty. Do they stay with us out of the water?"

I nodded, "They want to be my primary suit, but I haven't tested what it's like to have only them on."

"They *want*?" Lucy asked.

"Well, that's the impression I get," I told my friends. "They won't stay if you don't want them. I found that out the first time, but they do want to help. As you can see." I turned, realizing my friends were no longer listening. Lucy stayed until she saw that Melanie and Cleo had begun to swim off. I was left looking back up, hoping to see the pool, but seeing only the rippling surface. So, I went to join them.

3.8   Explorers

The current was strong, it pulled us along. It hadn't taken my friends long to orient themselves, and by the time I caught up to them we'd traveled a ways, leaving the pool behind. It was great to be in this water. It felt different here than my brief plunge in the Atlantic. Here, it wasn't so deep so the water was a lighter blue and full of light and color. It wasn't like the last time I was here either – then, it had been a struggle in comparison. Now, I was floating along.

It was as if I'd become part of the ocean. I closed my eyes to feel the sea better, and through the sea I felt and saw my friends around me. Around us as far as I could sense were schools of fish rising and falling from the depths. Also, I could sense my friends undergoing a similar change to what I had experienced and continued to undergo.

Before, the change had resulted in me crying in the shower. Now, the same was happening to my friends. Their hair became resplendent, attractive and richly colorful. Somehow, they were experiencing the change that had swept through me. The vision lasted a second, and then I opened my eyes, hoping my friends would take the change better and not become embroiled in tangled emotions.

We were adapting, but at least I didn't have flippers this time. I felt stronger, more in tune with the sea. I saw my friends transforming in similar ways. Even though we had been swimmers since we were babies, they still had to change. They were growing their own fins until the necessary changes were finished. I'd always thought that swimming was glorious, but it had taken on a supple grace that had everything to do with being able to breathe water and not having to go up for air. I was glad my friends were getting this adventure, enjoying the sea as I had last night.

Swirling around one another, we danced, relishing in one another and the moment. Not needing air, we circled and circled, passing before each other, laughing and listening to Lucy orchestrate us as if we'd become instant underwater ballerinas and could perform as she directed. Often as not, failing to execute the maneuver and in my last crash with Cleo, we couldn't stop laughing. Lucy got so mad that it took the rest of us to swirl tornados of water on her so she couldn't talk while concentrating on trying to orient herself. "Ok, stop," she complained and we went back to swirl dancing on our own.

Out of breath, we hovered and then turned toward the surface, which was only about ten feet above. We emerged into the rolling sea.

"This is so awesome!" I said to them as we floated. "I'm so glad you guys are here with me." Apparently, it was no dream after all! I turned in a circle, looking at my friends, seeing the astonishment on their faces. I had been pretty sure it was no dream, but now I was certain it wasn't.

Melanie echoed my thoughts, "This is no dream. But where are we?"

"It's barely light. Almost morning," Lucy said, figuring it out quickly and thinking out loud. "So we're probably in the Pacific somewhere, way west. Probably near Indonesia or Australia. There are a lot of islands around there, and there's one over there," she said and gestured to the island I'd seen before. "I didn't see any sharks either," she stated.

I'd never thought about that, but then again I'd presumed it to be a dream at first. I never had scary dreams, so the thought had never crossed my mind, but now that she brought it up we started looking around.

Determined to be hopeful, Melanie added, "Sharks leave mermaids alone, unless provoked I guess. Even then, it wouldn't be worse than getting bitten by a dog."

"Where did you get that from?" Cleo asked her nervously, looking about anxiously for danger. Then, she saw that the other two were getting their signals from me. I was relaxed. At first, we'd looked about, but our eyes did little good. I had to open myself up to that other vision, and I sensed no danger. Indeed, there were a pair of sharks near the point of the island, but I didn't bring it up. Sensing the sea around me, I could tell that the sea creatures mainly seemed to be friendly.

And above, the morning breeze was full of the day's promise. Seagulls were flying here and there, while other seabirds floated about riding the waves. The fish that had become our covering had no problems keeping with us, no matter how much we twirled, dove and swam. At times, it seemed like we were like gumball machines to them, and they gumballs inside our glass. They became indistinct, their colors overlapping, to create interesting designs. And now that we swam in the ocean, other fish shadowed us. All the sea seemed to greet us as we swam among them, including us in their activities and not fleeing as we had expected.

"So, you're a mermaid," Cleo said when we gathered in a grotto of coral. And there was no use denying it, but I still shook my head refusing to believe it, saying, "I'm not." Indeed, I could choose not to be.

"Do you have fins again?" Lucy asked. I shook my head, not wanting to mention that they looked like they had fins now. When I held my hands up, there was nothing to see, so I showed them, "See? No webs."

The longer we stayed, feeling it, the change that made us fish in water would keep affecting us. When I'd thrown my suit away, I'd opened a door that wouldn't close again. We weren't becoming fish. I could sense us, and we remained people. Fish couldn't breathe out of water, nor walk on land as we could. They'd never know what it was like to explore the heavens. Mankind had gone to the moon and flew through the sky.

Nor were we one of the many other aquatic life forms that could pass the barrier of the surface, like turtles and birds. We remained human with some freakish water breathing ability. And I was experiencing a transcendent sense of life beneath the surface of the sea. It seemed a lot like intuition, and it greatly reduced my fear of the unknown, but I had to activate it. Sometimes, I forgot.

"How cool is that!" I heard Cleo cry out, pulling me from my thoughts. She was pointing to the sunken ship I'd discovered on my previous trip, as we weaved our way through the coral reefs. "A real pirate ship. We have to explore it!"

The three of them swam up and over to the ship, no longer staying near me as they had at first. They probably thought I was there alongside them. They were in as much awe of the sea as I'd been. Not that I'd lost the joy, but I was having more fun seeing the aquatic life in these coral canyons. Around every corner, a vista awaited. Exploring the byways of the coral canyons was more fun to me now than hovering over the whole scene with the vast ocean disappearing into the distance.

I watched them, through "the sight," as they swam about, doing loops and swimming about the ship declaring themselves in turn "Captain" of their pirate ship. "Hoist the sails, swab the decks, load the cannons, ahoy, land ho" and many similar shouts rang out from them.

I couldn't bring myself to follow, for I was still wrapped up in the changes taking place in me. Even though I tried to redirect my attention to the life around me. But, I kept returning to the thought that I was changing. I wanted to say I was the same girl, but my perspective was growing to include a horizon much greater than that of the gym. At least my heart held to my awareness of myself. Even if I were to grow a fin like a shark on my back or head, I would have to remain true to myself. Drawing on my friends' wonder, I finally put the thoughts aside and went to join them.

It didn't take long to become enraptured with the sea again. I hadn't taken time to explore the sea before, so now it was a delight to carouse with my friends. I shouldn't let myself get separated from them, or I would become moody. Moving from the ship and from one coral reef to another, we played tag. After a while, we sought out the burning sands of the island to soak up some rays. I might be immune to the cold of the sea, but I'd never tire of sunning with my friends.

3.9   Deserted Island

Standing up again was a nice change, as we walked inland through the coasters that rolled past us, feeling the sea surge and with a light breeze in our face. Cleo was the first to remark that the fish were staying with us, on our bodies, but no longer as fish. As I'd noticed before, they somehow were stretching out and connecting to one another becoming the swimsuit bikinis that they'd promised, minus the stitches, tags and emblems, and ultra-comfortable.

We played a moment in the waves, riding them in, but we were tired of the sea and made for the soft sand ahead of us. As if we were the first to ever arrive on a beach, we danced and spun, excited by the novelty. The air felt so good as I leapt, wanting to be caught up in the breeze and soar like an eagle. Then the breeze carried an organic aroma containing the scent of every island flower imaginable under our noses, making me want to stay and breathe it forever. As if there were some kind of enchantment on the island keeping us here, I felt that I could live happily ever after in this heavenly place.

Crawling onto the dry sand, we scooped out some alcoves for ourselves beside one another. The awareness I'd felt beneath the sea had nearly disappeared once we left the water. No longer did I feel the heart beats of my friends, or their skin as if it were my own. But when we laid down together, shoulder to shoulder, inadvertently holding hands, that sense returned. It had to be coming from the water that flowed through our bodies.

Again, I felt their hearts, and our breathing synchronized before a sense of giddiness took over. Nobody said anything, but before long we were hunched over laughing for no particular reason, which was the best kind of laughter. "Anyone have a Coke?" Melanie asked. "What I'd give for a Coke," she said and we laughed some more before quieting again and laying back down.

For a time, we were enraptured by the tranquility, but then Cleo sat up casting a shadow across me. I'd fallen asleep. I awoke to a crab crawling across my stomach. The crab and I had a moment of looking each other in the eye before she mozied onward as if I were simply another dune. Why wasn't this crab or the others crawling around on the sands near us afraid of us? Or us them, for they resembled giant spiders. I didn't know, yet it made me feel at peace, and I put my head back down. This had to be a part of the changes I felt occurring. The more we embraced this life, the more such changes took place; not freaking out about the crab was apart of that.

"It's too quiet," Cleo finally said, distracting me from my thoughts. "Except for all of these," she said, pointing to the chattering crabs.

"Go to sleep," I said, rolling over, but she was right.

"A place like this, shouldn't exist. There should be people, hotels, something," she went on. "I'm not complaining that we have it to ourselves, but really. A paradise like this doesn't exist on its own without people."

Lucy added from her prone position, "I noticed that too. There should be hotels, or a dozen yachts and sailboats around it with tourists playing upon it."

I looked up from my position towards the trees and brush that rose up not far from where we laid. There were no huts or any other sign of human life. What they said made sense. My senses were greatly dulled and I didn't expect to find anything, but I reached out anyway. There was nothing nearby I could sense. "Yeah, it's weird," I said agreeing with them.

"I could live like this," Cleo said expressing what I'd thought earlier. "The air is so fresh and stimulating that I believe I'm detecting pink, purple, yellow and blue flowers," she said laying back down. I glanced over at her as she tucked her arms under her head, practically poking me in the face with her elbow.

"Me too," I told her, and she looked over and smiled a second before closing her eyes to the sun.

It bothered me to know that out there was someone who was suffering and that maybe I aught to be doing something about it. Sleep evaded me. I tried flipping over and gazing out at the greenery, but that only made me want to go explore it more, so I turned again and sat up, pulling my knees up and looking out to sea. We'd chosen a spot that was to the side of where the boat sat, but it was still visible off to our left. It drifted around its anchor with no sign of life aboard.

Unable to go help right then, I gathered up my weakened senses and darted towards the yacht with my vision hoping to satisfy my curiosity. Like a seagull spreading its wings on the wind, my sight rushed outward, but then it stopped as if I'd hit a wall and I knew I was draining my powers. My mouth was suddenly parched.

I rose to my feet unconsciously and, like a zombie, walked into the sea. As I was searching for a way past the wall, my feet touched the water, and I surged out in every direction and suddenly blew past it. An influx of information slammed into me, and I crashed to my knees, falling forward. I had one second of omniscience before I blacked out, and I saw the man below decks of the yacht with the medical kit spread about him, doing his best to treat his leg.

It was fortunate I couldn't drown, but the sea was doing its best to choke me with sand. The waves rolled me back and forth before the undertow pulled me into the depths. Like a dress in the washing machine, I rolled over and over, dreaming and knowing I shouldn't be, but I couldn't wake up. I felt my friends calling and looking for me. "Over here!" I cried, but the cry went unanswered. They turned and walked into the trees away from the beach, leaving me to the dregs of the sea. The dream changed and I saw dad, picking up my swimsuit from where it had fallen after I threw it. He called to me too, encouraging me, "Wake up!"

I awoke with the remnants of a splitting headache dispersing into the sea. I gulped air about six feet under, feeling rotten. With a shove, I pushed up from the sea floor, kicking for the surface. How long had I been out?

I'd last seen my friends on the island, and hoped they were still there, but I didn't dare reach out towards them and see if they were. Had they really gone looking for me inland? I had to find them. Also, the diver would have to wait, because my friends came first. Plus, I now knew he was alive and treating himself. That would have to comfort me until I could return.

I paused during my swim back, *would I really return?* It wasn't at all certain that we'd get home as there was no easy way back to the pool. Partially, I thought, as I resumed my swim, it was the island and its many beaches, rocky outcroppings and tropical forest that drew me onward. Mostly though it was my friends I longed for, I couldn't wait to rejoin them.

3.10 Stretching Their Powers

Even though I hadn't sensed that people had ever been on the island before, that sunken ship had certainly sailed these waters and it was highly probably its crew had been ashore. How long ago had that been? Cleo calling it a pirate ship made me wonder. It was a wooden sailing ship of old, but not ancient, origin. As a result, there could be a thriving modern-day community somewhere on the island, even if we hadn't seen any sign of one.

When I emerged from the water, my friends practically tackled me like a bunch of overgrown puppies. I hugged them back, so glad they hadn't left me as I'd seen in the dream. "We were so worried!" Cleo exclaimed and then asked exasperated, "Where did you go? Why did you leave us?"

Lucy said at the same time, "We thought to scout the water but decided to wait a while longer." Her voice trailed away as the other two nodded in agreement.

"We also found fresh water," Melanie added. "Do you think it's safe to drink? I mean, we're all thirsty." I shrugged. "Come," she said, waving us inland, and we all went. Apparently they had gone inland, but they had returned to await for my return.

They walking before me, I noticed something strange – tanned streaks down their backs where there was water. Especially where I'd hugged them. The rest of them being sunburned, but as I watched it was disappearing as the water ran. I could sense the water and there was nothing magical in it, but knew it had to have been a combination of the water and my touch.

What was happening to me? More changes, more freakish abilities, but to keep their healing from being uneven, I one after the other put my hand on their shoulder and encouraged the water to spread over them, the healing moving with the water. Then I didn't want to touch anyone less something else unexpectedly happen. But I ended up observing them and was pleased with the resulting even tan.

Lucy and Cleo were fair-skinned, Lucy being chalky white and never able to tan, always burning. Melanie was the darkest of us all, yet she had burned as well. Now I saw that the water was changing it all into a tan, Lucy's skin becoming light caramel in color. The healing taking place rapidly where they were wet, and it passed down their backs to their legs right before my eyes as I'd encouraged it to do.

"Here," Cleo said, interrupting my thoughts. We ducked through a tunnel of branches my friends had woven to create a small passageway. On the other side, was a small creek that disappeared into the ground. Around it were rocks that prevented it from reaching the sea, but it ran so close to the sea that it had to be merging into it at some point. I knelt beside the stream and pushed my hands in. Immediately, a cool sensation rose up my arms, cooling me from our brief walk up the sunny beach.

I knew the dangers of drinking unfiltered water, and wasn't thirsty myself. I had another ability revealing itself just then – the water was entering me through my hands, satisfying any craving I had.

"Here," I said, "Kneel and do as I'm doing."

The three of them dropped to their knees, Melanie dropping down beside me and the other two across from us. When their hands dipped into the water, I felt the water go into them as well. I felt a similar connection to them as I had when we laid on the beach.

"This is amazing," Melanie exclaimed. "I can feel you all!" Our hands weren't touching. Excitedly she went on, "I can feel your breathing, your skin as if it were my own. Even more," she added, blushingly pulling her hands from the water to look at them. "Oh, it's gone!"

"I feel like a doctor," she said thrusting her hands back in the water again to confirm that it was real. "The knowledge I have of each of you is intimate." Looking at her knees, she continued, "I'd know if any of you were pregnant. It's that intimate. How is this possible?"

I had my ideas, as I had been more sensitive to it all for a bit longer. I expected it was because we were friends. Lucy, the smartest of us, summed it up. "When we were back in the pool," she explained. "We couldn't experience any of this until Jill removed her suit."

I wanted to say I'd been wearing the fish, as they had been too. Had they forgotten? Still, I didn't want to interrupt her, so I let her finish.

"It wasn't apparent, but we must have passed some test that permitted us to breathe as naturally as we breathe now – even though we ourselves remained dressed. When we each began to remove our suits, I noticed a dramatic rolling back of the natural; the pool's walls disappearing before my eyes. I didn't grasp what was taking place until suddenly we found ourselves in the ocean. I'd seen the walls of the pool disappearing, and once we were all undressed" and fish-covered, "it was suddenly no longer the chlorinated pool water but salt water. Above us, I had seen the diving board and someone walking along the edge of the pool."

"Something, and I'll call it 'magic,' transported us to some part of the Pacific Ocean. As I said before, I'd hazard to guess we're near Australia, but without instruments I can't be sure. It was morning when we arrived, so some nine-hour difference or so. It should be relatively easy to calculate our position from that."

"Ever since our immersion in this culture that Jill carries; the fish suits and all of this, we've been on a journey of transformation, and it is probably both biological and society-bound. The biological seeks to advance us to a place where we can experience what would be normal for those of the society. It's possible through the event Jill experienced some microbe that has touched her and has now spread to us."

"So far, it has been benign and therefore I don't expect it to plague humanity. Until we can be sure, though, we should isolate ourselves..."

I thought about what Lucy had said, putting into words a lot of what I'd been thinking and what I'd experienced. But this last part about us being biological terrors I didn't buy, so I decided it was time to interject. "We don't have to do that," I interrupted. "It is clearly, at least to me, smarter than a mindless disease. How smart it is I couldn't say, but it will only spread to friends, and as far as I can tell you're not contagious. Only I am, if anyone is."

"How do you know?" Lucy asked.

How was I to explain the spiritual sense, as it reached out from me to them? Melanie only guessed at what I knew. We'd removed our hands from the water, but being so close to them I still felt them. It was as if I were each of them. Their hearts were open to me, but their personalities remained their own.

"At least for now," I said. "There may come a point where that won't be true," I shrugged, unable to explain better.

3.11 Island Fever

"I want to explore more," Cleo interjected, "before we leave."

"Let's meet back at the beach in two hours," Lucy suggested and stood up. She looked to Cleo, and the two of them grabbed hands and followed the stream further into the island.

Melanie reached out for my hand and I held on as she said, "Let's explore the beach," and led the way back to the beach and into the water, deep enough so we didn't have to bend to get our hands wet. "I wonder where we are," she said standing sideways as one of the taller waves broke around her. Raising a hand to shade her eyes from the sun, she gazed out to sea.

"I don't know," I admitted, doing the same. "This feels so much like a dream, it's all so perfect." Then looking sideways at her, I admired her relaxed poise and then asked, "You don't accept Lucy's explanation on where we are?"

She smiled back a second and then went back to scanning the sea, "Oh Lucy, always has an answer. I meant more specifically, though, I suppose her answer is good enough."

"I'd guessed something similar, but Lucy can articulate my thoughts better than I can. So, do you think its my fault we're stuck here?" I couldn't help thinking I'd brought this on everyone.

"You can't blame yourself," Melanie said turning to look down the beach past me. "Lucy means well. Even if this thing is biological, I don't mind being infected with this thrill though I know you don't like it. I too feel like this is a dream. Even though I've heard of mermaids all my life, I admit I never thought that any of this was possible." She was so overjoyed by this. I was thrilled when I thought it a dream, but I wanted the changes to stop. I'd be fine with breathing water and diving in tropical waters. I didn't need to be a cover girl, or heal the world.

"What do you mean?" As I turned to her, the sun was over her left shoulder and I shaded my eyes with my hand. Out of the four of us, Melanie had the darkest skin and the darkest hair. In this light, her Latin features stood out beautifully.

What I couldn't get over was Melanie's attitude, or that of my other friends. They were all taking this in stride. Spending time on the beautiful beach with them, without miraculous abilities, was all anyone could ever want. Cleo and Lucy were off exploring like they were at an amusement park, one we had all to ourselves. That we were comfortable here in this amazing wilderness on our own surprised me. With no adults, unsupervised, I thought we were handling it rather well.

In fact, my friends were even more accepting of it than myself. They were trusting me, but I had no influence on the biologic or moving us about across the globe. I certainly had no hand in finding this island. I really had no idea how these things were happening.

"So, what do you mean?" I prodded when she didn't go on.

"Let's walk," Melanie said, spinning me about by my hand to dive from where we were back towards the beach. When we left the water for the beach, we held hands again.

"You know how I've mentioned Aunt Anne," she asked. I nodded. "All my life, she's told me tales of mermaids, dolphins and fairies." As I looked back over our shoulders, the waves were erasing our footprints like we'd never been here.

"What I haven't told you is that Aunt Anne is friends with them." We climbed over rocks to slide down into a new moon-shaped cove. We had to slide down into the sea and then side stroke for the shore before resuming.

I wasn't sure I believed her, but then again here we were somewhere else in the world where anything was possible. Talking animals? That seemed farfetched, but then again so was going through the bottom of the pool into the ocean and talking under water. What we'd done seemed so natural now, but what was she saying? I wasn't listening.

"Wait, what?" I asked.

"I know you don't believe me," she said holding tightly onto my hand, afraid I'd run away. "I hardly believe it myself, and I've been there."

I squeezed her back, sliding my hand around her waist and holding her close, "I believe you. I do," I said, trying to believe and failing.

We stopped to eye the next hurdle in our path. The forest jutted out to sea at the other end of the half-moon beach. "Shall we go through?" she asked, our noses practically touching. Our eyes met, and we could see in the other's a challenge still to go further, so we let go and scrambled up a steep dune. Once on top, we looked back, hoping to have a view of the beach we started from, but we couldn't see beyond the rocks on the other end of the cove. We smiled and shrugged, and then turning our backs to it, pushed under palm leaves that reached to the ground, doing our best not to scratch ourselves on the undergrowth. It did us little good, for after about ten steps our feet were scratched and bleeding, but then the undergrowth gave way to the shade of the bigger trees and there were softer plants underneath.

"Let's go to the right," Melanie suggested. I'd been following her lead, so we turned towards the point, but we didn't get far before she stopped to pull a thorn from her foot. "You know," she said, "I've always wanted to do something like this." I knew what she meant – explore an untouched tropical island. "But it hurts worse than anything I've ever imagined. In my dreams, I would walk sunlit beaches and in cool forests just like this without a care – with a friend." She held me close and we turned again to find our way out to where we could hear the sea pounding like a distant drum. "I do hope this isn't the only time we ever do this."

"I can't promise anything," I told her. "I don't even know how it works, except being open and willing seems to trigger these trips." That was true enough as far as I knew, "But I don't know how to control the destination. During the swim meet, my suit fought with me and I found myself floating in a windy sea as a result. I'm not even sure if I'd ever have been able to return if I'd let my suit get away."

"You would have," Melanie said squeezing my hand. "You would have found a way."

"I'm not so sure," I said under my breath helping her climb a big rock that had risen in our path.

"What?" she asked, looking down from the rock.

"I'm not sure," I repeated. "I feel myself changing with each outing, and my heart feels more at home here than at the gym."

"Either you'd find a way, or I'd come find you," she said looking me in the eye. "You're my best friend, and I'm not losing you."

"Okay, thanks," I said trying to have the same determination as her, "Up the last little bit and we're over this," I said and formed a cradle with my fingers into which she stepped and I hauled her up.

"Yep, this is the top," she said from over the ridge before returning and looking down.

Kneeling and then lying on her stomach, she extended a hand down for me. I leaped up, caught a hand-hold and then took her hand as she pulled me up. "What a view," I thought looking around from the summit.

Looking back down the way we came, we both said together, "We're not going back that way." From there, it was some more scrambling across the ridge to the point where we could see far and wide with the sea before us. We sat shoulder to shoulder, enjoying the view, the sun, and each other's company. Eventually, we had to take to the water to swim out and back to the others.

3.12 Make a Way

We found Lucy and Cleo sitting on the beach with flowers woven into their hair staring out to sea. They were so beautiful. We ran up and settled down next to them. "Here," Lucy said, "Turn around." She was holding up flowers to weave into my hair.

"So when are we leaving?" asked Cleo. "I should be getting back to the sport shop soon."

Looking out on the turquoise water, the sun, the wind coming off the island, it was hard to imagine that the day had to end. I still had no idea how we got here, so I didn't know how to leave, and I told them that.

"Well, if we sit here all day, nothing is going to happen," reasoned Lucy.

I shrugged, but Melanie responded, "And you know that how?"

Giving her a look and tugging on my hair as she wove in another flower, Lucy said, "If it was going to happen, wouldn't it already have happened?"

Melanie wouldn't let it go, "So shall we swim around hoping to? I'd rather stay here where it's nice."

There was no figuring it out. Lucy finished my hair and I told her thanks, sighing inwardly with relief. Lucy didn't have Cleo's gentle fingers, and my neck was sore from holding back my flinches when she tugged my hair too hard. Conversation turned to the swim meet, but when another argument was starting to boil, Melanie said, "I'm going to swim," and stood up dusting sand off her legs.

The rest of us got up and followed suit. Then Cleo ran up the beach, and returned a minute later with a bundle of flowers, "For the shop," she said and then looking at the incoming waves added, "I hope."

Then we all walked, ran and dove into the water, Cleo doing her best to protect her flowers. A barren sandy slope guided us down to where the sea life waited about fifteen feet down. The sea continued to grow deeper.

"Jill," Melanie suggested, "concentrate on home. See if you can feel home the way you can feel the ocean."

We swam along while I tried as she had suggested. It was true, it hadn't been hard to feel the sea while we were at home. But that hadn't been something I'd conjured. It turns out it wasn't too difficult to feel home with the spiritual sense I'd been using today.

The funny thing is I felt the connection as soon as I put my mind to it as Melanie had suggested, but I had no idea how to bring it into reality. So I brought it up with them to discuss.

For a while the subject was tossed around, but it was finally Cleo that thought of it first. "These things aren't happening randomly," she said. "There has to be someone in charge of it. And we should thank them for the fun we've had while we're at it."

"Is that praying?" asked Lucy with a sour face.

"We're communicating. Isn't praying usually to a god? We don't know what we're doing at the moment, but let's be polite..." Melanie said trailing off and holding up her fingers crossed. We didn't know if it would work, but it felt right.

"So who wants to begin?" I asked.

"Cleo should go. It was her idea," suggested Melanie after a period of silence.

"Thanks, Mel," Cleo said. "If I get struck by lightning, it's your fault."

Lucy laughed sharply at that, saying, "If you get struck by lightning, since we're underwater, we're all dead."

"Thanks, Lucy. You all are the bestest friends I could ever want," Melanie said sarcastically.

" 'Greatest,' or 'nicest,' but 'bestest' isn't a word," Lucy corrected her.

"So, are we going to do this?" asked Melanie, "Or are we going to float here all day?"

I raised my hand and said with a smirk, "I vote for floating here with my nicest and greatest friends." I winked at Cleo.

She floated over and we rubbed shoulders, "Thanks Jill. In that spirit, I propose we begin." Seeing that there were no more comments, she opened up, and I "felt" around in that spiritual sense for "who" was in charge and for home. After a pause, Cleo began to speak, "Thanks for the fun day the four of us has had. Um, sir. We ask for the way home to be opened, please." Then she waved at the rest of us and we all added, "Please."

I waited for the rest before saying my "please," as I sensed that it would happen when I did and I wanted them all to feel a part of it. Lucy was reluctant. I knew her feelings about praying, but she finally conceded. Then I added my voice and soon we were looking at the floor in the deep end of the pool.

With one voice, we cheered and then swam for it. Cleo in front, and with the greatest delight, carried her prizes still intact from the pool to the shop to fill it with the aroma of the island.

4 Red Deer Lake

When the day finally wound down and I was able to crawl into bed, I was beyond exhausted. The changing of time zones, a full day at the gym and the extra exposure to the sun had wiped me out. I lay back thinking of the wonderful day, marveling at what great friends I had to share it with. As Uncle Arden tucked me in, he ruffled my hair and kissed my forehead. Before he was gone, I was asleep.

When I awoke at 2 am, moonlight filling my room again, I knew I wouldn't fall back asleep, "Not again..." I complained yawning and stretching. I looked out at the moon across the top of the gym. Funny thing is, instead of reaching for my pillow, I was wanting the feel of water for a bed.

Reluctantly I pulled myself up. I almost grabbed my suit, but the thought of wearing it sleeping, I'd just end up struggling with the thing. I couldn't struggle and be sleeping at the same time, so I left my room without it. Leaving the apartment I climbed down the many steps to the gym, practically sleepwalking. I had one goal – the pool. When I got there, I dove in. I barely discarded my nightshirt in time, as on the night of my birthday.

I slid, or swam, I don't remember, to the deep end, knowing that once I arrived I'd immediately be "somewhere else." I begged and prayed for tranquility with no emergencies this time, but I realized I should take what was given.

When I arrived at the deep end, it wasn't what I expected (a tropical island and someone needing rescue) – instead, I was somewhere in the mountains above Boulder in a lake I'd been to before. It was a long hike to the place. There were camping spots around the lake, but I'd be undisturbed if I stayed some feet down in the chilly waters.

I lay on my back, cozily wrapped in watery sheets, viewing the few stars that were visible between the clouds. *Am I a mermaid?* I wondered. That was my last waking thought before the rays of the morning sun awoke me. Again, that had been the best sleep of my life. Sleeping underwater was without a doubt the strangest thing ever – the most glorious and the most restful.

I'd enjoyed the camping trips Uncle Arden took me and my friends on, but this was way better. I rose up to the surface and scanned the shore. There was nobody around and I estimated the time to be about 7 am. It was either return to the pool for laps or stay here...

Not a difficult choice. At home, I would have to pull my punches and swim nice. Here, though... I started to swim, giving it my all. In seconds, I had covered an impossible distance and had to flip before returning the other direction. I had almost finished my normal morning wake-up exercise, when I suddenly became aware through a side glance that someone was watching me.

I dove immediately, panicking for a way out before I remembered how we the day before in the ocean had gotten home. I stilled my heart, then pictured where I wanted to go in my mind, trying to find home. Nothing came to me. "Please," I said to the water, "I need to get home." There it was, the pool shimmered into view – an image of home. I raced into the opening. In a second, the lake was gone.

I forgot to slow down, though, and had only a split second before I had to shove off from the bottom before crashing into the side opposite. I literally sprang out of the water several feet, windmilling my arms to keep from crashing. My agility might have worked in the water, but I had no such skill in the air. Then it felt like the water molecules in the air became a sort of pillow for me as I smacked into them and then the wall before falling to my butt. It took me a second before I could regain my feet. "Think, Jill, next time," but I couldn't get out of my mind the panic I felt at being watched, reminding me of the freak I'd become.

I didn't have the pool to myself this time, so it was lucky that I had entered along a lane instead of across the pool like a wrecking ball. But there was no one to see my aerial display. Whenever the five swimmers noticed that I was sitting on my bum at a distance from the pool, they would hardly think anything unusual had happened.

Getting to my feet, I had composure – but not my shirt. So, I hastened around the pool to the deep end to retrieve the shirt and slip it on. Either I was going to have to prepare something in advance or get used to this. Being caught out in these fish was becoming a regular occurrence. It was obvious now in hindsight, but when the moment came, it felt better wearing only the fish. It was bound to get people talking. I just hoped it would be a little while before I got it from my parents.

4.1 The Competition

When I returned to our apartment, I walked in on a discussion between Uncle Arden and Mom. Mom gave me a little wave. Uncle gave a friendly smile.

Mom was saying, "It's her territory now. She'll have to handle the problems, too."

"Don't you think that's piling too much on her? She's just started," was Uncle Arden's exasperated reply. He looked at me, before continuing with mom. "A client halfway across the world," he continued, "and a client here as well. There's no chance it's a mistake? Why don't you take this one?"

Were they talking about me in parent speak? The way parents say things around kids to make them think they are talking about someone else. It sure seemed like it.

"You know that I can't. Competition is severe enough as it is, I have my own troubles."

"Competition," Uncle Arden said with crossed arms and a serious expression. "I don't know if you noticed, but one of them is registered with the gym."

Mom lifted an eyebrow. "That's bold, but then we should have expected it. Do you know who it is?"

It looked like their conversation was going to take a while and they weren't going to include me in on it, so I moved into the kitchen to find something to snack on. There was nothing as boring as office talk, and I heard it all the time. They were always worrying that the "competition" would find out about our little operation. The gym was well known in Boulder, or so it seemed to me. But I guess they were worried about the big players trying to shut us down. That didn't seem likely to me, though. We were doing pretty good. In fact, so much so that Lucas had been scouting out new locations for a new gym.

I picked through the apples, selecting a Fuji. Fujis were my favorite, big and juicy. Then, I returned to the main room to hear out the rest. I was going to ask mom if I could hang with her, but now I wasn't sure. She was busy. Still, I hadn't seen her since breakfast yesterday.

"I have my suspicions," Uncle Arden said. If the competition was really trying to understand our success, then we were doing something right. "But before you suggest we get rid of them. I think, let them stay or they'll send someone else and we may not figure out who it is."

"Still I don't like it," mom said and I agreed with her, my right eyebrow rising in imitation of hers. Like mother like daughter. "And where there is one, there may be two."

"Possibly," Uncle Arden replied. "So we're agreed?"

"No, but you're right. A known is better than an unknown, but I don't like influence on our operations," Mom said. Then when uncle was about to walk off, she added "Hold on a second. You need some time off. Why don't you take Jill for a hike. Lucas was going to Lyons. He could drop you off on the way. And I'll check things out here."

"Mom, that's unfair," I said joining in heatedly. "I haven't seen you in a while. I was hoping we could hang."

Blowing up at mom was never the best policy, but she was amused at my response. "You have a champion, Arden. Very well." With a grin, she put her hands on her hips, and turning to me she added pleasantly, "Jill, go get ready and you can go on a hike with your uncle. Oh, and I bought some new clothes I think you'll like. They're on your bed. Pick something from them to wear. And hurry, Lucas needs to get going."

4.2 Westward Bound

I was off to my room before she'd finished, and I caught the last of her words as I turned to examine the garments mom had laid out. Sometimes, mom had no fashion sense, but these clothes were okay. I pulled out a nicely cut running top. My chest was growing, and I needed new sports bras. I wondered if the fish would do a dance for me and I asked them, "Can you look like this?"

The top fish pulled away from the bottom, revealing my belly and swimming around to reform as the bra. It was a close enough approximation that I felt I could be comfortable going without it. I told them, "Nicely done, but Mom might check and I don't want to lie to her, so I'll be putting it on. Sorry…"

It went on, not nearly as nice as the fish made it feel, and then the fish cunningly moved about as needed. It reminded me of my previous thoughts about appearance – Lucy was jealous. She seemed to be stuck looking boyish, which made me sad. But there was nothing I could do about it except hold her hand and hope she would get what she wanted.

I had my choice of skirts and jeans made of the softest material I'd ever felt, but the weather was going to be hot. I imagined being hot on the trail, so I picked the yellow pleated skirt. It was cute, but I did the same thing again, asking the fish, "Can you do this?" and I held out the skirt for them to examine. I was curious if they could do a hem, but then remembered the dream. At that time, they'd been a gown, so it was with little surprise that they duplicated the skirt from the one I held. They had to borrow fish from the top, though.

"You all are amazing," I said and I wanted to hug them. How far I'd come in so short a time. It was just yesterday I'd been squeamish about them being on me. "Okay, good job, but I have to put this on as well.

Once dressed, I looked at myself in the mirror that hung on the back of my door. Now that I had to worry about "mermaid" activities – even if that wasn't the right label, it was the only label I had for it. So, pretty much from now on, it was likely I would be getting wet on any outing I went on. I had the fish, and they'd proven their abilities to me. I should probably go without the garments Mom provided, but now I had them on.

My hair was too perfect. I twirled this way and that before the mirror. I'd been swimming in the lake above Boulder, and now it was dry and smooth, instead of wet and tangled like it should be. I applied my brush anyway, but it did little good. Did my hair feel softer? That didn't make sense, but in a hurry, I shrugged satisfied with my appearance, I sat down to put on sandals then grabbed some socks and jammed them into my trail shoes, which I would put on when we got there.

No one was in the apartment when I emerged, so I headed down to the car. There, I found Uncle Arden talking with my stepdad by the door. When they saw me, they gave a look and Lucas said, "You might get cold."

"She'll be fine," Uncle Arden said. "Besides, she has to figure these things out on her own now. She's an adult. Isn't that right, Jill?" He nodded with a grin, encouraging me to agree with him. Apparently, he was referring to the discussion after the night swim, where I was entrusted with swimming alone at night.

"Right," I agreed smiling back and standing up straight, like that would make me taller. I wanted more than anything to be considered an adult, unless it meant having boring conversations like the one I'd just witnessed between him and Mom.

"Okay," Lucas said, "But don't say I didn't warn you." I shrugged in response. And with that, we headed for the car, got in and headed up into the mountains up through Boulder Canyon to Nederland and then north.

I used to envy adults who could drive, but with recent events, it wasn't such a big deal that I didn't drive yet. There are several pleasant trails in the mountains surrounding Boulder, and Uncle Arden had picked the trail to Red Deer Lake roughly above Jamestown, off of the Peak-to-Peak Highway.

During the drive I felt adrift, like the car was a boat and the air was rushing by the windows. If I looked out, I'd see waves. If I hung my hand down, it would get wet. So it was with surprise that my hand got wet when Lucas passed through some water that was crossing the street from where it ran down off the hills. I glanced up in surprise. I was shocked to find that I was still in the car.

It wasn't long before we arrived at the United States Forest Service campground. During the car ride, I'd taken my sandals off. So when I swung my feet out, it was with surprise that I found the ground marshy feeling, not the hard dirt and sharp rocks that it looked like. Wanting to go barefoot like I had with Melanie yesterday, I left the shoes in the car and stood up to stretch out before our hike.

When you head into the mountains, you can expect the temperature to be twenty degrees cooler, so the obvious thing to do is be prepared for cooler weather. Then if you are going to be out all afternoon, it is good to be prepared for sudden storms. There wasn't going to be a storm, though – it would probably be clear all day. How did I know this? I hadn't a clue, but I could sense it and once I put my feet on the trail, I knew.

My friends were convinced I was a mermaid. I didn't understand the whole thing, but now suddenly I was having weather awareness in addition to everything from yesterday. I felt like breaking down, but I couldn't get moody with Uncle Arden there or we'd spend all day sitting on a bench talking it out. Now that we were here I wanted to hike. Nothing was the same anymore.

When we said goodbye to Lucas, who was on his way to Lyons, he assured us that he'd pick us up in several hours.

4.3   The Mountain
I loved the smell of mountain air, so clear and full of the fresh scent of trees and bubbling brooks. Things were greener here above the heat of the plains. I wiggled my toes in the packed soil, feeling the sense of earth and green grass, my toes disappearing into the ground. I pretended not to notice. A few pale yellow butterflies fluttered past as Uncle Arden tied his shoes. I turned my eyes to gaze down into the valley beside us, hoping to see some deer, elk or moose, but there were none.

Turning around, I heard Uncle Arden grunt as he picked up our things. He handed me my camel pack sloshing full of water. After strapping it on, I took a sip then let the beautiful mountain become part of me again as we turned to the mountain road. Since we didn't have four-wheel drive, Lucas had driven us as far as he could. I saw it as a good thing, as we got to hike up the valley that I'd been scanning for wildlife.

Uncle Arden took the lead, guiding us down off the road into the valley. Then he took his camera out and began snapping pictures of some columbine. I'm normally a follower, but as he paused, I passed along. He never could get enough photos of mountain fauna and landscapes. It was like he'd never seen them before, as if he would never be here again.

It was usually my job to stand beside him, or kneel near some shrub or flower, but really I was more interested in the rocks I found in the brook which I'd proudly show off in some slideshow later. One of my favorite things was to tickle one of the fish from the various pools we passed into my hand for photographing. It was much easier after having experienced the fish from the suit. They were practically leaping into my hand to be photographed.

"Hey, look," Uncle Arden tapped my shoulder pointing. I followed his gaze as we watched a doe with a fawn in tow come from the trees on the other side of the valley. After we'd watched them a while, the baby looked right at us. Then the doe looked to her baby. Where they talking? They seemed to be. As they reached a conclusion, they walked towards us but stopped halfway.

"Go to them," Uncle Arden encouraged me.

"Really?" I asked. Holding up the camera, he wanted a picture. "Okay…" I said getting up from where I'd been kneeling beside the stream. Dusting off and straightening my skirt, I stepped gently towards them, expecting them to flee at any second.

The mother lifted her head once but then went back to pulling some of the grass from the meadow. The baby fawn didn't wait. He jumped and then tottering walked over to me. I was sure he was trying to say hi, but his voice was so high that I giggled in surprise, bending down on one knee and holding out my hand.

He stumbled into me, and I helped him stand, tears coming to my eyes. "Hi," I said in return, "There you go." I was smiling from ear to ear and my face was wet as I turned to Arden, stroking the fawn's brow.

"Born kind of late, weren't you?" I asked the fawn. Fawns usually were born in late spring, but here it was mid-July. "I do hope that doesn't hinder you, though you may be shorter than your fellows for a time." As I held his face, we stared into each other's eyes. I could get lost in those brown eyes. He seemed to understand everything I was saying, so I added. "You grow great and strong, but be kind where you can. I do hope we see each other again."

That was enough seriousness for him, and he bounded off to circle around his mom's legs only to turn and stare back at me. "Bye," I said. I stood up, about to return, but Arden wanted another picture. Then we went on.

"That was wonderful," I said gushing my delight and wiping away tears. They wouldn't stop, I was so happy. "Stop it," I complained as uncle snapped picture after picture of my smiling wet face.

"That was kind of you," he said lifting the strap of the camera over his head, "to bless the buck so."

4.4   The Trail

It was quiet on the trail, tranquil compared to the constant hum of the city. You could hear the birds singing as they happily conversed. A black squirrel decided to chide us for making too much noise. "Hey," I replied, fists on my hips, "Good morning to you, Mr. Squirrel, but your complaining is even louder than our footsteps." I could swear the birds applauded then went about their songs in a different tune. The squirrel huffed and stormed off up a tree.

Arden laughed, "I think he listened to you."

"Yeah, it's a mystery," I shrugged happily. First the deer. Now I was having conversations with a squirrel! Plus, I talked to fish. What next, an otter?

Some five minutes later, it felt like a rock hit me on the head, "Ow."

There, rolling down the trail was the offending nut. I glanced up at the trees expecting for them at any moment to unload more nuts, but there was nothing to see. It didn't occur to me until later that it might have been that squirrel. If I'd listened closely, I'd probably have heard it chittering in laughter.

On the way up, we crossed the creek we'd been following from the campground. Several times, we stopped to splash ourselves with the cold water. I didn't really need to splash, simply touching it sent the water all through me, cooling me as it went, but I did it for the sake of appearances. When I was cool enough, all I had to do was remove my hand. Because I was pretending to be normal, I ended up cooling off more than I needed to be as I was now wet as well from splashing myself.

"It's too bad we can't drink it," I said.

"Why can't you?" he asked. "See?" He put one hand in, and out his thumb on the other hand spurted a water-fountain-sized flow. He bent down and drank from it. "Yum, fresh," he declared, and I stared at his hands trying to see the trick, but I didn't get it. "You try it," he suggested.

Um, right... I bent at the knees, put my left hand in, and felt the water enter me as before. "Now, hold your other hand up, thumb up," and I did. Still nothing. With a palm to his face, he looked pained. With extra patience, he suggested that I "let it go through."

"You know?" I asked in surprise.

His expression didn't change, he told me only, "Let it go through." Now, it was a command. He never spoke that way to me before, so I was shocked to hear him now. In an instant, a stream like a fire hose shot out of my thumb and hit me in the face, knocking me on my butt and soaking me to the core! Thankfully, when I fell down, my other hand came out of the creek, stopping the flow.

Uncle Arden fell back laughing so hard that he pitched over on his side. Tears streamed from his eyes. Then, taking a look at my expression, he burst out again with a full belly laugh. I took that opportunity to put my hand back in the stream and give him a soaking. He only laughed more, so I gave up and sat down in a sunny patch to dry off while he recovered himself. I couldn't help catching his mood and I laughed some myself – it would have been hilarious had it not been me.

Recovering enough to sit up, he said, "Again, but this time don't empty the creek. Let it just be a simple flow. And angle your thumb to the side... God, I love that. I wish I'd thought to film it." *Oh, his camera!* But he didn't seem to care as he brought it out and took some photos anyway.

"You've taught someone how to do this before?" I asked, but he shook his head.

"No," he said, "Go ahead and try again."

I stuck my hand in and then with what seemed like simple common sense, which I lacked, turned the thumb of my other hand to the side. I could feel the water there, ready to be shot out as before. I could feel how I wanted to grab it all at once, like it took all my effort to do such a simple thing. Instead, I relaxed and let go of the creek, and it all left. No, not that much. I let it in and then didn't release it but cut the flow. I felt bloated, but then when I let it out my thumb, it was still like a garden spigot. This time, it didn't pull from the stream, so it dwindled until I was empty.

Practicing that, I soon had a steady flow, like a fountain, and I was about to sip it when uncle said, "Wait. That lesson is later." I nodded. We stood up and walked on. Soon, we were dry.

We were nearing a crossing of the creek when uncle raised his hand saying, "Hold on." He turned, looking around and then back down the trail. Listening, I heard the sounds of running feet. Turning, he looked around for a place to hide. I'd seen that look before when we were camping, but never quite like this. Seeing the stream, he told me, "Quick, jump in. Come on," taking my hand and hurrying us up the path.

He wanted us to hide, why? Usually we might try for a quite private place, but this was a public trail. His tone and expression were enough to get me moving, but when I didn't move fast enough he'd grabbed my hand and hurried me along. We rushed up to the stream ready to swim, expecting a pool of water, but it was barely a couple inches deep down an embankment. "Jump in and get under the bridge," he gave me that stern commanding tone again and I leapt, expecting to land hard. We jumped in together. With a surprised "Woop!" my hands went sky high as the bottom dropped us through the rocky water with nary a splash into a river beneath the stream that followed the same course, but much deeper than was apparent. He fell through right after me.

I watched as the world above the ground rushed past, the water below absorbing our jump and we were left floating in a strange realm below. We had both fallen through the surface of the stream, where we could see up through it here. I'd seen a moment of panic on Uncle Arden's face as the water came up over our heads.

It felt strange going under, obviously – to be under the stream. It was so quiet that I felt like I was hiding behind a bush, but so secret nobody would see me. There were only the sounds of the deep stream, the fish swimming by and ourselves. We were both strong swimmers and maintained our position without much effort. My eyes followed the trout, turning a circle in amazement, trying to understand what I was seeing. The fish were making the most of the Underriver, a name I invented on the spot to call the river under the river.

Completing my turn about, Uncle Arden was still freaking out. "Why the panic?" I asked, focusing on him. His eyes went wide at the sound of my voice. Since he knew about me and my abilities, helping me be better at them I'd expect him to calmly accept all of this. Seeing that he was not, I used my "spiritual sense" trying to ascertain why – he was holding his breath. The great Uncle Arden couldn't breathe water.

I had to get him air, and felt the barrier caused by my clothes as I tried to help him as I had my friends and the diver. I'd helped my friends by removing my team swimsuit, but I've changed since then and perhaps now for one person I didn't have to shed my clothes. So I tried. It wasn't easy. I tried reaching out with a feeling of air, but I could see it wasn't working.

Working through this, first with the diver we'd connected heart to heart, but it hadn't happened automatically. I'd been going to give him air physically and then as best that can be described, a link was established and as a result he'd had air in his lungs instead of water. He'd also begun to breathe naturally. But Uncle wasn't drowning, yet, and if I had too I would give him air mouth to mouth. So because of my willingness, why wasn't he having air and breathing!?

I frowned internally and continued to "monitor" Uncle. I could sense that he still wasn't breathing and that he persevered in holding his breath. I'd wanted the diver to live, and when I reached for him, he'd had his air. Remembering it all over again, I'd really cared that the diver lived and had wanted to give him the air I breathed. As a result, I'd gone to him to do it in the only way I knew how, as a lifeguard at the pool would.

Now I knew differently, I could give Uncle air magically. Still, I knew it was a matter of the heart, so I reached for him both physically and with my love. When I did, effortlessly, the barrier between him and me caused by my clothes was pushed aside. With delight I sensed the connection with him that would let my abilities flow to him be established and suddenly he was breathing. I wanted to cheer.

Like what had happened with the diver, I could sense I was being drained of energy as a result of this bond. If we stayed much longer...

"Jill, thank you. What did you do, and what is this place? How are we breathing, and talking?" It made no sense, he who could order water out of his hands the same as I but with greater skill... couldn't breathe water? I was glad I could be his life support, but his confusion was infecting me.

Also, what did he mean, *What is this place?* He's the one that had instructed me to jump in, hadn't he expected this place? I had only done as instructed.

I looked at him strangely, asking "You don't know?"

"Where are we?" he was freaking out and freaking me out with these questions!

"Uncle," I said, sliding close and putting my hand on his shoulder. Since we were swimming, he didn't tower over me. "I was just doing what you told me to do." I felt the tension flow out of him at the touch.

"We were going to hide under the bridge," he said calming down and now looking up in wonder. We could see the bridge arching over the creek above.

Soon, we saw three runners approach the bridge, thunder over it, and continue up the trail. They didn't see us.

"Can we leave?" he asked. I didn't know, I hadn't a clue but nodded yes anyway.

"Good," he said regaining his confidence. Then, he pushed off with a kick, rising upwards and I turned to follow. When I surfaced next to him he said, "Perhaps we could swim from here because... Wait this is strange."

I turned to look at him and saw he was waving his hand through the rocky bottom of the stream. That was indeed strange, and I copied his gesture. The bottom went through our chests, feeling like water. But beside me, he had one hand on a boulder in the water of the stream. I reached out and touched it, it was solid, but the rest of the stream wasn't. Both solid and not where it needed to be, "Hmmm, well, maybe we could swim from here, but we're here for a hike." I could read in his expression, that this magical effect was more than he wanted to deal with and he then hoisted himself out of the stream.

Curious to see if only the rock we'd touched was solid, I put my hands out taking a hold on the bottom of the stream, it was oddly solid while the rest of me was through it like it wasn't there – definitely strange. Then I hoisted myself out behind him and then turned to look down at the stream. I could now sense the Underriver and I tested the "sight" by putting a foot in, feeling a different rock, it was firm and I could put my weight down on it fully. But then reaching through it for the Underriver, I almost fell in again as my foot went through it to the river underneath. Rocking unsteadily, my foot swung through the rocks and sand of the stream, it being unexpectedly normal, especially because I regained my balance by placing my foot again on the bottom of the stream.

"Uncle, am I a mermaid?" I asked turning to him.

"What's a mermaid?" he asked confused by the question as we resumed the hike.

"You know, girls with fish tails from here," I said holding a hand at my waist, "down."

In a light tone, he said, "I think you can answer the question yourself, I see no tail."

"Thanks, Uncle," I frowned. Was he deliberately being obtuse? "Except my friends seem to think I am."

Climbing up some steep boulders and holding a hand down to me, he replied, "On what evidence. I thought you said mermaids have fish tails instead of legs."

"Um, it doesn't sound likely, but how do I explain being able to breathe water?"

"And your friends know this?"

I nodded, "And they have, too. Add to that, we were... You may think I'm crazy. I half-think I am. We were in the pool talking underwater, then um, we were in the Pacific Ocean the very next moment. Then we went up on a deserted island. We spent the afternoon before returning. Before that, I was there by myself..."

"The night of your birthday, go on..."

"I'm not going crazy.... Yeah, it was that night. I rescued a drowning man. I had thought it a dream. I did unbelievable things."

"As you continue to do," he said with an air of disregard and a wave of his hand, considering it all obvious. He was good for me, but I was getting exasperated.

"Yes!" I pounced on that, trying to grasp some sanity amongst my feelings.

"And so your friends think you're a mermaid because of that. Does that make me a mermaid, because it would seem we both did 'unbelievable' things just now?"

"No. Um, no. I don't know." I was so confused. He was right, but I suppose that was a good thing because I didn't want to be a mermaid.

"And as you see I have no tail," he went on as if I hadn't spoken.

"But you knew..." I tried again.

"Ah, yes. I knew. So?" and he doffed his hat and scratched his head before putting it back on.

"I guess there's more to being a mermaid than just a tail," I admitted. "They are known to rescue people. And, and... breathe water." I was talking to myself now. "But that proves nothing. I guess I need to learn more about what it means to be a mermaid."

"Now that, my dear, seems like solid reasoning."

4.5   Run, Jill, Run

At about the halfway point, we passed several hikers coming down and carrying light packs and sleeping rolls. This group of college-age people, two men and two women, caught my attention. They'd obviously spent the weekend, and their easy chatter seemed so normal I found it comforting. I noticed the two women and their carefree laughter. I felt so different, but they only nodded. One of the men said, "Good morning."

"You didn't freak out. I'm so proud of you," I told Uncle Arden after they passed.

"That's because I didn't want to hide in a creek again," he joked and we both laughed lightly.

Then it was the beautiful morning all to ourselves again, but it wasn't long before we were passed by another set of four joggers going our way. By then, the trail was steep, and we walked single-file. As we waited for them to pass, we looked down on a creek that wound through the rocks below. The four of them, three women and a man, were all in their late teens or early twenties, and they were just like the others we'd hid from, wearing university cross-country T-shirts, shorts and light hip packs. They were breathing heavily but looked to be enjoying themselves.

The view was beginning to become spectacular – we were above the trees now on a switchback trail. "Follow them," Uncle Arden whispered, gesturing for me to step it up. Running wasn't my sport, but I wasn't going to let that stop me. I was used to the treadmills in the gym, and Uncle Arden's camping trips usually included forced marches. I turned, bent my head down, and pushed off. With a quick deft twist, I pulled a hair tie from my wrist and got my hair in a ponytail, then all I heard was our quick steps as we followed the fleeting foursome.

We kept far enough back that we went unheard behind them, but not so far that we would lose sight of them. Fortunately for me it wasn't more than a few miles of rugged steep terrain before we arrived at the lake. Like a hound, Uncle made sure we didn't lose the runners, and I had to dig deep, which required me to tap into my reserves. Then when those failed me, I found myself grasping for anything, perhaps the water in the air or the soil could sustain me.

The trail became like a river to me, and I pulled on the seemingly marshy ground I'd felt at the beginning of the hike to gain some strength for my burning thighs and starving lungs. I transcended somewhere to a place like home and among close friends. Was I hallucinating? The runners ahead of us were anticipating a dive into the chilly mountain waters of the lake as their reward. I could hardly wait to do the same. That's what kept me going.

I ran so fast in order to be among them, to be like them, that I unwittingly started to catch up with them. I'd nearly

---

caught up when the lake came into view. The four of them like arrows to a target headed straight for the water, leaving a trail of shoes, packs and other things in their wake.

With a tap on my shoulder, I became aware of Uncle again, like a sudden splash of cold water to the face. How had I forgotten him?

"Over there," he pointed, steering us around to the left. There was a formation of stones that seemed natural and man-made at the same time. By the time we reached them, we could hear the loud whoops of the four runners now entering the water, followed by their laughter and shouts.

Uncle Arden hid as I followed in the swimmers' steps, shucking my clothes. Guessing that my fishes would enjoy the swim too, I took to the water. There was nothing that could keep me out, not even myself. I dove down the steep sides of the lake until I was some twenty feet under. I pretended I couldn't see the four sets of legs treading water above me.

I stayed down just long enough to make Uncle worry about me if I were a regular American girl. I couldn't help but be upset that he kept his own counsel. How long had he known?

I was glad for the fun, and I was glad he and I had finally spoken. It seemed a miracle that he not only was understanding but encouraging as well. I'd thought I might lose our close bond when I wasn't able to tell him about what had been going on, but I was relieved he could teach me instead. I laughed remembering the water to the face, and how he'd been as surprised as I was at the creek incident. Whatever I had was different than him. It was a surprise that he hadn't known what to do. I was just glad he was there to share it with me.

What about my parents? The casual way Uncle had raised the subject made me wonder, but then again neither of them had ever let on that I was different. I guessed only time would tell if they knew or not. There was no easy way to say anything to them. That I had them completely fooled was impossible. They must have all been complicit in it somehow.

Finally, I surfaced and looked around. The other swimmers had left the water, the cold finally overcoming the heat of their run. The water was freezing, but to me the cold was at arm's length. I'd given up on using the word "impossible" for this anymore. *I could swim in icy waters!* This felt as wonderful to me as the warm sheets I'd experienced the night before.

In an attempt to provoke him, to get him to talk more about what was going on, I left the water, literally leaving the water, showing that it had no hold on me, my hair or skin. He was unphased. Nothing could irritate him, his lips were sealed. It was a quality that had its benefits, but was irritating me now.

"How was the water?" Uncle Arden asked pleasantly as I stepped onto a boulder to sit across from him. He'd been packing my things, and I saw the last of them disappear into his bag. Suddenly, I was glad for the fish suit, glancing down to be sure I was wearing it, feeling insecure.

I lifted my eyebrows and managed a light pleasant tone in response, "Refreshing." He'd set out a towel, which I didn't need now because of my behavior in removing all the water from me when I left the lake. So I wasn't sure if it was right that I use it. Then I decided that since he had been kind enough to offer it, it wouldn't hurt for me to use it as a wrap. In an attempt to soothe my ruffled nerves, I pushed back a strand of hair, leaned over and picked the thing up, pulling it around my shoulders as I sat back.

A pot was steaming over a travel heating can. From it, I could smell my favorite tea. As I sat down, he lifted it and poured us two cups. I liked the blend for its orange twist flavor intermixed with dozens of other spices that Uncle had created especially for me. The tastes seemed to go off like delayed fireworks for several seconds after each sip. I could drink a gallon of the stuff, hot or cold, anytime, anywhere. The tea leaves he carried with him, and the brew was fragrant, making the mountain air smell like a flower-filled meadow.

In the distance, I heard a girl's laugh – it was one of the four runners. I turned to look over at them. They were huddled together like the two of us. I wondered at them briefly. The dip in the water had brought something out of me, and it was suddenly like I was sitting among them. The girls I saw, on close inspection, were weaving flowers in their hair, laughing at some comment one of them had made. The guy was pulling out trail mix and sharing it with the others. He wasn't laughing. Maybe he was the brunt of the joke.

"What are they saying?" Uncle asked softly, so as not to disturb the moment.

Sound carried easily over water, and I turned to listen. I'd been among them in sight. Now, I heard them clearly, as if a microphone were hanging above their heads.

Listening, I heard them speaking of us and I relayed it. "They're speaking about us, wanting to do something here," and I looked at the seeming random placement of stones, really more like pillars of varying heights, ranging from small stepping stones to oddly bent waist high swim noodles with flat tops. "They want us to leave and wish they had picked this place first as their camp."

"Well then, we should get started and let them," he suggested and swept up the remainder of our things, plucking the tea cup from my hands. Looking up at the angle of the sun, he commented, "The sun is about right." Then in aside to me he stated, "We need a distraction." Drawing my attention to the water and sun, he asked, "Do you think you could blind them?"

Blind them... "What, how?"

Taking a sip of my tea, he spat sprays out of his lips to the side in demonstration saying, "All air carries some water. If you still the wind, the lake water will reflect the sun in their faces." He tossed the remainder of the tea in the lake and packed away the cup in his bag.

I knew what he said was true, *but what he asked, was... impossible!* I was getting tired of that word. I turned to fully face the water to give it a try, letting the towel slip and dropping my feet back into the lake.

"Concentrate, Jill," I told myself. I was going to need everything for this. All I knew up to this point was that anything was possible if I believed in it. I let go and hung on to every word as he told me what to do.

"Focus on the water in the air," he said as my mind raced everywhere. The runners' presence was comforting, perhaps because they liked nature too. Turning as if I were one of them, I saw the sun glittering off the water from the ripples. I imagined the surface of the lake turning to glass, but I was still everywhere and nothing was happening.

I tried reaching for the particles of water in the air, but it was like grasping at straws. The more I pulled at them, the more they escaped my fingers. I must have been moving my hands, because Uncle suggested, "Wave the wind back, like you might fan yourself, but extend it out from yourself."

Like seeing water in the air on a humid day, I saw that now. I'd been trying to order the individual motes to do what I wanted, but as I moved some into position, others would drift away. Extending my hands as Uncle told me, and waving them had a greater effect on the whole. Trying different hand positions, and waving the water in the air they became strands that stuck together, somewhat like shaping cotton candy. What I wanted was a wall and slope, which would lift the incoming air over the lake. I heard the startled exclamations of the young runners and pulled myself back. I was exerting myself too much and I sensed that I would soon be exhausted if I kept it up.

"Just a little bit more. Hold back the wind, Jill," I told myself. I set myself in my mind between the oncoming wind and the lake. In my mind, my hands became a wall, but that was too much, as the river of wind that swept over the Rockies carried with it a force I hadn't reckoned with, and I felt the air begin to slip over my defenses. "Just so long as it doesn't touch the lake," I reasoned. Focusing my eyes I exerted myself for the last part, shaping the now visible misty ball into the skateboard ramp shaped cloud I had in mind, letting the air channel over us. The lake stilled and became blinding to those on the other side. And just in time because I had nearly collapsed.

"That's good, Jill. Let go. It will hold long enough."

Uncle lifted me to my feet saying, "We must be going now." I was about to help him break camp, but he'd done all that already. In fact, he already had my pack tied to his. "I'll carry it for now. No not that way," he added as I turned towards the trail. As I turned back to him, he held out a hand for me to grasp.

He led me to a pillar of stone no more than a finger high, one of the ones I'd noticed on our arrival, and had me step on it. Then guiding me to a higher one, he finally let go, gesturing me to take to a pillar higher up. From one to the next I went until I was balanced on one of the tallest stones several feet up, Then it was on to a fat rock that looked like it had crashed down amidst these standing stones. This fat rock led down to the lake. Down at the water's edge, there were three more submerged pillar stones that went out into the lake.

"What you've done is attune yourself." I heard him, but now I saw him too even though I was facing away. It felt like the previous spiritual vision I'd just been using to hone in on the runners, but now it was clear as diamond.

He went on, "For you, that comes easier than for most. You probably feel like your skin is on fire. Your heritage is tied closely to the basic properties of the world. Magic – as most people without a thorough schooling in the subject call it, and even those that do know still use the term, just with greater understanding – is the manipulation of the world. Someday you may be given the opportunity to study. Until then, you'll have to apply some basic principles."

Each word was a revelation, "First, your body is more attuned to the world and clothing inhibits it, naturally." I was stunned. With those words he summed up every issue I had.

The towel, clothing, it all made sense now. And my body was burning up, I'd thought that a result of what I'd just done, like muscles felt after a good workout. He was telling me, it was my connection with the world. What did he mean by that?

"But there are other factors. Mostly, though, it's repetition. The first few times are the hardest." I knew just what he meant, I was exhausted. Repetition of what? Then he began to lose me, "The greater the skill, the less, but we're in a hurry so I'll skip all of that." He wasn't making sense.

"What about my suit?" I asked, interrupting him, "Should I remove it too?" But I was not at all sure that I could, as it wasn't exactly a swimsuit anyway.

He frowned at the interruption and sighed, "You should be okay as is, but until you learn to control your skills, anything more could have complications." Trying to interpret him, I think he meant it would be just be plain harder. As I'd discovered trying to get him to breathe earlier when we'd hidden under the bridge and had been determined to do it while I was still wearing my clothing. I smiled at that little triumph, and nodding making the connection in my mind. *If you want the greatest effect Jill, it was the fish suit alone.*

He continued with the instructions. "Now, what matters is connection, understanding and practice. You have connection, which is the second half of attuning. Though you can have attuning without... never mind. More on that later. To effect a transfer you need understanding. First, you are not in charge of it. Your strength is water, and thereby the Lord of the Water is to whom you must apply, just keep in mind he wants this to take place more than you do. Otherwise, it couldn't happen. Last is practice, which is affecting the change. These stones resonate with another place, their destinations are already set. By using them, accepting the connection, understanding the application and then affecting the transfer by practice, you will arrive." Whew, that didn't sound easy.

"Go ahead," he said, encouraging me to take the first step. I thought about what he'd said, at first shocked by the sudden massive change in subject, and then lastly that he meant what he said. Then, I really felt the change from spiritual vision to attuning. Once I knew it, I'd never go back. It was the difference between a candle and a flashlight.

As I stepped to the first stone out from the rock and onto the lake, it felt like taking a giant step sideways, and then to the next the same until standing on the third I had my back to the runners. The bright sun shimmered off the lake so bright I saw only white. Now, it was too late to ask questions.

This would be my first transfer above water, though my feet were still a bit wet from the lake. I could feel my connection with the water spiraling up around me like my head was the top of a chocolate kiss. Though it couldn't be seen, I felt it for sure.

Uncle Arden's voice came from far away. "Since the application is approved, you merely have to step into it to complete the practice. I'll see you at home." Wait, what?

Expecting to fall into the water, I stepped forward, and indeed I did step into water, but the transition was like falling through a trapdoor, knees jarring as I landed. It was not nearly as fluid as the previous ones, but those I hadn't commanded. Then, I was standing on a shimmering disc of water upon water. There was a haze all about me like a fog, though I saw clearly through it. I recognized the location almost immediately. I was down in Boulder, near Boulder Reservoir at an adjoining lake called Coot Lake.

I felt Uncle's presence at my shoulder, but he wasn't there in person. "It can't be helped," he said and I saw why. A man sat on a flat-bottomed boat, binoculars trained on a nesting pair of eagles, but his eyes had found the mist that was partially obscuring me. Before he could understand what he was seeing, I felt exhaustion overcome me and the disc of water evaporated as I could no longer maintain it. That's when I fell face forward into the water.

4.6 Coot Lake

It was funny as I fell; it wasn't a simple dive but a full belly flop. I laughed as I hit, thinking of all my diving and swimming training flying out the window. I simply had no flying skills. I earned a perfect four out of ten as I fell, windmilling my arms and legs, but it didn't hurt as I expected. The water spoiled the fun – as I was about to hit, it reached out and took me in. "Let me wrap you up and hold you secure. How was the trip? Fine, thank you," it seemed to say.

Was that "trip" as in you just fell in, or "trip" from Red Deer Lake to here? In either case, "I'm fine, thanks."

Underwater was nothing like the mountain lake, but the waters cleared from my splash and became beautiful. Oh this was wonderful, how was it that I was so lucky to see and breathe underwater?

Elated, I finally understood the missing piece that we – my friends and I – had been trying to figure out. I ran in place, overjoyed and hopeful. How great was it that the Lord of the Water wanted us to do great things? "Thank you," I told him and thanks to Uncle Arden for showing me. I couldn't wait to show it to the others. I wonder where we're going next.

I turned to rise but saw that the eagle watcher's boat was headed my way. I swam a bit underwater, skimming the bottom, towards him and rose up to part the still waters before him. "Hey," I said, swimming by his boat as he paused in bewilderment.

"Beautiful day, isn't it?" he replied not quite sure how I'd covered the distance so quickly.

"It is," I said rolling onto my back and swimming around his boat casually.

"Why were you watching the eagles?" I asked sitting up near to where he sat, turning to face their roost and nest. "They're beautiful," I added seeing two of them standing tall. "Are they watching us?"

He nodded and smiled, turning to follow my gaze. "Hmm, yes they are." He beamed to be sharing his delight. His passion was evident in his voice as he added, "I like everything about the sea, and eagles are the most elegant of all that fly and fish from the sea. They're watching us because they find us interesting."

I laughed, "Are you sure they don't find us amusing? I'd laugh at anyone that couldn't fly."

"So, do you laugh at anyone that can't swim?" he asked in return.

Aghast, I turned back to him, and he was watching me, "Goodness no, I teach them. Goldie's Gym, heard of it?" I didn't meet his eyes but turned back towards the eagles. I kept my gaze down as I looked to the horizon.

"No, not really," he replied explaining. "If I'm not out in the wild, I'm at my lab at the university or teaching a class. So, you're okay?" he asked. But I could see via this new attuning skill, his expression, that he wanted to ask if what he'd thought he'd seen was true. If I said nothing, he'd probably think he was imagining it.

"Alright, cool," I said, forcing the conversation to be over. For a bit, I hung out looking at the eagles, but I was really more interested in exploring the bottom of the lake.

The lake was teeming with aquatic life. It wasn't very deep, about twenty feet, but deep enough for me to make my escape once I'd said goodbye to the researcher. Since he was now touching on that which I couldn't share, I waved and said, "Later." Then I dove and debated what next.

I couldn't exactly stay under forever, no matter what he thought. That wouldn't be smart. So I kicked out the way I was facing, which happened to be towards the eagles. Surfacing, I turned on my back to look upward until I came near the shore. I was tempted to rise up and say hello to the eagles, but instead I angled away.

I worried for about two seconds how I'd get out of the water and onto dry land, for there was marsh at one end, and there were joggers and bikers making their way along the trails overlooking the lake. At least there were a few trees along one edge. I made for the trees, surfacing and scrambling over some rocks. Some seagulls squawked a greeting at my appearance before turning their attention back to their fellows. I found myself saying hi in return before realizing I was talking to the birds. Just as I'd thought I might have done with the baby buck.

Did I imagine their eyes acknowledging me? I must have. A biker was coming, and I ducked behind a tree, facing out at the lake. *What am I going to do? How am I going to get home?* Uncle Arden was at ten thousand feet and Lucas was supposed to be picking us up at the end of our hike. I suppose I could wait for nightfall and then try to make it home. I had no bus pass, money or shoes. Besides, I was too exhausted to give it a go now. It had seemed so natural in the mountains to go barefoot. Here, not so much. Wait a second, Uncle wouldn't have sent me here without a plan. They probably would pick me up on their way back. That had to be it. So I just had to wait. Waiting didn't bother me nearly as much in light of the strange travel that had just happened.

A mere journey of a few miles seemed like no great feat, but for the first time it had been done on purpose. It struck me as interesting how deep and ancient this knowledge was, and those stone pillars up at the lake had probably been there for a long time. Here, I was a fair weather sunshine girl, a kid that my parents barely considered an adult, and I was being shown the wonders of the universe. Permanent spells fixed to stones. Perhaps there were runes or ancient writings on them as well. How many of these places existed in the world, and could I do it without the stones? Uncle Arden had hinted that it was possible.

I stood there behind the tree for a few minutes before sitting down in a patch of sunlight, hoping that the surrounding tall grasses would hide me, but knowing that they did not. At least there were flowers here. They smelled wonderful. I liked this place.

The people were noticing me as they went biking, jogging or walking by on the path away from where I hid. Seeing that I wasn't going to stay hidden this way, I went to lie down on some soft grasses. The man in the boat had returned to his bird watching and I followed his gaze up to a soaring eagle. Rolling onto my back, I put my arms under my head and decided to enjoy the afternoon while observing the eagle in his lazy pursuits. I'd figure something out later.

Soon, I dozed off. The sun had moved by the time I awoke. I was getting used to these adventures. If lying on a beach soaking up the sun was a "mermaid" trait, especially with friends, I could get used to the changes. I didn't believe I was one, but all the same this was nice. The air carried the scent of aromatic flowers. The wind in the leaves as they rustled was everything I thought of summer and an easy afternoon. I'd rolled onto my belly at some point, head on my forearm. The grassy ground felt like a soft bed. I didn't want to move, but then I heard the cry of the eagle soaring on the wind. It sounded a lot like, "Lady, wake up…"

I lifted my head to gaze at the eagle then rolled onto my back to keep it in view as it soared by quite low before zooming high in aerial acrobatics that made my heart soar, wishing I could be up there with it. It circled a few times lower and lower, until it swooped so low and headed over the water right towards me. Several people around the lake had stopped to watch its antics, including the bird-watching researcher I'd visited with. He had to be out there by special permit, for there was a sign nearby that read "no boats," and one saying "no swimming." If he forgave me my trespass, I wouldn't say anything in return.

I fully expected to be treated with another aerial display as the eagle flew over, but instead it suddenly flipped out its wings wide, back-winging and set itself down on the grass no more than three feet from me. He'd given me such an amazing display of his great wings and talons that I sat in awe as it looked about, and then he set to preening. Sitting up on my elbows, I waited until I was sure it was waiting for me to say something. Then, I greeted it like I had the seagulls.

"Lady," he replied with a duck of his head, which looked more formal than a gesture of his had any right to be. With the blink of his eye, he turned towards me, "Your arrival is known, and welcome. It has been sometime since your kind graced these lakes. The air itself is refreshingly clear, as is the waters in which you sojourned. The fish no doubt thank you, as do I, for fish is a favorite dish of mine. I'm to tell you, your conveyance comes. If you have any questions, now is the time."

That was pretty long-winded for an eagle. But then again, I guess I didn't know too many eagles. They were seen from time to time around here, but to talk with one... unheard of! What questions to ask? There were so many!

I probably should have asked something else, but I said, "How are we conversing?"

"That's not actually something I know." Somehow, I could tell he was frowning. "I don't really know how the things you do are done, but I know known things. Or at least a few things, since I suppose someone somewhere knows that, you should ask them. There, that does it. I suppose

I should get going…" He raised his wings pivoting around to fly off over the lake.

"Huh, wait, I thought you said I could ask several questions."

He looked at me. "Oh, I suppose I did." He turned back around and lowered his wings, ran his claw over his brow, and looking me straight on, asked, "Alright then, what would you know?"

"Um, why are you helping me?"

With a twist of his head, he looked at me sideways before turning back the other way and starting to pace. His wings were crossed behind his back. When he turned back, he stopped and looked down saying, "That's complex. Simply, helping you helps me, everyone, the earth, sky, and I suppose even the gods. That's not very simple, I know. What I know is that I like you, the rest is… extra. Now can I go? My wings itch to taste the wind."

Then he added, "He comes," and turned his head to watch, pointing out the single person strolling along the path. All the others had stopped to watch the eagle and now me. They pretended to look elsewhere, but it was obvious that this situation was uncommon. They probably thought I was putting them on. It was Lucas approaching.

When Lucas was near, the eagle turned and made ready to fly. "Wait," I called, and it turned back a second, saying with its expression that it was leaving before he arrived, no matter what I wanted. At a loss for words, I finally said, "Thank you," and smiled my thanks.

116

"Lady," he said again with a dipped bow. Lifting his head and then with quick steps he ran towards the water, at the last second extending his wings to fly low over the water before taking to higher air.

Lucas was there with a, "I'll never get used to that." *What did he mean?* Then, seeing my appearance, quickly removed his shirt and tossed it to me. "Arden didn't say–" he left the rest unsaid. I caught the shirt as I turned it back right-side-out, and my nose guessed the story as I caught a whiff of it – he'd had a long day, but his eyes gleamed with news. I knew better than to ask now, he'd say after he talked with mom and uncle. Giving me his shirt was a bit overboard in my opinion. The fish outfit would have been adequate, even if they had changed to a bikini, which would have fit under my outfit, when I swam in the mountain lake. I wondered if he thought it indecent. Misjudging my expression, he suggested, "Go stand in the water, holding the shirt." *Did he want me to wash it and wear it wet?*

I was used to doing what he told me to do. Yet I had to complain, "I'm dressed as I am at the pool every day." Holding the shirt out before me with two fingers like it had the plague. It didn't smell that bad, it only smelled of his sweat. I should have had the fish become the top and skirt again, but it was too late now. Besides if I ran into Uncle Arden with a duplicate outfit, there would be other questions to answer, so it was just as well. He only nodded and gave me a look, "Be considerate," he said, looking at the other people.

The water wasn't far and I turned to look at him as I stepped in. This must be another "lesson," and then him saying that he "never got used to that" must have meant he had seen the eagle before. "Dad, what's going on?" I wasn't holding the shirt up anymore as thoughts rushed in. Dad knew, and had known perhaps, as I had guessed. There remained only Mom, and she was gone much of the time.

He came and sat on the dry grass before me, only a few feet away, but he said, "I can't say, you'll have to figure that out for yourself," admitting that he knew more than he was willing to share. "Remember what Uncle Arden told you," he suggested.

There I stood, remembering. The first bit had been about connection. Understanding was the first step of that. No it was second. Attuning was first, but it was more than simply sensing what was around me. It was making a connection to the basic elements of the world, for me water was easiest, but it applied to the here and now. For a transfer it would include where I was going, though that had been done for me with the stepping stones. Next in magic then was Understanding, via an application with The Lord of the Water and then lastly Practice. The act of making it happen.

So starting with attuning, I opened myself as I had discovered to do early on. Now I had a name for it, and it was more than just a vision now. It was like discovering a bike had more than a single gear. I was no longer stuck in first and I felt like I was the center of an electromagnetic pulse wave, as my senses could overlap with everything. I could feel the shirt, Lucas like an iron pillar before me, while the passersby were light figurines and the many varied insects and birds going about varied wisps of colored energy. I inhaled as my skin burst into flame. If the passersby were light beings, I was the diamond in the rough, a bright torch that shone through the night. It was overwhelming to hold open for more than a second.

I had to let go without being given any directions. I felt like I was about to explode. Uncle Arden had said it would increase. I hadn't understood him. Was this what he was talking about? But he also mentioned something about "less." I wasn't sure.

It was everything out here, the connection in this instance. I was thankful for that, but I wanted to know why. That, he couldn't tell me. So I asked instead, "Why am I standing here then?" gesturing at the water.

"Smell the shirt," he told me. I really didn't want a whiff of it again. The air here was refreshingly clear. Tentatively, I held the shirt up to my nose, wrinkled it only to get a tiny smell when I inhaled. I breathed in, my eyes opening in surprise. It smelled nice, and faintly like Lucas, just as he would smell when freshly groomed. That smell faded though as I continued to hold it.

There was more going on because of me attuning than simply a shirt being cleaned. Until dad had arrived, people were noticing me and the eagle, and that had been bothersome. Now they were going about their business like I wasn't there. Again, why? "Lucas, they're ignoring us. Why do we have to leave so soon?" With his arrival, I knew we'd be leaving and now that he was revealing things I didn't want it to end.

"It's complicated, and not here. Still, look around you, where you've been, where you're standing, but say nothing."

Looking with new eyes, and not taking for granted what I had looked over on first glance. There had been bits of trash all about, something I took for granted around places where people commonly went. It was all being wiped clean, and the cleansing was spreading. Prickly weeds were giving way to lush grasses, barren ground was producing and everything else was perking up as if after a fresh rain. Yet, not all at once. It was emanating from the water that circulated through me. The sudden refreshing air that I'd delighted in, was itself a consequence of my being here attuning.

I could feel how I'd been feeling since that first night, in touch with life, but I'd no idea that it was in me producing more life and that life was spreading from me to the plants. The people, however, were not so easily touched. Remembering the eagle's answer to my question. He had been talking of this, like it was known. Even when out of the water. Where I'd lain, where I'd walked – the flowers blossoming and the harsh plants disappearing.

I left the water, almost dropping the shirt in surprise at flowers that were suddenly blooming, as if becoming visible from some other place. I started walking, watching behind me. Even more life than before. I turned about to Lucas, spinning in place, "How?" I mouthed. He only shook his head and held out his hand for the shirt.

I misunderstood his request thinking he wanted to get going, I didn't really want to put it on, thinking that putting it on would slow the effect, but I did as I thought he'd told me to. It hung low.

Together we walked the path away from there, I aware that the shirt was indeed stifling my connection and the effect was restricted to a narrow space around me. It was a one-piece garment, light and airy. What would jeans and a jacket do? I would have to remain barefoot if I could, and in sandals if I couldn't. That should help.

I looked for the eagle and saw him soaring above the roost where his mate sat watching the non-flying humans. I imaged he was definitely amused at the sight of the non-flyers.

I'd made Lucas uncomfortable – that much was obvious. We walked for a while. I kept trying to feel everything even if it was muffled. I had a tiny victory, I remembered swimming with the swimsuit after hitting the submarine. It wasn't all or nothing. Someday I may have the sense I had just experienced even while dressed. I wondered when I got there would I want it. Just yesterday I'd not wanted fish for clothing, and now I preferred them over the shirt. How I was changing!

When we were safely in the car, I put my feet up on the dash and tried to open some questions. Lucas had admired the eagle, so I thought I could get him to talk about it, "You've seen that eagle before?" I asked softly.

He expressed only a little surprise at the inquiry and dodging the question stated, "You must be hungry," and pulled a pouch of beef jerky from the pocket in his door tossing it to me. In truth, I was ravenous.

As I chewed at the peppery jerky, I realized what he'd said before. I was going to have to figure it out, whatever it was. Interesting though, the cleansing bit. I'd like to test it out more. Trash, and more generally, pollution always had bothered me. Apparently, it was in me to do something about it.

I wondered as we drove home what Melanie and the others were up to. Perhaps they too were having adventures. We'd have to compare notes.

5 Native Trouble

I had trouble sleeping again and went to the pool, where I fell in, not even attempting a graceful entry. The water reached for me, wrapped me up and carried me away. Every fiber of my being relaxed into it. I was unconscious before I was swept away to who knows where.

I awoke lying on my back in water, floating as easily as if it were a bed, my head resting on a wave pillow that drifted away as soon as I sat up. I was back at the island. The water was tranquil, and an early morning mist rose from it. It was hard to believe I'd been sleeping in the ocean. Whatever brought me here, was it totally unconcerned about my safety? Wasn't I supposed to be afraid of anything? I tried to get worked up about it, but it was so glorious waking up here. It was hard to be mad at something that kept bringing me to these beautiful places. It was breathtaking.

The stars were disappearing in the west over the last bit of shrouded sea. South was the island, but I was too far from it to hear the morning songbirds. I could imagine them, though, in full song and I could understand why – the world was alive with wonder! How the sun cast the world in glorious relief, hidden through the night, now renewed I could not say, but it was amazing. Turning about to the east to continue admiring the show, I happened to see a dark silhouette floating on the horizon and knew then the reason for my visit. The dark form, out over there, about the same distance from the island, was that yacht still drifting at anchor. It appeared not to have moved since I was last here.

I didn't know much, but seeing it there made me shake my head. How had I let it go for so long? The man had seemed so capable is why. Admittedly, I'd been reluctant. Instead, I wanted to walk the island again with Melanie. That was what I wanted to do, but I reasoned; so far, the mysterious hand that guided me to these locales had given me fun; my bet was on The Lord of the Water who I had been told about. It was he I thought who was responsible for bringing me here. And because of "him," I'd had wonderful times with Uncle Arden and Lucas. They'd been teaching me its ways. Perhaps now it was time I repaid this Lord of the Water for its kindness.

But first, a swim...

Arching, I flipped my feet into the air and then arrowed downwards. Kicking my feet to gain speed, I began welcoming the early morning risers out for their cup of joe among the aquatics. Swimming, any swimming, was my morning's cup of tea. I was invigorated after only a few minutes. About me swam the creatures of the sea; there a group of jellyfish, and over there a giant manta ray; was it the one from that first night when I thought it was a dream? Below me, a few eels oozed out of the coral for a race, and over there a late-night octopus looking for somewhere to sack out.

When I found the sunken ship, it was much as I remembered. I settled onto the deck. Leaning on the railing, gazing out at the wonders that lie beyond, imagining salt spray and the wind in my hair. "Ahoy!" I cried. The grumpy octopus gave me a wide berth, "Not so loud," he complained using a couple of his suckers as earplugs and wrapping one long limb over its head.

I pouted. Nobody would play with me. "Fine," I said looking upwards where the dark form of the ship lay, *Waiting for the friendly neighborhood mermaid...* I laughed at the thought, at me being a mermaid. Its dark form, dark since the day I'd first seen it, pulled at me. Even though I wanted to do the work, I was hesitant because of the thought I'd just had, "friendly neighborhood mermaid," indeed. I'd overheard girls talking about mermaids before, especially those on my swim team. Several wanted more than anything to be one or see one. "Let them be one!" I called out to whoever was doing this to me, The Lord of the Water or whoever.

Me, *I'm going to sink yon ship from over yonder.* "Load the cannons, Mr. Bones," I ordered the skeleton hiding in my imagination. "It's time to bring her down to the deep!" I smiled as the cannons lit up the sea like fireworks. "If only," I sighed, leaning on the railing, eventually choosing it for a seat. I still had my imagination and could imagine the galleon cruising the surf and riding the hugest coasters the sea could throw up. I strode, in my imagination, out to the bowsprit to stand mighty, as we dove through the waves to rise up triumphant. Shouting a challenge to the sea.

Try as I might, I couldn't blast the aforementioned yacht from plaguing me. Even if the battle was only active in my mind, I was having fun anyway. I'd always loved the water, and here any bucket could be a pirate ship. How thrilling the world could be with sunken ships to explore, and to imagine sailing upon them to far horizons. Until recently, I'd never been to the ocean, or even to a lake I couldn't see across. This was too good to be true, yet here I was.

In the spirit of the moment, I thought, I should share this. Who better then than the guy I'd rescued? And he was right above me. I jumped off my seat on the railing and pushed off for the ship above. There was no way I could stay down in a sea as glorious as this. I rose up spinning, exulting in the freedom of swimming unhindered. Leaping like a dolphin, like I'd done the first day in the pool, I spouted from the water smiling. A couple more leaps and I saw that the deck was empty. The boat looked forlorn and needed its captain at its helm. It was time I got busy and stopped fooling around. I would have to see this out and get the guy to safety. Hopefully, he wasn't too bad off, and still in a mood to share the adventure.

The last time I was here and surveyed The Lazy Cloud, I'd had fins on both my hands and feet. It seemed so long ago, but it was just the other day. Having continued to adjust, my hands were only hands as I reached for the hanging ladder. The fact that the ladder hung there was useful, and I pulled myself up quickly and over the side, but it worried me that the deck look the same as I'd last seen. The artifacts the diver had unearthed were still laying where they'd been dropped, undisturbed. Maybe the guy really did need my help after all.

Boat, ship or yacht, I was unsure what to call the craft. It didn't have the look of a pleasure yacht, yet the captain had called it a "yacht." I suppose it had similar qualities. Since ships were huge vessels in my mind and yachts were pleasure craft, I found myself thinking this as an overly large boat. It was at least fifty and no more than seventy feet long. I wasn't very good at estimating length. Being as big as it was, it had plenty of room for storage or cabins within, and on the main floor a large cabin with a full-sized command deck and an upper deck for fair weather steering above that. And the back deck where I stood had observation equipment and instruments for sea study. The yacht was too big for just one person if it was for pleasure, but then it clearly was dedicated for research. I suppose there had to be a few extra automated features.

I thought about the research equipment for a moment. They looked to be functioning. I wondered what they were doing. I might understand the sea better than I'd ever had, but what all this tech-wizardry was doing was beyond my ken. I'm sure in some way I was under observation, but I presumed most of the research wouldn't be about what was happening on deck but what was going on below the surface. Which had been me and my friends at one point. A small part of me wanted to take a sledgehammer to it all. I shrugged it off thinking that it could be completely benign. Fat chance of that, but I had no sledgehammer.

Besides he wouldn't be looking for mermaids, because mermaids don't exist. Whatever was happening to me wasn't because I was a mermaid. Melanie's attempt to cheer me up about mermaids didn't help, because I didn't want to be one. Her explanation of how they got their tails, like it was said about angels getting their wings because of helpful actions left it open to the possibility that someday I could still get a tail. Exasperated, I muttered at my one track mind that kept revolving around mermaids, "I give up." There was no making heads or tails of what it meant to be a mermaid and if tails were a requirement to being a mermaid. It would either happen or it wouldn't. And I hoped Cleo had been right, that I could choose not to be a mermaid.

The weather had been kicking up since I awoke and the deck was starting to pitch in the rising sea. I felt a storm system a ways off. Again I was sensing the weather patterns, seeing how it was moving. It would be a pretty big storm before it dispersed, but if I was reading things rightly, I felt fairly confident it would pass by us. That didn't mean we wouldn't be affected by it though. So I went in search of the guy before things got rough.

It wasn't long until I found him crashed on the floor in the lower area, a bin of food spread out in a mess where he'd fallen. His leg was bandaged in a splint. Thankfully it was intact, and I didn't have to tend to it for him. I knew basic first aid, but anything beyond that would be a stretch. The attuning I hoped would help. I'd healed sunburn and scratches on my friends and me on the island, before I knew about attuning.

I knelt by him, and noticed first that he was breathing, or moaning. His head was sweaty, and I felt his forehead – hot and moist. I had to get him up and to a bed. There were several doors off the main room, and I checked them for a sleeping area. They were mostly all fit for sleeping, but only one was rigged with a hammock and had the leftovers of several meals on a desk. Yuck, this was probably the place.

It appeared he preferred a hammock to sleep in, which would make sense in a swaying cabin, but I doubted I could maneuver him into the thing. There were also two canvas cots that pulled down from opposite walls for beds, so I pulled one down for him after clearing a space.

Unhooking the hammock from one end, I hung it out of the way. I studied how I would walk him back and hopefully onto the cot. Moving a couple things that looked like they might get in the way, I went to see what

I could do. There was strength in my arms, shoulders, back and legs that I didn't normally feel. Hopefully this new found strength was there for hoisting beefy sailors, or else I was going to have to drag him and that wouldn't be fun.

I bent, and then rolled him over onto his back. He was probably ten inches taller than me and probably a hundred pounds heavier, yet here I was with nobody else to help. When push came to shove, we women were tougher than we looked. I applied every bit of that, the strength and more, after I got him into a seated position. I stood up with his arm over me. He cried out in pain, awakening. Surely, the room was spinning in his mind. The wall was too far away, but he tried to reach out for it anyway.

"You've got this, Jill," I told myself, feeling like I was going to pull his arm off. Ducking, I reached around his waist, wishing I had suckers on my arms like the octopus to make holding onto him easier. My arms were too short. "Lean on me," I ordered. "I've got you!"

He finally got the message and shifted his weight back to me. We moved back and forth until we got a rhythm. I carried his weight easier than I should have, he was no featherweight and carried a lot of momentum whenever the deck shifted.

"We have to get my experiments, and my cameras," he said urgently. Even though that was far from the most pressing issue at the moment. Did he want me to just drop him?

"I'll get them," I promised. "You'll tell me where they are, but first we have to get you onto a bed."

He nodded wearily. Holding on tight to whatever was at hand, he held as steady as he could on the one good leg. He kept trying to keep his weight off me, but the deck kept shifting too. It wasn't working. I was fighting him as well as trying to carry him. He was unsteady and ill. When we got to a wall, I stopped us so we could take a breather.

"You came back," he said, when we were taking the break. "When you left, I thought I would never see you again. But seeing you I feel better already." Right, I'm thinking. Get a move on Jill, he's delirious, soon he'll be saying he loves me.

Rae's mom, Laurie at the gym, was always telling me stories of how men at the hospital were saying such things to her. She worked there as a nurse. She was good at her job I could tell, it made her smile to help people. I was feeling the same way now. It was a good feeling to be helping this guy and I was glad that I'd come back.

After we'd rested long enough, I encouraged him and said, "Let's keep moving."

"You a nurse?" he asked hesitantly, shifting his weight back onto me, assured in his mind that I was stronger than I looked.

I laughed at that, "No, but I have a friend that's a nurse."

"Well, I'd love to meet your friend."

Here it comes I thought, but it wasn't what I imagined. "How is it you have a friend that's a nurse... Wait, never mind, of course. I'm not the first human you've helped, or talked too. You see, I'm a researcher. I still don't get it, how you, a mermaid, came to speak the language so well. Do you know many humans?"

I froze and about dropped him. The gall! Perhaps he sensed I was about to abandon him. "Wait, don't answer that. I'm rambling, prying... And about to collapse, can we continue?"

He tried to take his weight off me again and nearly fell as a result. I was left bracing him up. "Don't fall," I begged, but he had nothing left. I had to suck it up. It was all on me, so I ducked my head down and put my back under his shoulders and pushed upwards. I misjudged the angle but caught us before we went over the other way. Hopefully, he was too delirious to know what was happening.

Morning came and while I was walking him back, a bright shaft of light lit up the cabin and the sun began pushing its way over the horizon. The cot had seemed forever away, but then I was dropping him onto the bed. "Look," I said with relief, propping him up with some discarded clothes. Thankfully, I was able to give them a once over as Lucas had taught me to get rid of the odor, while trying to encourage him "It's a new day. With any luck, you'll be feeling better after some rest."

Standing, I looked back the way we'd come. I shouldn't have been able to haul him back here. He'd leaned on me more than he realized. This was all too much and I found myself shaking my head at the incredulity of it.

"My stuff!" he said, echoing his previous concern. I let him talk me into retrieving his gear from the sea. I wanted to get back into the water anyway. Being aboard his boat was a risk that I'd been willing to take, until he started calling me a mermaid, but how could I say no. He'd probably die if I left him. The boat would be fine, it was anchored and likely safe, but in the condition he was, I'm not sure he could make it on his own. I couldn't turn my back on him. If the tables were reversed, he thinking that I'm a mermaid, would he be so kind?

I knew enough about mermaid stories, in most of them there was some scientist that wanted to study the mermaid. How was I to know he wasn't one of them? He was already thinking I was one. He'd asked if I knew many humans, how pathetic.

Looking up, I realized while thinking I'd walked out to look over the back of the boat. I had one foot placed on the edge, ready to leap over the side and not return. I would be walking a fine line in staying to help this guy. Lifting my eyes from the water, but I thought, I never regretted helping people, so. Who knew where this might lead? Still, I was going to have to play it safe.

By leaving him initially, I wasn't off to a great start. But I had a chance now to correct that, and make it right – to help him. In some stories the good guy was always saving the bad guy. So, would I be doing the right thing in helping him, however he turned out? Oh, how I wished Uncle Arden was here. He'd know what to do.

At least I knew what needed to be done – retrieve this guy's stuff. "Come on, Jill. It'll be fun," I said turning, taking my foot down and making my way back inside, trying to convince myself I'd be okay.

When I spoke to him next, he mentioned a map of the sea floor he'd put together identifying where everything was laid out. By his directions I was able to find the map and the computer he had linked to his equipment. The large cabin on the main deck, had been converted to a lab, and had the map. There were all sorts of containers in the cabin as well. They were filled with liquid and samples of sea life. He was a researcher, definitely. I wondered briefly what his main project included. I doubted the wreck I'd found him in had been his main area of research. Because, the samples were nothing like what had been there.

With his help, I was able to get the computer to let me see what each camera was filming. This helped in locating them. It was clear with the various camera's I'd pulled up, my friends and I had to have been on them. But there was no simple process of erasing them. I didn't have the skills. Computers were foreign to me, so for me to try and erase their recordings was out of the question. I barely got by on my phone. I started feeling that urge for a sledgehammer again. There should be enough evidence here to have us all bottled up.

After retrieving the first two underwater cameras, I checked up on him, he was burning up. His fever had taken a turn for the worse, and I went in search of some ice. Putting the ice into a towel, I went back and put it on his head. "Hold that in place," I advised him, unsure whether he was lucid enough to understand. But he held it in place. I kept hoping he would get better, so I could leave, instead he seemed to be slipping away. And he kept muttering about his equipment.

To put him at ease, I spent the better part of the day pulling up his equipment. The weather was shifting with the nearby storm, the yacht's pitching grew worse as the heights of the waves rose. It began to rain and I turned my thoughts to getting his finds undercover. I wondered briefly at the collection of artifacts he'd found: statues, pots and chests – they were remarkably intact. Most of the items I was able to secure, but the chests were heavy. What was in them to make them so heavy? I figured probably nothing more than water and rotten clothing and besides the chests were difficult to move. Then, I thought if they got wet, it wouldn't be a lot worse than they'd experienced lying at the bottom of the ocean. So, I left them alone. Besides, nothing would be worse than if I broke one of them.

At one point, I took a break and went to his radio. I tried to call out on it for help. I thought I heard someone pick up, but then nothing. Since there was no answer, I left it on in case someone would respond. Then I made us something to eat. I managed to get him to eat. I tried again on the radio, then switched it off. It was now late evening and the sea had settled once more. I sat out on the back deck watching the sunset. Reminiscing about home, I wondered what mom, dad and Uncle Arden were up to. I thought about trying to make a call, not knowing what I'd say if I had gotten a hold of them.

I imagined my conversation would've gone something like this.

"Hey, Mom, Lucas, Uncle Arden," whoever I would have gotten a hold of, "I'm on the other side of the world. Hope everything is great – sorry, I had to go and rescue a stranger and not leave word. No, I'm fine. This guy is sick and needs my help. How did I find him? I was swimming with my friends, and the bottom of the pool opened up into the ocean. Next thing we knew, Lucy, Melanie and Cleo and I were all swimming in the ocean and the pool was just a mirage floating in the sea. Sounds strange huh? Well, after a bit they went home, and me, the reluctant hero, came back to save the day. I fell asleep in the pool and woke up here. It's impossible I know. Seems like he'll die if I don't stay. I can easily see that you, Uncle Arden, would have a fit about this situation. So, it is probably good that you're not here, and that we're not having this conversation. Anyway. I love you…"

I was glad I didn't have to make up a story, at least not yet. I felt tears on my face and wiped them away. Thinking about my family, on the other side of the world, made my heart reach out for them. I wanted them here with me. How was I supposed to explain any of this? I didn't think I could. On that note, I stood up to go inside, but lingered to breathe in the night air for a minute longer. The sun was gone, and the sky had finished with the last of its orange and purple fireworks. With the last bit of light, I went inside, navigating my way by feel. Determined not to waste this guy's electricity. Walking through the yacht to where he lay resting, I pulled down the other cot across from him and laid down, blissfully at peace. I fell asleep immediately.

I woke once to the guy crying out, and for a minute I was lost as to where I was. Then I heard him moan in his sleep, it yanked me back to the moment. I jumped out of my cot and went to him. His forehead was still hot. I went to replace the towel with another one filled with more ice. Then I sat with him a bit before I sat back down on my cot, overcome with sleep.

I woke again to the rocking of the boat, comfortably listening to the beautiful sounds of seagulls floating in the sky above and the sound of the sea. "I could get used to this," I thought aloud, but it wasn't nearly as nice as waking in the sea.

At the sound of my voice, the man stirred and I moved over to sit beside him. In the better light, I studied him. He appeared to be approximately thirty-five, with dark hair and dark stubble all over his jaw. The stubble made him look disheveled and handsome, too. Realizing I had been staring at his lips, wondering what it would be like to hear him say my name, I got up and went to look for something else to do. The last thing I needed was to fall for this guy. He was like a father to me in age.

I turned my thoughts to Lucas, who wasn't my real dad, and then to Uncle Arden who wasn't my real uncle. But that wasn't helping, because somewhere out there I had a real dad. For a skipped heartbeat I imagined this guy could be him. No, he was much too pale. Nor was mom dark naturally either, though she tanned easily. No, whoever my dad was, he would have a dark complexion. I still held to the idea that he was tall, dark, handsome, fun and a bit comical. He would always be making me laugh.

"Better get a grip, Jill," I said talking to myself again. I wanted to be sure this guy was okay. Besides, I knew I couldn't stay away. So I went back to check on him. (Also I wanted to reassure myself that he didn't look anything like me.) It had been a long time since I'd pined for my real dad. It was smacking down on me again. I sat down beside him, studying his face some more. No there wasn't the faintest resemblance. He wasn't looking very good either and he didn't rouse when I changed his compress. I sighed as I stood back up – I would have to get him help.

I wasn't thinking clearly as I dove overboard and headed down to the anchor. It was a relief to be in the water again. But, once I had the anchor in hand and was swimming up with it, I wondered what I was going to do with the thing. Surely, the boat had a mechanism for lifting the anchor up. Finally, I ended up climbing back aboard with the anchor, shaking my head, and searching for some sort of switch. As it turns out, the anchor switch was by the steering wheel. I flipped it and the mechanism started whirring loudly. Alarmed, I went back and tossed over the anchor. After a minute, there was a clunk and the thing shut off. "Now, where to go?"

"You should have thought of that before pulling up the anchor!" I chided myself. I checked the wind. The water was clear to all sides, and the wind was blowing from the island. We would slowly drift out to sea and we wouldn't crash into anything. I felt better for having checked. Looking upwards, I saw that the storm from the day before was now replaced with a blue sky and scattered high clouds. It would be nice here for a while, though I thought it might rain come evening. Hopefully, we'd be gone by then. With a satisfied smile and a swing in my stride, I went up the back steps to the command deck. I was looking forward to getting this guy taken care of and to getting home.

Beside the pilot seat were all kinds of charts and a pair of books. I was faintly surprised to see that both books were up to date. The first book contained all his finds, cataloging his course, dives and instrument readings. The other being a personal journal that summarized his journey. Reading that one, two things jumped out at me, the first being his name – Arlo McKenzie. There couldn't be two people with the same name. Wasn't Melanie's uncle, on her dad's side, named Arlo? Also her uncle was a marine biologist – was this a coincidence, or was her uncle below? I'd have to ask her to be sure.

The other was the word "mermaid." It jumped out at me off his last entry. An island he'd stopped at named "Syreni" was his last port of call. I reread the entry before trying to find the Syreni island in his charts. They would know him there. I too was curious as to what I would find there, because his journal mentioned they had something of an affection for mermaids.

Digging through the charts, it didn't take me long to find it. He had a line from one stop to the next. But, what was missing, was how he had gotten himself here. Several times I looked out the windows to be sure we were drifting without problems. It was still calm in the lee of the island. But, it wouldn't remain so if we drifted for too long and got out beyond the island's protection.

I reread both books to see if I could find some clue to our whereabouts. I was reading his personal journal when I saw he was currently lost. His instruments had not been working correctly. If he couldn't find his way, how was I supposed to? Still, there had to be something I could do. Not sure what I should do, I went to check up on him, hoping he might have revived to help me decide. When I saw he was further gone than before, I grew worried.

Did mystical powers of healing come with being a mermaid? I had seen my friends' sunburn healing, and minor scrapes on Melanie's legs and mine disappeared when we entered the water. I attuned, I sang, but so far there was little change in him, even with melted ice water spread on his face, it wasn't enough. If it was even helping at all. Swims always revived me. Feeling his head, I thought a swim would do him good too, but it seemed cruel to dunk him on a whim, and it might not help.

Thinking that perhaps I could find that Syreni island or other help by spiritual vision searching, I got up from the cot where I'd been watching him. I went back out to the back deck, leaned on the railing and tried to feel for the island. I felt outwards by trying to attune a vision of what I wanted, but it was no more than the sea beneath and not much beyond. I had to get into the water.

Going overboard with a rope attached to the bow, to climb back up with, I lay back and opened myself to the sea and distant images. We'd drifted further than I thought. The sea below was much deeper, and the types of sea life had changed. I sensed great turtles flying by on a deep current and watched them go. All around me there were overlapping images of fish and no fish, the turtles and empty sea. In the sky nothing but clear sky and also a faded out jet coming our way. The world of man seemed to be near, but just out of sight. It didn't make sense to me. Until, I realized, I'd been experiencing these things before. That this wasn't the first time I, or the things I was experiencing, came from… I was hesitant to say "another world," but a place so real and just out of sight, like you might blink and say there it is.

The flowers, I'd noticed, when I'd spoken with Lucas at Coot Lake had been growing from some other place. Had they been coming from here, where things were untouched by man? There had been no trash on the island when we'd searched, but then thought, there was the wreck of the ship. So mankind did occasionally breach the barrier between the worlds. Then there was also, my experience under the creek, while Uncle Arden and I had been hiking to Red Deer Lake, it too was another place. Impossible. But then again, so was I.

I came to the conclusion, this guy had somehow come across from the world of man, to here. How on earth did he get here? It was probably like the Bermuda Triangle, people disappearing in boats and planes never to be heard from again. Like the galleon, it too had arrived and had never been able to return home. There had to be a way back. Uncle Arden had taught me what to do, to move myself. The first would be to make a connection to the here and there, then by getting understanding of what needed to take place and the permission to do it. Then lastly to practice it, completing the spell. The process of sending myself from place to place still sounded complex, but it hadn't been all that difficult when I'd gone from Red Deer Lake to Boulder. Now though, I had a whole yacht to take along with me.

I didn't have the experience, but I knew what to do. I would envision there and now, but in the world I lived. Knowing I had to do this, I reached out, attuning and making the connection. I could feel the yacht, the waters in which it sat, and all about. Even the wind was measured for speed and direction. I then knew the yacht's measurements. Also I pictured where I wanted to go, the same place in my world that I could see faded out all around me.

It was time to get the understanding, and so I asked, "Lord of the Water, you know what I need. Can you help me get there?" It was like when my friends and I had asked, but now I knew to whom I spoke. I felt different as the understanding came. I saw that we existed in a parallel place, beyond a veil. I was then able to practice it by swimming through. It was similar to the time in the Atlantic, after my encounter with the submarine. Here, it was a steady moving, of leaving one place and arriving in another. Swimming through the veil, I glanced up to see the contrail of the jet now plowing the sky above. I'd made it! That wasn't terribly difficult. Now what?

I looked back. I saw the rope I held disappear in mid-air. I could "see" the yacht as it drifted in that other place, on the other end of the rope. I would have to "practice" it through as well. It wasn't going to be a simple swim.

Pulling the rope taut, I got ready for the real work. Tugging, I kicked, giving it all I had. Slowly the yacht began to move. I was watching as I swam on my back. Seeing it pass through the veil, it looked to be coming whole into existence from front to back. What a sight that would have been for an observer. It was a lot harder than taking just myself. I was sweating from the exertion but couldn't give up. I had to believe I could do this. So I kept kicking. In the Atlantic, my legs had seemed like twin jets propelling me along effortlessly. This time we crept along as they created a fury in the water.

The yacht seemed to resist me, the last little bit, like it wanted to stay in that other place. But all of a sudden, it rippled through. With a cry of triumph, I relaxed letting the water go all through me, replenishing my strength and cooling me off. I was still pretty tired, but felt remarkably good. I looked back the way we'd come, but here and not there. There was no island in this world, just empty water. The sea here was deeper and colder. Too bad there was no island, as they may have been able to give us aid. I would have to continue with the same plan, find the Syreni people and their island.

Climbing up the rope to the deck, I turned to coil it back up and stowed it away where I'd found it, then went to see how my patient was doing. He was out cold and gave no response when I changed the compress again. Then I went to see what I could do about getting us to the Isle of Syreni. With the expectation of success, I went up to the wheel house, sat down in the captain's seat and looked over the many instruments. One of these has to be for turning the yacht on. It wasn't that hard once I found the switch. I was simply fretting, for the engine turned over with an easy rumble, and I hoped I pointed us in the right direction as I gunned the throttle forward.

He was awake when I checked on him, which gave me hope, but he had trouble focusing on me. "What's going on? Where are we going?" he asked. I tried reassuring him, telling him I was taking him to get help. When I mentioned Syreni, he relaxed, so I knew I was doing the right thing. I just had to find it!

It was mid-morning when suddenly the dials and navigation equipment burst to life happily chirping away as if nothing had happened. Apparently, the computer needed time to reorient. The pilot chair was too comfortable and I'd been dozing. My sense of direction was good, but not exact, and now with the help of the equipment I was able to plot a course. We'd been going almost in the right direction, and it was late in the afternoon when we arrived.

5.1   Syreni Island

The island was sizeable, but the navigation plot to get me to the harbor had me going around a ways. The harbor, when I got there, was beautiful as the rest of the island appeared to be, a sheltered cove with a brilliant river flowing into it. There was a long pier, and I headed towards it once I had cleared the breakwaters and the tiny lighthouse. Apparently, the sea life liked the place too. I sensed their presence as we went in. The waters were crystal clear – not an ounce of debris floated in them.

Coming out from a wooded and weather-beaten hut, a wrinkled and deeply tanned old man greeted me with a wave while raising a flag with colored streamers that looked like fish scales. He came and helped me tie up. By gesture, he taught me what to do. His warmth and honest face reassured me, but before I could say anything, he asked, "Where are they?" Seeing my confusion, he said, with slowness so I'd understand, "Those that you rescued."

"Uh," I found myself at a loss for words, "How did you know?" I finally asked.

"You," and he pointed at me. "You came. You here," and he pointed downwards, "Show me," he added with as much deference as he could muster, but he didn't move from the pier until I stepped back and let him come aboard.

He disappeared down into the craft the way I had pointed. I was hesitant to follow and instead looked about and up at the flag he'd raised, which was snapping in the wind. I heard excited voices and turned to see three people perhaps as old as the old man. They were all dressed like, well, like Mom, which was very strange and I thought I might see Mom among them. They were all different, wrinkled by the sun, and mom tanned easily, the same as me, but had no wrinkles except at the corners of her eyes from smiling.

Once they arrived, they waited quietly on the pier. They seemed afraid they'd spook me into diving overboard. If they hadn't been dressed like mom, I surely would have. All this was too much for me, all these strangers. This time, though, I would see this man safe before I abandoned him; yet, what could I do from here?

Pretty sure that we would be leaving the yacht soon, I set about tidying things up, stowing away anything that wasn't tied down. After a bit, the old man came out with the diver draped over his shoulder as I'd done before. I stepped up to help him get the guy over to the others. Of the three, there were two men and a woman. One of the two men stepped over to the other side of the pier and what I'd taken for a part of a painted piece of artwork was a cot, which he lifted down. All business-like, the men got the guy onto it and started to carry him to shore.

"Wait," I called, I wanted to go with them. Using the key, I locked up the craft. As I stepped ashore, the key was suddenly gone, I couldn't feel it and feared that I had dropped it in the water, I turned to look around the pier. What a dumb thing, Jill. To lose the key right off the bat.

The woman calling and gesturing for my attention held out her hands palms up. She wanted me to do the same, but it was a mystery why. When I did, right there on my palm was the key. I was sure I'd checked my hands, but it hadn't been there. I turned my hands over, fingers still out and the key was gone again, as I turned them back upwards, still gone. Yet, I knew if I wanted it, it would be there.

I had no pockets. What a clever trick. I wouldn't be able to carry much that way, but it was something. As I smiled at the woman, she nodded and turned to the one remaining man, and took a bundle from him. When she turned, she bent low holding out the bundle as a gift – it was clothing.

"Please," she said, "Take it – you like," and then trying again she said, "It, it be made for you." Then going on, "We honored you come. See him safe, then come – we celebrate."

I felt like Mom, a naturalist hippie, as I pulled on the garments. I was hesitant at first, but if I was going ashore, this made sense. Mom used to dress me up in such garb, but I'd long switched to polyesters and nylons. But after the outfit she'd gotten me for the hike to Red Deer Lake, these seemed acceptable. The light brown skirt was actually quite comfortable, and the natural white top equally so. Then they offered me two sandals made from durable natural materials, such as they were wearing. They were all a tiny bit big but fit well enough.

Seeing so, the woman apologized, "Sorry, it be long time since a child..." and she looked to the other gentleman that accompanied her.

"...visits," he added in unaccented English.

"We will fix," she said, "please stay," but then she gestured for me to follow the men. So I wasn't sure what she meant.

The two men, straining with their load, were glad to resume their journey, and I felt ashamed for having made them wait. I offered to help carry the guy, but they would have none of it. So I followed, ready to jump and lend a hand if they stumbled. Soon, I saw their destination, a modern ambulance just pulling into the port. The thing looked barely used. The cleverly hidden road, on which it had arrived, gave the quiet harbor a grander appearance than at first impression.

The old man returned to his pier, leaving me with the woman ambulance driver and the other man that had carried the guy. The man sat in the middle, giving me the door. He started to teach me how to operate the door, but when he saw me put the window down with the switch he gave up with a confused smile. *This mermaid,* I thought to myself, *isn't a hick!* For he clearly thought me a bumpkin not to know how to roll down a window or close a door. But then on the island, there probably were not too many people who knew how to operate vehicles. He was just being polite, so I thanked him.

The two of them spoke in their Pidgin English, I caught maybe one word in ten as we traveled to the hospital. It seemed like natural banter between two people that rarely spoke. I felt like I was being whisked along on a fast horse, completely out of my depth. After the port, there was very little that was modern, but the street was clear enough for an ambulance without any siren or lights to get by. Then near the hospital, it grew quiet in the cab and the town began to look strange until I realized it looked like ancient Greek architecture with a modern twist. Everything here, I realized as I glanced back the way we'd been traveling, was strangely out of time and colorful with flowing streams, fountains and cultured gardens blooming with fragrant flowers everywhere. I could live here, even more than the island my friends and I had roamed on, because there were modern conveniences. I would still like to visit that other place because of the privacy.

We followed the river up from the cove, the road winding up the hills of the island. The slopes intermittently passing into cool forest only to emerge alongside amazing vistas. There were lakes at the base of each waterfall we passed. Eventually though we made a turn into a modern complex, I half-wondered where the road continued as each vista seemed greater than the one before, and this one wasn't too bad. We rolled up to a hospital that offered a beautiful garden and view. The ambulance slid into a stall, and the two of them slid out the driver's side. I jumped out the passenger side and went to help, but they already had things in hand. Again, I felt useless, so I followed after trying not to get in their way.

A doctor and nurse appeared in white and green. On seeing me, they gave me a little nod of the head in greeting then helped guide the guy onto a wheeled gurney they'd brought out. The ambulance driver blushed and did a little bow to me as well before departing in a hurry. Suddenly, I was all alone. Everyone made themselves scarce and I began to put two and two together. There were symbols of mermaids everywhere.

It was inconspicuous, but looking back at the ambulance, I saw mermaids in the place of the typical snakes on the health symbol that was painted on the back door. I'd seen one on the side of the ambulance, but I suspected what I'd mistaken for medical symbols were mermaids as well. They were taking it a little too far in my opinion, but so far they were courteous. I ran to catch up with them but got distracted by all the imagery. I'd seen a few things on mermaid lore over the years, but in just this one hall there was so much that I paused to take it all in. They also seemed crazy for hummingbirds, it was all too much. Here in this picture were two mermaids talking with a couple brightly lit hummingbirds. So, they knew I talked with animals?

Looking at the pictures more and more, I fell behind and had to hurry to catch up. The hospital was a veritable museum of such art. If I were to stay, I could spend some time enjoying that alone.

They wheeled him into a room, and more people descended on him. I stood at the doorway looking on, until I felt a gentle hand on my shoulder. It was the man who had accompanied me from the pier.

"Excuse me, miss," he said in nearly unbroken English. "They have it well in hand, there is nothing more you can do here."

"But..." I didn't want to let him go, but I saw he was right. *Would I take him back to his home, tuck him in, and then what?* "You're right," I nodded. "Here," I said handing over the guy's key. "This is to his boat. Please see that he gets it." Then I added, "What will happen now?"

"We will be sure he gets this," he said, holding up the key. "As for you, we will take you back to the sea where you may go or stay. We'd like you to stay, to know you are welcome among us. It has been years since we've had a sea lord amongst us, and we hold to the ancient pacts. We enjoy clean waters and plentiful fishing. In return, we are a refuge for any of your kind and those that you send us."

His expression said he had much more to say, but by then we were outside and an old uncovered jeep from a past era was waiting to give us a ride. The driver, a young girl not much older than myself, was waiting for us. There were no doors, but she stood beside the passenger side to give me a hand up, and she'd put down a stepping box. That was helpful as it was a big step up and my skirt would have made it difficult.

I decided to sit in the back, letting him take the front seat. That gave me time to think. I thought about what he said and what he hadn't said, likewise with what I'd seen. Who did he think me to be? Presumably they thought me a mermaid, but I lacked the telltale mermaid body. A mermaid was half-woman and half-fish, or perhaps all fish but only looked like a woman. I didn't know enough. Up until now, I had pushed away all the fancies because I had other things to think about, and I didn't want to be "their" mermaid. Or anyone's for that matter. How was I to fulfill their expectation when I didn't know what it was to be a mermaid? Maybe I could coax Melanie to give me more information about them.

Then he'd referred to ancient pacts. How far back did they go? "Ancient" sounded like it should be more than hundreds of years, maybe more like thousands of years. Who held to such an agreement for so long? Though it could be like a constitution, a set of laws that they decided upon. It was probably something like that, though he made it sound like it remained unchanged. He'd reassured me that they still held to them.

We drove back a different way, down an avenue with great trees lining either side of it and a colorful river flowing between the lanes. The curbs were painted white, and every fifty feet there was a statue of a merman. Men with fish tails holding what must be tridents, spears with three prongs instead of one. Stranger and stranger, and cute.

Their upper bodies resembled those of strong men, and their hands were webbed. I wonder if their webbed hands gave way after a time, like mine had. The stone statues might have been white at one time, but now they were covered in lichen, giving them a pale green look. Instead of menacing, they looked like they were honoring all that passed with one arm raised, the trident held up in salute. Not the image I would have imagined.

"There are many such things here, if you'd care to stay, I'd show you," the man offered, seeing awe in my expression.

I shook my head in disbelief before hearing him then again saying, "I shouldn't stay long."

"Of course," he said trying to hide the frustration in his voice. Instead, he extended an open invitation, "You are welcome back any time. Can we at least offer you food? I'm sure there is a feast being prepared in your honor. There will be music, dancing..." he tried once more. This time, I relented. The island was beautiful. I would stay – night was approaching anyway. If all he said was true, I had nothing to fear. I was tired, and hungry. He gave orders to the driver and we drove down to the sea.

5.2   Beach Party

I'd seen old movies of Hawaiian luaus, and this resembled one in many ways, except there were modern grills loaded with foods. The music was all live, big drums and guitars, reed flutes and whatever else made a melody. There was also singing. They didn't seem to need an excuse for a shindig. It was in full swing when we arrived, thankfully. I didn't want to be the guest of honor.

I was whisked away by girls who were my age and they exchanged the clothing I'd been given for colorful outfits, loose for dancing, like they wore. Then they sat me down, brushed and braided my hair, weaving in bright aromatic orchids. Laughing happily, I found myself smiling along with them. There was no threat here, only merriment. Soon, they had me up and running after them. Like moths to a flame, we went down to the fires where the dancing was already going on. They headed straight into the midst of them, rolling their hips, and I did my best to imitate their movements. I had thought there might be speeches or ritual, but it seemed I was accepted as one of them, though I couldn't help feeling apart. The girls stuck close to me, making sure I never felt left out. Whenever they talked, they included me, though I couldn't understand a word and when they stopped for food and drink, I thankfully went with them, too. There was laughter, cheer and singing all around.

We sat in the midst of the singers and gobbled up our food and drinks. The songs seemed to be ones they loved, and the girls joined in the singing as I tried to hum along with them. The song was soothing, uplifting and enchanting all at the same time. My hum found words, and I had no idea what I was singing, but it came up from my belly like a fountain. The music took on colors, splashes of blues, purples, pinks, greens and white diamonds. It became like the sea, ever-moving, powerful, wonderful. I could feel its spray as it leapt up in the dance. I saw dancers imitating the song like ballerinas. I was lost in the tune for what seemed an eternity. The stars were out in profusion. It was a moonless magical night, and at last I fell silent to listen to the night's song. It was entrancing.

Along with everyone else, I was wiping tears from our eyes, I was unaware at first that I'd been alone in singing for some time. Until I realized they were all looking at me. "What?" I asked happily, "Did I do something wrong?"

The music thrilled my heart. I couldn't keep down my happiness no matter what they thought. I heard the night sky singing. Unable to stay silent any longer I joined in and sang some more, as surprised as they were at my desire. The sea surged and became the base drum to the melody. Soon the drummers started up again, and the flutes, followed by the guitars. Lastly the singers lifted their voices in tune with it all. Together, we sang and gathered in the elements around us in harmony.

If only the night could last forever, but it was late and I was yawning uncontrollably. The older crowd had already called it a night and faded away. The girls who had seemed inexhaustible were now drooping. A signal was given, and those that were left said their farewells. Then the girls gathered me up and led me to a beach house, where they offered to stay with me. I thought I would send them away, but instead I didn't. Being alone on an island of strangers wasn't right, especially at night.

There were enough beds and pillows for everyone to be comfortable. The sea was just down the beach from the front porch. I sat up watching it, amazed at how beautiful it was, how endless it appeared. Two girls sat up with me, leaning on me because they wanted to sleep but wouldn't go inside unless I did. It was terribly endearing. At some point, I let them lead me inside and they pulled me down onto a bed, where sleep finally claimed me.

5.3 Nightmare Island

I awoke to quiet, moonlight and the hair of one of the girls, cuddled close, in my face. They were close about me and we were warm, and the moon now risen shone through the windows. I could hear the ever-restless sea, and it called to me.

Disentangling my face from the girl's hair, I lifted my head and listened – really listened – and heard the sea's lullaby. It hadn't been my imagination from the bonfire song. No wonder it was a favorite for so many to rock them to sleep, especially if they heard what I heard. The night and the sky each had their interweaving verse woven into the peaceful melody.

Inwardly I knew it was time to go. An inner clock told me it was now morning at home and if I didn't make an appearance they would notice. I was deluding myself. I'd been gone two or three days. I was missed, even if they were calling me an adult now. Surely I was in for it.

Pushing myself up and out of the embrace of the girls, I crab-crawled sideways over them until I had a clear place to stand. They'd all pushed their way to be near, and I was gladly surprised I didn't wake a single one. It was time to go, and I let go the binds that held the skirt. I pulled off the top. I had the fish suit for the swim home – I couldn't swim in the beautiful outfit even if they wanted to gift them to me. I wouldn't presume they were gifts, I'd only borrowed them. I then ran my fingers through my hair, unwinding the braids they'd wound, and let out all the flowers that I'd crushed in my sleep.

It was with sadness that I gathered up my things, folded them and set them on a chair. The flowers that I could see in the moonlit darkness I gathered and set next to the clothes. Turning to leave, I walked quietly away. The way to the door was brighter, lit with the moonlight. All was quiet and peaceful. The screen door opened with the tiniest sound and closed just as quietly. Thankfully.

I lifted my eyes to the sea beyond. It was a welcome sight reflecting a trail of moonlight off the incoming waves. As if calling me home, there was the faint image of the pool lying as a solid rectangular cube out beyond the breakers. I glanced up at the moon as I descended the stairs, which blinded me. I stood looking up at the white orb and the endless stars. Even the stars over the mountains at home didn't compare, they had too many city lights obscuring their brilliance.

Glancing back down at the sea, I saw the pool winking at me, its light reflecting through the oncoming waves. Then I noticed an odd sight, dark blotches in a large semicircle around the building, like freckles upon the sand as far as could be seen. It took a bit before my night vision returned and I could see in the moonlight a variety of people kneeling, sitting, and lying prone and everywhere in between. How I'd missed them when I first left the house was a mystery, but then I'd been looking primarily at the sea and sky.

Then closer in and radiating out from the house in a strange geometric pattern were men kneeling with their backs to the house and armed with weapons, and not just island swords but modern weapons. They started from the walls of the house out to where the others were. A path went between them out to where the first line of non-warriors waited, and I expected it was for me to use, so I walked down along them angling roughly towards the sea. There were probably a hundred with weapons, maybe more, for I couldn't see those that might be behind the house.

At the end of the path were the first three that had greeted me when I'd stepped off the yacht. They'd given me clothes and tried to make me feel welcome. They'd tried, but it had been with their children that I'd danced, played and sang. Their behavior now was very strange.

They uncovered bowls that radiated light upon them, and not on me so I'd keep my night vision. It looked very practiced and formal. Then they stood with eyes cast down at my feet, and the woman spoke saying, "Good morning, Lady," and then with a nervous bow and a tremble in her voice that made no sense, "Was your sleep not restful?"

Huh, what? It had been very restful, and I was about to answer so when I heard a disturbance behind me in the house I'd just left. The sound of frightened girls, but I was so transfixed by the sight before and around me and their odd question that it didn't register.

Perhaps I'd been asleep when I came out, for I realized the warriors had been facing outwards. They were protecting me, from what? The guards had automatic weapons. They stood at my sides and back. Were they protecting me from their own people? Worse, they were trained for this – they had the look of the best-trained marines my country could produce.

I was caught off-guard. What was going on? This was important, and I took a last glance out at the pool in the waves and sighed, I was going to have to take care of this. They expected it of me. But what exactly I had no clue. I'd have to feel my way through it.

"I'm fine," I said, but a yawn betrayed me. "I was going to leave."

Now, I could hear the sound of the girls coming from the house, but I didn't dare turn. The girls were weeping and sobbing in fright. Why? What have I done?

"We've displeased," said the woman trembling as well, they were almost groveling and they were the ones with the army! Did they expect me to level a lightning bolt at them? They obviously thought something of the kind. Why should I be displeased? I was happy or I had been until a minute ago.

"These," the woman continued, meaning the girls as they were brought forward, "Were to care, provide and give you anything. They've failed and shall be hanged!" What? No! I wanted to shout at the injustice, but instead I was speechless. Hanged? Barbaric!

There was a beautiful Japanese gate halfway between the house and the shore, which I'd thought decorative and odd, being where it was. It was behind the others that knelt behind the three, and I recognized the doctor, nurse and the man from the pier among them. And the two drivers that had driven me on the island. They were all bent to the ground on their knees, face-down.

It was to the gate the girls were led. They were stifling sobs, sniffling, trying to not be afraid. They were going to their deaths on account of me, on some perceived slight! Yes, I'd been tired, and yes I should be getting home, but it wasn't their fault, and then I understood. The rings and rings of men surrounding the home. The girls had been the inner defense and they'd fallen asleep. I'd sneaked off and they had been my inner guard. If I'd but woke one of them, this wouldn't be happening!

While I'd been having my inner debate, they hauled six ropes over the fence and were tying them to the girls' necks. There were those waiting to pull them up and choke them to death, it would not be quick! Some of those holding the ropes had to be their parents, and yet they were going through with it all the same.

They were starting to pull, and it was past the time of thinking, "Wait!" I shouted. Would they listen? The girls' wrists were tied behind their backs and they couldn't save themselves, but then the girls were let down to where their toes touched the sand, barely alive. Could I save them?

"Why is this being done?" I demanded an explanation, now angry. What must they think of me that I'd demand the lives of their children and their own?

"Mistress, please," the woman cried, throwing herself down on her face, as did the other two. They'd fallen there, afraid. It was real fright. In apprehension, she spoke haltingly, "They must die to appease your wrath. It is the way, we serve and protect. We shelter and destroy. Our lives are yours."

What was this they spoke of? "Is this the pact?" I asked, still mad but finally getting some answers. The woman nodded, but there were two sides to a pact. Surely, my side wasn't to zap whoever offended me. "That's not all of it," I stated.

I was aghast at myself, but none of them were looking at me. *I was acting the part. I had to save these girls! I wouldn't be going home.* Mom, Lucas and Arden were just going to have to trust me. Mom and Lucas would, I knew, but Uncle Arden, if he knew where I was, he'd be here beside me. Perhaps it was good that he wasn't.

Uncle Arden could be fierce, and these people were frightened enough.

The woman looked up hopefully and seeing that I wasn't going to zap her on the spot, gulped then told me.

"When the god's raised the world from the sea, we were given charge over the land, but only so long as we protected the servants of the sea and air. We are to protect, serve and obey you, High One. Your word is law and life. In service there is life, in protection there is continuation, and in obedience there is structure. We all have pledged our lives and our children from the beginning of time unto the end of it in this task."

She went on, "In life there is joy, abundance and prosperity. Life without law is death. With law, we have new life, new joy and purpose. Please mistress, it is the law, these—" she pointed but couldn't bring herself to say *children*, "must die so that there may be continuation. They've failed to protect. I'd gladly take my own life and fully expect that you will demand it of us and will go willingly. It has been my life's joy to serve, and in this is the greatest service."

I saw sense in what she said, and that they believed the agreement was between them and their gods. Who could argue with that? It certainly wasn't my place to disagree. But this was life and death to them. They were ready to kill their own to satisfy its requirements, and they expected me to enforce it if they disobeyed in the slightest. So far, this mermaid business had its moments. I loved the time I'd had with my friends beneath the sea and I loved rescuing the guy, and with the doctor here I wanted to hear how he fared. Was I expected to make sure that the doctor off himself if he'd failed to make the guy well? This was too much to bear!

Somehow, I had to let them know that killing their children was a mistake, but without them taking offense, or someone else would die for that error in interpreting "divine" will. I yawned again. My mind barely able to process it all. I'd hoped to be home by now and in bed. It had been a super long day. Now, what was I supposed to do?

The woman had said my word was law. Staying their execution wasn't good enough, for that would not change future hangings, but I was too tired to reason it out. Perhaps staying the execution until morning would work, I decided. I was going to be here awhile longer, and I determined not to let them see how I felt about that!

Gesturing them up, I said benevolently, "Please stand. I haven't decided yet. I need until morning. Let them resume their duties."

There were no joyous cries at getting to see another sunrise, or at being released. They didn't run for their lives but marched up to stand around me, all duty and no playfulness. This was almost worse than before, but I kept my chin up. At least they weren't swinging by their necks in the breeze.

They were all duty, and I was about to take them up into the house with me, but I saw the doctor, the nurse and the two drivers. They were all still kneeling. Stepping around the three leaders, I stepped before them and they were about to do a face plant but I knelt quickly and took the doctor by the hand.

He, probably fifty years old, obviously studious and modern-minded still felt bound by all these traditions. Even though he'd had to have studied abroad and knew foreign cultures, maybe having studied at an American school. He didn't look unhappy as he looked up. These people were content with their life and did not feel that their ways were a burden. "Sir," I addressed him, "How is your patient?"

His eyes met mine briefly. "He has a fever, mistress. We are treating it, and his leg. He will have a full recovery. This much is certain."

I wanted to ask him how he knew, but I was no doctor. I barely knew the remedies for a cough. Surely he had thousands of solutions at hand, studied and practiced as he was. I would leave them to their work.

"Thank you, doctor. Are you returning to the hospital tonight?"

"No, Mistress," he said baffled. "My place is with you. All serve. On my shift, I will return, but there is much to be done here. In your presence is joy, Mistress." He was smiling and believed what he said.

This is how ancient royalty must have been treated, with endless people waiting at hand for a word to be directed their way – a whim to be fulfilled. I couldn't, shouldn't change them, but this could become stifling for them and for me.

I turned and went for the house. By the time I got there, those girls that had been to the room had straightened everything up. All except for the clothing I had left – that had been left untouched. I'd rejected their gift in some subtle fashion, and it all came from my relationship with these girls. I'd not tried for names, or even conversation.

Worse, they were jumping to attend to my needs with renewed vigor. Once I was seated on the bed, three gathered behind me and began to brush out my hair. It would surely fly apart from static electricity, but they brushed some sweet scent into it that kept it from doing that. They must have had to practice this on each other before being given this duty, for their movements were deft and I felt no hair-pulling. My friends were good, but nowhere near the skill that these girls displayed as they settled my hair over my neck and across my chest in a weave, where it would remain untangled while I slept on my back.

Waiting for me to fall asleep, they knelt with their legs to one side and worked with their own hair. It seemed but a moment and then it was day. I'd dreamt something important, but in remembrance of last night's events it faded before I could grasp it. At my stirring, the girls roused themselves to waken the rest.

5.4   A Die Cast

No longer pretending that they would leave if I wanted, they overtly took over everything I ever did for myself. If it wasn't for the momentous predicament I was in, this would have been something to get lost in. But I couldn't stand the sight of such pretty necks in nooses in so short a time. I felt responsible for them. I had to say something.

"Please," I entreated them. "You have not displeased me. I don't know how to explain it, but this has been – until now – the happiest night of my life. It would make my heart burst to lose even one of you. Tell me, what must I do?"

They smiled and I didn't think they understood me, but they all turned to look at one of the girls, the smallest one with the unusual blue eyes. They nodded to her, and she got up from where she knelt at the back and came forward. A spot was made for her and she knelt directly in front of me and put her arms out straight to either side, perhaps to show she was unarmed or for an entirely unimaginable different meaning.

"This one," she said, and I think she meant for them all, "serves. In joy, we know your happiness and in joy we know your discipline. All is joy." But that wasn't true, they'd all been frightened when called onto the beach. I could only guess at the cause. All their life raised on tales of mermaids and their religion, but until today it had all been a myth, a game to play for their parents. Something had changed in this community, a lightning bolt of a different kind had run through them, electrifying their beliefs. I couldn't put my finger on it, but it had to be something I'd done since my arrival, and yet my arrival put it into motion. I've done as they have – sang, drank, ate, danced, laughed and enjoyed myself. We brayed at the moon, enjoyed the night air and had our fill of each other. What has so changed their attitudes?

I was missing something, but even if I figured it out, they were still in jeopardy and I had to figure that out first. With determination, I stirred myself, nodded and said, "Yes, we all serve, don't we," and I bent over in a similar pose in response.

With relief in her voice, she said "So, you agree then," sitting back on her heels relaxed, but I could see the tension in her eyes because of what it meant. Then I caught up with her on it. She was relieved as were the others that their ways would be upheld and I wasn't casting them aside, and she would die along with the rest of them.

No! I wanted to pound that into her mind. It must not happen!

"I agree that you've served me well, and I agree that you slept beside me for I needed, and wanted, it. I did rise to leave, filled with sorrow to be leaving you, and yet letting you sleep. I did not want to awaken you. It was not your fault that you were sleeping, it was my wish that you sleep." Then I had an idea, "And therefore, you were following my will to be sleeping when I rose up and when I left."

She would not have so simple an argument and she saw through it, "Yes, those that were to be with you, yes, they would be sleeping with you. That was arranged, but it was I and these others that should have stayed awake to serve you were you to rise."

It made no sense that they should be ready to serve my every whim at every hour of the day! What could I say to such an argument? I didn't want servants, I wanted friends. Last night, they had been my friends but woke up as my servants. What had changed?

"Last night, you were my friends, you were friendly when I was a stranger. We laughed, sang and enjoyed friendship, and I love you for it. You all had your eyes on the boys and they on you. What happened? Are we not friends?"

"No, Mistress. We are most definitely not, but we love you all the same. Thank you that you love us in return. The elders called for girls of our age, raised all our life on the expectation that one day one of yours would visit us. Ashamedly, we had not believed it. No sea lord has visited us in many years, even our leaders, heaven protect us, doubt. But no longer. Forgive us, we're only humans."

"We all, from youngest to oldest, male, female and all professions and callings in life have but one purpose, one faith, and one love. In this we have prospered, never does a storm destroy or belittle us – always the most violent pass us by. The elders have always spoken of your kind, long have they been under the sun, advising, directing, teaching and loving. To be an elder, they must have met one of your kind and served. There is a connection between them and you that goes beyond time. Our leaders, like all of us, hope to attain to what they have enjoyed their entire existence. Our leaders are old, but not by your reckoning. Our elders are older but still young in comparison."

"This one is younger still. We have drawn breaths for short years. Unfortunately, we have become current in thinking. I, youngest of those considered ready enough to serve, the most vocal. I am ashamed, Divine One, but I will appease my unhappiness with joy in serving. This I know." She said this last with such purposeful joy it made me ill to think of what it meant.

They were all nodding in response. All were ready to die, to atone for the mistakes of a few. Oh, it hurt, the realization I had now. I was about to condemn some of them to die. The pain was unbearable, but I had to bring this to a close before I burst open in grief.

"Not, all of you will die," I said and they looked up at me hurt, confused. "Did not some of you have the duty to sleep with me? To be sleeping while I slept?" There were nods here and there. They understood me just fine. There was no pretended language barrier.

"Those of you that had that duty, behind me. Those that were to be awake, in front." Most of the room moved to kneel behind me, but more than I wanted to see knelt down before me. Gulping, I was about to condemn them before I remembered it had only been perhaps an hour or two that I slept before waking. "Those of you that were asleep, waiting for your turn to be awake or had already served your awake time and had returned to sleep, kneel behind me as well."

With reluctance, they all cast eyes on the girl that was speaking with me, she hadn't moved from where she'd been, right before me. They got up to kneel somewhere behind me and left her alone.

I nodded, but inwardly I wept. That this youngest girl should be forever parted from life, I couldn't take it and reached forward to embrace her. She held me while I cried. With tremendous grace, she was comforting me, which made me cry all the more.

5.5   I Am Lady Death

Full morning came. I dressed, but it was more like I let them dress me once they knew what I wanted. My hair and everything was in order when I went outside. It seemed as if none of those outside had moved all night long. It also appeared as if the whole island had turned out to witness the execution.

The leaders that I'd mistook for elders were there. Beside them were obviously the elders the girl had mentioned, for six others had appeared. They were more revered than the leaders and somehow looked younger and older all at once. They smiled and each one in turn stepped forward and hugged me, greeting me like an old friend. I warmed to them immediately.

As I greeted them in return, I got the feeling they were much older than they appeared, but I couldn't put my finger on why. It was a quality that the others lacked, and the oldest, their leader the kindest man I'd ever met. He seemed positively ancient. Perhaps it was because he did appear to be fifty or sixty, then I met his eyes. Clear blue and empty of all guile, warm and welcoming. What a strange meeting, for they clearly wanted me there, and I remembered the circumstance.

When we stepped apart, they waited, and I realized it was my turn. I lifted my voice, but there was no need. A wind that must have been prepared by some spell carried the sound to those furthest back. I explained my reasons, what I'd been told, and everything I'd concluded, ending with the judgment pronounced against the littlest, hoping beyond hope that they'd hold their child in their arms and not let her go.

Then when I'd finished, I was startled when they cheered in response – such a happy response from the entire crowd that the birds leaped into the air all about the island as with one voice they were yelling for joy. They were beyond elated, yelling their happiness, many of them leaping high into the air.

I was utterly confused. Here I'd just pronounced a death sentence on their child and they were happy. There was no understanding these people. Perhaps, if I could drum up that lightning bolt they were expecting last night, I could blast them from the earth.

Suddenly they all went quiet, completely, as if given a command and I looked around. Their faces were radiant and I had trouble locating the source of the command. Most had tears of joy streaming down their faces. Not all, though. No. The girl that was to die stood silently, stunned. Finally, she was awakening to the fact she was about to die.

All had become quiet. The second youngest elder, her hand raised outward, had reached for the sun. Her hand was on fire. She spoke to the girl, asking, "Will you serve?" The woman wasn't going to hang the girl but burn her alive! I wanted to stand between them, but I was transfixed by the sight.

The child was tongue-tied. She wept as understanding came to her, then unexpectedly laughed with the biggest smile on her face, a reflection of the joy I'd seen on the others. Her laughter was carried out to the rest by the wind, and the congregation joined with her, laughing for joy. Waves of it rolled up and down the beach. They couldn't stop. Even the elders were caught up in it. If I wasn't so upset, I would have been carried away with it as well. On and on the laughter went until they had all fallen over, holding their chests from the pain.

After what seemed like hours of waiting for them to recover and rise, I noticed their numbers had swelled. I had thought the whole island was here before, but certainly they were all here now. Food was being brought, refreshments, flowers and music. These people never missed an opportunity to celebrate, and murdering one of their own was causing them the greatest joy. I was disgusted.

Apparently, they were going to put off the execution just a bit, for they still had their feast to prepare. I was about to be swept up in it, if it were possible, but I had too much grief to bear. In the whirlwind of activity, there was a place of calm... well, two places – one around me and one around the elders.

It was easy enough to find them – the six of them and the girl. The girl radiated a light, a fire, seemingly about to explode from it. I guess they didn't wait to finish her off, for fire covered her from head to toe. Strangely enough, the girl was elated to be burning alive. That is the last straw, *I'm out of here!*

When I stepped up to them, the elders all turned to me as one, even the girl. She reached out to me with her fiery arms and hugged me before I could step back, and I was afraid my dress would catch fire. Then she let go and I was alright.

"Please, I'm going," I couldn't manage anymore. I was very displeased, especially with how they were taking the child's dedication to their code. They had brainwashed her, brainwashed them all. This place was creeping me out. I'd never come back.

The oldest one spoke, "Children," he said, addressing the girls that still flowed about me. So unobtrusive they were that I'd forgotten about them. "Please lead our honored guest to the sea." Then, he said to me, "Come back any time, dear one."

Not on your life, I thought but instead I said, "Of course." I couldn't quite manage a gracious smile, so I turned away and looked to the waters beyond the courses of people gathering around the banquet.

The crowd parted before me as I headed towards the sea. They were smiling and showering me with flowers. They all turned to wave goodbye, so I couldn't shed the clothes before going into the sea. I ran and dove into the waves and with several kicks was out a ways, enjoying the feel of water like it was the first time. I couldn't help but rise up and give them a wave goodbye. Then, turning, I dove away.

It was great to be under the sea, to hear nothing but the beautiful ocean, and finally to no longer hear their joy. I was so furious with them and horribly torn up by my grief for her. I swam for some time with no clear destination. Yet, after a while, honest tears came and I remembered the whole reason I was furious, I'd killed a girl. Not me

167

personally, but my action to save the guy ultimately resulted in her demise.

I tried to reason their behavior, and to justify that the girl had to die because of it. I could see how they could come to that decision, but I couldn't get past my belief that all life was to be treasured. How could the ending of hers be the attainment of something better? I'd be weeping and puzzling this out for sometime. I wondered if I'd ever understand.

On that thought, the pool appeared before me, it was time to go home. With a last look at the sea, I turned and swam into it. And when I left the pool, with water running off me like I was a seal, I was still wearing those clothes. They were damp but drying fast. My first thought was to rip them off of me, but then I thought I should at least wear them to my room.

It was a crowded day at the pool, and nobody noticed my appearance there or my disappearance into the locker room. I walked straight through and out into the gym, angling for our apartment. Once inside, I shut myself in my room and fell face forward onto my bed.

6 The Gym and Friends

I was frustrated, angry and grief stricken all at once. I lay on my bed in our apartment trying to process my emotions, but there was no figuring it out. They were a crazy people that condemned a child to die because she didn't stay awake while I slept.

Ground her, or don't let her watch women "of my kind" sleep, but don't kill her. How ridiculous is that! To top it all off, she welcomed it as the highest form of service. How could someone buy into that kind of belief?

I would have welcomed sleep as an escape. The problem was, it was noon on the island and I'd had a full night's sleep. So, instead of worrying about my emotions or sleep – no, I was upset that I hadn't shed the island clothes upon laying down. They were a constant reminder of the "crazies." Also, they were a constant reminder of my failure, of their dedication to a pact that made them sacrifice one of their own, even a child. I was never going back. Never.

Tears came to my face and I tried banishing them, but they wouldn't go away. It was small consolation that she went willingly to the headsman, or in their case the pyromancer. Dedicated to their code, seemingly even more so than the others. No, that wasn't fair, but she believed it to the core. It didn't make any sense! None of my arguments matched up. That I couldn't reason it out had me tied in knots.

What was worse was that they thought I should be enforcing their laws, the pact they'd made with the ancient gods. The girl had claimed that her people were protected because of their adherence to it, but couldn't that be coincidence? Primitive cultures oft-times looked to natural disasters as being from "god." As if their god were judging them, or punishing them for letting their Princess marry the Undertaker. But they recognized me, whatever I was, as a representative of their god. How scary is that?

The island... ugh! Why did they...? Everything about the island made me furious, and when I wrenched off the blouse, I tore it in the process. It shocked me, but when I finished undressing I sat on my heels looking down at them, hesitant to touch them. Distracted by movement, I started laughing, seeing the fish running from my hands where they rested on my waist. "I'm not mad at you," I pouted. Their actions were mesmerizing.

The clothes as I continued to ponder reminded me of mom, which is why I'd opened up to the people so readily. There was so much to enjoy about the islanders as I guess the fish were trying to remind me. I was too good-natured to stay angry long. Besides it had been their decision, not that I could grasp their thinking. It made no sense. It made the tears start afresh, thinking about the girl with the blue eyes – she'd been sweet and kind to me all night and the previous evening. I saw her laughing in my mind, her hair escaping from her braid as we laughed about something from the party.

It wasn't fair. I knew enough from my social studies to know that other cultures were different, but I'd never imagined them being so... so... *backwards.* "Backwards" was going to have to do until I could find a better word to describe how their thinking was all flipped over and squashed to the side, run through a grinder and spat out like a bowl of jello that tasted wacky.

I was stuck on the outcome, so sad and terrible, but they'd acted as if it was high praise and joy unspeakable. The whole island had felt that way, they'd fallen down from the joy of it and even thrown a feast to celebrate! Yet they'd been so kind to me. So kind, because they thought me a mermaid.

Everyone thought I was. I wanted to prove them wrong, that I was a normal American girl. But how to go about it? The first step would be to stop rescuing people. Yes, Jill, when some force in the world sends you to the opposite ends of the earth, refuse. Just refuse... that doesn't sound very healthy, even if it was sometimes fun. I'd have to refuse.

It's been three days, has anyone missed me? Surprisingly, I had the sudden desire to go to the pool and swim into the world. Surely, there was someone needing help, but that would mean embracing mermaid life. But being helpful did not a mermaid make. So what if I practically lived in the water, dove into danger on a regular basis, and was in over my head – a thousand feet! The stories I had to tell!

I wasn't doing very well at convincing myself to give up this life and be a normal American girl. There were too many perks – bonfires, singing, great food, tropical sun and beaches. Friends that went into the unknown with you and didn't care that you wore fish for clothing.

So what if everyone thought me a mermaid? Even if the evidence was strong, I had no mermaid tail so I was no mermaid. The discussion I had with Uncle Arden helped convince me that it was more than that, but that was certainly a strong enough reason to say I wasn't. But so what, everyone said so based on other evidence, than a mermaid tail. Why were they so convinced? I could list their reasons, but I wasn't swayed. The problem was, nobody knew for sure what a mermaid was. Would a DNA test prove it? That wasn't a route I wanted to take. The last thing I wanted was to put it on record and go from doctor to doctor.

6.1   Nothing to Wear

I turned to put my feet on the floor. I was even more conflicted than when I'd gone to bed. Mermaid or not, I had to get on with my life. I'm going down to the gym to see if I can pick my life back up. First things first – swimsuit. I couldn't walk around like a mermaid, even if I was one. Perhaps someday, mermaids and their swimwear could go as they like. In the meantime, though, I had to dress appropriately.

But then I couldn't find my swimsuit. Normally, it would be on the hook beside my door, but nothing hung there. Where did I last put it? Walking about my small room, I checked the hamper, under the bed, everywhere! It wasn't to be found. Then I remembered throwing it across the pool room. What an idiotic thing to do. Sometimes, I wondered if I had any brain at all. It seemed my hormones did all the thinking of late. Whatever had happened to it since?

I had other suits, but they would be too small. I was growing up and filling out. Still, with nothing better coming to mind, I started going through them and eventually pulled out my old favorite red-and-blue, and then my gray-and-white. Holding up one after the other, I initially thought I was looking for color, but found myself instead feeling for likeness. Even if I could fit into it, I found myself wondering if I'd be comfortable in it as *her*.

The word *mermaid* wouldn't roll off my tongue just yet, but it was clear that I couldn't wear just anything anymore and be comfortable. At first, mindlessly I tossed each one in the trash like a used candy wrapper. Then I thought "What about all the kids who would gladly use my old rejects," and started pulling them out again. Finding a bag, I stashed them in it for later. I even found a swimsuit that I'd worn when I was five in the bottom of the drawer. Definitely time I got rid of that. I'd let mom have the last word on these, but I knew she'd approve.

Finally, I turned to the empty drawer, disappointed that I essentially had nothing to wear. I had dozens of suits, but none were acceptable anymore. There was something in the fabric that said don't wear that, I'll suffocate – even if I could have fit into them.

Mom's things were like the islanders' clothing. I wondered if she'd have a suit that would fit. I'd never borrowed a swimsuit of hers. I'd always thought of them as womanly and, well, I was filling out... I did hope to be her size someday. As I looked at the reflection in the mirror, suddenly those days didn't seem so far off now. The thought of it got me moving towards the door. Perhaps I'd find something to wear in her closet. It seemed just yesterday I'd been a little girl wanting to be like her and trying to fit into her oversized shoes. Yet, the image of them being so big had stuck with me. I was now her height, and we nearly had the same feet.

My life waited for me downstairs. I should be relieving Cleo at the shop and closing it up. I looked at the time before leaving the room. She'd forgive me for being late, but first I had to find something acceptable to wear.

6.2 Mom's Things

Even if it didn't bother me to glide blithely into the hall dressed in fish, how quickly things had changed. Still, I was cautious. They wouldn't skin my hide if I walked to the kitchen this way, right through them as they talked to clients or with friends. But the last time, well, mom had given me this exasperated look that said, "Honey have *some* decency." She meant, at least wear a towel or a night shirt when we have company. How was I to have known? Apparently, I'd missed the memo stating that clothes were to be worn around the house when there was company. All my life I've walked the house in a swimsuit. Suddenly, it was no longer acceptable. What was the big deal?

Anyway, I listened for a sound but heard nothing. Then I braved it out of the room, across the living room, which was empty. All was quiet, but I found myself tiptoeing and hurrying it along anyway. Rounding the corner into the short hall to the adult rooms, I paused to listen again. I wasn't worried that my family would see me but that they might have someone over. It would be so much better if I could go back to being the innocent kid that had streaked past family and friends without a care. What had I been then, two? Now it was infinitely more difficult carrying this burden of propriety, and it was at odds with the circumstances of the last few days. It only got worse the older I got.

I leaned against the wall and glanced over at the opposite wall where pictures of everyone hung, as on the wall behind me. There was one of me at every birthday, but not my thirteenth a few nights ago. It wouldn't be long until that hole was filled. I didn't understand parents and their desire to catalog the years, but they saved every picture as if it would bring back the past. Even Uncle Arden preserved our hiking pictures.

There should be a picture of me ninja'ing through the house like this. I'd feel much better. Even add Lucas strolling by with his eyes in a book completely unaware of my presence. I smiled imagining mom off to a tennis game, cute white skirt and colorful top. There she'd be, coming out of her room, passing me and saying, "Give Mom a kiss, Honey. I'll be back for breakfast."

It took a moment for the fantasy to pass. I came to mom's door and poked my head in. She'd always said I could borrow her things, but I hadn't until now. Her clothes were hideously cute, in an old World War One style that had gone out of fashion years ago.

There had only been that one girl with sassy curls, pink bubble gum skirt and top – me – as I'd snuck into her room looking for five-inch spiked shoes to wobble around in. Her closet had been bare of shoes. I had found a pair under her bed and wore them around all day pretending to be fashionable.

Mom didn't like shoes, I could hear her complaining "They make my feet swell!" I had to agree with the sentiment ever since Uncle and I had gone for that hike. Barefoot has felt infinitely better, and I'd been so mostly since.

Sneaking into the room mom and Lucas shared, I paused to listen again. They could be coming or going at any time, but I heard nothing and went straight for their closets. My hands strayed from my initial intent of borrowing a swimsuit and instead found myself looking over her skirts and tops. Something comfortable to work in, completely forgetting I would be around the pool after leaving the shop. Mom had tons of natural comfortable tops and bottoms. Soon, I was pulling out a pleasant short white top with lacy flower frills on all the edges, the neck, shoulders and waist.

She liked to show her midriff, mom did. "Nobody showed skin when I was growing up," she'd say. If that was true, then where did she get such old-fashioned get-ups like this? They looked positively ancient. Then I pulled out a matching skirt to go around my hips. They felt right, snug in the right places, and loose and frilly in every other way. Perhaps I did fit into Mom's things after all. Glancing in the mirror, I twisted back and forth thinking I could walk the streets like a gangster's gal from the old films.

There was a whistle of appreciation from the doorway, and I twirled about in surprise. Lucas was there saying, "You haven't ..." but then he stopped in mid-sentence as he saw it was me. I blushed deeply. He'd thought I was mom and, wow, I blushed some more. *He'd whistled!* Ugh! What had he been about to say? *I didn't want to know!*

"Excuse me," he said with a reckless smile before the moment became unbearable. He cleared his throat, trying to put on the studious demeanor he always wore, "Your mom hasn't worn that in some time. I'm sure she'd gladly part with it." Some of the recklessness poured out. That was surely Mom's influence, "You must promise to wear it often as you are ... adorable." *Adorable!* I would punch him for that, but since I was still beet-red from head to toe I wanted to turn away, probably "pretty" was too much to ask for. I already knew what he thought and *I didn't want to think that again!*

What to do? Unable to resist, I twirled to face the mirror again admiring how cute I was and admiring the swirl of the skirt before turning and dashing for the door. "I have to work!" I said with too much emphasis as I scooted past him. *Adorable, cute, pretty*, such words as I'd never say, so why did I react so much? I craved his attention, and my scoot had required me to brush past. In the mood I was in, I should've paused to kiss him on the cheek, but my feet had a mind of their own.

"You haven't eaten!" he called after me, but I had. On the island.

"I'll get something later," I replied over my shoulder as I headed out barefoot but modestly. When I was out of sight, I couldn't help but stop and take stock. Mom's outfits were cute, I had to admit, especially now that I was wearing one. Yet, Lucas thought them (blush time) *amazing*. Men. There was no getting what they wanted. I tried imagining myself being fashionable in these. Instead, I felt like an-old fashioned geek. Retro maybe. Putting myself back into motion, I whisked through the gym towards the lobby.

6.3   Back to Work

Cleo was manning the gift shop as I rounded the front desk, and I waved at the evening staff as I went by. She was busy helping a couple look for something cool to sip on before braving the evening heat. I stepped past them and began straightening up, folding shirts, dusting and finding something to sip on myself once they had left.

"That your mom's?" Cleo asked. I nodded and she said, "It's cute, and it fits you. Did you go back? We haven't seen you for days, so what happened? Wait, never mind, I have to get going. Can you take over? Your dad said you might show, but I'm *so* glad you did! David is on duty and I want to swim. Call me later ok?" and with that she was gone in a whirlwind, sweeping out past me. It was a good thing I was thirteen like her or I wouldn't have caught any of that. She didn't even wait for an answer, her mind elsewhere – if she was even using her brain. I knew how she felt.

David was a fifteen-year-old, sandy red-haired, freckled, long-way-from-home x-surfer lifeguard. He liked to brag about all the waves he would catch. I'm glad Cleo saw something in him. She always said, "He's so nice, and his smiles are dreamy." But he's an idiot as boys go. As a lifeguard, I suppose he was okay. He was always glad to take all the shifts I was willing to give up.

It was either sit in a chair and watch the pool or be in the pool. I chose to be in the pool every time. I got to spend time with the little kids, teaching them swimming or just playing with them. I could spend hours with the kids, and the parents loved it.

The evening shift in the gift shop was quiet after about eight. Until then, there were people leaving the gym, picking up a snack, an energy or protein drink, or the rare shirt or hat. Until then, it was fairly busy. Afterwards, I set about inventorying all that had been sold and figuring out if anything needed to be ordered. Then I stocked shelves, rotated the perishables with the extras we had on hand so they'd be cold by morning, and then left. The front desk could handle all the gift shop items after that until closing.

I went to the pool area and began picking stuff up and straightening all the chairs. Cleo was in the water and I longed to join her, but I'd neglected my duties for long enough and then some. There were kick boards and towels everywhere. It reminded me of the mess I'd made and picked up with dad.

Hearing no conversation, I wondered how Cleo was getting on with her dream boy. Then suddenly, as I was bending down to get a board, a pair of boy's feet appeared before me. "I can get that," David said, and our heads banged together knocking me onto my butt.

"Ow!" I exclaimed putting a hand to my head.

"I'm so sorry," he apologized quickly extending a hand but awkwardly stepping on my foot.

"Get away from me!" I cried pushing away his hands. He was like a big overbearing animal on the loose! My emotions already brittle came to the fore, and I wanted to blast him. If only I could! I got up on my own, turned away and tried to go back to picking up the towels instead, but he tried to help again.

I looked to Cleo for help, but she was sitting on the edge of the pool opposite us across the room, clearly upset. *What?* I mouthed to her, and her glance at David spoke volumes as I turned and interpreted it.

He was fawning to help me? How had I missed it? I took a second glance at him and then turned quickly away. Perhaps he was cute, in a way. His curly hair. Then I looked to Cleo and back to David. If he wanted to help so much, I told him, "Go ahead without me."

I went to a chair and deposited the shirt and skirt away from any absent-minded tidal waves I might throw his way, in case I decided he needed drowning after all. Then I turned to walk into the pool, diving in where it was deep enough. The pool opened up to me, a shallow pond compared to the great sea I felt near, but I wanted to be with my friend and turned to swim for her instead. She slipped into the water and we sank underneath to have a quiet conversation.

"Why do they always go for you?" Cleo complained after we hovered underwater for a few seconds. She was pining away for him. I could see it in her face as her emotions bubbled forth.

I shook my head, saying "I don't know what you are talking about." I then glanced up through the water the way I'd come. The water still rippled from our entrance, and we were the only ones in the pool. But we could see David at work, and I gestured towards him, "Go help him."

"Me? It's you he wants," she complained again.

"Maybe, but it's you that likes him," I echoed back cheerfully. Then added sourly remembering the abusing I'd just received, "Besides, he's a dork." My head still hurt. "I want to drown him."

"No, he's not. And don't say that. Also, don't stay down here long or he'll begin to wonder. And thanks."

I stayed there another little bit, watching my friend flash across the water. I was a hairsbreadth away from slipping into the full sea, but I shouldn't, couldn't. I had to stay and be normal Jill. I smiled, at least as normal as normal could be.

Kicking, I made for the lanes. Cleo and David had mysteriously disappeared when I looked up after a couple of laps. I bid Cleo a farewell in my heart, and then let the fishes have their way. I'd swim for a while. If anybody saw me, they'd see a swirl of color about me, thinking it nothing more than a flashy swimsuit.

The fish swam about me as I surrendered a bit more to the pull of my underwater person, the sea and the pool merged. Most of the fish were from the "suit" but the rest joined me from elsewhere and I was glad for their company. They swam all about in a swarm and brushed against me as I had Lucas. Perhaps it was okay to be me, happy and glad for my friend Cleo at the same time.

Smiling for my friend, I rose and flipped to my back and continued doing back strokes in the lanes, enjoying the sweep of water cascading past. There was the sound of thunder, and I paused to listen, to determine its source, afraid what it might mean. I was starting to recognize the signs that I was requested somewhere, hoping that this wasn't one of them. Since I had the pool to myself I loosened my hold to here, just not so far as to lose my connection with home and felt for the storm. I needn't have bothered, for I'd been feeling the pull to return to the water since my room. Once I relaxed, the storm in my mind shut out all else. Then it cleared for a second to show people struggling in it through the rain. I rolled my eyes, "of course" I complained. Another situation that required my attention but I was busy being Jill, the American girl. Wasn't there someone else that could save those people? As if in response, there was a flash of lightning, the storm reaching through the divide that separated us, and the building shook in response. Boulder was suffering a monsoon summoned from across space. Was this my fault?

I turned over, face-down like I might ignore the outside world, but the lightning strikes resonated through me with each blast. As I watched the time between laps, I noticed that my pace was better than ever. That turned my attention back to practicing being normal Jill and I tried shutting everything out. Even though I swam normally, the water twirled off my feet and legs. I tried matching my pace to what I knew my times to be. Even my *best* time was slower than molasses compared to this. Ugh, even coasting I was going too fast.

There was no way I could stay on the team if I didn't get this under control, and I wasn't about to give up swimming on the team. Until now, those girls were my lifeblood, accepting me, even the older ones. Especially the old captain, Colleen, who was now off to college. Practice! Practice harder at being slower. How ironic!

Somewhere in all of this, my mind slipped to the events that had preceded this moment. It was relaxing, letting go, but then I was speeding up, so I went back to a slower backstroke – the one I'd used to pull the yacht. Who was I kidding?

Frustrated, and it being late and all, I decided to call it a night and headed for the showers to try and release the pressure developing in me, hoping I could sleep when I got to bed. So I got out dripping from the pool and headed for the lockers. I was confused. Sometimes when I was water girl, I didn't always swim with turbo speed, so how and why couldn't I handle it now?

7 Save the Night

Standing in the shower, not doing anything excepting letting the water soothe my nerves, I had no answers, except to allow the source of my problems to continue to have its way. Again, the building shook as a result of the thunderstorm overhead, and I felt fire creeping along my neck and down my back. A not-so-subtle reminder that there were people in trouble out there that wanted help, whether they knew it or not.

Lifting my face to the spray, I tried to drown out the sound and closed my eyes to the flickering lights. It was too soon, I complained. Every nerve of mine was saturated. I wasn't sure I had it in me to experience someone else's problems right then. Didn't I get a day off?

The fire was spreading. I could feel it run down my arms like I had butane instead of water cascading from them. I ran in place, trying to keep my legs from catching. That lasted perhaps a minute before I stopped and the flames reached my toes. *No*, I begged, knowing I was failing, reflexively hitting the wall and flinched watching it crack. Absentmindedly I was rubbing off the flames with one foot and then the other. Unable to withstand it anymore, I was free-falling into the fire, but in my mind I was still closed up and my eyes shut.

Wham-Boom! The room shook as if a truck had slammed into the wall making me stumble away from the wall. I opened my eyes to steady myself and could barely see the room for the steam. The rain was reaching down through the gym roof. Great cracks went all through the roof and walls. Trees grew from them and the floor was no longer tile but dirt.

Fine! Okay! "Don't destroy the gym on my account! If someone dies as a result, it will be on your head!"

Why was I yelling? The fire was at last relaxing my muscles, the rain soothed my nerves. A true tropical downpour that drowned out all other sounds except the crackle-booms of lightning and thunder that rolled overhead.

Who was I to dictate when a transfer occurred? Nearly every time, I was whisked away to destination unknown. So far, the friend in charge of this thing hadn't put me in a situation that was over my head. Like the first time, the moonlight, the pool bubbling, so mystical I was swept away.

Perhaps my reluctance to go on another adventure was why I was having difficulty controlling my swim speed. The transfers were not a random hole in the world that I was falling through – they were on purpose, just not by me. I suppose if I were ever in trouble, the friend would send someone to help me.

Some of the time, the transfers were quick, but they were never without warning. Even if I was still learning the signs. I'd become a paint brush in the hand of the Artist, my willingness the paint. Admittedly I'd run from the islanders, but there was only so much I could handle. The fire on me was becoming unbearable. There was a need for me to do this, a need beyond me. I think that was my understanding. Still I kept thinking I wanted to be normal Jill, but truly I wanted both and if I kept saying no I might get my wish, and only be plain Jill and I definitely did not want that. Or I'd burn up, for I was melting under the heat and the connection was forming.

The gym was disappearing for real, cracking apart. The walls falling into a jungle with giant trees reaching up to block the sky, but doing little to stop the rain. Now I felt the wind on my face. I let the understanding of the place surround me, I was becoming attuned by doing so. Then the showers disappeared completely. The last shower head disappearing like a silver flower. I was left standing on a disc, like the transfer to Coot Lake, with nothing but a light mist between me and there. But I hadn't practiced yet!

Turning about, I saw a river jammed tight with downed trees. Around it were villagers trying to free the logs, and I saw why. The river was backing up behind it...

A familiar hand suddenly took my shoulder, a touch I was well in need of. Melanie! I wanted to kiss her in relief, but instead took her hand and held her close. "Let me come with you," she said stepping in beside me. The disc growing to hold us both. Taking it in, she asked, "Is someone trapped?" She was fresh and ready to take on the world. Silently, I thanked the Artist for sending me a friend.

I shook my head, "Look there," and pointed to where the river was leaping its banks and flowing towards the villagers' homes. "I think, if we're to get involved, we have to free those trees. Alone I don't think I can."

"I'm here," Melanie said. "Together we can help them. They just need help tying their ropes out in the dangerous current. Let's try." I looked at her in astonishment, and she realized I still held her hand. "What?" she asked searching my eyes. I couldn't let go.

7.1 Jammed Together

I wasn't nearly as confident surveying the logjam. We could be squashed like bugs by those huge beams, but Melanie squeezed my hand. "We can do this," she reassured me still trying to determine what was bothering me. "We'll be together. Come on." After thinking about it, I decided if she was willing, we could do it. I nodded that I was ready. Together, we stepped down off the disc into the lushest, greenest environments I've ever visited.

I'd thought I'd been feeling the jungle and its thick rain, but now that we'd used the magic to arrive, it exploded around us, taking us fully in. The humidity was thick, and it went right through me. As an aftershock, I felt the fire of the place wash over me, too. The ground was alive with it, as was the air coming from everywhere. It was forcing us to grow our sensitivities.

Immediately upon our arrival, I felt the villagers' eyes track to us. For we were two white girls and they were dark as the night, and we had appeared out of nowhere. I sensed in them fear at first, but then seeing we meant no harm, a desire to worship us. Neither would be helpful!

Standing there, we were surrounded by eyes, both unseen and seen. The awareness that came because of the magic let us see them. The whole world seemed to be watching. Around us were panthers and other creatures hiding in the trees, and in the river were crocodiles. Until now, they hadn't quite known what to do, as frightened as the villagers, but nature stood to benefit from our help as I'd been taught. Even beyond what we'd been sent here to do.

To move from where we stood was difficult. Besides the obvious larger creatures there were thousands of creepy crawlies – snakes, turtles, spiders, lizards and things I had no names for – all holed up, lying low and waiting. They were tense. I just hoped we could alleviate some of it and that there wouldn't be another disaster to figure out.

"Let's get started," I suggested. Melanie agreed with a nod, and we both walked through the watching eyes to the water's edge. Beside the river stood some of the villagers trying to hook the trees in the logjam to pull them up and out. I didn't think we had a word in common, but Melanie asked, "Can we help?"

I thought it foolish to try to talk to them but Melanie was not bashful. I figuring they spoke some other language and any attempt to do so would be met with blank looks. But then the man beside us replied frustrated and upset, "We cannot properly affix the ropes." Huh? He spoke English well enough. Though, he was a little hard to understand, like my first moments on the island of Syreni. But it seemed the difficulty lay more with his overflowing emotions, and not with the lack of a common language. At least we were speaking and it was all because of Melanie.

Continuing, he explained, "If we could just tie a rope to the trees out there, we could lift them up and out." He gestured to where there were pulleys attached up high, with ropes looped through them that could lift the logs. And at the other end of the ropes, "Our animals stand ready, but we're not quick enough to tie the logs off and more trees come and pin the one we're about ready to hoist out."

The man was speaking with Melanie because she spoke first. I was perfectly fine with Melanie leading. Emotionally tired, I willingly gave her my attention. I also liked it when she led and I could enjoy the trip. She'd likely be the next swim team captain when we were old enough anyway.

Giving me direction, she told me, "Jill, why don't you survey the jam and I'll help them up there." With an acknowledging nod, I dove into the rapids. Entering the river felt sweet despite its strength. I was seeing colored bands and lines flowed through the water indicating strength and direction, a result of the change we'd begun when coming here. I was seeing the way the water was moving, like a bird might read air currents. Using this new understanding, I flowed up the river to the jam very easily. It really was magic, and it energized my efforts. If I hadn't needed to stop at the dam, I would have tried jumping it as a salmon might.

Lying underwater where the water was still, I watched the raindrops hit the surface. It was so pretty, the overlapping circles that reminded me of falling leaves, making me look forward to fall. Melanie was up there basking in the hot rain and making a plan with the people. A few were watching my antics, but I paid them no mind as I continued to watch the rain and wait for Melanie to begin.

Seeing Melanie spider-crawl out over the maze, I surfaced and observed the torrential spider web of water jetting around, intermixed with crisscrossing branches going every which way. It took Melanie a moment to spot me. Popping out of the water like a cork, I made a gesture patting a log to direct Melanie as to which one to remove first. I couldn't help but make a "Pop" sound as I rose up to my toes. I felt like a pogo-stick as I did the trick. I was halving my salmon moment. Unable to fly, I went down and performed a backward somersault underneath in order to "pop" again. Sputtering through the layers of water jets, I followed it up with a half-twist dive to avoid them. This was fun.

Melanie grinned at me as she ran over the log, knowing just where to place the tie so that the hoisting teams could leverage it free. As it came free, a waterfall buried me so I dove down to escape it.

From underneath, it wasn't hard to see the problem – several beams, probably the legs of a bridge, were driven into the ground. I swam under the trees and around the poles, examining the complex weave, finding their pattern. It was like unraveling a tangle of yarn. Here next, I thought and followed it up and through, ready to point it out to Melanie. Again, I had to call out to get her attention. By then, they had freed her rope and she was riding the spinning rope back to the jam. Noticing my antics, she leaped free; performing her own summersault roll to my applause. She bowed and then turned to watch another tree that was plowing into the dam.

The whole dam shook as a result and I jumped up onto the log I had chosen as next to observe, pushing my hair back from my face. Melanie leaped to the new log and gave it a frown. In a second though her eyes lit up with a plan, and she dove under, disappearing from view to attach the rope. In a minute, she returned to give the crews a thumbs up. Now it was their turn. As they put tension on it, the log spun and took up the weight just right. How had she known where to place it?

Tossing her a rope, another crew was ready from the opposite bank to take the one on which I sat. Melanie quickly ran down past me, jumping from log to log to get to the tail end of it. Then, laying down on it, she reached around, tied the rope off and signaled the crew. Turning, she looked at me, yelling "Come on!" The one on which we rested started to rise upwards. "We don't have all day!"

"Right, boss!" I said and gave her a salute before diving off my perch to determine what next.

Somehow in the next few hours my anxiety disappeared as we had success after success. At one point, we exchanged a frayed rope for a new one, but we kept at it. All the issues of the morning dissolved in the heat of the moment. No amount of swimming laps could have done that.

After a while it became obvious that the logs on the river banks were growing higher than the dam. We were making progress. I watched as Melanie tied off another log and jumped free. It rose quickly and was guided over to the river bank. There it was cleaned of branches and stacked. Dozens of men and animals worked on each side to get all of this cleared, more than when we'd first arrived.

Apparently a whole neighboring village had come to offer help, but nobody could help the two of us, though some tried. They just got in the way and needed to be rescued themselves. A couple of them even fell in and were swept along by the rapids. If it wasn't for the seriousness of the situation, I would have gone and done the rescuing – but I couldn't take my mind from the task, and it was their fellows that ended up fishing them out.

Somewhere in all of this, I noticed debris that was manmade. Trash being swept along by the river. You'd think in this natural place there would be no pollution, but there it was. It made me sad to think there was nowhere that was untouched, except perhaps the island with the sunken ship. But even that had the sunken ship and somewhere the lost sailors. At least while we were here, we could influence it for the better. This was a good reason to embrace this new life and if one person could have a positive effect, what about a hundred? Or a thousand?

Perhaps the reason mermaids left was a human reason in its essence. Who would want to be responsible for cleaning trash? Especially if it was no fault of your own. Certainly, mermaids' responsibility wasn't to be street sweepers. A part of me wanted to find those responsible and drown them in their filth, but that wouldn't solve anything. These thoughts were making me angry, knowing there was no solution, except to attune and watch the debris dissolve and disappear.

I had time to think about that as we worked, but I got nowhere with it. The truth was I didn't get my purpose yet, even here and now helping these people. If I'd been just normal Jill, I'd like to think I'd have come to help had I known, but these people were thousands of miles away. It would have taken a week or so to arrive by plane and then to hike in. I would have been too late to lend helpful assistance. That is if I was aware of their need in the first place. By the time I would have arrived it would have been disaster relief, their village washed away and no more. It seemed all impossible how I had arrived – I had to settle on being me and go where I was sent, arriving magically in time to do something about it.

No, my job wasn't to simply clean up after others. But if I wanted to live in a world where it was better for all, I had to do some of that. Once again I was in an impossible situation, a croc-infested river, with huge panthers watching us from above and among complete strangers. Still, they didn't have to remain strangers. All of my friends were once strangers. We could remain afterwards and strike up friendships, but after the debacle on Syreni I was hesitant.

There was steady progress as we worked with the villagers. The frantic activity gave way when water began flowing freely again. With each log removed, there was a ragged cheer until the last was pried from the mud and rocks. The cheer was especially loud when the water lowered to a point that it was no longer threatening their homes.

While we worked, women for the village brought the workers and us hot food wraps and other delights. These were passed around to keep everyone's spirits up. When all was finished, there was a small celebration but everyone was too tired to make much of it.

7.2   Take Me Home

The villagers had been leaving for their homes in dribs and drabs through the night, until only the dedicated remained. Of the women, only one old woman stayed, and when she saw we were done, she roused herself from an old stump to invite us to stay. I demurred, remembering my stay with the islanders, how that could have been avoided had I left earlier. Melanie was mixed in her feelings, but I nudged her along and she surrendered.

"Why did we have to leave?" she asked as she had developed friendships with several of them.

Honestly, I wanted to get home. I'd left the shower running. How dumb is that? I could hear Lucas complaining about the wasted water. He has me well trained, what can I say?

Seeing that I didn't answer, she stepped up, giving a last glance back and taking my hand. We rubbed shoulders and she said, "It's beautiful here and we have each other," trying in her own way to lift my mood. "Besides," she said with a smile. "I'm glad we came, and I am tired, but I don't want to go back just yet." Then, bumping me with her shoulder, she caused me to skew sideways then pulled me back, saying "We did well. You can stay moody, but I'm not going anywhere."

Thanks to Melanie, I had left that deep mood behind, but with her antics and our hand-clasp, it was banished. I smiled back at her and echoed her happiness with a laugh. "You're right. We did do well and I'm glad we got to do it together."

This time I wanted Melanie to do the transfer. I was thinking of ways, feeling the rain, knowing there was a connection between it and the shower at home. For me, it resonated when I began thinking about it. Yet, each of my friends, if they chose to pursue this, should learn for themselves how.

We walked for a little ways along the jungle path beside the river. It was totally tranquil, including the sound of the rain in the trees, and the soft padding of several cats as they shadowed us from above. The jungle and river came to a small cliff, which in daylight must have been a spectacular view. The storm had passed and moonlight shone through a gap in the clouds in the distance, reflecting in silver highlights off the jungle canopy below, even through the continuing rain. The view was pretty amazing.

"This must be what the world looked like in the dawn of time," Melanie breathed out, awe in her voice. I had to agree.

I felt the padding feet of the panthers descending from the trees, the great cats coming alongside us. "Oh, hi!" Melanie said, kneeling beside a younger cub and running her hands over his broad wet shoulders.

The two largest came and rubbed their sides against my legs. Melanie moved through them, greeting each with hugs and affectionate rubs. She was so happy, tears came to my eyes to see it.

Then there came shouts and light. Three men ran out of the trail behind us, shining their lights about. The panthers roared and fled, disappearing quickly into the brush.

"We thought..." they said, seeing the panthers disappearing before they could train their weapons. The men were the more afraid, but bold enough to have hazarded the jungle at night.

I wanted to tell them to go away, but instead I took Melanie's hand and jerked her about, heading for the river. "Hey," she cried as we plunged into the river and then swam over to the far side staying underneath. The pull of the water was tremendous as it swept out into space over the waterfall. I held to Melanie as we strained against the pull of it together. Reaching the far side, we waited for them to go away. In the meantime, I explained my idea of her doing the transfer.

"What? Wait, what's the matter with you?" she asked, pulling us into a deep swirling eddy that had us revolving around one another. "You have us running scared. Were we not here just helping them?"

"Not scared, but every time I get 'involved' it's so much more difficult than I could have imagined. Besides I want to get home."

"Fine, and I get that we have lives of our own," Melanie said and then paused thinking about what I'd said. "Anyway, ok I'm ready. I get that we arrived here somehow, but I don't understand how you do it. Still, it can't be that hard – sorry. I mean, if you think I can. But I don't get what you want me to do." She gave me one of her serious happy looks, practically looking at me cross-eyed as we'd changed to lying flat, and we twirled and our hands held us together. Since I didn't answer, she clarified, "So, you want me to take us home?" When I nodded she bubbled with excitement, "How does this work?"

"Remember when we were on the island with our hands in the creek?" I asked.

After a second, she nodded. "Oh, I remember that. Is that what you mean?" Turning so we could link our feet, she gestured with her arms, "At the time, I felt fire everywhere on me, it was changing us. I've felt it tonight some more. If it wasn't for the panthers the whole time telling me where to place my knots, I don't know what we would have done. They understood and I didn't. They are such good people." With a sigh, she added, "I wish we could have done more for them, but what?"

My eyes were wide, I'm sure. She'd been hearing them and I hadn't. So not every "mermaid" was alike. I liked that. I'm not sure why I had thought we should have been. Especially since not everyone had felt the same at that stream that day. So as not to break the mood or change the subject, I let it slide. Maybe sometime we could talk about it, but for now I wanted to feel the shower at home more than the "mere" connection. It was so real,

195

I could taste it, but I wanted Melanie to experience it for herself.

"Maybe we will sometime." Could I let it go at that?

"You're right, I just wish... I don't like making friendships that feel like they should last a lifetime and then to be saying good-bye so quickly. I wonder if it is always like this..." She trailed off, then asked me, "You've had more experience at it, what do you think?"

I wanted to be thinking of home, and had a hard time following her, but as my mind caught up I had to agree. I nodded, saying, "Recently I was on an island. I haven't had time to tell you what has happened since." As the emotions started rolling back in, I pushed them away saying, "I don't want to talk about it yet, but what you are saying is true. I've seen it at the gym as well, and at swim meets. You meet someone, and then they're gone. Maybe you might 'Friend' them, but it isn't the same."

"I suppose. Yeah, I guess I've done that before. But these people, and I mean the panthers, are more real than most people I know. Let's hope we'll come back. Oh, sorry, you were teaching me about transfers. You were telling me about when we were at the creek on the island."

I tried explaining it as Uncle Arden had explained it to me. "We must be attuned first to our surroundings for 'magic' to occur."

"Magic?" Melanie asked interrupting me adding even more excitement in her expression and voice.

"I'm told there's another name for it," and I held up a hand to keep her from interrupting me again. I'm not sure I wanted to say who taught me. I expected it was a secret, as even Lucas hadn't wanted to discuss it openly. I was suddenly glad we were underwater where nobody could hear us. I wondered if I should even be sharing it, but they hadn't said not to. I was supposed to figure it out myself. We must be cautious.

"This reminds me," I continued. "Care should be shown as to who you share this with. Each time I've heard about these things, it was in strictest confidence." None of my friends were gossips, and out of them Melanie and I were the closest, had known each other the longest. I trusted them all, but I was sure of her confidence, at least until we figured this out. She nodded, saying she'd keep it to herself.

"The way I heard it described, is that we're better off like this," and I gestured to our appearance wearing our fish. Something that meant so little, but I now knew was important as I'd felt the difference between wearing a swimsuit, shirt or blouse and skirt, and not.

"It makes me uncomfortable to say it, but it's like a glove, clothing. Or shoes, anything that removes us from our environment. I'm given to know that, in time, we may get better at it, but in the meantime, and so far most every time I have one of these adventures, it is like this. The fish are a kind of magic themselves, so they are perfectly suited for this. I've come to accept them as being just the way it is. They are always with me."

"I wonder if it's because mermaids are fish from the waist down," Melanie postulated, "Do you think their connected? Unless of course it's a children's tale. I'm okay with never having a tail. Though you'd think that all those tales contain an element of truth. I suppose we'll find out."

"Still," she continued. "I'd rather be here like this, meeting people and those great servants of the jungle that the panthers are, than be home and dressed having cake and ice cream." It was hard to argue with that. When I'd delivered the boat, it had felt the same.

I was always changing my opinion on it. Melanie added thinking out loud, "It's just that I want to look pretty, and that's harder to do when our appearance never changes. I guess I've always wanted to put my best foot forward. Somewhere I'd come to equate that with being dressed prettily. But so far, in no way had being like this been uncomfortable." At least Melanie was comfortable with it. I couldn't be sure of anyone's reaction. I could see Melanie exceeding me, she took to this so quickly.

Continuing the explanation, "So that's for being a 'mermaid,' " and I put that in quotes with my fingers. "I really don't know what the right name is. But we have to be like this," and I meant the fishes. "Then to do magic, you reach out to your environment – attune, by making a connection. You may feel fire or spiritual power upon and within you. But, you will always feel it changing and preparing you. Next is Understanding, which is as it sounds, knowing the difference between here and there, understanding what you have to do. It's The Lord of Water that we apply for that knowledge, and it is he that approves all transfers. So it is like we had first thought, but knowing now helps immensely. Here's the best part, he wants us doing these things more than we want to. Or so I was told, so the approval is automatic. But there it is. Lastly, is Practice. That doesn't mean trying it over and over, but the actual doing of it."

"Remember when we arrived, it wasn't until we stepped off the disc that we practiced – effecting the transfer.

Until then we were still in the shower, but I'd like to know what you saw."

"That's easy," she said. "It was like when we were in the pool that first time. It had felt like we were in two places at the same time, yet definitely still in the pool. So it was, Cleo telling me you were swimming. But when I came to look for you, you were not there. Your clothes were, though, so I thought to check the showers. You retreat there to think, you know," she said with a smile and a wink. I just loved her and couldn't get enough of this.

"So when I came into the showers, it was like walking into a steam bath. You weren't visible. I thought at first it was just a lot of steam, but when I came to the only shower on, you weren't there. The fire was. The closer I got to you, fire blossomed all over me. Now I know it to be the attuning, on my skin. I knew then you were transferring, but I couldn't see you. I concentrated on you, wanting to be with you but couldn't. I even waved my hands all over where I believed you to be. You weren't there."

"I almost gave up, thinking you were too far gone. Then remembering how it had worked before when we were in the pool, we hadn't been thrust into the sea until we joined you by removing our suits. So I removed my things, tossing them onto a bench, ready for anything. Thankfully we were given these fish suits, it didn't feel weird even if we were in the women's room. The fire increased tenfold when I returned to the showers and now I understand why."

I moved again towards were I thought you were, reaching out hesitantly, not sure if the space would be empty again and afraid it would be. Then my hand touched your shoulder, and there you were. I stepped in beside you and the shower was gone and we were looking at this place."

We drifted in the eddy circling about each other contemplating – me what she had said and she putting together the pieces she'd been missing. I felt our friendship growing and I didn't want this feeling to end.

"So how do we begin?" Melanie eagerly asked, interrupting the moment.

Glancing around at the underwater view of the river, I thought about how to express what I was feeling. Seeing an area of calmer water by the bank, I thought it might be nice to get out of this swirling water, and so I swam out of the eddy we'd been floating in. Melanie followed after me. You could get dizzy going constantly in circles. Sinking to the bottom of this new spot, I sat back and looked up at the rain speckled surface. I felt the showers at home, the feeling was all through me, and I felt the river, jungle and the rain hitting the water. All of it, but mostly it was with the rain that I felt was closer to the running water in the showers in the gym. Deciding to use that, I waved my hands up at the circular splashes made by the rain, I told her "I'm finding the connection with the rain and shower. How about you?" I was ready to return home, even if it meant ending our time here together.

I think Melanie was going to go blue in the face trying to make the connection. Then she finally admitted, "No, not so much." And I remembered Uncle saying I had a natural affinity for this, "But maybe up there," and she indicated the surface with a thumbs up. "Do you think it's safe?"

I shrugged. It had been a while. "I think they're gone," I said glad she didn't give up easily. He hadn't said others couldn't learn, so I wouldn't give up either. The water was going by so fast between us and them, I didn't think they could see us. Even so, I didn't want them to surprise us again if we emerged here, so I said, "Let's swim up the river a ways, and find a quiet place. It'll be fun." It would also give us more time together, and that was for the better.

Melanie asked as we started up river, "Do you really think those guys might harm us? I'd thought they were friendly enough before."

"I'm not really sure, but I'm of the opinion that once the 'job' is done, it's time to move out." I could see how she was frustrated, but I felt I had no choice, "Besides what could we do if they did want to harm us? Nothing, as far as I know. Why are mermaids extinct? Every movie about mermaids shows men trying to capture them. I'd rather not be captured."

"So you believe you're a mermaid now?" she asked as we rolled through the rapids, talking as we flowed around the rocks, sunken logs and occasionally skimming the surface over some shallows. As we passed the place we'd unclogged, we entered into new territory.

I shook my head, and said, "No," when she hadn't seen the gesture. "I'm not sure what is what. Of course this kind of activity makes me think it could be something like it. At any rate, this is way better than swim team."

"As it should be," Melanie said leaping up out of the water to pass some boulders blocking our way. I followed her over them, and she resumed, "Swim team is really just competitive exercise, a preparation for all of this. I wouldn't trade any of this for that, but I like swimming on the team, don't you?"

"Definitely, but I've been missing practices since this began and I now swim faster naturally than I ever had before. I'd have to pretend to swim slower and take some middling place in a race."

"Hey, don't think of it that way. In target shooting, if you want to prove yourself and not let anyone know you're good, you aim at a spot that isn't the center. It is your personal goal to hit that spot, even if it means losing if you hit it. It should be the same way with us, we'll just have to figure out how. For I too am swimming faster than I ever have before. The surface is whizzing by. We're going faster than a boat would travel, and that is something."

"A boat couldn't travel this, at least not one with a motor." There were too many logs, sharp corners, abrupt changes in elevation and depth. "But you're right, we'll just have to find some way to make it competitive for us."

We swam for a while more. It was too fun to quit, but we were tired and the rain was lessening. "Let's do this here," I said gesturing up towards some shallows we were weaving through.

We chose some rocks in the middle of the river as our spot. It was already day, I'd hardly noticed. Melanie was slow in attuning, and it was hard for me to be patient because for me, all I had to do was think about it now and it was there.

"Concentrate on the rain, how it feels, inside you as well as outwardly. Then think of the shower as we'd left it, hot as the rain," the resonance I felt was there, but it was a while until Melanie said she had it. "Now, get the Understanding that the Lord of the Water wants us to go home."

"What if he doesn't?" she asked. "Would we know it?"

"When I was starting, I'm pretty sure it was he who opened the way for me each time. It felt the same, thinking back on all those times. I just didn't know what I was doing, or what was happening when it happened. It seems the same to me as now. Only we're doing the spell, and he's not doing it for us, but it is the same."

"Then why not let him do it?" she asked again tilting her head back and opening her mouth to the rain.

I struggled to come up with a reason for that. In frustration I said, "Why tie your shoes, if your mom can do it for you? I don't understand it, but if we can do it, then perhaps we should. Still, before I was in the showers. I was in the pool when I felt the sea growing close. I had ignored it. I could have gone through that one had I let it. Also, the place resonated continually and in the shower I finally accepted. That wasn't my idea. I believe there will be more times like that."

"Okay, I get it," she said looking poised. I felt the fire building, as she had in the shower for me, but it wasn't until she started fading that I realized I wasn't going to sense her transfer and I better grab on. I did as she had, reaching out, and placed my hand on her shoulder. We were facing one another, but it wasn't until I'd done so that I saw what she was seeing – the women's showers and the one I'd left on, but they weren't empty.

It was like before. We were there in all but person. The three ladies there were carrying on a conversation oblivious to us.

"Can they hear us?" Melanie whispered, leaning forward. I didn't think so and said so, but she kept whispering. "What now?"

"I'm not sure," I whispered back. "I suppose we could wait." That didn't work out, though, for others came in and we wouldn't be able to go through without someone seeing us. Suddenly Melanie collapsed forward, I barely caught her as the showers began to fade. But I was already attuned, so why was it fading?

8 Steamed

"Oh, I'm tired," Melanie breathed out, exhausted from holding the transfer open. "You've got to stand," I exhorted her, "and let go of the transfer. I've got this. You did well. I'd forgotten that sometimes these things are draining."

"Well, they're always taxing I suppose. Mostly they are over so quick you don't realize it." I'd had my hand held up, fingers splayed as I tried explaining it. "You sound like Lucy," she complained. I laughed at that, but she was too tired to give more than a weak smile.

The fires intensified when she let go and I picked up the strain of holding the both of us magically. In a moment, the showers came back. Melanie leaned on me. I put my arm around her, chose a moment, and led her from the disc. I'm not sure what they thought as we appeared out of nowhere, but I didn't stay and led us out and around to the steam room, grabbing a pair of towels for us along the way.

Thankfully the room was empty, as it was multi-use. But it smelled of disinfectant. "Do you want to cleanse it?" I asked Melanie setting her down. She shook her head. She just wanted to lie down. So I gave her my towel, rolling it up to use as a pillow. "No, you," she said unwrapping her towel and giving it to me as she then laid down on the towel I'd rolled up. Then it dawned on her I'd said something. "Cleanse?" she asked closing her eyes.

"Smell the air," I told her. I set the towel she'd just given me aside, then attuned myself to the steam room. The effect was immediate. "Ah, oh wow," Melanie said looking up at me. I'd taken the bench above her. I rolled up the remaining towel and lay on my side so we could still make eye contact as we talked. I kept the connection, letting the cleansing pass out into the gym at large.

"Do you have anything to keep guys out? I know we were fine when working, but now it seems different. Is it because..." Just then the door opened, and we lifted our heads but it was only Ms. O'Grady and a young woman who vaguely resembled her.

"Oh, it's blissful in here," said the younger woman, who was perhaps twenty years of age. "Wow, beautiful suits," she said coming in and striking up a conversation when she saw us.

"Is that you, Jill?" asked Ms. O'Grady.

"It is," I replied.

"It's so hard to see in here," she complained though I saw her ease onto a bench across from us welcoming the humidity. "I don't get how you girls can just stay in here forever. This is my niece, Helen."

"I'm Melanie. We're practicing becoming mermaids and it's quiet in here," Melanie said piping up and introducing herself. I thought about kicking her for that. Ms. O'Grady was one of my favorite of the older ladies – very kind, understanding and insightful, but now she probably thought we were a little old to be playing "mermaid."

Moving over to sit beside Melanie, Helen said enthusiastically, "I've always wanted to be a mermaid," and then pulling up her feet beside her asked, "How does one go about it?"

"Well, first, you have to be like this," and she gestured at herself. "And we are," and Melanie looked to me for confirmation, and I nodded agreement. Why was I the authority in it? I had no idea, because I still wasn't sure of the whole idea. Ugh, did that mean I was slightly sure? Well, there were too many coincidences, but why me?

I suppose also I was agreeing that she could share about it. What harm could there be? I wanted to curl up and put them on mute, but I was listening as closely as Helen to all of what Melanie was saying.

Looking down at myself, there was no proof in the flesh. Except for the fires which couldn't be seen, the fish which could, and the many places we'd been. It felt like a lifetime. No, there was no visible proof. I still had two arms, legs and a head. If I really was a mermaid, where was the fish tail?

Checking out Melanie to see if she'd changed in some physical way, I leaned over to have a look. The steam was thick, it was hot and we were sweating, but it felt so refreshing. I could barely see her through the mist, but seeing her reminded me that there were physical changes. Our hair was radiant, as if we'd been at a salon all day, and we'd just come from the jungle not to mention the other places I'd been. Strangely, I had no hair on my arms anymore, and thankfully not on my legs either.

I thought of other things, like our skin being soft instead of dry as Colorado air liked to make it. Admittedly, I hadn't needed to use lotion all week. Was it affecting us as women? We were in the midst of puberty. It was hard to say, not knowing what the end result would have been otherwise. We were no taller or shorter, though I felt fitter than before. I knew that was due to the changes.

All of it had started with attuning though I hadn't known what to call it on that first swim. As I attuned, it cleansed and invigorated me. Something in that was adjusting me, and those around me. In and of itself, it wasn't the effects of attuning that made someone into me, or everyone in the gym by now would be one. Since we arrived in here, I'd let the ability continue to have its effect on my surroundings. Also, I had no desire, as I rolled to my back, to let it go. I breathed easier and felt myself becoming alive under its influence, and I think maybe I was feeling the presence of The Lord of Water as we discussed the topic, but I wasn't sure.

"You remove your suit and get these," Melanie continued and held up her hand holding up fish the size of goldfish, "to replace it." I glanced back down to observe the trick. Spunky Melanie, always the first to think of new ways of doing things.

Helen moved back at the sudden use of "magic" seeing fish swimming in the air in and above Melanie's hands. Then Helen bent close examining them. "What? How?" she asked.

Melanie gestured at herself, the fish disappearing to blend in with her suit, "The suit I'm wearing is made of fish. Oh, and look, Jill, I have a new one, and she held it up for me to examine." It looked like the others, and if she was getting more, then why did it look like she had less? Her suit was skimpier than mine, and I'd thought it was a personal preference. Maybe it was, so I acted the part of being surprised and asking her all serious like, "Have you named it?"

She looked down at the fish in her hand and then back up at me with a weird look. "You're kidding me, right? I suppose I could, I hadn't thought about it." I wanted to laugh, but she looked seriously cute as she contemplated what to call the fish.

"Is that it? Just be, um… be covered in fish? Because I've been that many times and nothing." Helen was trying to reason it out. I could hear her intention, because it wasn't just the fish. In fact, it wasn't the fish at all, but several factors most of which I was yet to understand. Nor was it being without clothes, as she was implying. But the fish were our clothing. We weren't undressed.

Melanie touched my arm to get my attention, because I was now staring at the ceiling and she wanted my tacit approval for what she was revealing. When she had it, she continued, "Well, for me, it's been going on mermaid adventures. I'm not sure I'd have believed it otherwise. A few days ago, the lot of us – Cleo, Lucy, Jill and I – were in the Pacific swimming around, underwater, breathing water. It's so natural when you're doing it, it's hard to explain. There was an old sunken wooden ship we'd swum around. Then we spent time exploring it. Without once surfacing for air."

"Then, just now, we were in… I don't know, the Amazon, or some jungle place like it. A heavy rain had caused trees to fall into a river jamming it up, causing the overflowing water to threaten a village. We worked all night helping the villagers free the fallen trees. I'm exhausted, or was… Huh? I'm feeling better, how strange. I guess I should get used to that. Is that how it is for you too, Jill?"

Ms. O'Grady spoke up before I could answer. I'd forgotten she was there, "So you're a mermaid, Jill? That's hardly surprising. You're in water so much, I'm faintly surprised you don't eat submerged."

No, I wanted to say, but I was laughing at her comment. Instead I replied, "I'm not sure. What's a mermaid? How would I know? What would be obvious would be a mermaid's tail, but as you can see... legs," and I kicked mine out for emphasis. "And if I'm a mermaid, wouldn't that mean Mom's a mermaid? She most definitely isn't."

Shooting a hole in my logic, Helen said, and I could hear the hope in her voice, "How would you know, if you don't know about yourself?" Oh to not be pessimistic! All these questions and reasons about me being a mermaid made me want to run screaming from the room like a child.

Besides, I didn't want to dissuade Helen, but I couldn't enlighten her either. What a depressing thought. If mom is a mermaid, was she lying to me by not telling me? I remember Lucas saying I had to figure this out for myself, but didn't I inherit this from at least one of my parents?

In my early years, I'd wondered who my real dad was, but over time I came to see Lucas as my father. As much as I loved him, though, I didn't inherit his genes.

"It could be from my real dad, whoever he is," I countered. "He abandoned me to loving parents. Lucas is my real daddy in every sense but blood." So was Uncle Arden my uncle. He had been there all my life, but he wasn't a blood relative. I loved him with all my heart, maybe even more than I would a natural uncle. And I trusted him with my life.

8.1 When in Rome

"So can we show her?" Melanie asked me in that sweet tone that made me want to do anything for her. I could tell she wasn't done, even as tired as she was.

"You mean more than you already have?" I asked, knowing I was giving in. Showing her would mean another "adventure" and I'd already had my fill. But it would also mean spending more time with Melanie, and I was all for that. "I'm sure there is another situation needing our attention." I thought aloud, "Why not?"

Then, turning to Ms. O'Grady, Melanie asked, "Do you want to join us?"

Ms. O'Grady asked, "Do I have to remove my things, too?" obviously not liking the idea of having to do so.

Melanie turned to me for an answer. I shook my head no. "The first time you breathed water with me, you were in your suits, too," I told her. And when I rescued the diver from drowning, he'd been dressed. I was largely sure it could be done without her needing to. "Oh, right," Melanie said thoughtfully.

"Neither does Helen, unless you want to try," I left the possibility open to Helen.

In answer, she made to remove her suit. Seeing as how Melanie had less fish, I extend my hand to her and several left me for her. She gave them a look much like I had the first time, but then on seeing the result, she exclaimed, "Hey, this is amazing." The suit appeared as a second skin even before her shoulder was bared.

"I can see we'll have our own designs," Helen said, observing that hers was a deep blue with yellow starbursts. Mine was a melody of colors and Melanie's resembled a starlit night. At least at the moment. I never gave it much thought. I'd seen them perform some interesting effects, especially as outfits go. So why not color changes?

I'd never opened a mass portal before, but knew it could be done. We've been through several already. It shouldn't be hard to start the process, "But where to go?" I asked them.

"I'm for France, a sunny natural beach for you aspiring mermaids," said Ms. O'Grady with an affected French accent. "I've always wanted to visit, but I abhor air travel. And I get sea-sick."

Everyone else sat there. Melanie and I had had our fill, but a sandy beach sounded much nicer than a steam room. "Anyone else?"

Helen said, "I wouldn't mind somewhere closer to home, a deserted mountain lake, but wherever Aunt Betsy wants is fine with me, and I could use more sun."

Ms. O'Grady stood up declaring, "If we're going, I better grab my wallet. We'll get hungry, and breakfast in France sounds lovely. I'll be right back. Oh, and I'll want a camera."

Helen suggested to her, "Just use your phone, Aunt. Everyone else does."

"Right, thanks! You're so smart, Helen my dear," and she whisked out. I couldn't help but giggle at that. Ms. O'Grady was a riot. I swam with her all the time. Sometimes we talked about fashion, she trying to understand. She didn't get how us girls dressed nowadays. It wasn't long before she was back fully dressed. The three of us, on the other hand, wore fish suits. "We better go before I melt in here," she said before anyone changed their minds.

I looked down at Melanie, she caught my glance and read my question. I'd never done it before either, but giving her the opportunity sounded like a grand idea. "How?" she asked. "Never mind, I'll try."

Nothing seemed to be happening. It was the same as in the jungle, but this time she was including us on purpose. "Stand," Melanie suggested, so we gathered in a circle. I had to assume she got the location from Ms. O'Grady, for then we were looking at a mysterious cloud bank that quickly dissipated after she brought us through. "This is it," Ms. O'Grady exclaimed. At the same time people were marveling at the sudden appearance of our cloud, right there on the beach, on an otherwise sunny and cloudless day.

Looking at me, Melanie explained to my unasked question, "I kept thinking about the problem with the shower room. A load of steam would have masked us then."

Now nobody had seen us appear out of thin air, "Genius," I told her. Again she was out-thinking me, planning ahead. Why didn't I have these ideas?

"Oh, it's beautiful," Helen effused, sounding five years younger. "The sand and water sparkles, the hills about the town are green, and such a beautiful collection of shops. Everyone is speaking French, it's lovely." Hoisting her towel, she said, "Let's find a place." Walking daintily, she pranced down the beach, taking the lead to find a place to lay our towels. With a shrug, we followed, prancing ourselves because the sand was pretty hot and made me feel delightfully girly.

The beach was pretty crowded, but it wasn't long until we chose a site, placing our towels. It was too lovely though to sit just yet, so we chose instead to walk the beach first.

"You go ahead," Helen's aunt told us as she waved over someone renting chairs and an umbrella. We returned after a while to find Ms. O'Grady who had bought us sarong wraps, hats and drinks. Handing us the drinks and holding up the outfits, she said, "These are for later when we eat. Enjoy the sun first." Gone were our gym towels as they were replaced with colorful beach towels and bags to carry our things. She'd thought of everything, and obviously enjoyed being busy organizing things. I imagined, given the chance, she'd have us sitting to tea. She was cutely old-fashioned.

Melanie said as we laid down shoulder to shoulder, "We're going to have to take her on more adventures." I smiled in agreement, "But since these 'adventures' are almost never of our planning, she'll have to stick with us like glue."

"I'm willing, dears. But you must let me read," she said opening a book. "Blah, it's in French. I'm so rusty."

"Ms. O'Grady is right," I said, taking Melanie's hand. "We fit in. I had thought that island we were on together was perfect, but it's people that I crave too, and shops." I grinned. "If we can come and be 'mermaids' anytime, I could learn to love this place."

Melanie scoffed at that. "You a shopper? That's a first."

"Of course I'm right dear," Ms. O'Grady said without lifting her eyes from the pages she was struggling to read. Then after a while, when I was just starting to drift off, she looking down at us, asked, "What does 'vine' mean? My French is rustier than I thought. Anyone?"

I raised my eyebrows at the question. Had I heard her right? It had to be a trick. "You mean the plants that grow grapes?" Melanie asked.

"Yes, vines. Thanks," and she went back to her reading. I was confused. It didn't take long to compound it. "Melanie, I don't suppose you know what a 'grape' is?"

We both looked at each other. Was she having us on? Melanie had just used 'grape' in a sentence.

"A grape?" Melanie asked.

"Ah yes!" Ms. O'Grady exclaimed. "A grape, I'd forgotten. Thanks. You're so smart dear." We stuck our lips out and rolled our eyes thoroughly confused. The odd questions continued, and Melanie far too graciously continued to answer the inane questions.

I, on the other hand, turned my attention to the sound of the sea, wind and the birds running along the beach. It wasn't long before I felt the tune of it thrum, and let the melody carry me to sleep. The ocean played such a lovely lullaby. You must learn to get your winks quickly in this business, I was realizing. I drifted off hearing Melanie answer another odd question and I was soon out cold and only a "roll over" nudge to keep me from burning on one side woke me briefly.

"What was that song you were humming?" Melanie asked me when I woke. "It had me wanting to sail."

"Huh?" Then I remembered what I'd been thinking. My thoughts had drifted to the beach party on Syreni, how we'd sung to nature's melody. It wasn't attuning, but it felt similar listening for it again. "You mean…" and I let the music flow through me.

"Oh, that's rich," said Helen swaying to it, "Does it have words?"

Melanie gripped my hand and looked pointedly around, and I noticed that Helen wasn't the only one enthralled by the music. I hadn't been humming very loudly, though, or so I thought. "What is that?" she mouthed.

"The ocean," I said. Wasn't it obvious?

"There's clouds rolling in," Ms. O'Grady said interrupting us. "Let's go get lunch."

"It's beautiful," said Melanie about the music, as we moved aside to pull up our towels and put on the wraps.

The sarongs were lovely and comfortable, the hats gave us shade. I felt like a complete tourist in the outfit, but Ms. O'Grady had sense – one thing we girls apparently lacked according to her. I would have dressed local, but then again we were tourists after all.

Helen and Melanie were becoming friends and I heard her ask Melanie, "Why is nobody swimming? What do these signs say?"

"No swimming, sharks," I read out loud, it was in perfect English. It didn't occur to me that I'd translated it. The sign and those like it were stuck in the sand up and down the beach, all in front of the high waterline.

"Oh dear, you read French fluently?" asked Ms. O'Grady. I had no answer to that, it wasn't French to me.

"No swimming?" asked Helen sadly. "Wait, but we'd passed some," and she pointed to where a few were daring the shallows.

A well-weathered man walking the beach turned to see where Helen had pointed, then said with a lilting French-accent in English, "A few brave the waters, and then more will join them. Eventually though, the sharks come and scare them off. It is humorous, except for the occasional attacks."

"How long has it been happening?" asked Melanie, "And your accent is lovely."

He gave Melanie a rakish smile. He had no problems complementing a kid, "Oh my dear, you are exquisite, as are your companions." To which we of course blushed. The French were over the top, but oh lord I loved the compliment. "I've grown up and fished these waters all my days. These sharks and their attacks – we locals understand they do happen, but until recently they were rare. Something has caused them to plague our waters."

"You make it sound like you know what is causing this," said Ms. O'Grady, stumbling through her French phrasing. He was speaking English, why was she complicating things?

"Well," and he changed subjects, realizing he was talking to tourists, "It's nothing. What you need, Madame, is to visit my son's restaurant over there. Fine cuisine, soft shade and wine to slake any thirst. You girls will be quite comfortable. Just request Pierre, he'll be sure you are well treated."

"Sounds delightful," said Ms. O'Grady taking charge, "Come along ladies," and walked off towards where he had directed us, fully expecting us to follow. I wanted to stay and pump this guy for more information. Helen followed after her aunt, and left Melanie and I standing there.

8.2   French Stir Fry

"So, shall we?" Melanie asked, taking my hand and pulling me after Ms. O'Grady and Helen. We strolled along the beach, crossing through the sunbathers towards where several villas overlooked the sea and from where we could hear sweet music. As I caught up to her, she gave me a look. Then she said with a head gesture back the way we'd come, indicating the French guy, before turning back and giving me a tired look, "We can't solve everyone's problems. And it truly is nice here."

It was nice here, and these outfits were pretty. They went with our suits splendidly, "True. We can't, but I'd like to swim and wouldn't be afraid of any shark. The waters look inviting. Who knows when we'll be back?"

"Well, I'm about to fall over from sleep deprivation," Melanie complained leaning into me, "I should have slept like you did, but how can I," agreeing that this was a once-in-a-lifetime place to visit. "But now I need food."

We were behind the others, but she steered us from where others were sitting before asking, "How is it we speak perfect French? You know that is what was happening before. Ms. O'Grady was asking words in French, but we heard her automatically translating it, so we thought she was asking us 'grape' in English. When really she'd said it in French."

"I can only theorize," I shrugged in faint surprise. "So that's what was going on, I was so confused."

"Do you think it has something to do with us being, well you know…" She didn't say "mermaids," as I didn't like to hear it. Though even I found myself using the term, for want of something better. She believed we were. It was obvious in everything she did, especially in how she was handling Ms. O'Grady and Helen. Still, we didn't know what it meant to be a mermaid. When did someone cross from being human to mermaid? How many adventures and people rescued? Or how much time spent underwater without surfacing? Was it even that simple?

I nodded in agreement "That makes sense. Last night, I thought it strange that the villagers spoke perfect English, but it's us that speak their language isn't it?"

Melanie nodded in agreement, "So it seems. If I listen closely, I can hear the real language, but it sounds far away. I don't know how we do it, or if we speak their language even now. We should probably be careful with what we say anyways, just in case."

Ms. O'Grady and Helen were reading the menu posted beside the porch steps around the side of the restaurant when we arrived. "This isn't what I expected," Helen said greeting us. "A French coastal paradise with all the amenities. I could get used to being a mermaid." A waiter came out to greet us on the heels of that statement.

I frowned, but couldn't say anything on account of the waiter. Being a "mermaid" was not dining at fine establishments and shopping. It was solving problems that normally included overwhelming amounts of water. Turning to look at the sea, I thought "that is where we will be going eventually."

I realized I was answering my own questions and I was continually doing these things. I felt it becoming a part of my life, and every waking moment. I was no longer trying to re-experience "the dream." If anything, just when I had been trying to be normal, "mermaid" life exploded in my face! I could no longer separate the two lives. I felt like I was surrendering inwardly at the thought, but I was this new person now. There was no going back.

There was too much about being a "mermaid" to like. Melanie and I were becoming better friends. I was having adult experiences with adults like Ms. O'Grady, but it went back to the Syreni's too. They'd not treated me like a kid, but with respect. Not counting their other faults, they had welcomed me. Then there were these French...

"Welcome 'fine' ladies," said the waiter trying to schmooze with Helen, laying it on thick and following it up with a dazzling smile that was meant to win her heart, but made Melanie and I want to gag. "Please come in," he insisted with his arms open wide. He guided us into the cool interior. There were quite a few people there, relaxing and enjoying themselves. "A view of the beach?" he asked and waved at the porch, then gestured to the roof, "Or a view of the hills. Most everyone is up top of course, and there is music and dancing."

He was wasting his spell on Helen, as she didn't understand a word, and before Ms. O'Grady could request the roof deck, I suggested, "The front porch sounds grande, oh and there was a man on the beach that said we should ask for Pierre."

"Of course, Mademoiselle," and he led the way to the elevated porch overlooking the sea. Stairs cut back over the roof. Melanie, Helen and Ms. O'Grady went to look. He added, "I guess your party prefers the roof view, it is spectacular as I'm sure you'll agree." Then he gestured for me to go up, and he followed after.

I stopped at the top like everyone else. The panoramic view was breathtaking. Forested hills and a continuous fresh breeze from the sea made it cooler than I expected. Even though the front porch was pleasant and quiet in comparison, the top floor was where it was at.

We passed the server's drink stations on our way to the table, and then we had to dance our way through the jumping, bouncing and swinging crowd. It was like a crazy French version of spring break. When I asked the waiter who was seating us, he said, "Oh, it is like this every day. Good music. Great sun. Fun people."

People were singing, dancing, playing cards, wining and dining. A lovely place to be merry. The old man had been right – we fit in perfectly. If I were a betting woman, I could also bet at cards, for people were playing for stakes here and there.

"I could spot you," Ms. O'Grady said noticing where I was looking when we finally reached our table.

I shook my head. "No, thank you. I don't play," I replied and took Melanie's hand, saying to my friend, "Let's dance."

Melanie and I drifted to the music, drawn to the dancing and singing, joining the people who were looking on. Helen and Ms. O'Grady were led to a table, and then Helen came and joined us. To get close to the singing we had to move through the dancers and I found my dance feet. The three of us with arms raised and hips swinging circled about and swung through the crowd losing sight of one another.

The rooftop was a long rambling affair over several other shops. It was probably easy to navigate when nobody was here, but filled with swirling and moving people, it was easy to get lost. Doubly tough to find someone when you're as short as I am. So when I thought to look for my friends, it was impossible, but I did sense them when I attuned, reaching out for them.

I shouldn't have done that, though. It was a double portion of good vibes, the sound of the sea again, and the thrum of the people. Everyone's feet dipping, shuffling and planking to the music. I came apart at the seams and was scattered into the music. All my senses alive as I too dipped, shuffled and planked along with those around me. I got caught up in a train or eel of people moving along in a long line that brought in more and more, then broke out in spontaneous cheer.

I bumped into this couple, the guy making a fool of his girl. With the euphoria I was in, I'd already likened the music and dance to an electric eel, it didn't take much to extend that feeling, let it become understanding, and brush a finger over the guy's arm. I only wanted to give him a carpet static type of shock, but he dropped like a stone. I stopped astonished in my tracks, mouthing an apologetic "I'm sorry," to the girl he had been dancing with. She didn't even dine to notice that he'd fallen, turning her nose on the fellow for his rudeness. She spun away and disappeared into the crowd.

Shocked to stillness by her actions and what I'd done, I kept forgetting the impact I had. It had started in the pool, creating waves that wrecked the room. Subtle gestures were difficult, and I tended to overreach as I'd discovered on the hike with Uncle Arden. It took me a moment to get unstuck, with people moving about me. Eventually I became aware that I was in their way, and realizing I was parched, I moved out of the crowd to the edge to get a drink. It was edging on towards afternoon, and we'd come up here for lunch. I wasn't very hungry, and the music and the feeling of the place kept my feet moving as I sipped some water. Tapping my hands on the railing I wondered where everyone else had gone. Then I heard one voice raised above the others, so beautiful, causing the writhing crowd to move as one.

At first I suspected it was Melanie, knowing how she'd been moved by my singing on the beach. I watched the crowd moving like a many armed octopus for any sign of her. The women among the dancers spun, their arms raised, swinging out and bringing everyone into the dance, it was mesmerizing. Even the stoic among those that had been sitting back were caught up in the dance, shouting along with everyone. But then I saw those at the center of it all lift up the singer, to carry the unassuming woman. She was plain by appearance and not my beautiful friend.

The singer's voice was anything but plain. Everyone was enthralled by her performance. I found myself humming along with her song, but not liking it so much that I'd want to carry her around. In fact, the more she sang that tune, the less I wanted to dance. Soon I was just standing there watching, with everyone moving around me like I was a post. I watched their animated faces, as they hopped bounding by. Try as I might, I couldn't put my finger on why I was uninterested.

Then the crowd moved down the steps and towards the beach, catching up everyone along the way in the dance. Melanie and I along with the fellow I'd stunned were left of the crowd. He was still out cold.

"What was that, and who was she?" Melanie asked coming alongside, "And look at that, belongings everywhere." Then she covered her face unable to believe what she'd seen, pointing. At our table was Ms. O'Grady's things, even her purse. As I looked around it was the same everywhere. The game of cards, forgotten. The cards strewn across the deck, and the pile of money in the middle abandoned. It looked like graduation, caps and loose clothing had been thrown about, discarded.

There was a sound of sandals, and we turned. A young girl came up the stairs, stared at us a second before moving through, and began robbing the people of their things. We beat her to our table and gave her a stern look, and she moved past without saying a word. "Hey, wait!" I told her, wanting to ask about the woman.

I had about a second, felt the girl attune, though it was crude. Then before I could react she cried almost a screech, and a bright light reached out. Blink. What had I been doing?

"We better get out of here," Melanie advised in a whispered aside gaining my attention. I brushed off the lapse, "Or when they get back, we may be accused."

"Who?" I asked.

It must have been my tone of voice. Melanie looked at me strangely and with concern asked, "Are you okay?"

I stood there wondering, "I feel like I'm missing something." I finally answered. "What was I just doing?" I was confused, knowing we'd come here with someone, but I couldn't put a name or face to them. "My head hurts," I said to myself.

"You're kidding right?" Melanie asked, taking me by the shoulder and guiding me to a seat. Taking a chair opposite me, she thought out loud "too much sun maybe," pushing a cup of ice water towards my hand. I sipped but spat it out.

"Yuck, tastes like swamp water," I complained. "Really, what were we doing?" I was getting upset, "The last thing I remember is zapping some guy. I'd tried to shock him like a carpet shock, imagining myself an electric eel but instead he fell as if I'd shot him."

"Is that him?" Melanie asked pointing to where a guy was laid out, not moving at all.

I looked at him. I'd never seen him before, but he had to be the guy. So I asked. "Is he dead?" afraid of her answer. Melanie closed her eyes, and I felt her attuning. The wave of it hit me and I felt better. "No, he's alive, but not fine. He'll be out for some time. What did you do to him?"

I shook my head, trying to clear up the cobwebs, and noticed a girl going around the patio checking, or going through some things left lying about that people had abandoned. I didn't pay her any mind.

"Look," Melanie said standing up and looking towards the beach. "I need to get you home, you don't look too well. Besides, we should get moving before they return," and this time she gestured towards the beach. I still didn't understand her reference, "they" who? Did she mean those that they had been dancing with?

Melanie picked up some woman's things, and then I recognized Ms. O'Grady's bag. Was she the "they" Melanie referred too? No, Melanie clearly meant more than one person. At least I hoped it was Ms. O'Grady, she'd know what to do. Why were her things just lying here? "Let's go," and she took me by the hand and led me down off the top patio deck.

"See there?" she pointed at the beach when we reached the porch. The whole of the beach was a swirling mass of people. "Oh my," I said with my mouth open. It looked similar to my time on Syreni, but these people were swirling around as a whole, like a giant maelstrom. Then as we watched, the crowd broke up and started moving normally. We hadn't quite left the restaurant by the time the people returned, animated and speaking excitedly. All in praise of some women's talent. The returning crowed swept us along, and we managed to step aside on the front porch, watching the rest move on to the upper deck.

I felt in a cloud. Melanie looked at me with concern on her face. I tried giving her a reassuring smile, but found myself looking inward trying to place why we were here. Absently I was aware that she was scanning the crowd as if she expected to know some of them. I felt like a lump as I pondered my feelings. I must have fallen asleep again. That made sense. Or else I would remember everyone going down to the beach and why I had stayed. Melanie stepped out and snagged Ms. O'Grady and, and... Helen from the crowd when she saw them. Melanie tried explaining what had happened to me. I was surprised to see them, but before I could ask a question, Ms. O'Grady said, "Nonsense, she just needs food. We've been here all day without eating. Let's sit and get some. Besides, I'm buying."

Melanie protested, but she was overruled, so we sat and ordered our food. The view of the sea was remarkable.

"I so wanted to sing before her," Melanie said in a huff, trying to lighten the mood.

"Oh. Don't feel bad dear. Next to a voice like that, there is no comparison. Anyway, you should sing if you want to. I wonder if she has an album, what was her name?" I didn't know and shrugged. There were similar shrugs around the table. "Oh well, I'm sure someone around here knows. I'll ask the waiter when he returns. Let's have a rousing tune. Helen, you start it."

"Hmm, okay," Helen brought her attention around from the view of the beach. "What shall we sing? Oh, how about..." and she started off on some tune I had never heard. I hummed along not knowing the words, but Melanie leaped in cheerfully, and I was glad to hear her sing. Perhaps she was attuning, for I felt a ripple pass over me, but perhaps not, for I felt it only distantly. The song was good, and I tapped to keep them on beat. Then the conversation went back to the events preceding the beach gathering, from that I gathered what had happened, but Helen and Ms. O'Grady had their own take on it. I really must have conked out. All this popping about.

I wasn't exactly glad to know there were others like us in the world, yet somewhat reassured that I wasn't alone in it either. I thought back to my time on the Isle of Syreni. The people there believed in the old gods, ancient pacts between mermaids and men. The old gods had according to legend created many creatures, including the Sea and Air Lords that the people of Syreni had sworn to serve. How had these beings adapted to living in the modern world? Some, like mermaids, were probably extinct or so radically changed as to appear "normal," and maybe were so adapted to have forgotten their pasts.

Whatever we encountered today was beyond my ken. Were they an ancient race lost in modern times and struggling to survive, or were they interwoven into society and influencing it? Those were tough questions. The "dead" girl on Syreni had admitted that they too had lost their way in current times. I wanted to believe the former, that they were merely drifting along trying to make the best of things.

Because of these events, at times like this, I realized that here was my place, even more than the gym. I knew I would always call the gym "home," but I felt that our trip to the jungle, and now here with this exotic experience, was where I belonged. How could I go back to the swim team and the gym?

Then my thoughts were interrupted when the food came. It tasted so wonderful and the company was so great I soon joined in singing along with everyone.

Then Pierre appeared, apologizing for not having greeted us earlier. He said, "Pape, says to offer you a sunset cruise of the bay," which Helen and Ms. O'Grady wanted to do, and I was all for it until Melanie threw a fit. Which reminded me that something was indeed up. How quickly I forgot.

Then, "Let's go for a swim," Ms. O'Grady suggested as an alternative. "Madame, there's no swimming on account of sharks. How about that cruise instead, complimentary, of course?" Pierre insisted. Ms. O'Grady ignored the last bit saying rather, "Hmm, well we can get our feet wet before we head back. That okay Monsieur? Or do sharks walk the beach, too?"

"No, Madame. Of course not," he said sweetly, rubbing his knuckles nervously. "Then, how about some dessert? Our ices are positively divine."

"I'll take some," raising my hand. Helen added in her bid too, but Melanie stood up and walked out. Shocked at her antics, I stood up to follow, "I guess we'll be going, kind sir, and I wish you'd call me mademoiselle..." said Ms. O'Grady flirtatiously paying up.

I caught up to Melanie who was walking down to the beach rather rapidly. Taking her hand, I asked, "What's up, Mel?"

She spun on me, putting a finger to my face, "You! You're acting like you don't have two dimes to rub together. Besides," she said easing up, as I stood there with my mouth open, "there was something fishy about him. Did you see how he was pressuring us to take that cruise? I suspect he meant to drug us with the ice cream." Helen and Ms. O'Grady joined us.

"He was very determined, wasn't he?" Ms. O'Grady asked thoughtfully. "I hadn't thought about it from that vantage."

"I would have liked the icy," admitted Helen. "But, even if you were wrong, at least somebody is thinking. You can't be too careful sometimes."

We'd continued to walk towards the sea, but then they stopped when we stood ankle deep, feeling the sand whisk around our feet when the water receded from a wave. The water felt so good and my feet had a mind of their own. I kept walking. The water called to me, an urge to dive in and let go rose up and consumed me.

I barely heard Melanie call after me, "Jill, wait!" I dismissed her in my need to go deeper.

8.3 Radio Waves
– MELANIE

"Where is Jill going?" cried Helen turning on me for answers. We caught the last sight of her disappearing underneath the waves after she cleared the breakers that were pounding the shore.

"How am I to know?" I answered, exasperated at Jill's behavior. In a matter of a few minutes, she'd become like a five-year-old and it was freaking me out. "But I sense her swimming off into the depths," and my heart was going with her. "And there are things closing in around her," I reported jumping up and down sensing their menacing presence surrounding her. "We have to go help!"

I felt disembodied as my vision was divided between Jill and my feet desperately wanting to fly after her. Not paying attention, I was leading Helen and Ms. O'Grady into the water.

"Wait," cried a voice. "You can't. Sharks!"

Two fins were bearing down on us. "You two wait here," I told Helen and Betsy pointing to the beach. They raced for shore. We hadn't gone far.

The two sharks were part of the others I'd felt, and they stopped between me and the sea, "Get out of the water!" they ordered me. I could sense them swishing back and forth in place, guarding the way.

"Let me through," I told them. "My friend needs me."

I think I puzzled them as I sensed confusion, and at last they decided, "Your word transcends, lady. Go through."

I wasn't sure I was pleased with that. As I dove forward and saw the meat-eaters in person, they gave me steely eyes, but then bowed and turned away as I swam towards them. Jill was out there surrounded by dozens of their kind. Would she be alive when I got there?

It didn't take me long to find her. I had only to follow the school of sharks that were creating a globe around her, and more were coming in. Those nearer greeted me with a terse, "Lady," in their baritones and contraltos. It was unnerving to be swimming into their pack surrounded by more and more as I went deeper. I had to remember I could outswim them if need be.

I swam down into a depression in a rock formation, a miniature Grand Canyon. The area was covered in sea life that could ignore sharks. Everything else was gone or eaten. Not exactly a comforting thought.

I came on a scene that took my breath away, so odd to find it here. A Greek temple, white pristine marble, giant pillars but no roof. At the back of the temple an altar on which I saw a black box about the size of an alarm clock. Around it swam several sharks of different sizes agitated, upon one of the sharks sat a miniature girl. Coming closer I soon realized that I recognized the girl as Jill. Not miniature, no. They were just that much bigger than her.

Jill was riding the great thing like it was a pony. It was giving her a tour of the fantastic place, diving around pillars, doing rolls and other things, when I suddenly lost sight of them. I had to put on the juice to catch up with them. Coming to a ridge, I saw that they'd dived over it toward the slope leading up to the temple from below.

Why was she doing this? There must have been a spell on her and perhaps on the sharks too. There had to be a reason for their behavior. Down here were more sharks and as I looked around I saw they had floated out over the depths where Jill had gone, the temple of an ancient city spilling into the depths. There had to be a connection.

Swimming back and down into the temple which bore none of the marks of decay that the rest of the city displayed, I checked to see if I could sense a spell, but I couldn't. Still, though, that didn't mean there wasn't one. No matter, I continued to search.

Really I shouldn't have had to once I saw it. It was obvious from its location. In the exact center of the altar was the squat device that I'd seen before. Square at the base, resembling a trophy. Getting close, I heard music coming from it and singing. It had the sound of the ocean crashing on a beach, with an elegant undertone sounding like what I'd heard from the first sharks I'd met, "Get out of the water or we'll chomp." Then the song ended and another began, like it was a radio playing a similar tune.

I floated closer to examine it, and a huge pile of sand moved from behind the altar, rising up and placing itself between me and the radio. "Don't touch it, Lady. It soothes. It calls to us. I can't let you turn it off, Milady."

Caught off guard, I backed away. Before me hovered a titanic sand shark, strong and covered by ancient scars. He looked determined to stand in my way, but at the same time I wanted to pat his snout and give him a hug. What was happening to me? Shaking myself out of the mood, I tried to figure out a way past it.

By its action, it demonstrated to me that the radio had to be shut off. Clearly the device was the source of the sharks actions, the poor helpless sharks caught in its web. Going out on a limb based on how it deferred to me, I said, "Who are you to give me orders?"

"Forgive me, Lady," it cringed but did not back off. "But Shrremmm," it referred to itself in an odd way, "purrs to the music. It's simply divine."

It was under the thing's spell. So now what was I to do? What weapons did I have? I couldn't drown it. But then I thought of the guy Jill had dropped. Jill had stunned him. What had she said, something about an electric eel? That had to be the connection. Reaching by attuning, I asked for the understanding, "Please sir, for Jill," and at the same time I felt for the eel in me. Then I understood with a thrill, feeling an electric charge building up until I was resonating with it. Surely I could handle one orca-sized sand shark.

"Out of the way, Shrremmm," I told the shark saying his name clearly with the power flowing through me and not wanting to kill him as I felt I was about to do. He didn't back off but swam to the side to come up under me. His mistake, for I saw the device and remembered my purpose. Extending my right arm and forefinger, I let go the bolt that was developing in me. The water exploded as lighting blasted through it. The device disappeared in a tiny flash overshadowed by the light I'd generated.

Then darkness surrounded me and I frowned realizing the shark had just swallowed me. Just as suddenly, the shark coughed and I was expelled. Gross.

"Sorry Lady," he apologized. "Forgive me, though, as I've never tasted mermaid." I thrilled at being called a mermaid, even given the circumstance. If I could only get Jill to see how wonderful it was. "You taste pretty good but a bit too spicy for me." Again, gross. Was I supposed to thank him for the experience, too?

I gave it a go, saying with a smile, "It's been a while since I've had the pleasure, too." I still had an inkling of turning him into canned tuna fish, but since he wasn't going to swallow me again, I let it go.

8.4 Anxiously Awaiting
– Betsy O'Grady

"They've been gone a long time," said Helen chewing on her nails. Helen and Betsy looked out at the empty sea. "How can they go under like that and not come up? It's not normal."

"Don't you fret," said Ms. O'Grady, just as nervous as her niece. It had been an hour, and they were getting restless. Pierre, from the restaurant, had followed them down to the beach, though thankfully there had been the witness who had called out to them about the sharks. Melanie's evaluation of the man was spot on. There was something underhanded about him, and it wasn't because they were in a foreign country.

A crowd had gathered around them. Too many had seen Melanie face down two sharks and then swim into the deep, parting them and then leading with them in tow. The word had spread up and down the beach. Nobody did that. Already people were talking about miracles and mermaids.

Now with the sun in their faces, it was hard to see anything. They were left staring at a gorgeous sunset. If Ms. O'Grady wasn't so anxious it would have been worth sitting on a plane for. Her stance against air travel notwithstanding, the sunset was amazing. To be surrounded by people speaking French, it was a dream come true. She pulled out her phone to take some pictures. Someday she was going to have to brave a flight to return, but now she was beside herself with wonder and worry. Thinking Jill and Melanie actual

234

mermaids, she remembered fondly her childhood dreams of wanting to be a mermaid. It closely resembled the here and now. If she could live life over, it would be to swim off with those girls.

Surely, those two girls could handle despicable fellows such as Pierre who she had seen poking around the edges of the crowd. If Ms. O'Grady was with Jill and Melanie, she'd be swimming with pretty fishes and leaving those sharks alone.

The brilliant sky turned all shades of rose and scarlet before turning purple and edging towards the black of night. It had been too long, and people were starting to drift away. What were Helen and her going to do if the girls didn't return? They were here without passports. She could fake it for a while, but eventually they'd have to confess to the authorities. How would they explain their arrival? Luckily, she'd used cash to pay for their meals and the things from the beach. The authorities couldn't trace them yet, but eventually she'd have to use her cards and that would leave a trail.

Any minute now, Pierre was going to step in and demand an explanation. Didn't he see that he was being obnoxious? If he wanted to ingratiate himself, he should have stayed with the charming French man routine his father pulled off so well. So far, he'd hung back, but eventually there would be questions and she had no answers. What was she to tell Jill's parents, even if she could get them to believe her? No, they had to wait. Melanie had told them to wait. They had to trust her judgment.

Unable to stay silent any longer, and to contain her fidgeting, she turned on Helen. "Still want to be a mermaid?" Ms. O'Grady asked in a whisper. "No, Aunt Betsy, not if being bit by sharks is any part of it." She had to agree. Being a mermaid was a fun fantasy, but any sane girl should stay away from those creatures.

Suddenly the air become clear and fragrant. Breathing in the refreshing air, she felt her muscles relax. "Ah France," Ms. O'Grady thought. "What a wonderful place."

Then someone was stepping up behind her. Here it comes. Feeling a tap on her shoulder she tried to shrug it off saying, "Not now," expecting it to be Pierre. When they didn't go away and she turned to look, it was Melanie with a twinkle in her eye, holding a finger to her lips. It took all her self-control not to fling her arms around the girl and start balling her eyes out. She'd never been so happy to see anyone in her life.

Melanie turned and slipped out through the loosely gathered crowd. Taking a hold of Helen's hand, Ms. O'Grady turned with Helen in tow to follow Melanie. "Aunt, are we giving up?" Helen asked, looking back at the sea. She cried, "Oh my gosh, I can't stand it!"

"Settle down," Ms. O'Grady told the distraught girl. "Not to worry, they'll show up. We just have to be patient. Let's walk, all this standing around is tearing me up." Pierre saw them walk away, he was torn between staying to see the girls come out and being a serious creep. Thankfully, he stayed behind where the story was. How entrenched their thinking was to think Jill and Melanie "had" to come out where they had gone in.

Mermaids were too intelligent for that. Melanie was living proof. To stay undiscovered as long they had, they would have to be discreet. Who would ever suspect that the girl they were following was a mermaid. She was as normal as anyone about. It made her giddy thinking about it, a real-life mermaid and she'd been swimming with one all these years. Who would have thought? Not her, no way. Jill was as normal as they went, sweet and kind to all the kids and parents alike. Jill was one of the many reasons she frequented that gym. There were other gyms closer, but Jill and her family were some of the kindest folks.

All Helen had to do was look up to see that they were following Melanie. Well, no – not Melanie as she'd been all day. Now she sported a bikini and her hair was up in a frizzy bun. Nor was she walking the same – she was strolling along, swaying to the breeze, like she was much older. As pretty as she was, nobody was paying her any attention. Pretty girls were a dime a dozen and it was late. Most everyone else was walking the shoreline to catch the last bit of light.

Spotting something sparkling, Melanie bent to examine a fancy shell before tossing it into the sea. It was so well done, to seem disinterested in girls swimming with sharks, or much of anything else around her. Seemingly lost in her own world. As long as she'd known Jill, she had known her friends, but this one was special. Head and shoulders above the rest, and she probably had a better head than Jill too. That one could be temperamental. It was good to see Jill surrounding herself with good friends.

Funny, she was thinking how Melanie was so smart, and it dawned on her as they followed after how she'd pulled them from the crowd without the drama that people were expecting. If she'd come from the sea as people were expecting, it would have been dramatic. How spectacular it would have been if she had carried out Jill draped in her arms, mortally wounded by the sharks.

At the news of a swimmer meeting sharks, there had been several ambulances called and paramedics had come. Some had talked to Helen and herself, but they couldn't say what to expect. Now, glancing to her left, she could see their whirling lights at the edge of the beach waiting. Given the casual way Melanie was proceeding, she could lay to rest all the anxiousness she'd been feeling. Everything was going to be okay.

8.5   The Youngest Elder

Kneeling, Diloa organized her thoughts, holding back the emotions that sought to interrupt the class again. She was still reeling from meeting the Sea Lord and the elders asking her "to serve." Nothing could compare to her joy, but she was also awash with sadness. They had managed to alienate the Sea Lord at the same time and because of it, she was bursting with grief.

It did little good to try and avoid her emotions, the tears came anyway. They'd come so close to having Her feel accepted and welcomed. The problem was, She didn't. They'd come close to frightening the Sea Lord. The fiery connection she had with the Sea Lord was shattering her self control. The Sea Lord's rejection made it impossible to hold back the tears and she tried apologizing for her fuss. She wanted to get up and run from the class, but that would do little good. Diloa couldn't run from the connection she had with Her. Nor did the fires that bound them together do anything to alleviate her grief. Who knew that serving could be so bitter sweet?

Mentally, she went through her training in an attempt to avoid her emotions. All of their training had one purpose, to serve. Night and day, she'd practiced their arts, of dressing, grooming and preparing meals. Diloa reviewed the songs they knew, cultivated to enhance the Sea Lord's voice. And what a voice, and what hair! Every day she'd practiced with hair so fine and not to break a strand. The Sea Lord's had been like butter, so soft. That was probably the worst, to never touch it again. They'd all taken turns, for the opportunity might never come again. Ugh, her emotions came back at the thought of the time spent with Her. We'd all seen how she'd taken the ceremony, but it had been too late by the time we recognized it. Banging her fist on her thigh, she tried to find a way to reverse their mistake! But, it was too late to fix the error of a lifetime. Alienating the one we lived for.

The eldest had seen it before anyone else, and had been the most gracious trying to undo the damage. They could only hope that circumstances would bring them back together. The eldest had tried to reassure Diloa, telling her that, "the Sea Lord will find little welcome among the world. We must always remain open and available, and hope She returns to us so we can serve Her." Diloa blamed herself for failing to communicate the joy of serving properly. She'd been left to communicate their ways with Her, everyone had seen to that. So poorly she'd been prepared for the reality of a living Sea Lord, all her past doubts rushed in to trouble her.

The Lords were fierce, demanding and powerful. Their words were Law. How their teaching had failed to convey the human girl that had been among them. A heart as pure as Hers that freely loved, played, sang and was kind. It was easy to see that now that she shared her heart with Her. They had been prepared for a warrior and they had so missed what was right before them.

Diloa tried to redirect her thoughts back to the class. She'd missed most of the lesson, but she caught enough of it to rejoin her companions. There were a few glances her way as she knelt beside them, but she studiously kept her gaze on the instructor, and eventually she felt their eyes return to their duties – leaving her alone in her thoughts again.

The day was the same as those that had preceded it, except now in every class everyone stopped what they were doing when she entered. Walking the halls, people that had been her friends touched her gently, each one carrying away a tiny bit of the flames that now consumed her from the inside out.

In less than a day, she'd met most of the islanders. When the class ended, she'd go out to the courtyard and kneel and let those that had gathered outside come near. The elders had predicted that this would go on for months as the connection she had with the Sea Lord was established. Even now, she sensed the Lady somewhere on the far side of the world.

There had been doubt that remained even after Diloa's conversion. How could there not? Disbelief was not banished in an instant, even though they had all felt Her. What must the people be feeling now? That connection would take a lifetime to develop. So many times she'd questioned the ember that had been hers since her sixth birthday. Every child was expected to serve, and when she was old enough they had a similar ceremony where she received the fire from someone older that carried it.

With each splitting of the fire, it dwindled. So much so that the spark she'd received couldn't be felt and she'd doubted. Not at first, though. She'd been too excited at first, believing all she'd been taught by her mother. The problem went much deeper, though. A cancer had taken hold of their society, to such an extent that when the call came she wasn't prepared.

A call from an elder could not be mistaken. It came mind-to-mind. There was no doubt, just clear communication. Only once before had she been so touched. On her tenth summer, all the children her age had met the elders on midsummer's eve to be taught of them, a tradition going back to the dawn of time, where they melded minds with the elders and saw wonders of bygone ages. Without fresh fire, the technique became less grand, less awe-inspiring, and by the time it had become her turn there had been only faint colors barely perceptible.

Only the Archivist never shared her flame, so that the ancient memories remained crisp. It was with her that Diloa had shared first and then with each of the elders. Then with the people, from the youngest to the oldest, so that any who served would have a connection with the Lady too. We all hoped it would grow, we needed Her as She needed us, but it was unknown if She would return. Had we lost Her for all time?

The only certain thing was that Diloa was now connected with "Jill" – a name both different and familiar. She knew Jill's name like it was her own, though she would never utter it. Practically the only lesson she'd received from the elders reinforcing what she and her companions had been taught as kids – was the part of the pact where they were to protect the identity of the Lords they served.

After the ceremony she'd been told to return to her life, that she still had to grow up. Once she was too old to serve as a maid, she would have a life, maybe a family. That seemed so far away, put in that perspective, barely just a kid herself. Her passions in life would carry on for as long as "we elders" carried the flame. It seemed unbelievable that it could dwindle to the point that she would cease. That was a long time from now, if the eldest's life was any indication.

The other lesson was that she must never meet the Sea Lord again. They had told her nothing more than that, but she suspected it had to do with the Sea Lord thinking she was dead. That sounded lame each time she thought it. No, there had to be something else.

When the class ended, she was the last to know of it, being so wrapped up in her thoughts. The quiet should have made her aware. Never had she been a deep thinker, always care-free and never still. Absentmindedly, she felt her peers stop to touch her on their way out.

Eventually, the teacher, after waiting to see if she would get up on her own, stood up uncertain if she should go to the child. Then once she'd finished preparing for her next class, she paced. It was so unlike the teacher to fidget, and she tried to keep her calm in the face of this child that sat so unnaturally still. Convinced that finally she must act, the teacher walked up to help the youngest elder in whatever way she might. How strange to see the child that would outlive her kneel there at her feet, lost to the world around her. At last, it was time to prod her, so she stooped to bow before the elder. It was a moment before the girl focused, and then she guided her to her feet. "Diloa, they wait," said the teacher.

Kneeling in the courtyard, her thoughts distant, she felt the hands of her people only peripherally. Somehow she'd gone from the classroom to the yard, but she didn't remember the walk. Her connection with the Sea Lord had taken on an odd cast, and she found herself seeing the world through thick lenses. It felt like a dream and the only way out was within. Shutting out the people and her school, Diloa turned inward and felt herself disappearing entirely. Her Lord's vision expanded to include her, and she found she was playing a game with adversaries both feared and loved. The Sea Lord fought bravely. Fending off those who were bigger and with rows of sharp teeth.

The contest became tougher as more joined. Diloa found herself pointing out to the Sea Lord those that came from behind. So embroiled had she become that Diloa could no longer distinguish between herself and that of the Sea Lord, and found herself jetting around the sea as if aboard the fastest attack submarine, but it was only herself. Her friends attacked from all sides in a vicious game of tag. Seeking to nip her, she narrowly dodging as attack after attack came from gaping maws that desired only one thing – to be the first to taste her blood. But none was as fierce or as fast as she was. Together, Diloa and Jill fought them off.

In an instant, Diloa understood a delight so great she started laughing. A love so expansive that with a touch she sent a dear friend to the surface and out of the contest. One after another they came, but combined the two of them were a match for any and all. Laughing again from the thrill, they stopped to survey the field. Their friends gathered just out of reach, and then receiving their orders they spun in with a new attack that had them sweating and taxing their wits as they fended them off.

Then, out of nowhere, an electric current arched through the water and through her. Her body was locked rigid as she tried to scream. The arched lightning was affecting all the sea life around her as well, stunning them for a moment. The intense shock affected her the strongest, it overwhelmed her and she felt her Lord-self go limp in response. All the sea life, including her friends, stilled, seeing her collapse, holding their collective breath. Something was wrong, but she didn't know what it was and tried pulling back, suddenly afraid. Diloa found herself rushing back into her body. She was weak and started falling to her side. Her throat was sore from screaming.

In a moment, five pairs of hands were there to catch her. "Stay with her," one of them said. She saw the elders gathered around her, as one of them instructed her, "Diloa, stay with her." They were anxious that she not fail, "Don't lose her. Stay with her, she needs you."

Then she felt their minds strengthening hers as she felt for Jill. With their help the connection snapped back into place. Back again, she felt the Sea Lord drifting. Circling around her were several sharks, the vision suddenly crystal clear. So these were her companions that she'd danced with, the ones that she'd felt, and a large one was nuzzling her concerned. "Take me," she heard herself say to it. She was talking to the shark. "Bring me to my companion," they, her and the other elders, told the shark with one voice. The shark, in the only way possible, scooped up the girl in its maw. "Slowly, carefully," they advised it.

With the elder's help, she saw the deep sea and around Her was the greatest gathering of sharks she'd ever imagined possible, the loved ones that she had sensed Jill played with, had been playing with. It boggled the mind, for she saw fierce predators but through the connection she saw them as loyally fierce companions. The size of them, the sheer numbers that had gathered to "play." What must it be like to be Her? Did She have doubts? Surely not.

Along for the ride, the elders guided the shark up over a ridge to where a mountain of a shark circled another sea lord girl of Jill's age. This must be the companion that the elder's had told the shark to bring Her to. The sea lord had been having a conversation with the mammoth being, but on seeing the approaching cloud of witnesses she leapt through the water to Her. She was there in an instant, arriving at Her side, and holding Her close.

"Syreni, doctors," she heard herself say through the connection she had with Jill. So in tune had she become with the Sea Lord, that she found herself referring to Her by Her name. It was dumb of them to use Jill's unconscious form to talk to the sea lord. She wouldn't be fooled, Diloa saw that immediately. Fool the shark yes, … but then a mind was pressing on hers and it was not nice. The elders soothed her, and bucked her up as Jill's friend examined her friend.

"She cannot feel us," the elders told Diloa.

But then the girl pushed hard, "Who?!"

"We mean no harm," the eldest said opening his mind to her. "Bring her to us as soon as you can."

8.6   There Again
– BETSY O'GRADY

Helen and Ms. O'Grady walked up the beach following Melanie part of the way, distancing themselves from the town, being sure they weren't followed. Then climbing over a sand dune they found Jill sitting leaning on her bent knees. On the way, Melanie had stopped to wait for them, and then explained that Jill was experiencing memory loss and may not remember them.

When they arrived, Jill gave them absent smiles. Good, so she remembered some recent things, but it was plain that what Melanie said was true. Then just as suddenly, Jill looked at them again, as if seeing them for the first time all over again, saying "Hi." Like she couldn't remember she'd just smiled at them.

"As you can see," Melanie said, "I can drop you off at home, but I have to take her to someone that can help her."

"No, we'll come," Ms. O'Grady said, and looked over at Helen, she agreeing with a nod. "Yes, we'll help however we can."

Melanie gave the two of them a look, as if to ask "Are you sure?" and they both nodded and gathered close. "Okay then." She took their hands and together they took Jill's, who just stared straight ahead.

There was no pause as Melanie brought them to another location. In an instant, they were in bright sunlight and Melanie's grip slackened. Then she collapsed. Betsy tried to catch her, but Helen beat her to it. It was a good thing they hadn't gone back to Boulder first. The strain was too much as it was, and she felt faint herself, as it had been a long day of wonder and frights. Now, their remaining guide was falling to the ground.

Taking stock, she looked at the tropical grounds of what seemed like a high-school football field. That's where the similarity ended, because around it were giant statues every hundred feet. And then lowering her eyes to a ring of island men in black military outfits, she saw that they were carrying on their shoulders automatic weapons along with swords on their hips. Was this a military academy then? Beside them were slender adults, dressed otherworldly in loose flowing colorful robes. Their eyes were piercing, knowing, wise and not someone to be antagonized. Though they looked like they did more smiling than how they currently appeared. Ms. O'Grady suspected that these others could be the greatest of friends. They had been waiting for their arrival. How had Melanie known where to come? A mystery greater than the book she'd been reading had greeted them.

Before she could figure it out, she felt the faintness she'd been feeling rise to her face as black vertigo swirled up to knock her legs out from under her. Her eyes cleared a second later to see Helen leaning over her, unaffected by the day's events. Was her heart finally giving up the ghost? Was the excitement too much?

Ms. O'Grady thought she was imagining things when she saw a host of teenage girls run forward, instead of the heavily armed men, to surround Jill and help her up. Quickly, they fixed her up in pretty clothing, did up her hair and a whole spa treatment in twenty seconds. Their orchestration reminded her of a play she'd seen. It was as if the king from the play had fallen from his horse, and all his merry men gathered him up. Then before it seemed possible, they were leading the tiny woman away, all done up and looking like an island princess.

Girls Helen's age came to help get Ms. O'Grady up. "I got her," Helen said trying to brush them off, but they didn't understand and soon had Ms. O'Grady onto her feet, leading her out from there. On standing, she saw Melanie lifted up by six of the army guys and placed on a stretcher. In a moment, they were trotting quickly off with Melanie in the same direction that they'd taken Jill.

These people certainly didn't waste time, nor was there anyone there directing them. It seemed so strange that she felt like she was an alien in another land, one so familiar but altogether different. While Ms. O'Grady was being helped from the field she saw one of the statues surrounding their sporting stadium up close. An old weatherworn stone Greek or Roman figure of a woman, in a toga. The stately women looked like she might glance down at any moment and talk with her, so lifelike had she been rendered. Between the statues were high risers made of stone, a kind of amphitheater. But there were American field goals, a running track and archery targets. The mystery grew in her mind, as she wondered to what kind of place she'd been brought.

Following the girls' lead, she was placed in a comfortable car and driven through paradise. It didn't surprise her that they had separated her from her niece. Helen had been put in another car. But what surprised her was that wherever they were, the people were happy. After they had left the immediate surroundings of the academy or school, those that greeted them seemed truly happy to be there and to be doing their duties. Several times she saw parents wave with their kids as they passed. It wasn't normal, like we were on parade.

Expecting at any moment to be brought before the inquisition, she was hardly amused when they brought her to a chateau, she was still thinking French. An at once old, and neatly placed sprawling mansion. She thought for sure as they led her into what appeared to be a modern resort to find the island magistrate ready to interrogate her and reveal the mystery. The place had all the amenities, of the rich and famous, but where were the guests? The island girls that had accompanied her on the trip, helped her in being overly friendly. At any moment she thought the hammer would drop. Why else bring her to this glorious location? The lobby was grand, but there was something wrong and it took her a moment to see why. There was no "front desk."

She was greeted by the concierge where she parted with the young friendly ladies that had accompanied her. The fellow led her to an expansive apartment with a view of the sea. From the balcony she saw a pool and floral garden with chairs here and there for relaxing. It was anti-climactic that the gentleman left her with promises of food, to be served by the pool or anywhere she felt comfortable. She chose the pool. There was no sense being cooped up when she could be enjoying their hospitality.

A delightful place for a family, but there was nobody about. Where were the vacationing families? This paradise was clearly under marketed. They could be making a fortune. Turning about, she walked into the apartment. It was cleverly designed, but what was soon obvious were the clearly displayed mermaids. She'd seen them here and there, but now it was apparent. This was a guest house for mermaids and their families or guests.

Her strength had returned to her on the ride here, so she went exploring and ended up down at the pool, pulling out the book but finding it of little interest without the girls around her. They were true to their word and soon had her sumptuously served. She felt sure that she'd solved the mystery. It was an island of mermaid lovers, and Jill and Melanie were the guests of honor. Their inquisitive questions that she'd expected had vanished, her overactive imagination getting the best of her. In its place were the islanders who wanted nothing more than to be seen as they were.

Within the hour Helen joined her. "Hey Aunt," she said, beautifully dressed. Gone was the fish suit and the attendant females. "They mistook me for one of them," Helen said. "I think it was the suit, but I told them I was no longer interested. When I told them that, they outfitted me in these glorious clothes, and brought me here. I saw Melanie, she came to tell me Jill was doing good and would have a full recovery. Though she may not remember much of it on account of some spell she's been under." Then looking around, as if just noticing where she was, she said, "What a fabulous place."

"True," Ms. O'Grady thought. Yes, it truly was. Which made her wonder, was it too good? Pushing aside the thought as being her imagination running wild again, she gestured for Helen to join her and then re-opened her book.

8.7   And Back

– JILL

I awoke on a comfortable couch that was instantly familiar. I kept my eyes closed not wanting to know for sure that I was back on Syreni, but it was too late. The smells, the quiet rustles of the girls my age waiting patiently, quietly talking about everyday normal stuff, not the serious duty of expecting a hangman's noose or a reverent worship of the ground I walked on. It was refreshing to hear their light chitchat.

I felt rested, completely at ease. How quickly I had grown accustomed to sea breezes and island freshness. The powerful sea but a step away sang of the glorious day, of the warm sun and the colorful fish swimming its shores. The hot sands cooled along with the sandpipers running away from each incoming wave, only to then chase after it looking for their favorite food in the retreating waters.

Apparently, I'd been asleep for a while, for I felt rested ... Had we been in France? It seemed like we'd gone – Melanie, me and Ms. O'Grady and a twenty-ish woman that was her niece. Helen, was it?

It was vague, like we had gone to France and then I'd fallen asleep on a beach to wake up here. Something must have happened, but I didn't feel any different, I poked around in my mind, feeling out to my extremities – all without moving. The snap and rustle of a strand of hair across my face that had escaped the carefully wrapped and scented weave was loud in my ears. The weave spoke volumes to my location more than anything else. Nobody cared for my hair like these girls, not me, not Mom, not my friends or any salon attendant.

Nothing was certain, though, until I attuned. Casting out with the spiritual sense like it was a giant net, which was knowing without looking. Six girls knelt around me, with many others nearby, prepared, quieting immediately, and outside were gathered a variety of people. I didn't want to use the word "servants." But they were there to serve. Then beyond them were the strange patterns of armed guardians ranging out into the surroundings.

Prepared, they all sensed I was awake the moment I cast out, and gone was the light banter. One of the girls with me leaped up to adjust my sleeping weave, to tuck away that stray strand of hair, and then when I didn't get up, settled into waiting again. Those outside seemed to ease up a bit from their vigilance, but nobody left their posts. The girls with me looked ready for a sprint down a track, sitting waiting on an ankle, one knee raised, hands beside their forward foot. All alike, all ready.

They were a hair's breadth away from leaping up to surround, dress, feed and brush out my hair. They were poised like gentle butterflies ready to spring forward to nectar. Apparently, there wasn't going to be any mistakes on their end this time around. Not one person to fall asleep by accident.

All this time I'd been unconsciously aware of the music of the sea. It lilting in the background. Suddenly it pushed out everything else and I sat up to hear it better. Then I realized it was because I was singing. In a moment, I transferred, carried away magically by the tune to the beach outside, feeling the sun on my back, and water on my feet. The tropical waters filled me with such joy. I continued singing, filled with endless melodies of the boundless waves, of the beautiful deep and the sea breeze. It was a magical moment, much like the first dance I'd done beneath the waves, but this time I pirouetted and leapt on the wet sandy shore – the sea dancing around my legs like an extension of my dress. The dress flowing down and becoming part of the sea.

There was something wrong with my actions, I noticed. It was not me to be so unearthly, and I tried reigning myself back. It did little good, my whole life was this moment, and forever I could enjoy the fullness I felt from the sea. I turned and ran through the incoming waves along the beach, knowing my actions was causing the water to splash higher. I laughed unable to stop myself and smiled an apology to the girls that had come seeking me to only have their fine garments wrecked by my antics.

Taking a hold of the girls by the hand we ran down the beach until we were all breathless. Then walking back the way we'd come, I began encouraging them in the song, and I was glad to hear them carrying the melody along with me.

Falling in place, I pulled some of them down with me, continuing to sing softly. Then in a break, I happened to mention, laying all askew like a puppet that had lost its strings, "I'll speak with an elder now."

One of the girls bowed saying, "Your will," and then disappeared to speak with someone. It was nothing mystical, though. They used cell phones. The sudden mundane snapped me out of the mystical, and I sat up cross-legged looking about. So I was back on Syreni. How my two worlds had collided, the sea at my side an ever present ally ready to carry me away in its arms, and the Syreni islanders a connection to the world at large.

In the middle was my heart. My family, friends and life at the gym. The cool Colorado rivers and mountain lakes called to me just as much as did the sea. I found myself wrestling with who I was in the midst of these. Then, here I was again with the Syreni people. It seemed I wasn't done here.

"Do your thing," I said to them releasing them to their fun. So they helped me up and led me to a beautiful flowering tree that had been prepared with their things. I felt cruel having withstood them for so long, but they settled around me, a mix of the first night and duty. Leaning on me, and holding my hands, we settled under the tree facing the turquoise waters. I'm glad we had stayed near the ocean instead of retreating to the house.

Removing myself from the sea didn't remove the song from my heart and lips. I found myself humming to the tune, and felt the attuning take care of the salty deposits on us. What a little troop we formed, each carrying a different line to the melody. The whole melody pervaded around us, and the guardians beyond us were tapping their fingers.

The elder had arrived without my notice, and had seated herself beside the girls leaning on me. She joined in with the song, and it was her artistry that drew my attention. Otherwise, nothing gave her away from the others, and if I hadn't met her before I would not have remarked on any differences, though she must have been hundreds of years old. Well, one thing I noticed that was different from the purposefully still girls waiting to leap at my request, was that she accomplished the gentle stillness with patience.

We greeted one another with a kneeling hug, and she commented when she sat back, "It's good to see you've lost none of your touch dear one, you gave us a fright." Then to the girl who handed her a drink, "Thank you, Aromi."

She then moved and knelt in their sprinter pose next to a small table beside us on which rested some cut fruit, cheeses and meats – ready to serve. All was covered so as not to disturb the other aromas, and probably to protect it from flies. I was glad of the first, as I was really enjoying the sea and everything about it. Though food could be a part of that, too.

"High One," the elder said drawing my attention, dropping her eyes a moment. "You know we serve, but we erred on your last visit, which brought you much grief. It has been many years since we as a people have had a chance to practice what we believe. We want you to truly know, you are welcome here."

No matter her speech, I wasn't going to let her affect my mood. I was happy, and I felt the sea breeze on my face. She was not going to spoil my thoughts with their actions. No matter how she couched her words, they only spoke of how they'd killed one of their own because of a moment's transgression.

Closing my mind to the woman's words, I concentrated on the hands that every once and a while touched my neck in their work to weave my hair into colorful braids. Then remembering it was I who had called for the woman to visit I caught her last words. I knew she meant well, I just wasn't sure of their traditions. Though I stood to benefit, since it was all about serving "mermaids," and everyone here thought I was one.

It took more effort to be mad at her, when I had this breeze and the attention of these beautiful girls. They were so warm, these elders. She brought acceptance with her, but then I sensed the conversation turning. She was probing me in an attuning way, evaluating. Then she asked, "What do you remember, dear one?"

"So something did happen. I fell asleep on a beach, thinking it France and now I'm here." I was going to ask Melanie how she'd mistaken France for this place.

Nodding, she thought about that a moment, then said, "Then it isn't as bad as it could be. What has happened is you were assaulted with a mind-erasing virus and your companion received collateral effects. Hers were minor, yours included some hours of memory. She brought you here before it could get worse."

"Assaulted?" I asked surprised.

With a patient smile the elder explained, "As far as can be determined, by a girl you encountered. More than that we cannot say. The spell was imprecise, but effective. Rendering you unable to use your magic. It also halted your higher-order thoughts, reducing you to instinctive actions."

"We've studied the results, but there is nothing we can do to restore your lost memories, as they are gone. Nor do we know a way to counter its effects, not knowing how it was done. What we do know is that we effect similar results often on your behest."

"There is this," and she held up a hand. On it she held a many-faceted ray of light. Somehow she'd captured light into her hand, and though it sent out small rays of light, it didn't leave her. I was mesmerized. It was breathtaking.

"When I said we couldn't restore your lost memories, I spoke true, but not all was lost as you are currently experiencing. It is best to let the mind rejuvenate on its own, to piece together as much as it is able. We worked with you on this," gesturing with her other hand to the sparkling sun piece. "These memories are up to about the attack, minus an hour or so. Those that remain are too fragmented to be more than elements that may show up in dreams. Your conscious mind won't be able to make use of them. In time you may gain back a tiny bit more. So here," and she gestured for me to lean closer, wanting to place the light on my forehead.

I leaned forward and when she touched me; I was there reliving our first moments in France. How we'd spoken with the man on the beach, and the restaurant up until we were shown to our table. I could only guess Melanie and I went dancing, as that seemed the natural thing I would have done knowing how I'd felt.

Then I leaned back as something she had said registered. "Wait, you said you wipe people's memories when I ask you too?" That was a new one. "Why?"

"Throughout history, your kind brings us people, and it's best if they go back to where they come from with little knowledge of how they arrived. Like the man you recently brought us, without you saying otherwise, or any of yours, then he'd go about his way thinking nothing more than he convalesced after an injury. He'd be happy, and you safer."

"Can you teach me this?"

Shaking her head, "No, Mistress. In fact we'd thought it unique to our ways until now. We don't interfere. You learn your ways, develop as needed. But there isn't much need for you to learn the ability for you only need bring them to us." She sounded like Lucas and Uncle Arden, but at least she offered answers.

"And my companions?" She seemed to be avoiding names, so I chose vague words too. The girls had finished my hair, laid out garments and were now serving us food. I was famished and grateful for it.

"Two of them are in comfortable accommodations, like unto a beach resort awaiting you. Your friend is attending to some matters but will rejoin you here. This question remains, the one you know as Helen turned aside and gave up her fish." Holding forth her hand the elder displayed the fish, I saw those that had gone to Helen in her hand. They leaped to my foot and swam up my leg to rejoin the others. "Do you want her and Betsy O'Grady remembering?"

Apparently there was no harm in her using human names. She'd also greeted the girl serving her by name. But she was avoiding my name, if she knew it, or Melanie's. Why? I wondered if it had to do with the girl that had assaulted us. Perhaps it was a magical version of identity theft or tracking. It seemed unlikely, for at home our names were well known and neither Uncle Arden nor Lucas avoided using my name.

My first thought was to let them have this additional tradition. Ms. O'Grady certainly had been helpful, at least what I could remember. But Helen, having given up the idea of joining us, should probably have the treatment. "Will it hurt?" Even if they didn't remember the pain, I would reject it on that basis alone.

The elder shook her head, "They will go to sleep and wake up at home, or to the place where you last saw them with some memories to fill the gap as need be."

"Honestly, I'd like Ms. O'Grady to remember, but she's Helen's aunt."

"There would be complications as I'm sure you'd agree. You can always include her later and she'll have memories of her own without her companion. You don't have to do this, and chance it. There won't be witch hunts as in the old days, but there are today's hazards. You really don't want to have to go into hiding."

"Hiding? You mean on the run? Surely, it wouldn't come to that."

"Unfortunately, Great One, it could. Or you'd find yourself in battle with those that would ignore you otherwise."

Battle? A few lost memories seemed hardly a cost considering that. "They won't remember us?"

"Oh, they'll remember what they knew before your encounter today. Though we could always kill them for you. Then you..."

It took a second for that to sink in before I rose to my feet throwing aside my dishes, "What! Kill them?"

The elder was so dispassionate about it that I felt she was quite capable and probably had done it herself before. I apologized to the girls now scrambling for the things I'd scattered.

The elder continued, not put off by my reaction, "Usually you do that yourself. Mostly you send us those that you've saved from a situation and want to live." That explained their ready behavior at the dock when I'd first arrived. Prepared to lend a hand. Did that old man on the dock carry a shiv ready to do the other, had I been squeamish?

"Oh," I felt dumb. Mermaids were known to drown people, in fact it was rumored a mermaid's kiss gave water-breathing to the one kissed. Otherwise, I guess they drowned. Ugh, did that mean I was a mermaid? I still didn't buy it yet. Besides, they called me "Sea Lord" and not "Mermaid." Oh man, I was in the nut house and I was the head nut.

Reminded of the diver Arlo, "You mentioned the guy," I said reseating myself. "There's a complication. He's my friend's uncle." She raised an eyebrow at this but said nothing. She'd told me all I needed to know. I had to make a decision. "I guess if, um, unless my friend says otherwise, proceed as planned. What has happened?"

"He's made calls using our lines, used a laptop, but there is no Internet for him to use. He has images of you on his equipment. He believes you either to be a mermaid or an angel, based on what he journals. But he's shared none of it. In his position without a captive to experiment on and to offer as proof, he has only his images and ideas. He either intends to do experiments, or to do nothing and chalk it up to good fortune."

The elder added, "Without his data and memories, he'd only have the latter."

8.8   Have Some Fun
I paused to ponder what the elder had told me. They erased people's minds, and would even kill them. And all I had to do was, what, snap my fingers and say do it. Were there no restraints on what they'd do at my request? At my back was a small army to likewise command. This was more than any thirteen-year-old girl should be expected to understand.

On my former visit, they'd said my word was law. I didn't want to be judge and jury. Then I realized that the silence was stretching beyond a polite pause and told her, "Hmm, thank you. You've given me lots to think about, but unfortunately I should probably be getting home."

"Sea Lord, please wait." I hadn't made a move to leave, yet. "You arrived together, you should leave together. Your friend, I understand, should be with you soon."

Well, I guess I had time. I hadn't had my morning swim and felt it in my bones. Deciding to fix that, I suggested, "Alright then, who's for a swim?" Besides, all this nicety was getting to me. Formality was cramping my flair. Seven voices rose as one. I was faintly surprised to hear the elder's among them. "Then let's go..."

Going would require a state procession as Sea Lord, "Hurry, unwrap me and yourselves. I might have a spare fish or two now." They all stopped becoming round-eyed, then the six looked to the elder. Uh oh, had I overstepped another taboo? "Alright, never mind the fish. You're okay with a swim still?"

When they got me unwrapped and themselves situated, we ran for the water. The elder and I ran together. "I don't get to play much," she explained when we hit the water. Behind us came more girls and not a few others, to happily splash into the warm sea.

I could hardly believe how many people had settled in around us. The elder had explained to them, "We're going swimming," with such a surprisingly cheerful tone that I determined to add more reasons to do such things on subsequent stays. "Anyone's welcome," I'd called.

The elder happily ran about spreading her cheer, and the soldiers duty ended once I was in the water, some even joined us, but others went to sit and get refreshments, awaiting my return. Diving under, we explored their undersea waterfront. I'd never had to keep so many breathing underwater at once. Uncle Arden had explained that water was my strength, and I needed it then as there were so many to supply with air.

8.9   Shark Eyes

Melanie found us jousting on people's shoulders after we'd spent an hour or so in some coral canyons. She raised up a wave ten feet tall, which knocked me off my partner's shoulder's, bowling us over and washed aside two other pairs as well. It was refreshing to be in the water, and this wave never tasted better as I spun head over heels. Suspicious of the unusual wave, I surfaced, and searched about. Seeing a new group of girls body surfing on large custom-made waves, I looked for the wave's creator. Spotting my friend, I saw her making wave motions with both hands and sending up the rolling waves with the push of her hands.

Where did she learn to do that? I was a tiny bit jealous that Mel was developing abilities separate from me. I had a desire, which I stifled, to raise up a wave ten times bigger to send at her. What would it take to really get me mad like that? For behind her was the beautiful island, dotted with homes and families hidden behind the screen of the jungle and rocky outcroppings. Melanie would be unharmed, but not those caught up in my whim.

Silently I wondered if I could indeed summon such a wave and I was tempted again to try, but I passed on it. Anything I did now would be upstaging my friend. Sensing that those around me were ceasing to play because I'd gone silent, I dove and came up on one of Mel's waves. Soon some of the other girls joined me, but the rest were leaving the water where I observed a fresh set of girls waiting to serve. A double set, and I looked sideways at Melanie, my rescuer. She'd graduated to "mermaid" in my estimation. The Syreni people were treating her with respect. Melanie no longer needed me, and I was happy for her. Swimming over to her, she gave me a happy to see me smile and then swam forward to ride in on a wave. I swam after her.

Together we rode another of her waves, coasting in on a beautiful ride, one that eventually ended. It took me a second to push myself to my feet, and I saw Melanie seated gazing out at the receding waters as the tide rolled out, but that wasn't what was on her mind. I could see that in her expression, neither sad nor exuberant, just wonderfully content.

I stood there in a K-stance before her, but she refused to be baited and I finally settled down beside her. But as soon as I sat, she came out of her trance and she stood up, saying "Let's walk."

Picking a direction where the beach seemed to end in rocks we could climb on, Melanie took the lead. "You know I love you," she said, taking my hand and just about made me cry in one statement. Then I thought there had to be a "but" to the statement. Yet, she strode off swaying and pulling me sideways, then stopped so our shoulders bumped and gave me a smile.

That was it, no long speeches of what an idiot I'd been, or how she'd worried. I knew my friend Melanie, she should be lecturing me, but instead she was being sweet. So I stepped out sideways and pulled her after to bump shoulders again and she laughed out loud. Then it was her turn, and so we gamboled drunkenly down the beach.

Reaching the rocks, we scaled to a large boulder and sat facing the sea. After about ten minutes, I had to ask,

Steamed

"Please, tell me what we did after I fell asleep on the beach."

Leaning forward on her bent knees with her feet before her she said, "I want you to remember all our shared times, but unfortunately that isn't possible. We're so naïve you know, simple. I've been thinking and wondering if we're up for it."

"You're not making sense, you know."

"Yeah, and I don't want to tell you because I like you the way you are. Did you know when we first met, I thought you a bully?" My eyes shot open and I sat up at that. I tried to remember what I'd done to cause her to think that. We'd been friends since we were six. She didn't even notice my expression. "But now you are as sweet as raindrops, though at times I've seen your eyes go steely. Until now, I didn't have a comparison. But then on meeting those sharks, never mind…" Wait, what sharks? But I didn't interrupt her. Melanie was reminiscing and she was bringing me along with her.

"Back then, you used to win at everything and were a brat to us new kids. The girl with the Gym. Of course, you'd be better. Back then, I used to think you were part fish, spending so much of your time in the pool. But after a year of being every day at the pool myself, we fell for each other and I gained similar swim legs. Though it was a few years before I saw you get happy for a teammate who beat you."

"In that time, we became like sisters, doing everything together. We met Cleo. Meanwhile you took over the children's swim classes. That's where you thrived, and it was your love of children that awakened the girl I love today. Because of you I become a teacher too. That's what I thought I'd grow up to be, but I never saw that for

263

you. I thought somehow you'd join the Navy as a diver. Now, because of this," and she waved her arms about meaning the tropical island and why we were here, "I might be the Navy diver. You will probably be the Admiral and I'd gladly serve with you."

She smiled, thinking out loud, "Over time the steel has never left, as girly as you can be, you never go for the pinks or lace. It just hides for a time behind your good nature, one that replaced the old. Admittedly, neither does your mom like pink stuff, so it's no wonder you don't own makeup."

"I've worn makeup," I interrupted saying. "And, and I was wearing frills earlier…"

"Ha, my makeup," she jumped on that.

"Oh yeah, right. I forgot. Do I really have steely eyes?" I asked while I had a chance to talk.

She half-squelched a laugh, "And why haven't you been asked out? You always…"

"Um, David tried," I rubbed my head remembering. "But it's Cleo that wants him."

"But he tried with you?" I nodded. "Hmm, there's hope yet."

"Hope for what?"

"That you don't punch the first guy that asks. You didn't punch him, did you?"

I shook my head. "No, but he about trampled me. Cleo was upset."

Melanie looked out at the sea saying, "I don't want to see you hurt."

Now I was confused, was she talking about boys, my friends or what happened. I tried to pry it out of her. "So, I have steely eyes?"

She looked at me and then turned to look back out at sea. "Yep, you do."

8.10 Sweet as Rain

"What's that supposed to mean?" I laughed. "What happened to me being sweet as rain?"

"To be sweet as raindrops, you're going to have to do less talking."

I stood up in a huff, crossed my arms, stuck out a leg, frowned. I looked down at her, but she was just gazing at the sea. "Fine," I said sitting again. "I'm shutting up." When she next looked at me, I batted my lashes and gave her a sweet smile. She wasn't buying it, but opened up anyway. Telling me about France, the patio with the dancing. The guy I'd zapped, that I'd taught her about the electric eel connection. "Sounds like I had fun dancing."

Then it got interesting with the diva carrying away the crowd. "You say it had the feel of a spell?" I asked interrupting her.

"Not like I could sense it, but literally it carried off everyone but the two of us. There has to be a reason for it. She was good, but I was attuning at the time, so I wasn't interested. I had assumed you were the same."

"The elders helped me see, though, it was the girl that came up later to rob everyone that was the trouble. Whether the two of them were in on it, there's no proof, but it's likely. We stopped her from robbing our table, as Ms. O'Grady and Helen had left all their valuables. But then you stopped to talk to the girl. Afterwards, she went on doing her thing. But right then she did something to us, we're not sure what. Probably the intended effect, to distract, to make us leave her alone. But you took the full force of it."

"I think it was Sirens from folklore. That's my personal opinion, because of the singer," Melanie concluded.

"When I first came here…"

"You've been here before?" she interrupted. I nodded, "Sorry, go on."

"As I was saying," giving my best steely eyes. "I sang with everyone one night. It was quite magical."

"So you think they may have been mermaids?" Melanie asked baiting me.

"I'm saying I don't know. We should be careful is all."

"How are we to know?" she asked as concerned as I was.

It was obvious Melanie had been thinking about this a while. Answering her own question, she said, "I guess we'll know them by their results, their motivation if it can be determined. It's hard to say on the singer. Did the people truly enjoy the moment? On the whole, they were robbed, but that's not necessarily the singer's fault. We'd just have to see. Besides I can't convince myself that it was beneficial unless the singer had stayed at the club, nor is it something we have the authority to intervene in, right?"

So far, we'd just sat there talking, with seagulls flying intricate patterns around us and white pelicans flying even higher. That girl had robbed me of my memories as well as stealing from the club's patrons.

I shrugged in reply. Part of my memories were a complete blank and I only had Melanie's recollection of the events to go by.

Melanie suggested since I said nothing, "It's possible that the attuning is a kind of shield. It at least kept us from falling under the sway of the singer. Perhaps it could have been effective versus the young girl's attack."

Trying to push aside her fears, she added, "I like it, but I'd like some way to test it and be sure."

"Drowning one's opponent seems pretty effective," I suggested as an alternative.

She gave me a look that told me I wasn't being helpful. Looking briefly back to the sea, her expression changed back to thoughtful. "Which reminds me," Melanie said turning to face me again, "How do you control who gets air and who doesn't?"

I thought about that a second, thinking back to the first time with her uncle when I'd rescued him and then when I'd been with my uncle in the mountain stream. I knew it came from my love or compassion for the person. Supposedly, it was a mermaid trait as well, to give air. I really hadn't put much thought into it since, but I tried explaining how it worked for me.

"What I do know, is it is a matter of the heart. For the diver I rescued, I'd felt compassion for him. I'd drawn close, like I was going to resuscitate him as we were taught in life-saving. Then through the attuning, though I didn't know what it was called at the time, a connection was made from my heart to his. Then, I sensed his lungs clear and he begin to breathe."

I shrugged, unable to explain it better than that. Then trying to explain how it works when using it, I added.

"Ever since, I guess I choose, but I didn't with you all when we first tried. It is an ability, as I'm more conscious of it now and it isn't automatic. I'm aware of choosing to give air now. Though it doesn't take much more effort than to say, 'Yes, "that" person gets air,' inside to extend air to them."

Melanie sighed when I finished, "I was hoping it was something you could teach me. But, at least, you've given me something to think about. Thanks."

Then she went on to explain the rest of what happened. I'd ridden a shark? That seemed far-fetched, well, not as far-fetched as her talking with panthers and the sharks had listened to her. That she'd solved the shark problem was as interesting as the cause. I was proud of her for that, and for keeping her head. I gave her my best "raindrop eyes" as I told her thanks for bring us here safely.

8.11 The Need to Know
Then coming to my knees and sitting on my heels, it was time I broached the subject of her uncle, the diver I'd rescued. I couldn't keep referring to him in third person, when he was a part of her heart. I needed to know how she felt about what the elder had revealed to me. I didn't want to live in fear, but for her I would. Melanie turned fully to face me with my change in seating, seeing that I was going to be serious.

Choosing my words carefully, I asked, "You know that 'guy' I rescued – the diver?" She nodded at the change in subject. In her eyes I saw she knew who I meant, and I could see she was glad I was finally opening up about it. "I didn't know who he was at the time, or really, I didn't recognize him. We've met, I'd almost guarantee it, but I don't know how or where."

Looking at me with her head tilted in confusion, she said, "Huh? I don't get it. How can you be certain you've met if you don't know how, or even recognize him?"

Time to be blunt, I couldn't mince words anymore, but tried easing in on it. "What do you know of your uncle, Arlo? I've met him when I was in the guise of a mermaid. Do you trust him?"

Melanie sat back blinking. Saying the diver was her uncle had shocked her. On another plane of thought she replied with the facts, "I've known him my entire life, but he's a marine biologist. He's always off on one expedition or another. Speaking of which, dad wanted us to go help him the other day. He has a broken leg and has been sick..." She looked at me in sudden comprehension as the puzzle pieces came together, but her mouth kept going, "I begged off, because I wanted to give this my entire attention. I know you are undecided, but for me, this is a once-in-a-lifetime opportunity that I'm not passing up."

Her reaction and what she said, confirmed his identity to me as well. Turning the question from me to her, I had to ask, "Would you trust him knowing about you?"

"Oh definitely. I could go on dives with him. Always in the past I'd have to sit on his boat and wait for him to bring something up or watch through the camera. He records everything. I've even got to dissect some of his finds. Gross, but interesting too."

Even though she saw the connection, I didn't think she understood what it could mean. "You don't feel he'd turn his cameras on you as a creature of the sea? Or turn you into a lab experiment to figure out how you breathe water?"

Her shocked look disappeared. "Oh, um. You'd think he'd do that? Wouldn't that be murder?"

"Not if he considers you a fish." It hurt to lay it out plain, but I wanted her to be careful and I didn't think she really understood it yet.

"But I'm family, surely he wouldn't. Dad wouldn't let him... Wait, you haven't said Uncle Arlo is the diver, but you said you met him. You're not asking about me but you." Leaning forward, she asked, "He's not 'the guy' is he? Wait, don't answer that. I don't want to know."

Melanie held up a hand, denying the possibility but she couldn't avoid it either. "Honestly, saying Uncle Arlo is the diver you rescued," she went on unable to stop herself. "You saved his life, surely that has to mean something."

"What's more important – a find that rocks the world or saying, *thank you for saving my life*, to him?" I was holding out hope for the "thank you" answer, but I could feel the steely eyes around the corner if it was the other.

"I feel like I'm giving a death sentence in saying it, but the former. I used to send him birthday cards, draw pictures for him, so he'd have something of home. But really, he just wants to talk about his work. Don't get me wrong, he's my dad's brother and I love him."

"Well, get used to those hard decisions." Wait, I was coming on too strong, and tried to soften it for my friend. "In this life, I'm having to make decisions I'd rather not make that affect people's lives." Then I got to use a little humor and watched her eyes go round at the next bit, "But cheer up a little, he doesn't have to die, as long as he doesn't hurt any of us. The elders have a method of removing memories similar to the mystery girl we encountered, which they will use on anyone we rescue without our intervention."

"Are Helen and Ms. O'Grady included in this list?" she asked. "Because of the two, Helen was useless and Ms. O'Grady invaluable. If I had to decide, erase the guy and Helen, but keep Ms. O'Grady. He'll just have to not know you saved his life, there is no need for him to know that, even if he is my uncle."

Turning, I looked down at the beach. I'd been pointedly ignoring the girls and the elder that had followed us. If they wanted to follow, then that was up to them. I gestured the elder forward and relayed Melanie's decision, introducing her to Melanie.

"Let's go see how Ms. O'Grady takes it. I bet she even endorses it," Melanie suggested.

She was right, Ms. O'Grady took it in stride. "I have hopes for my niece, but being a mermaid, I guess isn't going to be one of them. Don't worry, she has aspirations of being a singer and she'll never miss these things."

Then we had only to wait a little while, before the elders returned telling Ms. O'Grady that Helen was waiting for her back at the Gym. So we gathered hands, and Melanie hovered to be sure I was capable of bringing us through. Borrowing Melanie's trick, we arrived in a cloud and then went our separate ways.

9 Boulder or Be Eagled

Uncle Arden pulled me aside after practice the next day. "Do you know anything about the clothing we're finding here and there?"

"Maybe," I answered coyly. "I probably can't speak for all lost items, but… sometimes it can't be helped. You know, as you explained, we have to ditch our things to exercise our abilities, I'm not sure what to do, if I could. Mostly the transfer will only take place when were undressed. Except yesterday was the first time we took someone along dressed. It was quite the experience."

"You could put them in a locker like everyone else," he said before his eyes went round with the rest of what I'd said. "Wait, you've been doing transfers?" He turned to look down at me. I always forget how tall he is until he stands right next to me.

I nodded. Wasn't I supposed to be? "Like I said, sometimes it can't be avoided."

Changing the subject, he said, "I need to take a trip to Denver for supplies. Why don't you come with me? I'd like to discuss this more."

"Sure, I'll be right back." Did he now disapprove of the transfers? It had been his idea in the first place, at least the controlled ones.

"Meet me at the car," he called as I ran off to change. I picked a white flowery top and matching skirt, with tan flip flops. Mom had disappeared again, but she'd left me a host of things to try on. I almost left my room before grabbing my phone. It had been a week since I'd touched the thing. It seemed such a remote and archaic device now. I'd been attached to nothing for so long, no devices or even clothes. They'd become a mere convenience, or did I have it backwards – inconvenience? With phone in hand, I went to join Uncle Arden. He'd picked us up a couple of sandwiches. He tossed them to me along with the keys, saying "I'll meet you outside."

It'd been one of the hottest summers that I remembered, but today wasn't too bad, only ninety-three degrees. Even so, I went wide around the parking lot, afraid I'd get burned through my sandals. Hearing the sound of water made me pause and look aside. Seeing the agriculture ditch awash alongside the property, I had to think about that. Usually it was dry. I'm not sure I could ever remember it having water, but today it was a bubbling brook. It called to me to get my feet wet. It wasn't very deep, and I thought why not. I ran to the car, opened the windows and put the sandwiches on the floor out of the sun.

Going to the culvert, I leaped down into the water, expecting to hit bottom, forgetting the experience from a week ago. It was only a few inches deep but instead I splashed in and was over my head in an instant. Oh no, my clothes!

Get a grip Jill, you're a... Sea Lord. Wet clothes are no problem! Whew, I almost thought "mermaid." I'm definitely not some girly mermaid. Flipping about, I scooted quickly to get my sandals that were floating toward the tube that ran under the driveway. Picking them up, I stepped out of the water. Feeling the water drain from me, and then attuning, I saw to it that my clothes were dry and set to right and smelling fresh. Deciding on a swim while I waited, with the whole Underriver to play in. I removed the clothes. Seeing them on the ground, I was reminded about the conversation I'd just had with Uncle Arden. Fine, I wouldn't leave them just laying about. After picking them up and folding them nicely, I edged along in the shadow of the car to put them inside it, and then returned to the brook. Now I would truly enjoy myself.

With a whoop, I jumped over backwards grabbing my thighs and fell deep into the water with a wonderful splash. No swamping the neighborhood, Jill, I chided myself, and then jackknifed into the water arrowing down into the depths and shooting along it upriver.

When I'd been with Uncle Arden on the hike, I hadn't gotten a chance to experience the Underriver very much. Here I found I could, and was swimming in essentially inches of water. And because of the Underriver, I believed I was swimming unseen by those above.

After a bit, I saw this child playing in the shallow stream, his toy duck getting away from him. I thought it might be funny to propel the toy upstream from under the stream. But the kid ran crying to his parents seeing the duck move fast like a toy motorboat. The kid's parents, a young couple, were having a picnic under the trees by the culvert, and looked up at their child as he came crying into their arms.

Rising up to my shoulders before them, I told the boy, "Hey, I'm sorry to scare you. Here," and I held out his yellow duck. Their faces were priceless, beyond bewildered, but I really wasn't trying to scare them. The kid surprised me by accepting my offer and came back down to the water and took his toy, and started playing right near me. "Hi," I said to the parents, "Where am I?" I asked, to make conversation.

I could tell from my position that I was up near the foothills on open-space land. I'd gone further than I thought in just a few minutes. "You're in Boulder... Colorado... USA..." said the woman.

"Is this the planet Earth?" I added, and on seeing their expressions I laughed, "Never seen a mermaid before?" They shook their heads no. "Well, if you see one, you let me know. Okay?" They nodded their heads up and down together, wide-eyed and in sync.

Before they could say anything, I turned and dove into the apparently shallow water heading back towards the Gym. On the way, suddenly a soda can splashed down before me, *trash!* How dare... Something caught my eye and I stopped to observe the can. The last remnants of the drink was flowing out of it to mix with the culvert's water. Eww! Glancing up at the polluter – this guy smoking a cigarette on the bank. I decided he should keep his can, instead of me simply attuning the can away for him. Taking aim, I sent the can, along with a small tidal wave, back at him.

The time I'd splashed the whole pool room had been an accident. But now I emptied the fifteen-foot-deep creek on him. "Oops," I thought, too much. A tug at the water and most of it returned to the brook, though not before he'd been knocked backwards and practically drowned. Then I frowned at myself for my reaction, and then shrugged it off figuring, "He'd think better of discarding a can in the creek next time."

It was only a few moments of fleeing, giggling the whole way, before I came back to our car. I had to surface a couple times to figure out where I was, being careful not to seen. Just peeking over the edge of the culvert, to find our place. I wasn't used to navigating waterways through a city.

Internally, I now had a map of where I'd been, and a sense of where the creek came and went. Almost home, I felt better for having explored. I now had a better understanding of the Boulder waterways. In my mind, I could picture the City of Boulder pretty well, and I could pencil in the waterway. It seemed appropriate that I should know the waters around my home.

Uncle Arden was waiting for me by my sandals, eating his sandwich, drinking a soda from a can. "Hey!" I barked raising up so that my head and shoulders were revealed. "Don't you dare litter," I teased. "I just about drowned this guy two seconds ago, back that way for tossing a can in," and I hooked a thumb upriver. Uncle Arden's eyes and mouth became O's.

"You don't have to worry about me," he said in response holding up his hands innocently. "I won't litter." Then gesturing to my lunch, he asked, "Hungry?"

"Sure," I said and he threw the sandwich to me, plus the soda which I let splash into the water first so it wouldn't be shaken up.

Leaning against the bank opposite him, and with my feet on the other shore – the middle of my body between my chest and feet hidden under the "bottom" of the brook. I opened the can and ate the sandwich. As I looked for someplace to set the can, Uncle Arden said, "Use the water, and don't let it tip. You could keep it cold too if you wanted too."

I set the can down in front of me, so I could keep it in view. The water here was only two or three inches deep, and you couldn't see any of me underneath. Essentially I was setting it in my lap, but really it was over dried grasses and stones. Very strange, but I didn't invent this.

Anyway, the can went down into the water and flopped over. Naturally it would float, tip over and then float away. Now I wanted it to stay upright. My first attempt of holding it up with a finger, and then using a tiny push of water from downstream flipped it over. Trying again, I tried pulling the water away from it. Successful, but now the creek was dry there and it still wanted to tip because now it had no flat place to sit. It did have an interesting effect, as water went around the spot, the can was dry. I felt like Moses splitting water. Uncle Arden laughed at my expression, and I gave him a frown.

Who would have known this was so hard? I thought of hurling a wave at Uncle Arden in frustration. Why did I have to learn to float a can? Though, when he'd taught me transfers it had proved incredibly useful, perhaps there was something to this. Then of course, he had been the one to teach me magic, perhaps it wasn't a good idea to get in a magic duel with him. Returning to the problem, I let the water return to the can, holding onto it lest it spill. I then tried stilling the water, similar to the last time and let the excess water spill around the area. The water did still, but the can still floated and wanted to tip.

"I know you contemplated splashing me. Why don't you use a little touch of that?" Uncle suggested.

"Ah, okay." Nifty idea, hold the can up from the bottom with a tiny, tiny, micro-splash of water. But it didn't take much effort to send a big splash, it was so much harder to make the splash rise only to the surface and keep the can still on the water, supporting it from the sides. In the end, I soaked myself a dozen times and managed only to keep water out of the can with my hand. I nearly had it once but then Uncle said we should get going.

I got dripping from the water. Arden gave me a "Will she ever learn" look, then turned and popped the trunk and pulled out something dry for me to wear. Tossing me a team T-shirt and towel, he suggested I dry off before coming up. I wondered what he'd meant by the look as I dried off, pulled on the shirt and then my sandals. After a second, I realized that I should have dried off using my abilities instead of using the towel, but my mind was still on the problem. I really thought I was close, and had a dozen ideas to try and perfect it. Still, I relied too much on him to think for me, I'm a Sea Lord – I could have dried myself without a towel. "But I'm still also a kid," I thought, as I wiped the last bit of water off with the towel and then handed it to him. He stowed it in the trunk and then asked, "Do you want to drive?"

"Sure," I said before my mouth could say, "I'm only thirteen." We passed each other, as I changed sides and then got into the driver's seat. I was so excited. I knew enough to adjust the seat and mirrors. "I'm letting you do this," he said sliding into the passenger seat, "because it will help you with control. Not everything is full power all the time. You must learn to do things in increments."

I nodded. I already knew that, but it wasn't as easy as he said. Putting the car into motion, it was stop, start. Start, stop, jerk, jump and it was an automatic. "Easy, Jill, use the gas a little at a time and don't stomp on the brakes."

After a few troubled minutes, I sat there close to tears. The work of floating the can was fun, as I was in my element, but this was frustrating. I wasn't even out of the parking lot.

"Hold on," Uncle Arden said after the last knee-bracing jerked stop. Thinking about it, he said, "You can do this. You're good with water activities, why don't you try attuning. Find your place in the here and now." I tried as he said, but it was difficult. Reflexively, automatically, I reached for water, but there was none here with me, I had to let go of even that desire. I had to attune to the car and its environment, to drive it. It really took a while, much longer because I was wearing the shirt, but I'd proven before I could work around that. A few cars came and went around us. Then he suggested, "Think of the path before you like a river with multiple course options." I immediately thought of the trip to the Amazon with Melanie. We'd swam up the river, and it had many branches with water coming in from all over due to the rain. *Think of the road in the context of the roads being like streams*, I told myself.

We were not logs in the river, but self-propelled boats as it were. Not letting go of the sense, I tried again. Thinking of the car like a boat helped a bunch, as I'd already driven a boat – a yacht at that. And pretty well, I'd managed to dock it without much trouble and it had been huge. Feeling more confident we soon zoomed out of the lot. It was trickier though, the car was more responsive, turning faster and it had brakes. I couldn't believe it, but soon I was moving through traffic, and while staying attuned, like a pro. Though I was tiring and it was either remove the shirt and stay attuned, which I was tempted to do, or stay dressed as expected and lose the sense. I chose the latter, unable to hold onto it anymore. In water, I could do it indefinitely.

When I let go, everything seemed to be moving faster. I had less time to react and let more space open up in front of me, which other cars then moved into. Uncle was patient, and at least I was doing it. Though I wondered if he had a big save-us spell ready to go. I'll never know, for we arrived at our first stop safely, My shirt was soaked with sweat. I would have exchanged it for another, but Uncle Arden waved me off. "We have more driving to do, and you need the practice," and he might have said, "and I don't want you ruining another shirt."

I helped him carry the supplies to the car and when I nearly caused an accident on the way to our next stop, we thankfully traded places. Given the breather, with my feet propped up the dash, I pulled out my phone and saw it blinking – new message. There was a text from Cleo.

9.1   Duck, Duck... Mermaid

Cleo had sent me a video link, "Check this out, it's gone viral... This isn't you is it?"

I was afraid to check it out. My finger hovered over the link as I imagined a hundred ways someone could have filmed me in the last few days. None of them pleasant, but then if there was a clear shot of me it would be all over the tabloids. There was the possibility of footage from the researcher I'd rescued, and perhaps dozens of other ways.

Until now, I hadn't processed the idea, but with every outing and the ubiquitous cellphone, pictures of me, even videos were liable to surface. I didn't even want to think about the possibility. Everyone was subject to voyeurs, but now I was up to extra activities. Who knew, even the submarine I'd encountered may have recorded the encounter. Though it wouldn't be on YouTube.

Sooner or later something was bound to surface and a reporter or government agent would come knocking. What was I to do?

If I continued in my actions, my anonymity would come to an end. I'd taken for granted the pool where I could be my normal self and nobody cared. But each night I was seeking out quiet natural locations for rest. It was only a matter of time until one was recorded.

I finally clicked the link.

At first the video showed ducks and their young with voice overs, "Come on, hurry up, Wraannq," a pleasant female duck-accented voice said. I laughed at the thought of the momma duck talking and the baby's name. "What's so funny?" Asked Uncle Arden from the driver's seat.

"Coming, momma," the last duckling piped up from the back of the line, and I laughed again. "It's a video of ducks that Cleo sent me. The ducks, they have voices for them. It's hilarious. It's like a Disney movie."

"I hear only quacking." Uncle Arden was either having me on, or telling the truth. I knew I heard animals sometimes, so this might be one of those times. Still, I couldn't help laughing at a couple more duck quips before…

"Hey momma, is that a mermaid?" I looked sideways at Uncle Arden. Had he heard that? He didn't seem to have.

The ducks were watching something off screen. "Yes it is hun," replied the momma duck, "Praise the Sea Lord, a rare sighting indeed. Food will be plentiful, Lraaangn, dear, you should spread the word, I'll stay with the babies."

I wasn't laughing anymore. I was reading duck expressions and their faces... And the Sea Lord, was that the same as the Lord of the Water, or was that a direct reference to me? Then the daddy duck took off, he must be named Lraaangn. It was all so surreal. I certainly wasn't worthy of praise, but they were calling what they were seeing a mermaid. I had a decidedly uncomfortable feeling and was afraid to watch any more, but I couldn't stop either.

"I'm not a baby, mom," said Wraanng and "Me neither," repeated some of its siblings.

Momma replied full of love, "You're my babies, and..."

Wraanng interrupted her, "Can we say hi? I want to say hi. Can we, mom? Can we?"

Before she could reply, her eyes shot real wide and then she was panicking, flapping wildly and trying to take off. Then remembering her babies, she flipped in mid-air coming down with wings wide to land and scoot by with her kids, screaming, "Watch out, get to shore. Ignore that human."

The focus zoomed closer and closer until the ducks splashed ashore and ran up and through the cameraman's legs. There was a sight of hiking boots before the camera rose up and panned zooming back outwards to the lake. After a quick focus, the man's hands shook on seeing a big boat wake coming towards him. The man didn't move. Turning the camera out further, his hands steadied, and he panned to view a torpedo-like object underwater zipping away creating the wake. It went about a mile to the other shore before flipping and coming back. Well, not directly back, aiming more for the longer distance between shores. Going out of sight around a bend in the shore before returning a moment later.

At its closest, it appeared to be a swimmer. That should be impossible, the speed they were going. The photographer knelt down, putting the camera in the duck blind and filmed for about an hour more of this phenomenon, me. It was amazing watching the speed and resulting waves.

I recognized the place now. It hadn't been obvious from this vantage, and the camera had mostly been on the ducks. It seemed to be me from yesterday morning.

I replied to Cleo, "It looks like it might be. I think it is, but I'm not sure." What about the ducks?

I checked the date of the upload... Yesterday, and over 3 million hits. What did this mean? It couldn't really be me, could it? And why add voices for the ducks? Then we were arriving at our last stop for some new towels.

9.2   Four Kisses

Loading up the car, I stood beside it and looked longingly at the South Platte River that flowed down below from where we were parked. It was a muddy river. I felt like a fish out of water in all this steel and asphalt, driving around in a car. How quickly I had gotten used to and preferred open seas, rivers and boats. When the last bags were placed, I asked Uncle, "Can we go for a walk down there?"

There were people strolling and biking up and down the cement path beside the river. There were also wide swaths of green grass. I just longed to put my feet in. He came around the car to look where I was looking, and then gave me a glance, "You can't stay away, can you," he joked. "Especially when it's ill."

"I don't know what you mean. It just looks so peaceful."

Seeing that the river had a hold on me, he made a split decision and grabbed my hand before I could wander away. He then locked the car and said, "Sure." Then, to hammer home how I was feeling, added, "You know it's a long swim back to Boulder."

"I'm not going to swim..." I said and then realized that a swim actually sounded good. But, oh, the water was so dirty. As we got closer, I could feel just how dirty. Could I get some help? Thinking of Melanie. I knew that Cleo and Lucy would help too, but we hadn't had a chance to develop their skills. Melanie, I thought, could make the swim, meeting me halfway.

I pulled out my phone and began texting her. By then, we were standing at the banks of the river. Uncle Arden leaned over and plucked the phone from my hands. "Not that way," he said.

I reactively said, "Hey!"

"How do you expect to communicate with someone when you're halfway around the world?" he asked. I shrugged pointing at the phone. "Without service and underwater?"

"Point taken." I was afraid to ask, but knew it would be another training exercise. "What do you suggest?" I

285

asked. He pointed for me to get in, saying, "And no transfers."

I kicked off my sandals and stepped into the water. Yuck, the river bottom was muddy. There was so much pollution in the water, any attempt I made wasn't going to make much difference.

Shouting for our attention, "Hey!" It was one of two police officers on bikes coming up the bike path. "There's no swimming!" he called again as he got closer. Had we passed any signs that said, "No swimming"?

"Are you going to be okay?" I asked Uncle Arden. He nodded picking up my sandals. Doffing my shirt, I backed into the river throwing it to him. It caught a lucky breeze, floating right into his hands. More than lucky I'm sure, but by then I had everyone's attention and I couldn't ask. Nobody was swimming, but there were several groups of people watching from benches and tables.

I attuned and opened myself to the river. Like a drop of soap in an oily tub, clear water spread out from me in a circle. By then, the police officers had arrived, "Hey, come out of there," one called to me, while the other radioed for help. "We have a crazy girl swimming..."

The river surged toward me, coiling up around me like a giant serpent. Desperate to be rid of its filth, it was going all in to get clean. It covered me from my head down in a spiraling cone of water. The rest of what the officer had meant to say was drowned out by it and the shouts of the people that gathered to watch. The river wasn't letting me move at least while attuning, so I used that time to figure out how to get a hold of Melanie. Since I was restricted from transferring, I had to think of some other way.

Obviously, Uncle Arden wanted me to "talk" to her in some fashion. Therefore, it was possible. Using a modified transfer, I thought of her, like I might travel to her, and knew she was at the gym, on a stair exercise machine showing someone else how to use it. But I didn't want to transfer. Well, the second part of any magic spell was called "understanding." Did I ask The Lord of the Water, too? I tried, and I guess he said okay, but I still didn't know how to practice it.

I knew sounds and light moved in waves as well. Could I use them like water waves?

Keep it simple. How about a text like message, but how? I couldn't exactly send a message in a bubble, or could I? My phone sent and received messages in bubbles, why not a real bubble? It was far easier than I'd thought. Cleansing the river was giving me unbridled power and even if my attempt was crude, I attuned to Melanie again and sent her a bubble message? "Can you meet me?" I was going to add where, but realized that was conveyed in the wording, "meet me" meaning here at the river.

Understanding was a shot in the dark, but in a moment I felt her attune back and she practiced a reply. It was far clearer. She was better at thinking things through than I was. "I'm on the way," her bubble said.

Uncle Arden hadn't said that she shouldn't transfer, so it wasn't but a few minutes before Melanie was at my side, along with Cleo and Lucy. I was surprised and glad to see them.

Seeing the tumult, and then suddenly being wrapped in it as the river surged into her as well, she cried out, "What's going on?"

"You don't have to shout," I said because this close our attuning was carrying our words to each other, "What do you feel?" I asked, wanting her perspective.

"Sorry, I feel charged," Melanie explained from the top of her mud spiral, "and I can't move. The river, has it gone mad?"

"Just the opposite," I gestured with my nose upriver. "It has been sick and we're the cure."

"What can we do?" asked Lucy. Both Cleo and Lucy were free of the river's demands.

"Um," I wasn't in a mood to explain Attuning again, but Melanie came to my rescue.

"Do what I showed you. Attune to the river. It's what sets this off."

Soon, two smaller upside-down water spouts appeared up to their shoulders. Already I felt the local effect loosening its grip as a result, and with Cleo and Lucy there to help it was soon over. There was a ragged cheer from those watching.

Many had stayed to watch the phenomenon. It seemed really strange to me, all of this. Being tied up by the river and then having people cheer when it let us go, I wanted to get out of there. As I'd told Melanie, once the "job" was finished, it was time to leave.

"C'mon, we should go," I said gesturing us downriver, but Cleo said, "I want to stay, this is fun." She then raised

288

her arm to wave and smiled back at the crowd. Lucy joined her in smiling and waving. They shared some laughter. I felt like a spoil sport. Was I the only one concerned that our faces would appear online? It was probably too late for that.

"I have to go," Melanie said next to me. "What, you just got here?" I complained.

"Remember, I told you about Uncle Arlo? Well, he's hurt, and you know the rest. Dad wants me to go, so I have to. The original flight was cancelled mysteriously by the airline and is rescheduled for later today. I want to go now after what you've taught me. I want to stay too, but anyway be safe," and we embraced. She then turned, dove and transferred. I wanted to go with her, but that was impossible.

I didn't need to ask where she was going. Her uncle and the guy I'd rescued with the broken leg were one in the same – Arlo McKenzie. Lucky her, off to perfect waters.

9.3   Breaking Eggs
The river was looking far better than it had been, and there would be more dirty water coming from above, but right now it was swimmable and people were taking to it again. Too bad we hadn't cleansed the whole thing, but that would take forever and many more mermaids. Every major tributary would need a full-time resident mermaid, if people didn't take better care of things.

Hearing laughter, I turned, Lucy was playing ball with a kid – the boy throwing the ball here and there, and Lucy playing fetch. Cleo had disappeared, but then I spotted her flirting with a teen. Didn't she know the effect she was having on him? I guess she did, and I think she liked that he was enamored with her. I shook my head. Melanie was gone. I was suddenly bored, and sank down into the water to my neck.

What happened to the police? Surely, they hadn't abandoned their duty to keep me out of the river. Looking about, I saw no sign of them. Also, the crowd was breaking up, uninterested in mere swimmers.

I was nervous, but there didn't seem to be any problems. I felt better about doing something for the river. My friends were having fun. Why couldn't I enjoy the moment? It was a nice day, the weather was hot. A frisbee zipped by, others had entered the water. On the next throw, the frisbee curved and landed out in the deeper water. "I'll get it," I told the two guys who had been tossing the disc, swimming on my back towards it, reaching back to pluck it from the water.

This is nice. I wasn't very good with frisbees but my throw was accurate enough for the guy I threw it to for him to make a diving catch. Soon, I was included in their game. Though I wasn't getting more accurate, "Sorry," I called after my throw went in a high arc that caused it to land halfway between us, closer to me, but he'd already been running after it. I dove forward after it anyway. I purposefully reached it just before him, "Got it," I said laughing and hurled it towards his friend, twisting up my face in an attempt to correct its path, but that didn't help.

"Hey, what's your name?" the guy asked staying near. We were in about three feet of water, but I was ducking low like it was deeper. Only coming up to throw it as needed. "Jill," I replied.

"I'm Clark," he said, catching the next one, and then leaping up to wing it under his leg. It flew with speed and accuracy. The next one came between us, I dove after it and missed. I swam after and then came back with it, giving it to him to throw. I liked watching him, he was good. After he threw it, he squatted down in the water, "Where you from?" he asked, catching the next toss easily and sending it back the other way.

"Boulder," I said, then watched him catch another. Tossing it to me, he said, "You're a long way from home," and then pointing at me, "Your turn."

I wanted to do a leap up, with an under-the-leg toss, and I did manage to get it under the leg but it went wide and way short. We had a little moment while his friend waited for it to float to him.

"Not really," I replied thinking of all the places I'd been in the last week. Stating, "Denver's not that far from Boulder."

"True, but isn't it far for a thirteen-year-old kid?"

"I suppose," I replied wondering how he knew my age, probably just a guess.

"You're not concerned?" he asked puzzled. There was a chip on his shoulder in his expression and voice, like he had to prove himself to these guys.

"About you?" I laughed at the suggestion. Was he being serious? I had the wide river at my side, and a great depth below if needed. He was in for a surprise if he tried anything. Besides, I was probably misreading him. He's only being frisky. Still I could toss him into the depths if he got rough. I laughed again thinking of how he'd look at me when he realized he couldn't breathe. Not that I'd do that. I've never denied anyone air.

The disc landed between us. I scooted over to pick it up, brandishing it between us. He made a grab for it, or was it playfully for me? I laughed, "Nice try," jumping away to send it towards his buddy. I couldn't help but wonder what his strong arms would feel like around me. A thrill went through me at the thought.

He probably thought of himself as tough. I examined him, his cut body, a few tattoos. Not my kind of thing, but his biceps, ow. His hair was dark, doubly so when it was wet and zipped close. His friend was taller with sandy hair. He wasn't grinning anymore, but then why should he. The friend had a twinkle of humor in his eyes as I played coy. Teasing me, he lifted the disc gesturing that he would throw it my way.

When the frisbee flew my way, I leaped up, missing it again. It flew overhead to land before Clark. I smiled at him, now I was "caught" in the middle. Pretending he didn't notice, he sent it just over my head to the tall blonde, where it landed short.

Coming closer, the guy I'd been talking with asked, "So how come you and your friends aren't wearing anything?" He stopped about five feet away. We were in about two feet of water. He probably thought I was all crunched up to have only my head exposed, but I was comfortably treading water.

"Oh, we're mermaids," I said to put him off. "Clothing only gets in the way. Besides we're wearing suits." I double-checked, well, the fish suits were cream-colored. Was something going on? I knew I didn't always have control of the transfers, and of course I didn't get to choose how the fish acted, but they always resembled suits.

He fell back laughing, which caused him to miss the next throw. It made me mad that he laughed, but then why shouldn't he? Usually that was my reaction. Seeing that he was going to be a while fetching the disc, I took that time to sweep around looking for my friends. Cleo had left the water to sit on a park bench, unaware that a guy was now between her and the water. He was facing the river. But where was Lucy?

"Let go!" That was Lucy. Her voice like a beacon, as all eyes traveled to her. Sometimes she did that, usually blushing when she became the center of attention. Now it was a boon, though I now saw her struggling with two guys near the upriver bridge. If those guys were like the two "friends" I'd been tossing the frisbee with, then she was in trouble. How'd she get so far away? What was I to do?

"Now it's our turn," said my "friend" as he put both hands on my shoulders and pushed me under. What he didn't expect was that under was better for me, and not for him. His expression had turned from friendly to something else, one I didn't recognize. Well, it was about to be surprise as a feeling overcame me, something cold. The thought of my friends in danger flipped a switch in me.

I kept going through the river bottom. He'd thought to pin me in shallow water using his body weight. Instead, we dropped way deeper.

His surprise was evident as he fell forward, falling past his depth. Thrashing, letting me go, he tried to swim for it. He pivoted, but before he could kick free, I took ahold of his wrist, and turned kicking for the depths, dragging him after me. He was no more than a tiny doll for all his wriggling to get loose in my strength. I could have let him have air, but for the first time I denied someone the privilege.

"Poor, Clark," I taunted him as I drew him deeper and deeper. His face turning all shades of desperation. "You're going to drown, you know," I told him. "You and your jock squad along with you." His eyes were bug-eyed seeing and hearing me, but unable to respond. When he finally gasped for air, choking on water I let him go, wondering what had overcome me as I floated clear. Then hearing his partner splashing above, I turned to look upward at him. He had ropes that I had mistaken for a belt in one hand and in his other hand, he held a knife.

He was looking for us, splashing back and forth in the shallow water unable to see that we were much further down. Angry, I went to him, leaving Clark choking on water. How dare they try? Grasping him by the foot, I dragged him under and down to his friend who was now floating limp. "Thought to take advantage of young girls, did you?" I said, dropping him by Clark. "Welcome to your grave," I told him waiting to see him gulp for air only to realize that this was his end.

This was taking too much time. I couldn't believe my bravado, it was not me, but they had my friends and were going to do something too awful to contemplate. I sped upwards and surfaced near the shore, to stand some ten feet from the water's edge, water rushing out from where I surfaced. The river was probably as furious as I was.

The wave from my breach reached the shore as I saw the situation. They had brought Cleo over to where Lucy was, near the bridge.

I walked towards them and offered them a trade, I wasn't gone in my anger, but I was getting close.

"Let go my friends," I called to them, "Or yours will die," and I waved back behind me to Clark and the other guy.

"You're bluffing! Get her," one of them said. Four of the remaining seven ran towards me, splashing into the river. I held out my hands, feeling the thrill of electricity flowing in my palms. The shock of the electric eel was about to be theirs in full. Seeing that I was surrendering to their overwhelming force, they grabbed for my arms.

"Too easy," I said to the first two when they touched me. As they did, twin jolts overloaded their nervous systems dropping them in place as had happened with the guy in France. They fell face-first, unconsciousness into the water beside me. "Next?" I said to the two a couple steps behind. They stopped, mouths agape, seeing their brute friends seemingly dead at my feet.

With a shared look, they turned to flee, "Too late for that," I told them, coming on them with a leap from behind. They fell just like the last.

Dusting my hands off, I looked up at the remaining three, feeling almost sorry for them. "Now I have six," I told them. "Though I think Clark is dead now, but you could save the others."

They looked determined. Somehow I expected their bosses weren't going to accept excuses. "Come no closer," they order me. I was walking towards them.

Stepping out of the river wasn't my best idea, but then I had to reach my friends.

When I didn't stop and stepped onto "dry" land, I expected grass, but instead my foot unexpectedly splashed. Looking down, the river had bowed out overflowing its banks of its own accord to keep me within its bounds. It wasn't letting go of me. How delightful!

Seeing this was the last straw for these guys as the river swept out towards them at an ever-increasing pace. They let go of Cleo and Lucy and fled. I ran to my friends, hugging them. Then just as if the river understood, it fell back into its normal channel as if nothing had happened, leaving the park untouched. I was at a loss to explain it, but we were glad to be rejoined.

"Are you okay?" Cleo asked me, blinking back tears. "Those guys were huge, what did you do?" she asked looking at my hands. Unable to contain the flood, she gripped me with renewed determination. "Teach me," she pleaded, "As you've taught Melanie. I never want to be afraid again!"

"Me too," said Lucy beside her, shaken by the experience, but holding up much better than I would have had I been her.

9.4 Making an Omelet

"It's too bad they got away," sniffled Cleo between tears, but Lucy caught our attention pointing. "They didn't, look," and Lucy nodded to where the three were now in cuffs. There was my cop friend coming down the ramp. "Hey, a word," he called to us.

There had been a small crowd when we put on our display earlier, but they'd vacated at some point. Nobody was even going by on cycles. I'd been too busy having "fun" to take notice of what was going on around me. I really was naïve, and after what's happened I didn't want to lose that feeling. I liked thinking of the world as fun, but around me lay the results of reality.

What were we going to do now? Getting back in the water had to be priority one. From there, we would have options. Releasing our hug, I let my hands pick up theirs and pulled them after me towards the water.

"Wait," the officer called. He was huffing it.

"Gather those four," I said pushing my friends ahead of me towards the floating bodies. Face down in the water, they weren't doing very well. I let them have air, but they were still limp when Cleo and Lucy rounded them up. The officer, in his mid-twenties, strolled my way, seeing we weren't going to flee. He was probably thinking that a girl my age wasn't going anywhere fast, especially barefoot. With the water at my feet, I could be down and under before he could even blink, if it came to that. As much as I'd disliked the thugs, taking on the law wasn't my idea of a good time.

"Can I help you, Chief?" I asked as he came up and saw what my friends were dragging along behind them.

"Um, are they dead?" he asked, uncertain. "Not yet," I replied, "But their friends are. Do you want their bodies?"

9.5   Scary Teens
– OFFICER JACKSON

"Friends?" Officer Jackson asked looking around for more floating corpses. The river was fast enough in the channel that they could be a ways away by now, or would he need to call for divers? Then turning on the tiny girl he'd seen drop two men without seeming to move, wearing only a swimsuit. How had she done it? Then she'd made a leap, dropping another two that he wouldn't have attempted, and they'd fallen like the previous two.

Because of her actions, he was keeping his distance. She seemed to be their leader and the one he wanted to be careful with. He'd moved out with his partner when the Tang Gang had moved in around the girls. The international gang had recently been sighted in Denver, but this was his first exposure to them. He wasn't naïve enough to see what had been going on here, but was glad of the outcome. Even if he could pin the charge of assault and attempted kidnapping on the gang, they would go free with their lawyers anyway.

He and his partner had been slow when everyone had started to move off, but they eventually had and had figured the girls would as well. His mistake, but then public safety didn't mean risking his life, especially considering that the gang had seemed to be in a good mood. He was wrong about the gang and the girls. The gang were now in cuffs or dead. Not bad for girls in swimsuits.

"There's two more dead at the bottom of the river. I can bring you to them," said the leader, she was self-assured, standing in a foot of water. Obviously she was the kid she appeared to be and not simply short. Her emotions showed someone trying to buck up under trying circumstances. He'd watched them move to the river after everything was over, and once in it they felt secure. What was it that made them feel that way?

His partner had the three thugs who had tried fleeing, but really, unless these girls testified it would be a waste of time to arrest them. But at least for the moment they were out of the way. There were four more here and two more dead below, so she said. For the sake of his sanity, he hoped these seemingly innocent girls hadn't done something horrible to the thugs. He'd seen too many horror movies. Checking the area, he decided it was time to deal with this.

"I should have you arrested," he said, clearly uncomfortable with two teen girls dragging around the bodies of four grown men and the possibility of two more dead ones no less. This was out of a horror movie gone bad where the bad guys ended up dead, having encountered a worse kind.

"She saved our lives," Cleo said interrupting his thoughts, his eyes were wide seeing her dragging two floating bodies. That they talked made it worse somehow. He looked at her, she was lining up the bodies with the other girl's find. Those two girls were spooky, so what did that make their leader? He only had her word that they were okay, though they surely would drown if left face down in the water, but he wasn't about to touch them.

"On what grounds?" Lucy asked after making the four bodies line up perfectly.

"Murder... and resisting arrest." He obviously was speaking just to hear himself speak. He was only a traffic cop. Being the first at a crime scene wasn't his thing, but he was doing okay.

Lucy wouldn't let go, though. "Murder, and on what evidence?" She was coming to the leader's defense. That one threw back her shoulders and crossed her arms, assured in her superiority.

"She just admitted to it. Said she had two bodies," he said facing down the argumentative one.

Lucy stood up to that saying, "Saying there are two bodies and admitting to killing them are different things."

9.6   Diplomacy
– JILL

Well, I did kill them, though, as only a mermaid could.

Chuckling at the idea, I thought why not say we were mermaids. I'd used the same on the thug and he hadn't taken me seriously. Perhaps it was time I started admitting to it. The ducks had gotten to me. Mermaids should be immune to prosecution, what defenses did we have anyway? Besides, if we were an international organization...

"Diplomatic immunity," I said smiling, inwardly laughing at the idea.

"What?" asked the three of them. I couldn't help it and laughed at their expressions. Cleo's was priceless and the police officer's wasn't so bad either.

"Diplomatic immunity," I repeated. "As a mermaid, from mermaid kind, I can't be arrested. Sorry, I don't have my credentials on me..." I thought I was being funny, but suddenly I didn't just feel mirthful, I felt giddy and a certain feeling of this guy's integrity came over me. He could be trusted.

Then at the same time the world tilted, became wobbly and I was having problems standing for no reason, "Whoa! What's happening?" I couldn't stay upright and fell onto my back with a splash, unable to move my feet to adjust my balance.

"Oh, my God!" Cleo exclaimed looking down at me. "No, it can't be," gasped Lucy.

"What's going on?" The guy asked. The three of them were staring down at me.

"What?" I asked them, feeling strange. My first thought was that my legs felt curved and stuck together, which was impossible. Then I looked down to my feet and about passed out at the sight. A tail, a curvy mermaid tail! My body from the waist down was a beautiful, colorful tail. The "scales" mimicking the bikini top fish suit that still wrapped my chest in appearance. I had to agree with Lucy, it couldn't be. And I felt everything!

Normally, I had to mentally reach out to attune, but now it was just there. The water was like a second skin, another muscle, an instrument to be played.

I laughed merrily, my voice taking on an otherworldly tonality. Oh, I wanted to sing, but Lucy stepped in before I could as I was getting carried away, "See, she's telling the truth. So, do you want the bodies of the two men?" He nodded dumbly. "Take him to them, Jill."

He realizing what was about to happen, "Why should I trust you?" he asked us.

Recovering myself, thanks to Lucy's fast thinking, I told him, "I give you my word, you won't be harmed. Follow me," and I dove under, the water sliding over me as I effortlessly glided into the depths. This is what swimming was supposed to be like, and what we only pretended at with legs. When I glanced back, he hadn't followed. I heard Lucy encouraging him, "Go ahead, you'll stay dry."

Hmm, I thought. *Sure, why not? Indeed, with this new water sensitivity, I could keep him dry.* A bubble for messages, why not one for him. I had only to think it, and the water formed bubbles here and there, some growing to the size of a man before I let them go. I sped up and jumped like a dolphin, arching up some fifteen feet, and then swam over to him.

"Come along," I said stepping to him, my legs magically back, and taking his hand, led him into the water. Already attuned, I moved air about him, and even his feet stayed dry. He walked along the no longer muddy river bottom. I guided him deeper still.

He looked up at the receding waterline commenting, "I had no idea the river was so deep." In a moment, Cleo and Lucy were swimming alongside. Kicking out away from the sloping bottom, I pulled our new friend towards where Clark and his friend's lifeless bodies were floating.

Looking at them, I started having second thoughts about having killed them. They may have been decent guys at one time. I wondered what their families would think.

"Don't regret it," the police officer said, reading my expression. "I recognize him," he said pointing out Clark. "His dad is the head of their crime ring. He's on the FBI's list. There is probably a reward for information about him."

"I don't need a reward, Chief." So Clark did have something to prove, but now his expression was empty as he stared into the waters of the unknown. Looking into eternity, leaving all the old expectations behind.

"Sure you do," Cleo said coming in close. "Who couldn't use a reward, you'll be famous." She then rattled off saying, "Jill's parents own Goldie's Gym in Boulder. You can find her there."

Interrupting her, I couldn't believe she was giving away my home address willy nilly, "Let's get these up shall we, Chief? And I'd appreciate nobody knowing where I live."

"I've got them. I don't know how I'll report this. Any chance this thing will work down here?" he asked pulling his mic from his shoulder. I had no idea. This realm was a total guess. Either we were terribly short, sort of two-dimensional, or we were somewhere else. "Nope, I didn't think so," he reported after trying. "It doesn't surprise me, because this is clearly impossible." I'd kind of guessed that, since it was like the dream island place where instruments didn't work.

In the Underriver, the current was nearly as strong as on the surface, but the two guys were there as if tethered to the bottom, having not moved from where I'd placed them. I think the river was holding them. How strange to think of the river as being intelligent, but then I was learning more about this world that I'd taken for granted, such as animals talking.

The three of us girls were swimming into the current beside them, though it wasn't difficult, and he floated nearby unmoving as well. It could have been described as picturesque, for the walls were not simply canyon cliffs, but windows into an idealistic vision of what this river would have been like hundreds of years ago when open plains surrounded it instead of a city. Just then, bison were coming off the hills down to the river and across it, and a distant storm gave relief to the summer's heat. Was this a true vision of the past?

Reaching out, the police officer took the two thugs and started swimming towards the bank. I heard him muttering on his way out, "I really should let the M.E. see them first." He was looking to the windows into the past too. "But at least I won't have to include this place in my report."

9.7   Swim Home

We were left there alone at the bottom of the river for some time before Cleo grew restless. I was happy to just sit there in a custom-made "mermaid" tank with a beautiful view. But it got me to thinking, it would be a drag to be only a fish in a tank and never to go outside.

"So, are we going back to Boulder now?" she asked.

Lucy crossed her arms at her, saying critically, "Have some more boys to flirt with? If it weren't for you we wouldn't be in this mess."

"How was I to know he was a creep? And it isn't my fault their behavior," Cleo protested. "Besides I just wanted to enjoy the river. It's pleasant enough. You two were having fun, too," she added pouting and probably would have stomped her foot if she could have.

"It's nobody's fault," I said, coming to her defense. "Creeps exist. What can be done about it?"

"Actually," Cleo said changing moods, "You're in a position to, well to do something."

"Can we get onto going home if were swimming the whole way? We can continue talking while we're on the way." Sure, we replied, "But I want to swim up in the sun," Cleo said and we moved upwards, surfacing in the rolling river as it narrowed to pass under a bridge. We surprised a pair of fishermen who were unaware of what had transpired upriver. We waved laughing and passed on by, letting the current do most of the work.

I wanted to show off my new tail, but it had disappeared and since I didn't know how it came, I didn't know how to bring it back. Just as well, neither of my two friends had tails. At least some of the new effects of the tail remained, so when we passed the oil refinery, it had one of the cleanest air days it had experienced in sometime.

Then we were sweeping northeast out of the city proper, under the interstate 76 bridge and past several gravel ponds. Each time we passed hikers on the trails and fishermen plying the waters, we were quite a surprise to them. Sometimes, we appeared like three girls floating on a big inner tube, but without a tube, or floating along separately. "Crazy kids," said one old fisherman as we swam by.

So used to modern conveniences like cars, I tried to imagine the days when river travel was the main way of getting about. I guess I was glad those days were over or there would be nowhere to swim with the river clogged with all those who would have been coming and going.

"If we're to get home by dark, we should get moving," Lucy said interrupting my thoughts. "True," I replied, though this had been fun so far just drifting with the current. Picking up our pace, we made good time and it reminded me of the Amazon River Melanie and I had swam in. Though this was an entirely different river, here we had open land on either side and an occasional well-maintained bridge. There it had been the opposite – a looming jungle and no bridges worthy of the name.

In practically no time, we made the hard left turn into the Saint Vrain combined with Boulder Creek, then we were into the much smaller Boulder Creek not much further afterwards which was more uphill and definitely smaller. We had to spend more time in the Underriver under the normal flow, but it was still fun to jump out in a dive to surprise people enjoying the river.

Some girl of four or five shouted after us, "Mommy! Mermaids!"

The three of us stopped in our tracks to wave and smile. Again, I wished for the tail to show off, but I was only sporting legs. The kid's parents were sitting there dumbfounded, staring at us in just a foot of water. "See mom, mermaids are real," the kid said turning on her mom. Then mom was pulling her purse towards her, fumbling in it a second before coming up with her phone. With a last wave to the kid, we turned and dove.

Then before we'd gone far, I felt something suddenly hard in my hand. It was a fabulous seashell. What was this? Immediately, I had the thought that the kid would enjoy it. "Hold up," I told my friends.

Casting my attention back to the family, I saw the parents had walked out to where we had been. The dad was splashing about, shouting, "Impossible!" The woman was scanning to take a picture. There was the girl looking forlorn in about an inch of water. She was my goal.

"Hi," I said softly rising to look her in the face with a finger to my lips, "Shh. Here," I held out the shell. Taking it in gentle fingers, she stared at it and then at me with wide eyes. Then I whispered, "Come to Goldie's Gym for swim lessons and I'll teach you."

"To be a mermaid?" she piped up, forgetting to be quiet. Her parents spun, "There!" But it was too late, I dove flashing away to rejoin my friends.

"That was sweet," Cleo said, and "Awe look at her. She is crying for joy," and holding her gift closely.

When we passed 55th street, I realized we weren't getting to the gym from here. We were too far into Boulder and the river continued on into downtown before going into the mountains. We'd have to meet Uncle Arden somewhere for a ride. I flashed him a message, wondering if it would work. I suggested the Boulder Band Shell as a meeting spot, but he suggested Eben G. Fine Park close against the mountains where it would be easier to park. He didn't want us leaving the safety of the river. And after the day's events, I had to agree.

Then we passed Boulder High, where we'd be going to school in the fall. I was a little leery of the whole idea. Especially being a mermaid-like person in school. Hopefully, it wasn't going to be like some mermaid stories – get them wet and out pops a tail. Then again I wasn't exactly sure how mine worked either. But it wasn't water, for we were swimming now. I could easily imagine the horror of a tail appearing at the wrong time.

In math class, "Area of a curve," the teacher would ask. Then someone would say, "Oh, let's use Jill's tail..." and the laughter. I would die.

Passing tubers, swimmers and the occasional kayaker on our way up past those cooling off in the summer heat. I'm not quite sure what they mistook us for, but there was the occasional greeting along the way. "Hey, you're going the wrong way!" called some college-aged guys and girls who were tubing the river. Then, "Don't you feel the cold?" two thirty-something women asked us, but we said no. Honestly, I didn't.

Then we were passing the library and shortly thereafter we arrived at the park. People were out in droves, barbecuing, sunning and playing in the water. We fit right in. This time, I hung back from mingling. The three of us angling for an unoccupied rock in the deeper part of the water opposite the others. Pulling myself up, I sat with my back to the rocks going up to the road into the canyon, with my feet in the water. This was surprisingly nice and relatively quiet, considering the crowd. Cleo and Lucy stayed in the water and leaned facing me with their elbows on the rock.

9.8   A Wise Bird

We'd been there maybe a minute when I heard a pleasant tenor say, "Excuse me," from over my shoulder. Behind were the rocks going upwards to the road. I jumped out of my skin hearing a man so close that I fell forward, tumbling between Lucy and Cleo. I hadn't even heard him approach. Lucy and Cleo hadn't even looked up at him to give me warning.

"Why didn't you warn me?" I complained, coming up some distance from the rock. "Warn you about a bird?" asked Cleo eyeing the rock above where I'd been sitting. Then in mock humor, she said, pointing to a swallow as it swooped by and exclaimed, "Hey watch out!" Then she pushed me under saying, "Duck, a duck!"

Coming up spluttering, I said "Ha ha, very funny." Then I twisted about to look back towards where I'd been sitting. There, on a rock was the bird that had spooked me. Not just any bird either, but an old golden eagle. He looked so positively decrepit that I was surprised he could still fly. I was unafraid of eagles, and remembering the kind eagle I'd met at Coot Lake, I swam back to my rock and hoisted myself back up.

"I'm sorry, sir," I apologized, pulling my feet around to look up at him, and asked, "What can I do for you?"

Using mannerisms similar to those of the bald eagle I'd met before, he ducked his head embarrassed saying, "I get that all the time." Then popping up his head apologized, "I'm sorry for frightening you. It has been too long since I've had the pleasure." Which probably meant it had been some time since he'd last seen a mermaid, and I wanted to ask him where else, but he continued on and I soon forgot.

He turned to look down at the river, again embarrassed, holding up one of his wings, "But what I was getting at, was would you be so kind as to call me one of them fish under that branch over there. I'm getting too old to fetch one myself. The wings are not as deft as they once were, and my claws, well I could use some help." Then with his chin up, he clarified his request. "I'd still like to catch the thing myself, an eagle has to keep his pride where he can. I'm sure you understand." He said the last with a nod and such sincerity that I was nodding along with him.

How could I not want to help him? My heart went out to his plight. What was I supposed to do? He said I was to "call it". If he'd said for me to catch one, I'm sure I could have, but it probably would have been as funny as me trying to catch a chicken.

Seeing my confusion, he let me know, "You do know that all sea creatures help the guardians of the sea, don't you?" Then unashamedly, he added leaning forward and letting his eyes go round, "And of course anyone else with half a mind would be silly to refuse a request from such a beautiful creature as yourself."

I hadn't known that, squirming in place from his directness. "Such flattery. But who are the guardians of the sea?" I returned his question with a question.

He tipped his head to the side trying to see me from another angle. "What shell did you crawl out from that you don't know that? Maybe I'm talking to the wrong person, but where am I going to find someone that will listen?" Then, pointing over my shoulder, "Your friends there." He meant Cleo and Lucy. Then his next comment was cryptic and made no sense, "Even she doesn't understand. It's too bad, because I'm mighty hungry."

Huh? The eagle was addled for sure, but I did want to help it. I just wasn't sure how.

Then Cleo touched my leg, interrupting my conversation and getting my attention, "Hey, can we talk about what happened today."

Lucy shrugged saying, "Skip me on that. I'm going to explore," and swam up the river some. Sitting idle wasn't her style anyway.

"Hold on, my friend here needs some help," I replied, indicating the eagle. She looked up at him and then back to me. "It speaks?" After I nodded, she settled into asking, "What's it want?"

"I'm a *he*, dodo brain," and then seeing she didn't hear him asked, "Why can't she hear me?"

I wanted to know how I could, and what Cleo was hearing me say, so I asked him, "You're the wise one, Sir Eagle, don't you know? And please don't call my friend dodo again..." He wasn't the only one that could get their feathers ruffled. I'll have to lookup "dodo," but I'm sure it wasn't good.

"Hey, easy," he said hopping back a couple steps. "I meant no harm. There's no reason to get feisty. I'd forgotten how temperamental the guardians could be. Seas boiling, tempests brew, whirlwinds, hail, nothing pleasant for a bird to fly in mind you. Remember that the next time you summon a leviathan or storm a port will you? Us birds always get caught up and sent who knows where."

Pacing he explained, "Why one time my cousin's uncle twice removed ended up in Portugal after a big one. He complained for weeks before he discovered the fish there were better on his digestion. Then he wanted the whole family to migrate over yonder. I can just hear my

311

old man complaining as if it were yesterday, 'He wants us to live on a rock! A rock!' Like he had it any better. We eagles live in rocks and on rocks. My pop wasn't too smart, but he taught me all I know about fishing."

This guy was too much. Did he realize how funny he was? I still wanted to have answers to my questions. Then, what he'd said sank in. Summon a leviathan, me? Weren't they giant creatures of the sea said to drag ships into the depths? Until today, I'd never drowned anyone, and mermaids were known for that. I wasn't even sure how to summon a fish let alone a tempest. One thing at a time.

"So, you'll answer my questions if I do this for you?" I wanted to do it anyway, just to see if I could, but he didn't know that. The thing I was missing was information. Every time I discovered something about this business, it doubled the number of unanswered questions I had.

He cocked his head at me again then came to a decision, "I'll answer them now, because after that I'm flying away with a big fat fish. Don't expect answers then, so. The reason your friend here is slow to hear me is she only embraces this because of you, not because she wants it for herself. While she travels with you, she will have shared experiences but rarely on her own."

"The guardians are the ancient shepherds of the sea, not herding but caretakers as humans would say. From time immortal, the seas and everything within were given to them as companions, protectors and as helpers. But that isn't your question is it?"

No it wasn't, "I have thousands, where to start…"

"I'm going to expire if I don't eat. Only one more will I answer," it complained.

"Earlier today," I began finally settling on the question, "I killed two people..."

"I heard. I'm famished, but I sense unless I answer you how I know, you'd die of anxiety and we can't have that can we? In short, birds are gossips. The smaller the bird, the less he can keep his beak shut. Every morning, birds wake sharing with the world everything that has transpired, the whole world over. It's why we eagles seek high nests and perches, or their prattle would drive us insane. Thankfully, we get to eat them, now on with it. I know about the two, the four and three. Tell me and end my pain!"

He wasn't kidding about birds talking. Did he know he was gifted with the same gab? Maybe it was a blessing to us earthbound creatures that eagles soared so high, as he put it, or we'd never hear the end of it. "So, my question is, earlier while talking with someone briefly, I had a tail like a mermaid, and my abilities have expanded because of it, but I have been unable to make it appear ever since... why?"

"I will answer you with another question... are you a mermaid?"

"I'm not sure," I replied with the truth and not as I'd boasted earlier. "My friends seem to think so. Everywhere I'm deferred to as if one, and even sometimes revered, but I myself doubt it. I have abilities like I said, and I'm learning to trust them. But nowhere is there a guide that says you're a mermaid if you do A, B and / or C. So, how am I to know?"

"I promised one answer, get on... You're not listening! The worse plight of we birds is no one listening, so I'll shut up and hope I don't expire."

Indeed I wasn't, I didn't even hear this last so caught up was I in memory. "This afternoon, I treated a child specially, I live for such experiences above all else. I was only able to do it as you see me." Then I did "hear" what he'd said and pondered that. With regret, I put the questions aside and told him, "You've been patient, kind sir, and I indeed could pester you for ages with my concerns. So without any more delay I'll figure out how to go about your request."

9.9   Fishy Talk

So did I say, "hey fishy fishy," but wondered how would it know that I spoke to it? Turning about again, putting my feet back in the water and looking for the fish, I saw that there were indeed a group of five rainbow trout sitting in the shadow of the tree he'd pointed out. I could feel them, and many more up and down the creek. I suppose I could single out an individual, but would I be like, "Hey Bob, come over and be this eagle's meal."

Then I realized those fish were in the prime of life. Was there no other way that would be better suited? Did I just talk to them? Seeing that nothing would happen until I opened my mouth, I decide to try. Here goes, "Excuse me, do you mind coming over here?"

"Oh, now we're talking," said the eagle spreading his wings and leaning forward as all five of the fish came from across the river to swim around Cleo to hover by my feet. "Hold on," I told him.

Cleo's eyebrows rose when I talked to the fish, "I think I got that," she said. "The fish hear you."

"How can we serve, Mistress?" they said after a second and I saw Cleo's face light up at as well. Good she was hearing them too.

Looking at them, they were like a pack of dogs wagging their tails, ready to chase a ball or get a treat. They swirled around each other, happy as could be to swim at my feet. It was difficult to keep track of which was which, but if they wanted to confuse a mermaid they'd have to try a lot harder than that. How to tell them, "So, there is this eagle…"

"Hey Swish," one of them "elbowed" the one beside it with its fin, "What's an eagle?"

The forth one replied to it, "Swish, don't you remember cousin Swish? He was eagled!" Seeing that his friend didn't comprehend, he went on explaining, "It's when you're rewarded with the river in the sky!"

Two was enraptured, "Oh Swish. That's divine. I want to be eagled."

"So, um, Mistress, is one of us to be taken to the divine?" asked the first one splashing out of the water in hope.

That would be one way of looking at it. "Isn't there another Swish," I asked them. It seemed "Swish" was a name, or how some people would use the word "dude." I wasn't entirely sure. "That maybe is more exalted, and that has lived a long life and is ready to go?"

"I'm ready to go now!" exclaimed three, and the others said something similar. I tried reiterating the point, but five explained, "We don't really live all that long, Mistress.

It's a fast life, filled with adventure. Sometimes we fight real hard to stay in this life," probably on the end of a fishing line, I thought. Then he added, "When we're meant for the next."

It really didn't seem like they were listening. I'd hoped to spare them, and they were nice enough. It was a shame when I pointed the eagle down to them. With a quick swoop, he landed on the back of number four, and then was off saying his thanks.

"Swish," One said to Two, "That was so amazing! Swish!"

"Swish," admitted Five, "I saw an eagle once."

"No way, Swish." I wasn't watching them anymore, watching the eagle fly off down the river and then hanging a right and out of sight once he had enough altitude.

Were they even aware that one of them had just been taken? "Thanks guys, you've helped me a lot."

"That's it Mistress? Thanks, and if you don't mind, I'd like to swim in your presence more. I'd feel more secure." I frowned, I'd just authorized one of them to be "eagled" and they thought being near me was safe. There was no understanding the mind of a fish.

"Hey, has anyone seen Swish," I recognized Three's voice, looking for Four. "No Swish, but hey check out ..."

9.10 To Be?

I tuned out the fish, getting Cleo's attention to ask her to sit beside me. Being careful of the fish still swimming beside us, she did a push-up on the rock to lift herself out of the water. She wasn't too comfortable with people she didn't know seeing us in fish-suits, but that was another issue and I wanted to address her first question.

"So you were saying?" I asked her.

"You know I don't like this... Well, after earlier..." she was having problems holding it together. I waited. "I can't stand being helpless, and you are so confident. You blasted your way through six guys! Six! I can't even fight off one."

She had her knees pulled in tight, afraid of her own shadow. I was sitting loosely, and I knew why. She was right, but then I'd never been so self-conscious either. Telling her that wouldn't help her though.

"Well, as long as you're with me..." I started, but she interrupted, "I'm not always going to be with you am I?" Did she mean how Melanie just went off on her own? I shook my head in agreement. Could I teach her to zap people? But then again would that really give her confidence? Honestly, it wasn't until a day or two ago that I'd been able to do that. Before then it had been pure guts going into places where there could have been trouble. Guts or luck.

Should I explain her error? That seemed the best, as it would serve in more circumstances. "You know earlier, when you started talking with the guys?" She nodded whimpering. "You left the water. As a 'mermaid' you need to stay in water the best you can, until you are sure of yourself. You saw where we swam, and you should do the same when you feel threatened. Don't wait, just go. You can always explain later, as you'll have a later, if necessary. People can't see the place... let alone go there."

"So, go under the river?" she asked to be sure that was what I'd said. I nodded, "But anywhere deep should suffice. People can't breathe water."

Closing her eyes, she admitted, "Neither can I. Both Lucy and I have tried on our own. We need you near to be able to do so." Peeking one eye open, she checked to see if I was mad at her, but I was anything but. Her trial taught me that it didn't come on donning the fish-suit, as I'd guessed. It had to come from experiencing mermaid life, as the more we did it, the more we changed. Perhaps even now she could, but how to prove it without her having to swim away from me to test it? Right now, I wasn't certain she could.

I remembered what the eagle had said about her, how she only wanted this only when I did these things. Well, that explained how she could only breathe water when I was near. "To get this," I tried explaining. "You have to want it for yourself. Otherwise, you'll be at the mercy of others, including me. Cleo, you're going to have to want it."

Nodding her head, she said weakly, "I know. It's just, I don't think I can. I mean, you and now Melanie are powerful. I'm a nobody."

I wanted to hug her, to hold her close, but if I was to get the message across, she had to accept this for herself. "Look," and she turned to look straight at me. "Magic, only comes by believing." I was talking to myself on this I realized. "To do it, like attuning, you must ask The Lord of the Water for understanding and then practice it, which is the actual doing of it. If you want to breathe water on your own, you have to start there. You can either try now while we're together, and I promise not to help with my 'powers,' or you can try at home. Either way, it is up to you."

Thinking that through, she asked, "You mean like we did that first time, 'praying?' " I nodded. "The Lord of the Water, is it He that has been behind it all?"

I wasn't sure of that, but I couldn't tell her that either. She needed faith and that depended on trust and not confusion. "He is behind all magic, that I know. Without Him, it can't be done. But on a positive note, He wants us to do these things more than we do, so you just have to want to, and to ask and do."

"I think that has been my problem," she excused herself, looking to see if I was upset again. "I always rely on people, trusting them too much. I've known it for a long time, and I don't know how to stop it. That's why I like you, Melanie and Lucy so much. You have always accepted me. So do you think He likes us?"

That stumped me, and she saw it. I hadn't thought about The Lord of the Water's likes or dislikes before, other than magic. That I knew He always wanted us to do, but did He even care about us?

I nodded thinking it through out loud, "He has too. If He wants us to do things more than we do. He probably likes us more than we like each other."

"How can that be? Never mind, I suppose I'll have to ask Him those questions. So, do I just talk to Him or is it in my mind?"

"It's both," as "I've definitely done both." How interesting. Explaining this to Cleo was so insightful.

"So, to do this – breathe water. I attune, ask Him and then do it? Is that the same with everything you do?"

"Hmm, I think that sums it up. When I attune, I picture in my mind what I want, then ask. It's probably the same. After a while, it becomes natural to do all the steps at once. For now though, if you want to try it, concentrate on each."

"Okay," she said looking bright-eyed and hopeful. Then before I knew it, she dropped off the boulder and into the water, disappearing but staying above the Underriver. I had to reign in my need to give her air, knowing she didn't have it naturally. Which explained why again, she could only do it around me. I was sharing air almost unconsciously.

Knowing she wasn't getting air from me, I wanted to dive in after her. I could attune to her, but that might, as a side effect, give her air also. One thing for sure, if she couldn't do it, she'd surface for air in short order. We all used to test one another for how long we could hold our breaths, and she'd always been the loser in the contests. She'd already passed that test so far. I'd give her another ten seconds and then I was going in after her no matter what.

Suddenly, she rose up in a jump that surprised me. I knew she'd succeeded before she said anything or her expression gave it away. Well, two ways I knew. The first is she didn't gasp for air, and the second was the fish of her suit had become permanent; rearranging themselves in a pattern I knew she liked, a weave of yellow and blue curvy stripes. There is no way I'd ever pick that for myself.

"I did it!" she exclaimed. "Well, He did it, or we did it. Anyway, thanks," and she gave me a wet hug. "Now to explore," and she dove under again disappearing for real this time. I felt her going this time downriver for a ways before stopping and looking around. Then remembering something, she came back. It was at least twice as long as she'd been down before.

"This is fun," she said. "But what am I to do with these?" and she gestured to the suit. "I mean, well, you know me. I feel undressed. I wanted to go up and talk to people. How do you do it?"

After today, sitting in the open in our fish-suits, I didn't care anymore what people thought. I told Cleo, "Well, it doesn't come easy. In the beginning, I didn't feel the 'fish' were enough either. What I didn't explain before, is it is super-difficult to do the things we do in more than them. Be thankful that we have the fish at all."

She gulped at that. "Right. I know the mermaid stories. It sounds fantastic being 'that free,' but in truth, who wants to be so revealed? Okay, another thanks to give. Anything else?"

"Well," and I thought about the attention we'd gained by the eagle being near. Everyone had watched the eagle fly off. "If you want this, you are going to be exposed to public opinion, even ridicule. Everyone wants the glamour of being a mermaid and ignores the other parts. In every movie or TV show on mermaids, there are scientists that want to capture us. So far, we've avoided attracting great interest. Keep these things to yourself, and don't show off until you are certain of yourself."

Did I tell her of the "scary" things I'd encountered? Maybe I should hedge at them, "Coming into this is almost certainly to have its thrills, as we're currently doing. But today is an example of being careless."

"I know, and I'm sorry. Lucy was right, I wasn't thinking. I can't help the way I feel when a guy pays attention to me. I'll try to use some wisdom the next time..."

321

I interrupted her before she could add, "If there *is* a next time," saying, "Good. I suppose guys can be okay." With her look of "guys are awesome," I admitted some could be, but reminding her, I said, "Not all of them."

She frowned, "Yeah, I suppose. But most are. I go all weak-kneed and my stomach gets butterflies when I share a glance. My hands go all aflutter like I'm about to launch into the air like a bird. Usually I just sit on my hands. Do you think there's a cure?"

I rolled my eyes, "Yeah, start thinking of them as dorks. The need to fly away will certainly cease."

Cleo gave me a smile, jumped up to then lean into me, resting her head on my shoulder before we fell back shoulder to shoulder against the rock the eagle had sat on, saying, "I don't think Lucy wants it. With me, I get so insecure. She is putting up a front so as not to lose your friendship."

"Well, I'm not quitting any of you. And you?" I asked.

"Honestly, I just want the good parts, sandy beaches, lying in the sun like this. But don't you think we should cover up?" Hadn't she heard what I'd said? "I mean we're lying here not wearing anything." I shook my head no, but let her continue. She felt naked unless fully dressed. I'd lived my whole life in and around a pool and now...

What must it have been like fifty or a hundred years ago for mermaids? Fish-suits would hardly have cut it. Perhaps the stories were true, but I was glad we didn't have to experience it that way anymore if so.

"There's all these people. God, and today. I may have nightmares if I spend the next thousand nights alone, spend them with me... I know that is silly and am now armed with what you've now taught me. I promise to do better. I will. I really will!" Was she trying to convince me, or herself?

I thought about it for a few seconds, "I don't care what they think. Ever since this began, I've been exposed, and really, for the most part I don't even notice it anymore. I'm never not aware, but it doesn't factor in. After today, anyone who messes with me is in for a surprise."

Cleo sat up, turning to look in my face, not quite moving away from me, but I could feel the distance as if it were greater than that. "You'd kill them?" and she waved at all those around us. Just opposite us were families and their friends of all ages but mostly kids and teens.

She was right, I was overreacting. I guess I was still furious at those men. Those I could drown without hesitation and said, "I'm not sure." I followed up with. "I just acted to save us today. They had ropes and knives, what were they going to do with us? I shudder to think of it. Thankfully, we weren't hopeless. They were jerks, don't dwell or even think for a moment it was your fault. You were right before. Stand on that."

"If one of them," and I nodded to those over there, "did something of the same... I just don't know." I knew I had my steely-eyed expression, so I did my best to calm down. We were in a beautiful place. Think of the eagle, and of the Swish fish. I felt the coldness leave as I thought on the positive.

"Maybe you could get them wet instead," Cleo suggested and I was reminded of the guy littering in front of me today with the empty can. I'd nearly drowned him for a two-cent crime. I told Cleo the story, and she suggested, "Perhaps we should work on squirts like a water gun and build up from there and only get them wet to the degree they deserve without resorting to violence."

"Excellent idea, but I'd just like to lie here for now." Maybe Cleo was right, I should have a variety of responses, and the other thing she mentioned. If I had the mermaid tail, I'd be more decent and yet more of an outcast. Perhaps one day a mermaid and her tail would be normal in a setting like this. But the parents of the kid I'd given the shell to were prime examples of how I could expect to be treated in the meantime.

The Syreni Elder had talked about this. She'd been right and was more than likely well-acquainted with how mermaids have been received in the past. I would be treated like a freak. What had we been thinking showing off while swimming here? But then again, should we hide all the time? It was unfair.

Even though we hadn't been quiet on our way into town, there was little evidence to support any claim of there being mermaids in the river today. That alone was a problem and one I wasn't fit to solve. Should I, if I could summon the tail, be displaying it? And by "it," I meant me? Exposing myself to additional ridicule and attention.

Cleo let the subject drop while I continued to not understand much of anything. Really, what could be done? I was attuned, and nobody was paying us more attention than we deserved, and that was little. The eagle had drawn attention our way, but I chose to ignore it, put my arms behind my head and closed my eyes.

There were dozens of things we could do, including fleeing somewhere else but this is where Uncle Arden had said to come. Instead, I turned my mind to the encounter with the eagle and then with the fish. By now,

I knew animals understood me and I them. I had to turn my attention to them to hear them. No different than having people talk near you, but you don't hear them until you attempt to listen in. Unless of course, like the eagle, talking so close that I'd not failed to hear him.

Reaching out, through the attuning, I felt the life around me, insects, grubs, and a line of searching ants. They all had conversations, but not worth listening to. Just like mom and I could gab on forever about clothes and I knew uncle and Lucas would tune us out in seconds. So I observed but didn't listen. I was more interested right now, as Cleo phrased, in sunning.

Fortunately, that lasted a while and I fell asleep. Cleo swam off to go exploring again.

Then she was back and touched my leg, waking me up and getting my attention. She held up the shirt and skirt I'd worn earlier today – all wet again. They were having a problem staying dry, and she was telling me, "Your uncle is here." Then she left them with me. So I slipped into the water and my things. Then I disappeared under and followed after to resurface on this side of the downstream bike path bridge where there was a natural shelf to the park. Rising up, I wanted to shed the water as I exited the creek, but there were too many watching. As I went to the car to slide in beside my friends in the rear seat, I was handed a mostly wet towel, got it wetter, then really dried us off and put it on the floor.

Uncle Arden asked as we drove east on Canyon, "Food, anyone?" And after the enthusiastic response, he handed back my phone to us saying, "Text your families, let them know where you've been and that I'll get you home after we've eaten."

"How do I explain I swam from Denver to here?" Cleo asked out loud as she texted her parents.

"And you're going to say you got to Denver how?" Lucy asked her.

Cleo looked thoughtful at that, "Oh, good point. I guess I better leave that out. I'll just say what I always say, 'I spent the day with Jill.' "

To Be Continued

"Matt. I don't get how Spock was both old and young. What did I miss?" said the Chief of the Boat referring to the latest Star Trek movie, as he leaned back sitting easily with the two junior men on watch. He smiled as he posed the question to the elder of the two. It amused him to watch the last few minutes of the movies that the younger crew members took so seriously and pose questions that required them to explain the details of the film. He actually knew the answer, as he'd seen this movie with his wife, but they didn't know that.

"Seaman Darin, why don't you take a crack at that? Chief obviously doesn't understand the intricacies of wormholes." He saw the hidden amusement in COB's eyes. It made perfect sense if you bought into time travel as many sci-fi movies and books postulated.

The two watch sailors were each listening with one ear of the headsets they had plugged in. Also they were keeping an eye on the several video monitors that displayed the sea around the submarine. It was a dark sea, but the computers enhanced the images so that it was near-perfect vision, up, down, forward and to stern, port and starboard. It was imperfect, though, as what they needed were wrap-around screens like the movies had.

Seaman Darin, tried thinking how to explain this. Wormholes were black holes where an infinite amount of possible possibilities could take place. But before he could voice his understanding, out of the corner of his eye he saw the strangest sight. He stopped with his mouth agape. It looked to be a shapely woman descending towards them, like she were jumping into a pool. Instead of saying any of that, though, he leaned forward pointing to the monitor. "What's that?" he asked the senior men. This was his first tour, and he wasn't about to say what it first looked like.

The other two looked at the monitor. "Can you zoom in on it?" Asked COB. "It's coming in too fast," said the mid shipman. "Flip that switch, there, so it zooms with its target," said the Chief, unwilling yet to step up and take over from the rookie. Darin flipped the switch that COB had pointed out and the image zoomed to keep the descending figure at full screen.

"It's not metal, Chief," said Matt. "There's no sound of a screw, but a rapid swishing sound. It is not a torpedo, but it is headed right for us. Contact in approximately one minute," he continued his report as the three of them stared upwards at the descending girl.

COB stood, flipped on the intercom, "Skipper, incoming, unidentified... torpedo? Contact in one minute. You have to see this, Sir."

In a second, the Captain was at the watch. Gone was the bantering between the three. Displayed on the biggest monitor was a sight none of them could explain. "This being recorded, Trapp?" asked the Captain of Matt.

There was a quick check, then a nod. "Yes, sir."

328

To Be Continued

"What do you make of it COB?" asked the Captain.

"Unknown, Captain. It appears to be a female swimmer, descending feet-first to impossible depth at impossible speed. Countermeasures are not going to do any good, but... Impact in, fifteen seconds. Brace."

The Chief was right, it was his call on countermeasures, but there was no time. The captain stood to the same intercom, "This is the Captain, unknown impact five seconds, brace yourselves." Thinking a girl couldn't harm them, he was slow to grab something and was thrown to his knees when she hammered them topside. The whole sub rang with the impact. Around them everything loose rattled, some spilling to the floor. Thankfully, there was no explosion. It was improbable he thought, staring at what now appeared to be a young girl strapping up a swimsuit, that she was there to harm them. And if she was?

"Well, I'll be," said seaman Trapp slipping into a southern drawl. From three separate cameras, they were seeing an American girl some thirteen years of age grinning happily, her hands at her neck, drifting astern. In a brief moment, she became aware of the propeller and with a kick, flipped over backwards in a wide arc to end up behind the submarine. Where it was hard to see her from the prop-wash.

"Full stop! Hard to port!" the Captain yelled coming to his feet.

Before he could stand, there came a voice through the ship, female, young and gentle, "Thanks, Sailors." Then, while they watched, she started kicking for the surface rising slower than she had descended, but still faster than anyone should ascend from such a depth, and faster than a normal woman could swim. This girl wearing a normal one piece bathing suit. Anywhere a thousand feet above and close to any shore this would be a common sight. Here, though, it posed a mystery. He wondered if he should stop their patrol to investigate, and if she stayed around he'd make contact. At her speed though, they couldn't keep up. It would be better to let her go. There were alternate ways of pursuit that were probably a lot more effective.

"For the record, Trapp, our depth?"

"One thousand twenty three point oh six, Captain." The girl had reached the surface and the four of them were now watching two feeds – the long range lens and a satellite feed – each of which showed the girl treading water in twenty foot swells as if it were a day at the city pool. Then, in a second, she disappeared.

"Wait, where did she go?" asked COB leaning forward to squint at the monitor.

"Both cameras are blank, and thermal shows nothing along with sonar, Chief," said Trapp.

"Thoughts?" asked the Captain. Several other officers were now crowding in behind. When no one was forthcoming, he continued, "Off the record then. I won't attribute anyone to what is said."

Seaman Trapp, rewound the feed to view it from start to finish. They all watched with astonishment the whole playback. Even the clear playback of her voice, as heard from the external microphone.

"Impossible," was Trapp's first thought. He was saying what everyone was thinking. "What do we really know of the world? Today makes this whole cruise worth it. Mermaid, alien, or a special swimsuit, we've witnessed something and nobody will believe us."

Seaman Darin added, "We were just talking about fictional wormholes. One of their abilities is travel through time, but not least is temporal travel. Now we've just witnessed something similar." Seeing everyone except Matt confused by that, he clarified, "Travel across distances, sometimes vast. At least in science fiction, it could be used to jump from one location, say our star system, to another. Perhaps in a blink or faster than light, but not instant. If merely faster than light, we wouldn't see her move away either. It would just seem to be instant."

"Teleportation?" asked first-mate Reynolds.

"Exactly!" Darin said, and then realizing he was addressing the first mate, added, "Sir."

"Then what about her ability to withstand crushing sea pressure? If any of us were to exit the submarine at this depth in our swimsuit, we'd die. I've a mind to report this as a hoax." Said the first mate with arms crossed. And if it were not for the Captain having witnessed the whole episode, he would've done exactly that. Then write up the two sailors for dereliction of duty. Teleportation, indeed, he grumbled.

A good man, the first-mate, thought the Captain. Knew his tactics, had a sharp mind and if the crew didn't respect him for his ideas, he didn't make mistakes. A good first-mate but not Captain material. Admiral Holsey had asked if he wanted the man. One reason for their late departure was the lack of a first-mate. Now, he wondered at his choice.

Their duty was only patrol, and to continue mapping the undersea with their enhanced instruments. Now only three weeks from port, the crew had settled into routine and a casual frankness he'd had COB instilling in the men. Reynolds wasn't likely to make friends with the crew, but he'd train them well. What he needed, though, was not only trained men but thinkers as well.

He wouldn't reprimand the man, especially in front of the crew. He had to step in and let the thoughts continue. He also had to pick his words carefully, as he didn't want people jumping to think this person was some kind of creature. Speaking up, he suggested "Teleportation is probably unlikely. Perhaps camouflage. Certainly there are enough natural explanations."

Then to appease the first-mate, "Back to your duties, but I'll want a write-up with your thoughts." Then when the room had cleared out except for COB and the two sailors, he gave a nod to COB, and then to the older of the two seamen, "Trapp to my office."

He took a minute to survey the bridge on his way through, and gave orders to resume the patrol. He didn't believe the girl had merely gone invisible. That wouldn't be enough to fool thermal scan, which was the first thing he'd checked when she disappeared. He had to get to the bottom of this, and fast. He and the man he met in his office had served together on several cruises, and he trusted his judgment. He was almost right – most wouldn't believe, as witness to it the first-mate who had seen it.

As a submarine captain, he was privileged to hear about the latest marine technology, this wasn't an advanced swimsuit. We've encountered someone, a perfectly natural phenomenon, or she wouldn't have been sweet, innocent and clearly dangerous. Contact needed to be made, but with kid gloves. Admiral Holsey had to get this right away, but first he needed to know if the girl existed.

"At ease, sailor," he said as he entered then closed the portal. "I know you think the girl is no hoax, so I'd like you to track her down privately. If you trust Seaman Darin, then the two of you. Consider this Top Secret. I'm sure COB could help, but he has his duties. When I have his report you'll have it too."

Matt stood, his mind already trying to figure out how he would proceed. That he could use Darin would help. The young man was gifted with computers. The two of them had bonded fast, as they both loved all things fiction and especially science fiction.

"In every way, be circumspect. You cannot use her image to search, I'll not have anything from this investigation appear on a search engine. Whatever she is, she clearly could be a threat if antagonized. Let's do our best not to do that."

"Then how would you have me to proceed, Captain?"

"You can start by finding that swimsuit. It looked to me to be a team suit. From there, a team photo will probably help. After that, you'll have to wait until we make port and I can have you check, in person."

The End...

Thank you for reading Mermaid Rising by C. L. Savage.

For more information about further Mermaid Adventures titles, please visit us at SeaRisen.com

About the Author

I spent my early years in a suburb of Chicago before our family moved to Boulder, Colorado while I was yet a teenager. It was a good move for me, and the town and location is beautiful.

During my early years I was introduced to fiction reading – I think every parent pushes their children to read, but I didn't really catch the bug until my High-School years. Afterwards, it was hard for my parents to peel me away from whatever book my nose was in.

I've never been a "good" writer. In fact I've failed most of my English classes – as may be apparent in the book. A friend of mine constantly complains of my "tense" problems. To date, I still couldn't tell you the parts of a sentence, except for nouns being a person, place or thing.

So… I didn't get any positive feedback from my (English or Creative Writing) teachers growing up, but everyone agreed I was good with computers. So, into computers I went and became a programmer – a very creative career. A career that went nowhere for me.

In my spare time, which I had plenty, I would read. After a while though, reading didn't satisfy my imagination enough and so I began to delve into writing.

Writing can be very creative, and so different from one writer to another. Complete this sentence and you will know what I mean: "Under the door, I saw a light – when I opened the door …"

... the door slid up into the ceiling – did anyone write that? Then a brilliant cotton candy colored unicorn was revealed. Her name was Tiffany, and she was inviting me to ride her...

... a dump-truck was emptying its content on the floor... It was my kid brother with his toy truck. "Mom! Danny is messing up my bedroom again!"

As you can see, infinite possibilities. Maybe I'll float down a river today, or climb a mountain tomorrow. Or travel on a starship the day after.

I've written lots of stories that sit on my computer, which nobody ever gets to read. Mostly because they are incomplete, some I don't even remember where I was going with the story. What they did for me though, is teach me to write. Good dialog, is not, I looked at Mike's brilliant red race car and asked him, "Hey, how's it going?" but descriptive, "Hey Mike! That's a beautiful race car. How'd you get that color of red? It's brilliant!" At least to me, description through dialog is better than a narrative on the subject.

Writing many incomplete stories can drag you down. I was honestly sick of failing to complete one. So when I got the idea that became Mermaid Rising, I was determined to see it completed. A little over a year later, the book is a reality.

I don't claim to be an expert writer, so if you find grammar issues – incomplete sentences, run-on sentences or what-have-you, I'm to blame.

About the Author

If you find errors, and you are reading this on the Kindle, there is an option to send a note to the author about it. Highlight the word or passage with the error. A popup of the definition will appear, there is a button at the bottom labeled 'More.' In there, report the content error. I'll do my best, if I agree with your sentiment, to get it fixed for the next printing / ebook update.

Otherwise you can leave a comment on the publisher's (SeaRisen.com) contact page. Please be as specific as you can, to where the typo / error is within the book, and which book it pertains too.